This Won't Hurt A Bit

This Won't Hurt A Bit

❧

Timothy Sheard

CREATIVE ARTS BOOK COMPANY
Berkeley • California

Copyright © 2001 by Timothy Sheard

No part of this book may be reproduced in any manner without written permission from the publisher, except in brief quotations used in article reviews.

For information contact:
Creative Arts Book Company
833 Bancroft Way
Berkeley, California 94710

ISBN 0-88739-313-6
Library of Congress Catalog Number 99-65732

Printed in the United States of America

For Dave

I would like to thank Paul Samuelson, my wonderful editor, who went over my manuscript with a fine-tooth comb and straightened out the tangled prose, and Jonathan Diamond, the literary agent who gave me thorough and enormously helpful critique of the first draft. I would also like to thank my mystery writer friends, Leah Robinson, Bill Chambers, Jonathan Harrington, and Walter Wager, for giving me so much encouragement and advice while I struggled to complete the text, and to my dear wife Mary, who puts up with my solitary habit—writing.

This Won't Hurt A Bit

Prologue

KATE Palmer gripped the scalpel lightly in her right hand, as she would the bow of a violin. With the forefinger of her other hand, she traced the cadaver's anatomical landmarks from the crest of the hip diagonally to the groin. Even through the latex gloves, the wet, rubbery gray flesh felt cold.

Her lab partner, Jennifer Mason, stood watching from the other side of the black marble dissecting table. Theirs was one of sixteen tables laid out in neat rows, each with its own cadaver flanked by a pair of medical students. The lights of fluorescent ceiling lamps reflected off the moist surfaces of the corpses, and the air was filled with the pungent odor of formaldehyde and decay.

At another table a beefy, blond medical student with a surfer's tan called out, "Hey, look at the dingus on this guy—is that an implant or what?"

"I didn't think rigor mortis lasted this long," a fellow at the next table rejoined, raising guffaws from several of the students in the dissecting lab.

Kate turned to the noisy table. "Letterly, couldn't you advertise your inadequacies somewhere else?" She stood five feet five in her running shoes, trim and graceful. Her short auburn hair framed a round face without make-up.

"Just doing a little comparative anatomy, love," he replied. "You never can tell when—"

"Crack!"

The blow of a wooden pointer against a marble surface silenced the class. Aiming his stick at a word on the blackboard, Dr. Anton Praxis intoned, "You will recall that the relative location of the femoral nerve, artery and vein can be remembered by use of the mnemonic 'navel,' meaning: nerve, artery, vein, empty space and ligament. Bear in mind that the femoral nerve is lateral to the vasculature. That is, away from the midline."

A wan, restless man with unkempt white hair and a drooping mustache, Praxis liked to prowl the classroom, gazing into the cavities of the bodies with the look of an animal that hunts, and pointing out flaws in the students' work. As he continued, the class stood poised over the cadavers waiting for permission to use their scalpels.

"When you make the incision, be cautious. Do not bisect the structures with the knife. After making your incision, probe the wound with your finger, or the handle of the scalpel, if you are squeamish, and locate the underlying organs."

The Professor paused to gaze disdainfully at the class as though looking at a lower form of life, then, with a little flourish of the hand, he said, "Begin."

Kate stabbed the rubbery flesh with the pointed tip of the scalpel. Despite months of dissection, she was still surprised that the wound produced no blood, merely a trickle of clear fluid. Each cadaver's bodily fluids had been drained and replaced with a clear preservative that filled the organs and blood vessels, keeping them plump and life-like.

Pressing firmly, she drew the blade across the groin, pried the wound open with her fingers, and peered into the opening, trying to recognize the layers of tissue.

Jennifer, tall and blonde, with raspberry red lips and a mouth that was born to pout, bent down to peer into the wound. "Gee, Kate, it looks like the meat in the back of my fridge."

"Remind me not to have dinner at your place again."

While Kate probed the wound searching for the femoral nerve, her partner looked over the body. "Boy, this guy's face really got mangled when he hit the windshield. I bet he didn't have an airbag."

"Or wear his seat belt," said Kate, glancing at the torso. "That circular mark and the 'X' on his chest is where he hit the steering wheel."

She felt a long, stringy cord inside the wound. "Got ya! Femoral nerve! Pour some more cadaver juice over the wound, will you?"

Jennifer grimaced at the nauseating odor as she poured a mixture of saline and formaldehyde over the corpse's groin. "What a bummer we got stuck with the worst cadaver in the class."

"They say Praxis hasn't given an 'A' to a woman student in ten years."

"He's has got to give it to you, Kate. You're tops in the class."

"Don't count on it." Kate pushed her finger deep into the wound searching for the artery.

Jennifer said, "After you finish the groin I guess I'll dissect the scrotum." She held the shriveled sack and felt the testicles. "I wonder if he had a vasectomy. Let's see if there's a scar."

Looking at the underside of the penis, Jennifer traced the cord from the sack up along the underside of the organ. There were three small, red birthmarks along the cord. She bent down to examine them. Suddenly she dropped the member, ripped off her latex gloves, and stepped away from the table, her face contorted in horror.

"Katie, I know that dick! I mean, I know that guy!"

"What's that?" her partner asked.

A few students at nearby tables stopped their dissections to look over.

"I'm talking about the cadaver. I know who it is!"

Jennifer grasped the corpse's head and turned it to the side. "His face is deformed from the auto accident and his hair should be blonde, but I'm certain this is Randy Sparks, the third year medical resident."

"The one who disappeared last December in the middle of his rotation?"

"Yup, that's the one. God! And we've been cutting him up!"

By now the entire class had ceased working and was staring at the two women.

Professor Praxis approached them.

"Is there a problem, ladies?"

Jennifer pointed at the cadaver. "Professor Praxis, this isn't an ordinary body. This is Randy Sparks, the resident who disappeared last month!"

Arching a single eyebrow, he glanced down at the cadaver, then turned his attention to the groin incision that Kate had made.

"Have you dissected to the femoral nerve, Miss Palmer?"

"Yes, sir." She pointed to a slender filament running through the wound. "It's that gray string, isn't it?"

"Correct. Continue until you have exposed the artery and vein."

As Praxis turned to a nearby table, Jennifer blurted out, "But, Doctor, shouldn't we, like, call the police or something?"

The Professor pulled a gold watch on a gold chain from his vest pocket, opened it to note the time. "There are thirty-six minutes of class time remaining. This man has been missing for—what did you say, a month? The police can wait another half-hour to find him."

As he cast an imperious glance around the room, all heads bowed to their business on the tables.

Kate hesitated, torn between revulsion and a desire to find the vessels hiding in the wound. She glanced briefly at the body's battered face, gritted her teeth, looked back at the groin. Taking a deep breath, she inserted her finger into the wound and resumed her probing.

"Honestly, Kate, I don't see how you can still work on him."

"Praxis isn't keeping me out of the Honors Program. I'm going on with the dissection."

Looking at the other tables, Jennifer saw Letterly wipe his brow on his sleeve, wink at her, and return to his dissection. She crossed to Kate's side of the table, leaned close to her partner and whispered, "Kate, what if somebody finds out I slept with Randy? It means I've been cutting up a man I had sex with!"

"So?"

"*So?* Why, it borders on necrophilia!"

"I don't know. Some guys would probably find it a turn on."

"Letterly would, but he's a pig."

As Kate cut deeper into the gray tissue, more fluid welled up in the wound, like water filling a footprint on the beach.

"Hey, I found the femoral artery, take a look," she said, pointing to something that looked like a thin white worm running through the wound.

Jennifer glanced nervously at the wound. "I think I'm going to be sick," she said.

Her finger deep inside the cadaver, Kate said, "Come on and probe the wound."

Pulling on a latex glove, Jennifer pushed a finger into the opening. As she felt the sinewy formations in the wound, she whispered to her partner, "You realize, Kate, if this gets out it's going to *destroy* my love life."

One

He was a man of modest proportions. Dressed in custodian's black shoes and blue work shirt and pants, Lenny Moss was the sort of fellow who went unnoticed on a crowded sidewalk. His black framed glasses perched on a broad nose beneath thick, arching eyebrows and coarse, untidy hair. He needed a haircut, but he always seemed to need a haircut. And a shave.

Having recently celebrated a thirtieth birthday, Lenny wasn't feeling old exactly, but he didn't feel young and energetic either. The custodial work in a big university hospital like James Madison could tax even the strongest man. On top of that, his responsibilities as a union representative wore him down. He was worried about the contract negotiations, which were stalled over the hospital's threat to privatize whole departments, eliminating union members.

He had been sleeping badly as well. A woman in the kitchen was on probation for missing work, and Lenny knew that one more slip would land her in the soup. A housekeeper on the night shift who had custody of her three grandchildren was sleeping on the job, which was inevitable, given her daytime responsibilities. Lenny functioned as a combination defense lawyer and salesman, bargaining, promising, sometimes even begging the administration to lessen a charge and save someone's job.

But the main source of his fatigue was not what he *did* so much as what he lacked. His wife Margaret had died nearly a year ago. Although he would be loathe to admit it to his friends, or even to himself, even after many months of living alone, he didn't mind staying late on the job talking to his co-workers; it meant putting off the moment when he stepped into his empty house and heard the silence there.

He set the buffing machine in the middle of the Seven-South corridor. It was six-thirty on a Tuesday morning, his favorite time of day, when the only floor traffic was an occasional technician drawing blood or a sleepy night nurse making a last bed check.

"It's a fucking war," he grumbled, moving the buffer in broad sweeps across the old marble floor. The enemy was the procession of careless pedestrians who scuffed up his work or marred it with food, coffee, urine, blood.

"Nurses are the worst," he decided. "They never pick an armchair up to move it. They always drag it. Why can't they lift it?"

He knew that as the shift wore on, liquid stool from soiled linen would leak onto the floor, and the wet wheels of the stretchers would spread it in long black streaks. By evening, the floor would look like the slushy Philadelphia streets in January.

Celeste, the unit secretary, came by in a fur coat and floppy wool hat. "Hey Lenny!" she called over the sound of the buffing machine. "Your number come up last night?"

"I don't play the lottery," he answered. "I'd rather just give more in taxes and know I'm getting screwed!"

"I choose to dream," she said with a smile and went on to the nursing station.

Betty, his housekeeping partner, came ambling down the hall on her bowed legs. She was a middle-aged black woman with short, gray hair like steel wool, thick hips, and a face that was all sharp angles and a long jaw. She tapped him on the shoulder

"Hey Lenny!" she yelled over the buffer.

"Huh?"

He snapped off the machine and looked up.

"They need you down at the office. Regis got his self in trouble again."

"Shit," he said, coiling the electric cord onto the handle. "Cover for me, will ya, Boop? I got a feeling this is gonna take some time."

"Sure," she said, smiling at the nickname Lenny had given her years ago. "You give them hell down there, you hear?"

After riding the elevator to the basement, he walked briskly by the housekeeping office to the locker room. The workers couldn't get to their lockers without going past the office, a layout that allowed the supervisor to keep an eye on comings and goings.

Lenny opened his locker, which was stuffed with paperback mystery novels, union grievance forms, extra clothes, and an umbrella. He dug out a yellow notepad and a dog-eared Employee Handbook covered with doodling, then he shut the locker and hurried to the office.

Entering the outer office, he walked past the time clock and the long rack of time cards, to a door labeled **ENVIRONMENTAL SERVICES SUPERVISOR.** With a curt knock he opened the door, entered, and found himself looking at a familiar tableau.

Slouched in a black leather chair behind a large, cluttered desk was Supervisor Norman Childress, a pasty-faced man with hair the color of wood ash. Standing at parade rest beside the desk with his chest bulging beneath a

This Won't Hurt A Bit

dark blue blazer was Joe West, the chief of hospital security. In front of the desk sat a young black man, Regis Devoe, laundry worker and frequent visitor to the supervisor's office.

Giving Lenny a sour look, Childress pointed a smoke-stained finger at the accused and said, "Mr. Devoe has been terminated for violating three separate work rules. Mr. West will collect his hospital identification and clean out his locker."

"Whoa," Lenny said, making hold it signs with his hands. "Do you mind if I hear the charges?"

Lenny pulled up a chair and had barely sat down when West stepped forward, placed his face inches from Lenny's nose, and snarled, "Devoe was fifteen minutes late *again* punching in. He disobeyed a direct order from his supervisor, and he called a Department Chairman by a foul name. You can't grieve your way out of this one, Moss!"

Lenny nearly gagged smelling the security chief's cheap aftershave. He pulled his head back, turned in his chair and looked with disbelief at his young coworker. "Regis. I can't believe you would do that. You, of all people."

"No way I could've been late this time. My watch said I was right on time, and it's got a frickin' quartz movement. See?" he said, thrusting a wrist up to West's face. The watch was big, gold, and said 'Rolex' on the dial.

West stepped away from Lenny, a pair of handcuffs jingling on his belt, and stood ramrod stiff, the creases on his navy blue pants as straight as a yardstick.

"It looks like a very accurate timepiece to me," said Lenny. "Did you set it by KYW, the 'all news' radio?"

"Of course," said Regis. "I love that little song they got. You know, the one that goes, 'K-Y-double-yew, news ray-di-o-"

"Can it!" Childress snarled. "At James Madison Hospital we go by the time clock. Mr. Devoe not only arrived at the office six minutes late, but he refused to report for duty as ordered by his supervisor, Mr. Docksett. He didn't even punch in til quarter after, *and* he called Mr. Freely a faggot!"

Lenny sat forward in his chair. "Let me see if I understand this. He came into the department at six-o-six but didn't punch in 'til quarter after. Why the delay?"

"Perhaps he can explain it to you. We don't understand Mr. Devoe's behavior one *bit*," West said, spitting out the last word as though it were a bitter seed.

Lenny looked from West to Regis and back to West. "I'll need a few words with my co-worker... alone."

With a nod from Childress, Lenny and Regis stepped out to the hall.

Lenny stood looking at the young man. He found himself thinking that his bag of tricks was not only empty, it was ripped to pieces, and there was no way he could pull out a rabbit this time.

Two

Gary Tuttle, RN, hurried to the Seven-South nursing station and picked up the phone on the forth ring. He cocked his head sideways to hold the phone to his ear. He was a stocky man of thirty with light brown hair beginning to recede and sleepy blue eyes. His features were rounded and soft, and they, combined with a disarming manner, encouraged trust in his patients.

"Seven-South, Mr. Tuttle. May I help you?"

The strident, nasal voice of Dr. Priscilla Gandy raked his ear. "Gary? This is Dr. Gandy. I've got a patient in my office I need to admit right away. Are there any empty beds on your ward?"

"Let me check the board, Dr. Gandy. Hold please."

Gary punched the hold button on the console and put down the phone. He pulled the Census Ledger over and ran his finger down the list, comparing the number of Seven-South admissions to the number of discharges. He also checked for Deaths, of which there were none.

He picked up the phone. "I'm sorry Dr. Gandy, but both our discharges have been taken by Admissions. Nothing is open."

"Dammit! I've got a sick patient here in my office. What am I supposed to do, dance around the room until somebody finds me a bed?"

Gary's free hand tightened into a hard fist. The fist trembled, then slowly opened. He spun his chair around to look at the census board on the opposite wall. As far as he could tell, none of the patients listed on the board was ready for discharge or about to die.

"I'm looking at the board, Doctor, and I don't see anyone else going out any time soon."

There was a long, awkward silence. Gary knew that Dr. Gandy would not give up until she got what she wanted.

He took in a long breath, let it out slowly.

"I guess I could call admissions and ask if they can switch one of our hits to another floor to make room. What is your patient's name?"

"Mr. Lewis. He's in a lot of pain and he's badly dehydrated. Prostate cancer. He needs the morphine pump and IV nutrition. When you get a bed, call the resident for orders. I'll be up to check on him after office hours."

"Okay, I'll see what I can do."

Dr. Gandy clicked off.

As he dialed the Admissions Department, Gary asked himself for the hundredth time, why did he ever do that woman a favor?

After two rings, a purring voice answered. "Ad-missions, how may I help you?"

"Hi, Ruthie, Gary on Seven-South. Dr. Gandy just called me all upset. She wants to admit a patient direct from her office, a Mr. Lewis, and we're full up. Is there any chance that you could switch one of our admits to another floor?"

"Let me pull your census up on my screen, Gary. One moment."

While he waited, Gary plucked a pen from the pocket of his white scrub suit and transcribed Mr. Oldenfield's medication order.

Ruthie purred back on the line. "Gary?"

"Yes…"

"Aren't you expecting an admission of Dr. Gandy's by the name of Louis Anderson into 6-B?"

Gary looked over the Census Ledger. In the Admissions column he found the entry 'Anderson, Louis–CA of Prostate/Gandy.'

"That's right, it's in the book."

"Could the Mr. Lewis that the doctor called you about be the same man?"

Gary looked again at the name in the Log: L-o-u-i-s Anderson–Prostate Cancer… Gandy had called her patient Mr. Lewis….

"That damned Gandy," he said. "Do you know that last week she came up and asked Betty—our housekeeper—could she put a patient in the bed she was *cleaning*! She never follows proper channels."

"Shall I change the name in the computer?"

"We'd better wait until the patient comes up and we'll let him tell us his right name. Thanks, Ruthie."

"Sure thing, Gary. Anytime."

Gary called Dr. Gandy and told her that a patient had been scheduled for a bed on Seven-South under the name L-o-u-i-s Anderson.

"Leave it to those admission clerks to screw things up," Gandy said.

"I don't know who screwed up, Doctor, but the bed's ready now. You can send the patient over."

There was silence on the phone.

"Actually, Mr. Lewis hadn't eaten anything this morning, so I sent him to the coffee shop for a snack. You know how long it takes the kitchen to deliver a late tray. Be sure and page the resident when he gets on the floor."

This Won't Hurt A Bit

The phone clicked off.

Gary felt as though he had been pushing against a stone wall. Unable to move it, he was left tired...depressed...defeated.

Lenny stood in the hall outside the housekeeping supervisor's office wondering how he was going to keep Regis from being fired this time.

"I'm not sure I can help you, Reeg," he said. "You've got too many strikes against you."

"What're you talking about? You handle those bozos real good. You don't get pissed off like me."

Lenny studied the young man in front of him: a slim and broad-shouldered knot of restless, angry energy.

"Regis, what the hell happened this morning with the time clock?"

"Man, I really thought I was on time today! I got this new watch from a guy hawking it on Germantown Avenue couple a' nights ago." He showed Lenny the watch again. "Paid twenty bucks for it. I figure it's only a knockoff, but what the hell, it looks great."

"And..."

"And when I went to punch in on the clock, Docksett was standing right there watching, and I see it's six minutes after the hour."

"So why didn't you punch in then?"

"I knew Docksett was gonna dock me fifteen minutes pay for violating the four minute grace rule, so I told him go ahead and dock me, you can't make it any worse, and I went back to the locker room."

"That's logical."

"Then he said if I didn't punch in and report to the laundry room this second he was gonna call Childress and have me suspended on the spot, and Mr. Freely in Human Resources would back them up one-hundred per cent."

"And you, being a calm, rational young man, refused."

"Hey, no way I'm gonna lick Docksett's boots. Just 'cause he's black and talks like, 'we all brothers,' and shit like that don't mean I'm gonna cut him no slack. No fuckin' way. I told him, call that faggot Freely and report me, I don't give a shit, I'm going back to the locker room and sit my ass down."

Lenny took a deep breath, puffed out his cheeks and studied his union friend. Grievances were like this more often than not. The worker in trouble was no angel. Not that Regis deserved his fate, but it was harder to win when the guy dug his own grave. A few even brought their own shovels.

Lenny considered the charges, searching for weaknesses. Exceptions. Precedents. He remembered a case with a similar charge, decided it was the best he could do for now.

"I'll try something. Stay put."

"You gonna get me off, ain't you? Cause if you don't, Salina'll kill me."

"You might have thought of that before you crossed swords with Docksett." He ran his palm over his chin. "Just stay here. And don't make things worse. Okay?"

As he reached for the door to the office, Lenny made his face a mask.

Three

Returning to the office, Lenny took a seat, opened the Employee Handbook and leafed through several pages. West stood stiffly behind the desk, while Childress pretended to read a report.

Lenny underlined several lines on a coffee-stained page of the handbook, stared at the page for a moment, then looked up. "Let's take the charges one at a time, shall we?"

Silence from West and Childress.

"Good. Now, I admit that according to the time clock Regis arrived two minutes after the four minute grace period that's stipulated in the contract, *but*—you know there've been problems with the clock for months. Sometimes it's off by hours, not just a couple of minutes."

"That's because some joker's been pulling the plug on the goddamn clock!" West said.

"Whatever. The point is, I called the number for the exact time on the pay phone out in the hall just now, and Regis's watch was right on the money. Purr-fect. So it looks like he was correct about the time and shouldn't have been docked in the first place."

"That clock is checked every time it's reset."

"Are you sure that Mr. Docksett didn't simply set it by his own wristwatch?"

Childress opened his mouth to speak, hesitated.

"For two minutes—that's two minutes over the grace period—an arbitration panel could rule in our favor. They might listen to KYW, too."

Childress shot back, "Even if you win on the two minutes, he still refused a direct order from his supervisor."

"Ah, but did he really? It says on page twelve, paragraph three, and I quote, 'All employees are required to obey any and all reasonable requests of their supervisor while on duty'"

Childress looked puzzled. "So?"

"So when Docksett spoke to him, Regis wasn't actually 'on duty'." Lenny answered, making quotation marks with his hands. "In fact, he told Docksett that he wasn't ready to report for work."

13

"Are you saying that Devoe was in the hospital but not on the job?"

"Exactly. It's just like he was at home calling in." He pantomimed picking up a phone and dialing a number. "Hello, Mr. Docksett? This is Regis Devoe. I'm sorry to report that I will be fifteen minutes late getting to work this morning. I hope that doesn't inconvenience you any."

"Bullshit!" West said. "An employee can't decide when he's on duty and when he's not."

"As a matter of fact, there was a case just like this last fall on third shift. A nurse's aide came onto the ward a half-hour early and was sitting drinking a cup of coffee. The nursing supervisor told her to answer a patient call-light, but she refused. She was suspended, and we turned it around at the third step."

"No comparison," Childress said.

"I think there is, and so might an arbitrator."

"What about the foul language? Calling Freely a faggot is insulting any way you look at it."

"Not if it's true. In that case, it's merely use of a common slang. Are you prepared to certify that Mr. Freely is a bona-fide, true blue heterosexual?"

Childress scowled. He raised a meaty fist in front of his face. Lenny noticed that the cuticles were red and swollen and the nails were bitten down to the quick.

Childress pulled a finger up with his other hand. "One: he was late on the clock."

"With all the time clock problems we've had, you could lose on that."

"Lose, schmooze." The supervisor pulled up a second finger. "Two: he disobeyed an order."

"*If* he was on duty."

"Three. The faggot thing. Docksett told Freely about it, and Freely's feelings are hurt. I can't let a thing like that go by."

"Even though Devoe didn't say it to his face?"

Childress laced his fingers together to form a tent. "Makes no difference."

Lenny doodled in the margins of his handbook while he considered his options.

"What if Devoe apologized to Mr. Freely? That would soothe his feelings. You could drop the charge for foul language and give him a three day suspension for the two-minute lateness. Three days for two minutes—that's still a respectable punishment."

"Is the apology in person or in writing?"

"In person, of course. Mind you, I'm not sure I can get Regis to do it. He's very proud."

West leaned over the desk and pointed to the January heading on the desk calendar, then he flipped the pages forward to June and tapped the number 30. Both men knew that it was a long time until the end of the fiscal year, when the disciplinary records were wiped clean and past violations could no longer be counted against union members; that Regis would never make it that long without earning one more reprimand—the one that would get him terminated.

Childress looked up from the calendar. "Three day suspension and a face-to-face apology to Freely. In my office!"

Lenny stood and stepped away from the desk. "I'll run it by him. I can't make any promises."

Dr. Leslie Odom, a senior physician on the gynecology service, approached the nursing station. He was a short, trim man immaculately dressed in silk shirt, pinstriped suit and soft Italian loafers. As he pulled a chart from the rack and began reading the history and physical, the residents and medical students on his service, two of whom were Kate Palmer and Jennifer Mason, stood behind him waiting.

Closing the chart, Odom stood and led the others down the hall to the patient's room, summarizing the case as he walked.

"Mrs. Grey is a thirty-eight year old black female who has had three full-term pregnancies and one miscarriage. She came to the emergency room complaining of back and abdominal pain not related to lifting or posture, nausea, and loss of appetite. She was initially seen by the orthopedic resident, who ordered x-rays of the lower back and a CAT scan."

Poker-faced, Odom looked at Kate with dark, unblinking eyes and said, "The results of the scan were…?"

She realized that the gynecology service would not have been consulted had the orthopedist's test been positive, so she answered, "The CAT scan was negative."

Odom turned away from Kate without acknowledging her answer as he continued down the hall. "Back pains are nonspecific symptoms which tell us little. If physical exam suggests an area of tenderness or a mass, an MRI may be useful."

The group entered Mrs. Grey's room. In the bed was a slender black woman with an oval face and large, dark expectant eyes. She was reading a bible.

Dr. Odom approached the bed.

"The orthopedic doctors asked me to examine you, Mrs. Grey. I am Dr. Odom, a gynecologist."

"Oh thank goodness, doctor. I wanted to see a gynecology doctor when I came to the emergency room, I was sure it was a woman's problem, but they insisted on sending me to the orthopedic doctor, and I've been so depressed with the constant pain, I haven't wanted to eat anything."

Odom pointed to the door, which was quickly shut by a medical student. The physician pushed the bed control to lower the head of the bed, then he lifted the woman's gown and began to press on her stomach. At two areas she winced.

"Discomfort?"

"Yes, a little."

The doctor continued pressing on her abdomen.

"Lower your panties and raise your knees. I am going to perform a pelvic examination."

The woman looked at the clutch of people standing around the bed.

"You mean here? In front of everybody?"

He gestured toward his entourage. "They are all physicians."

"But…"

Odom stepped away from the bed. "If you refuse the examination I cannot find out what is wrong with you."

She stared at the doctor's deadpan face. Odom's dark eyes did not blink.

With trembling fingers, she slowly pulled the sheet up to her chin, raised her knees and began pulling down her panties.

Four

Lenny stepped out of the supervisor's office and found Regis in the hall, looking pissed off.

"Here's the deal, Regis. The refusal to report to work I think we can win because of a case last Fall on third shift. As for the two minute lateness, I told Childress how we called for the exact time from the pay phone and that it confirmed your watch's quartz movement."

"How's that?"

"I borrowed a quarter from you for the phone when we first stepped out of the office. Remember?"

"Right, right," Regis said, catching on to the ruse.

"But calling Freely a faggot...I couldn't argue around that."

"You couldn't cut 'em no deal?"

"Oh, I got a deal all right, but I'm afraid you won't like it."

Lenny searched for a phrase that would soften the proposal. He decided that no amount of honey could make it go down better.

"If you apologize in person to Freely, Childress will give you a three-day suspension. Which I'll grieve right away, of course."

"In person? I gotta say it in person?"

"That's the deal."

"To the fruit cake?"

"Reeg, you can't go around picking on somebody's private sexual practices. Sometimes in a Step Two hearing Freely votes on our side."

"If I lose my benefits Salina'll kill me dead. You got to fix this for me, man."

"I'm trying, but you have to help me. We have to give Childress something."

Lenny took out a handkerchief and blew his nose, then stuffed the cloth into his back pocket. Watching Regis pace the width of the hall, he could see the emotions warring in the young man's body: the anger and the pride in his stiff shoulders and hard mouth, the flicker of fear in his restless walk and his squinting eyes.

After a long moment, he stepped up to Lenny and looked him in the face.

"I can't do it, man. I'm no kiss-ass."

Lenny nodded solemnly. "I understand. Let's go in and tell 'em."

Back in the office, Lenny told Childress, "The deal's off. Regis doesn't feel that his remarks warrant an apology, and I agree with him. We'll grieve the termination."

West plucked the photo identification badge from Regis' shirt pocket.

"You can pick up your terminal paycheck in the security office at three o'clock today. Otherwise, if you're found on hospital property you'll be arrested for trespassing…unless you come in on a stretcher." His thin lips betrayed just the hint of a smile.

West followed Regis and Lenny down the hall to the housekeeping locker room. Regis walked with a rolling gait that appeared confident, but Lenny knew better.

"I'll file the appeal on my afternoon break," Lenny said. "If we're lucky, we'll get to second step by end of next week."

As they entered the locker room, Lenny stepped close to Regis and whispered, "Is your locker cool?"

The young man winked as he stepped up to locker number 13. "My lucky number, man," he answered, twirling the combination lock and yanking it open.

The locker contained nothing more incriminating than old newspapers, a dirty styrofoam coffee cup and an old cloth coat with ragged patches on the sleeves. Lenny understood that this was a 'safe' locker that the workers used when ordered to face an inspection. Regis pulled out the coat and put it on. He left it unbuttoned, knowing it would be ludicrously tight across his broad shoulders.

Turning to West, he asked, "All right?"

West kicked the locker closed. "Let's go. I'm escorting you off hospital property."

They walked out of the office and down the corridor. When Regis stopped at the loading dock, West pointed to the stairs that would take them to the main lobby on the first floor.

"Ain't no rule says I got to go out the front door," Regis said. He passed through the wide sliding glass doors onto the broad platform where truckers unloaded their delivery, leaving West inside. The January cold blew his coat open. He paid it no attention.

Lenny put his hand on Regis' shoulder. "I'll let you know as soon as I get a date for the hearing."

Regis stood silently on the edge of the dock looking out along the curving driveway.

"You sure you're okay with this?" Lenny asked.

Regis glanced back at West, who was staring hard at them, impatient to be rid of the young troublemaker. "You know what the man says," he answered. "Don't get mad, get even."

He turned, jumped off the dock and walked briskly down the driveway toward Germantown Avenue, where he could catch a bus for home.

Lenny walked back to the sliding doors. West, who loved to surprise workers by appearing and disappearing suddenly and unannounced, was already out of sight.

Passing through the glass doors into the corridor, Lenny felt a mixture of anger and disgust. He understood Regis's anger, his pride, his hatred for the system, but he worried that some day Regis would push the wrong guy just a little too hard, and Lenny would be unable to save him.

While Mrs. Grey looked up at the ceiling, Dr. Odom pulled on a pair of latex gloves. He lubricated the fingers of one hand, and with the other pulled the sheet back below the patient's knees. As he spread her labial folds and advanced his fingers into her vagina, he pushed deeply on her abdomen with his free hand. As the doctor probed, Mrs. Grey grimaced and bit her lip to stifle a cry. Odom's face was blank. Reactionless.

When he finished, he pulled the sheets up to the patient's waist. Mrs. Grey lowered her hospital gown and began pulling up her panties.

"Do you know what's wrong with me, doctor?"

Odom peeled off his latex gloves and tossed them at the trash bucket. One glove fell in, the other slid down onto the floor. The same student who had closed the door bent down and deposited the glove in the bucket.

"We will need more tests," he said in a noncommittal voice. He led the group back out into the hall and down the corridor to the nursing station. At the station he sat and filled out the consultation sheet in the chart.

As the surgeon wrote in the chart, Kate Palmer coughed and said, "Excuse me, Dr. Odom. I was wondering, do you think Mrs. Grey has endometriosis?"

Still writing, he said, "It is more likely that she has pelvic inflammatory disease. Black women have a lower incidence of endometriosis than the Caucasian or Asian population. I'm ordering an MRI to rule out a mass or abscess."

Kate was puzzled at the suggestion of pelvic inflammatory disease—a persistent infection. She knew that some diseases were more common in certain racial groups, but even with her limited clinical experience she could not understand Odom's diagnosis.

"Does the patient have an elevated white count?" she asked, looking for signs of infection.

"Chronic inflammation of this type is not always marked by a proliferation of white cells," he replied.

"Then why do you suspect pelvic inflammatory disease?"

"Because black women have so many partners, pelvic infection is a more likely diagnosis than endometrial disease."

Finishing his note, he put his pen in his coat pocket, then stood up. Not much taller than Kate, he looked at her with disdain and impatience. His look reminded her that medical students were supposed to keep quiet and listen.

"Physical diagnosis is more complex than dissecting a cadaver," he said, his face a stony mask.

Kate felt her face flush.

As Odom turned away from her and led his entourage down the hall to see another patient, Jennifer pulled Kate aside.

"Kate, do you realize the whole medical staff must know about Randy Sparks turning up on *our* anatomy table?"

"It wasn't our fault," Kate said. "We didn't have anything to do with it."

"You don't have to make it worse by pissing off Dr. Odom!"

"We can ask questions, too, you know," she answered."

"But what if they find out I had sex with Randy? It's like the kiss of the spider woman. On top of that, the cops will be all over me with questions. How could I study? I'm barely passing as it is, even with all your help."

"Don't worry, nobody else knows, and you know I'd never say a word about it."

"I trust you okay. It's that damned Letterly that worries me. He always hears things."

"Well he doesn't know about this, so stop worrying. Let's get some coffee and look over our notes. We have an anatomy test, you know."

"I've got to go to morning report. I'll meet you."

"Okay," said Kate, and walked off. She couldn't help worrying about her friend. Jennifer was a little scatter-brained, especially when it came to keeping a schedule. Kind of like a lot of the doctors.

Maybe she was practicing for the job.

Five

Gary Tuttle stepped into the tiny medication room adjoining the nursing station and looked at his watch. It was ten forty-five—time to send Walter Oldenfield for his hyperbaric treatment. Gary unlocked the narcotic cabinet, broke the seal on a box of morphine and withdrew a 10 milligram syringe. Then he walked down to the patient's room.

When he entered, he found a slim elderly man with sunken cheeks and a semi-circle of white hair around the back of his head. He noted the many purple blotches on the patient's arms, a combination of numerous injections and a low platelet count, the cells most involved in forming clots. Oldenfield was rocking back and forth in an armchair, his left leg elevated on an ottoman and pillow.

Gary looked at the bulky dressing wrapped around the patient's foot. Fifty years of smoking and atherosclerosis had choked off the arteries in Oldenfield's legs until only a trickle of blood dribbled down to his feet. After an arterial bypass failed to improve the circulation, Dr. Galloway, James Madison's only vascular surgeon, had amputated the small toe of the left foot. Now, the two adjacent toes were black for want of a blood supply, and the whole foot was mottled and cold.

"The foot's bad, isn't it, Mr. Oldenfield? Dr. Galloway switched you from those pain pills back to the shots. I've got the first one right here."

Oldenfield looked at the syringe in Gary's hand. "How fast does that stuff work?"

Gary wiped a spot on the patient's upper arm with alcohol, jabbed the needle into the muscle and pushed down on the plunger. Oldenfield winced as the narcotic entered the muscle.

"You should be comfortable by the time you get down to the vascular lab."

Oldenfield rubbed his arm at the injection site. "You think Dr. Galloway will operate again?"

"He may have to take off those two toes, but right now he wants to continue with the hyperbaric treatments."

Oldenfield scowled as he eased back in the armchair.

"I don't mind going under the knife again, but I hate that goddamned tank. It looks like a big steel coffin!"

The nurse placed his hand on Oldenfield's shoulder. "I know you don't like the treatments, but they do seem to be helping you." He dropped the used syringe into a red needle box hanging on the wall, then glanced at his watch. "Do you want to fill out your menu for tomorrow? They'll be picking them up soon."

Oldenfield picked up a little portable radio, its back held on with nursing tape, and half the antenna gone. He turned it on and rotated the dial, searching for a station. "What else is there to do?" he said, looking old and frail.

The orderly came into the room with a stretcher, and Gary helped him transfer Oldenfield from the bed. He wished that the treatments would produce a miracle, but knew that the disease was too advanced and the patient too old. He hated when a patient's disease had no cure and it looked as if pain was going to be a lifelong companion. Why didn't Galloway just cut off the damn foot?

On his way back to the nursing station, Gary saw an elderly woman walking slowly along the wall. She was so bent forward from curvature of the spine that from the back she seemed to have no head. As he came abreast of her, she turned her head to the side turtle-fashion and eyed him.

"Oh sir'rr. Would you be so kind as to pick that up for me please?"

Looking down, Gary saw a shiny new penny on the floor, heads up. Bending down to get it, he noticed dried stool on the patient's old leather slippers. He realized that the woman's eyes had grown too weak and her sense of smell too dulled to notice it herself, and he felt a familiar rush of sympathy and affection for her.

He plucked the penny from the floor and handed it to the woman.

"Did you drop it, Mrs. Gold?"

With pale, trembling fingers she held the penny in front of her face. The little coin shone in the fluorescent lights, as did the woman's moist, good-natured eyes.

"Oh dear me, no. I was just hoping for a little luck."

Head bowed, Mrs. Gold resumed her slow progression along the wall.

It was almost seven-fifteen by the time Lenny left the housekeeping office and returned to Seven-South, where he found Betty, his housekeeping partner, and Celeste, the unit clerk, at the nursing station. "The bastards axed Regis for being two minutes late on the clock," he told them. "I had a deal for a three-day suspension but it fell through. Regis wouldn't go along with it. Not that I blame him."

"That poor boy's his own worst enemy," said Betty. "Always gettin' his self in trouble."

"You think you can get his job back for him?" asked Celeste.

"I don't know, this is a tough nut. I've got to talk to the area rep. She might know about an arbitration case we can use as precedent, but…"

"But he's been written up so much what chance has he got. Right?" said Celeste. She was a tall, slender black woman who always dressed elegantly in long, billowing skirts and blouses with bright colors. Today she was wearing her hair piled high on her head, showing off a long, willowy neck set off by a slender gold necklace and dangling gold earrings.

"It's a piss-poor case," said Lenny. "I'll file a grievance this afternoon and we'll see what happens. I just wish he could learn to hold his anger. He'd spend a lot less time in Childress's office."

"And if God delivered us all from our servitude there'd be no need to ever raise our voice but in prayer," said Betty.

"Amen to that," added Celeste, picking up the phone. "I'm calling Birdie."

Birdie was the hospital seamstress. Her sewing room in the basement was a major social center for the service workers, who gathered there to exchange gossip and blow off steam. One call to Birdie and within an hour half the hospital would have the news.

Lenny left the station to catch up on his morning chores. He spent the next hour working out his frustration on the old marble floor. Laying down a thick coat of wax, he guided the buffer in broad sweeping curves across the surface until it shone. When he was in a playful mood, he would work the machine one-handed, making the heavy buffer sail over the floor in elegant pirouettes, but today he only wanted to get the job done. The rhythm of the machine was soothing, and by the time he'd finished with the floor, he'd framed the appeal in his mind and was feeling a little better. He'd fill out the grievance form and deliver it to Childress after lunch.

As he unlocked the supply room to put away the machine, Betty called out to him. "Break time. You comin' to the cafeteria?"

"I'll meet you there," he said, wanting to put everything away before going off the unit. Besides, he wanted one more minute alone to think about how he was going to handle Regis's appeal. Not that he had a rat's ass chance of winning it. "I can't do the impossible," he muttered, all too aware that people in trouble expected him to do exactly that.

Six

Regis Devoe stepped out of the twenty-four hour deli on the corner of Germantown Avenue and Washington Lane, a sixteen ounce bottle of malt liquor in a brown paper bag clutched in his gloved hand. Normally he wouldn't have anything to drink until after work, and even then he usually went home and had dinner with his wife Salina before tapping a can, but today was a far cry from normal. He had lost his job at the hospital, maybe forever this time. What really ate at his gut was that he might have been able to save it if he'd listened to Lenny. But how could he do that?

"I'm not kissing no boss's ass," he mumbled. "No way no how…"

Unemployment was not, however, his biggest worry. His biggest fear was facing Salina, whose temper was as hot as his. In that way they were a matched set, except she had a habit of throwing things at him, or, if he wasn't home, of throwing his things out onto the sidewalk. The major difference between them was that he could forget a spite an hour later, while she held on to a grudge for a long, long time.

Like the Friday evening he'd told her he was going out for a drink at the local pub. She was watching a movie on cable and he wanted to catch some of the Eagles game, so he walked around the corner to the bar. He really didn't mean to stay long. Have one, maybe two beers and then come home, but he'd run into Stanley, a buddy from his old neighborhood in North Philly, and they'd gotten to talking and telling stories, and Stan invited him to ride in his new car and go down to look at the old places where they used to hang out. One thing led to another, they smoked some weed and met some more old friends and he ended up not coming home until early Sunday morning.

He found the locks changed and his name crossed out on the mailbox. Salina had thrown out all his clothes, his tapes and CDs and his weight bench and barbell. She must have been mad as a volcano erupting to lug that heavy bar bell with the weights on it up from the basement. Lucky for him a neighbor saw what she was doing and called his brother Lester, who'd dated the neighbor's sister on and off. Lester had come and scooped everything up before scavengers could haul it away.

This Won't Hurt A Bit

Regis got everything back except for a couple of CDs, which Lester swore were gone by the time he got to the house, though Regis had his doubts.

That wife of his did not play. That scared him and made him love her like crazy at the same time.

She was home, too. Had been throwing up half the night and called out sick, so he'd have to face her when she was already in a lousy mood. Maybe she'd be asleep and he could tiptoe in, make her some breakfast when she woke up. But she'd ask right away why was he home so early, and then he'd have to tell her.

He was up shit creek with no fucking paddle. He sheltered from the January cold in a bus kiosk and sipped his beer, the too-small jacket affording him little warmth. A bus lumbered up and came to a stop. The pneumatic door opened with a loud "whishhh" and the driver looked down at him.

"I'm gonna take the next one," Regis said.

The driver glared at him. "Fucking wise guy," he mumbled, closed the door and roared away from the curb, the huge wheels thundering on the cold cobblestones of Germantown Avenue.

By the time the next bus came he'd finished his beer, leaving the bottle standing in a corner of the kiosk. He entered the bus and sat in the back, staring out the window at the empty sidewalks and shuttered shops waiting to open, and wishing he had someplace else to go.

Lenny rode the elevator to the basement cafeteria for morning break. As he carried his coffee cup to a crowded table, his friend Moose Lennox pulled out a chair for him. Moose was a tall, powerfully built black man who had played football in high school and for a time taken up amateur boxing.

Watching Lenny take a slim sandwich out of a wrinkled paper bag, Moose said, "You still eating that peanut butter and jelly shit? On white bread?"

"Ahh, since it's just me now, I don't cook much."

Betty, eating a soft pretzel dripping with mustard, looked at him. "You still miss Margaret a lot, don't you?"

"Mmmph," he said, biting into his sandwich and wiping jelly from his lips.

"You were made for marriage, just like your old man," said Moose.

Lenny swallowed his mouthful of sandwich. "It's true. My dad liked nothing better than coming home and telling us about his day," he said. "His family was everything for him."

He silently stirred milk and sugar into his coffee and watched the swirling surface. For several moments the only sounds were those made by silverware striking plates.

Betty pointed a piece of pretzel at Lenny. "That was a shame, them firing Regis Devoe over two little-bitty minutes. You gonna get him his job back?"

"I almost had a deal cut with Childress, but it fell through."

Freddie, the old stoop-shouldered morgue attendant who always smelled of formaldehyde, said. "I bet ya that bastard Joe West was behind it!"

Lenny held his thumb and index finger an inch apart. "West put his nose this close to mine. I nearly gagged on his cheap-ass after-shave. I wanted to smash his ugly face in."

"That's right," Moose said, balling up his fists and holding them in a fighter's stance. "A few jabs to the head and then a roundhouse to the jaw. Stop him spying on us all the time." He dropped his hands to pick up a cup of coffee.

"The union gonna win this one?" asked Freddie.

"I don't know," Lenny said. "Regis' been written up so many times, it'll take a miracle to win this case. I'm gonna talk to the area rep this afternoon, see what she thinks. But I have a bad feeling about it."

"You can do it," said Freddie. "Remember those three guys last Fourth of July weekend watching the porno movie in the multi-media room?"

"Those fools," Betty said, laughing. "They didn't realize the dirty movie was being broadcast on the wards. Half the patients in the hospital saw couples bumping and grinding before Mother Burgess heard about it and ran down there and turned it off. God a-mighty, I heard she was spitting fire when she found them sitting there with their hands in their laps."

Lenny laughed, shaking his head. "The only reason those guys got off with a three-day suspension was because the youngest one was the Director of Nurse's cousin. Old Mother Burgess got him into the job knowing he'd lied about his age, which I brought up 'off the record' in a little sidebar discussion with Freely. I pointed out that they couldn't fire two of them and let one come back, it would be disparate treatment, and in the end they agreed to a three-day suspension and six months probation."

"You'll win Regis his job, too," Moose said. "Trust me. 'Member when Sidney stole that case of frozen chicken from the kitchen? You got *him* off."

"Now that was a tricky case," Lenny said. "Sidney had his car parked outside the hospital. West knew he was stealing food, so he ordered him to open the trunk of his car and the dumb schmuck did it!

"West saw the case of frozen chicken and went ballistic. Just as he called on his walkie-talkie for the police, old Sidney panicked and jumped in his car and took off."

"The way I heard it told," said Betty, "the meat was bad and the supervisor ordered Sidney to throw it out."

"Sidney swore it was two weeks past the expiration date. I argued it wasn't fit for human consumption, but the supervisor denied ever saying it, naturally."

"So how'd you get him off?" asked Freddie.

"It was like this. Sidney called me from a pay phone, all shook up. I told him to ditch the stuff and go to Murray's Steaks on Chelten Ave and buy a case of frozen chicken, and be sure to save the receipt, then go home. Sure enough, when he pulled up to his house, the cops were waiting for him. They ordered him to open his trunk, and when he did he had a case of Murray's chicken and a receipt to go along with it. West had to drop the charges. He knew I was behind it. The bastard's been trying to get even with me ever since."

"If you got Sidney off you ought to be able to get Regis off, too," said Moose.

"I wouldn't count on it," said Lenny. "It's gonna be a lot tougher nut to crack."

Seven

Regis turned the key as quietly as he could, but when he pushed open the heavy metal security door it creaked loudly on its hinges.

"Shit," he muttered, listening to the door. "I knew I should have oiled them hinges." The house was a well kept, two-story twin in East Mt. Airy, a tidy section of black, working-class families.

He stepped inside and closed the door as quietly as he could. From upstairs he heard Salina call, "Hello? Is somebody there?"

"It's me, sugar," he called, trying to sound blasé. "You still throwing up?"

"Reeg?"

"Yeah."

She shuffled heavily down the stairs, dressed in a rumpled nightgown and pink wool socks with pom-poms on the toes. Her feet were always cold, his, always warm, which meant that they fought in their sleep all winter long over the comforter being tucked in or pulled loose from the foot of the bed.

"It's so early...what are you doing home? Did you have an accident or..." She stopped at the foot of the stairs, suspicion darkening her face. She was a full-figured black woman with strong arms and a low, throaty voice. Putting her hands on her hips, she said, "Are you in trouble again? Don't you stand there and tell me you're in trouble again 'cause I don't want to hear it."

"It wasn't my fault, baby. There was this punk doctor jangling my chain and I just..."

"You *just*. You just had to let go with that mouth of yours, didn't you? How bad is it?"

He told her about the meeting in the office. About Lenny's efforts to save him and his unwillingness to go along with an apology. He hoped that his sticking by his principles would earn him a little sympathy from her, but he knew from the start his hopes were in vain.

"You had a *deal* cut and you didn't *take* it? Is that what your dumb mouth is trying to tell me? Lenny had it down as a suspension but you, mister Walk on Water...Mister I'm Too Good for That...*YOU* had to turn it down and lose the whole fucking job! Is that right?"

This Won't Hurt A Bit

"Not exactly."

"Of all the dumb shit, half-assed things you've done in your pitiful life, this is the worst."

"Hey look, I did what I had to do, okay? I'm no kiss-ass and I never will be. That's just the way I am. Do you want some Uncle Tom for a husband? Is that the kind of man you want? Someone who hangs his head when the boss gives you shit? Huh?"

"Fine. You're proud. Great! I'd like to know how we're going to make the mortgage payment on this house, is what I'd like to know."

"There you go always bringing up the damn house. Just 'cause your daddy gave us the down payment when we got married so his little girl didn't have to live in mean old North Philadelphia, you always have to bring up the house we couldn't afford on my paycheck."

"*I* didn't say anything about the down payment, you brought it up. But as long as you did, now that you're out of a job, what are we supposed to do, sell the place and move into some sleazy apartment on Chew and Chelten? Tell me that!"

"My uncle will take me on, delivering furniture. You know I always brought home a paycheck. I never failed you yet and I'm not about to start now."

"Four-fifty an hour and no benefits lugging fancy sofas and beds up three flights of stairs for rich white folks out the Main Line. That's just jim dandy. If we lose our health insurance I'm gonna have to go to the damn clinic. You know how dirty that place is."

"We'll work it out, baby. We always do. Okay?" He approached her gingerly, putting his arms around her waist and slowly drawing her toward him. He loved the way she looked in the morning when she first woke up, her hair all wild and her nightgown hanging on her heavenly curves. More than anything else, he was relieved she hadn't started throwing things. Probably too sick to start spitting fire at him.

"I'll make you some oatmeal. You think you can eat that?"

"I don't know, I guess so." She laid her head on his shoulder, then lifted it up and stared at his ratty jacket.

"Where's your leather coat? You didn't lose that too, did you?"

"No, it's safe. I had to clear out a locker. I couldn't open mine, so I used the safe one. I'll get Sylvester to bring it home for me."

"You damn well better get it back. I bought that for you for Christmas and it isn't paid off yet."

They walked arm and arm into the kitchen, where Regis took out a sauce pan and began making the oatmeal.

"I'm gonna put honey in it cause you're so sweet," he said, chancing a smile.

"Don't even try it," she said. "I'm not…"

Knock, knock knock!

The steel front door resonated with a loud pounding. Regis looked at the door, then turned to his wife, who shrugged her shoulders. As he passed from the kitchen through the dining room, he saw police officers in flak jackets carrying automatic rifles running through the alley beside the house.

"What the fuck," he mumbled. "Salina, get upstairs and lie on the floor. And don't look out the window!"

"What is it?"

"I don't know," he said, looking out the window, "but the house is surrounded by a million cops."

Regis squinted one eye as he looked through the peep hole in the front door. He saw a pair of plainclothes detectives flanked by uniformed officers standing on the front porch.

"What do you want?" Regis called through the door.

"Open up or we break in the door!" one of them shouted.

Salina had come into the living room and pulled the curtain aside to look out the front window.

"You better let them in, Regis."

He unbolted the door and opened it a crack. A beefy white detective shoved the door open and stepped inside. A black detective followed behind. The first one in said, "Regis Devoe?"

"Yeah, so what," he answered.

The cop grabbed Regis's wrist and slapped a handcuff on it before the young man could react. Quickly the detective turned him around, saying, "Put your other hand behind you. You're under arrest. Don't do anything stupid."

"What the fuck's goin' on!" said Regis.

The black detective stood in front of Regis, looking him square in the face. "Regis Devoe, we have a warrant for your arrest for the murder of Doctor Randy Sparks. You have the right to remain silent. You have the right to legal counsel. If you speak, anything that you say may be used against you in a court of law. You will be…"

Suddenly Salina leaped forward and put her arms around her husband. "You can't do this, this is crazy! Regis didn't kill anyone!"

"We've got the right guy all right," said the white detective. "There are witnesses who overheard him threatening the victim."

Salina buried her face in her husband's back and hugged him tighter.

This Won't Hurt A Bit

"You better let him go, lady," said the white detective. "*Now.* Interfering with a police investigation is a felony. You want to go to jail, too?"

"I don't care as long as I'm with Regis."

"Sweetheart, they don't put boys and girls together in the same cell, you know what I mean? Now let go."

Regis turned his head to look at Salina. "It'll be okay, baby, it's some stupid screw up. I won't be locked up long. You'll see."

As the two detectives led him through the door, she stepped out into the cold January air in her nightgown and said, "I'll call Lenny at work. He'll know what to do!"

Shivering with the cold and the shock, she stepped back into the house, closed and bolted the door, then ran into the kitchen and picked up the phone. She didn't know the number for Seven-South, but she knew Birdie's number in the sewing room, so she called that.

"Sewing room, good morning."

"Birdie, it's Salina! Oh God, Birdie, you won't believe what happened. The cops just came to the house and arrested my Regis for murder!"

"Arrested? Murder? What's going on?"

"They said he killed that doctor they found in the medical school last week. You've got to get hold of Lenny and tell him—he'll know what I should do."

"I'll call his floor—you sit tight. Everything will be all right."

"Okay," Salina said. She put the phone down slowly. Once the connection was severed, she felt the emptiness of the house. Fear made her tremble like a frigid wind was blowing through her nightgown. She ran into the kitchen, bent over the sink and heaved out her guts.

Eight

The discussion in the cafeteria turned to the problems the hospital was having with the budget cutbacks and having to close beds.

"Hey Lenny," Freddie asked, his face set in a perpetual hound dog look. "You think they're really gonna lay off all us old-timers? I been here goin' on thirty-six years. Even McDonald's wouldn't hire an old fart like me."

"Yeah, what's the deal?" Betty said. "All these rumors buzzin' around. Hospital gonna get bought up, closed down, turned into a fat farm.. It's crazy."

Lenny tasted his coffee. "I missed the last Board of Directors meeting, but you can bet they'll try and get rid of the seniority language in the next contract."

"Can they *do* that?" Freddie asked.

"Sure. They can't sell the hospital for a good price unless they cut their costs, and old guys like you are pricey. Why pay one man fifteen bucks an hour when you can get a couple of hungry part-timers for nine-fifty? Hell, they can get welfare workers for free!"

"Welfare workers?" said Moose. "In a hospital? No way. This ain't like sweeping the streets and cleaning the parks. We're taking care of *people*."

Exclamations of agreement rose from around the table.

Betty poked her last piece of pretzel in a puddle of mustard. "I guess all that publicity over the murder across the street don't help the hospital none." She bit off a piece of pretzel, "What do you make of that young doctor turning up on a table like a slab o' meat?"

"He probably got caught with his pants down sleeping with a doctor's wife," Lenny said. "Nothin' to do with us."

"I heard he was real smart," she went on. "That's a shame, a young man having his life cut short like that."

"Anybody hear how he got iced?" Moose asked, looking around the table.

Freddie said, "Down the morgue, Doc Fingers told me Sparks was made to look like he was in a car wreck, but the wounds were faked. Heard it from the M.E. himself."

"How in the world somebody could sneak a body into a classroom that way is beyond me," Betty said.

"They don't exactly come in with a UPC label," Freddie said.

"A what?" she asked.

"A Universal Product Code. You know, those little bar codes they scan at the supermarket? If you know how to work the identification, sneaking a body into the anatomy lab is cake, so long as you drain all the fluids and replace them with preservative. The slick part was mashing in his face so nobody recognized him."

"Somebody knew what they was doing," said Moose.

Lenny took a last bite of his sandwich and washed it down with coffee. "Let the cops worry about how some doctor got killed. We've got enough problems of our own."

"No lie," Moose said, holding a bagel oozing cream cheese, "though it *is* kinda interesting."

"A shame somebody didn't ice West," Freddie said, a glint of mirth lifting his doleful countenance .

"That'd be too much like right," said Moose.

Lenny picked up his empty cup and rose from the table. "Anyone want more coffee?"

Moose and Betty accepted, and as he took his tray with him into the serving area, he imagined what it would be like to not worry about his friends being fired and ending up out on the street. To not have any more Regis Devoes.

Birdie dialed the number for the Seven-South nursing station. When Gary answered, she said, "This is Birdie. Is Lenny there? It's important."

"No, he's gone to the cafeteria on break. Would you like to leave a message."

"Mmm, no, I'll run over there, it's not far. Thanks," she said, hanging up.

She hurried out of the sewing room, made her way along the basement corridor to the cafeteria, and was relieved to see Lenny carrying a tray of coffee cups to a group of service workers gathered around a table. Rushing up to them, she said, "Lenny, we've got big trouble!"

"Cripes, *now* what is it?" he said, passing out the cups and settling into his seat. He peeled opened a little creamer and stirred it into his cup. "I went one-on-one with Joe West this morning and had to walk Regis Devoe out the door. I don't think I can take another termination."

Birdie stepped closer to her husband, who put his arm around her waist. "Salina just called me in the sewing room, all upset and crying. She said the police grabbed Regis right in his own living room. Threw the cuffs on him and took him down to the Round House!"

Lenny stopped stirring his coffee. "They arrested Regis? What the hell for?"

"Salina said the detective told her they were charging Regis with murdering that young doctor. They said he threatened him just before he disappeared. They have witnesses and everything! She wants you to call her right away."

"That's un-fucking-believable!" Lenny said. "Regis never told me about an argument. I know he's hot-blooded, but he wouldn't kill anyone. Besides, how could he sneak a body into a dissecting lab?"

"Damn right!" Freddie's voice snapped out. "Draining the body fluids and filling the vessels with formaldehyde. It'd take a doctor to do something like that, not a man works in the laundry."

Lenny glanced at his watch. "Break time's up. I'll call the union office and see if the lawyer can find out what the fuck's going on."

After they bussed their trays, Moose walked out of the cafeteria with Lenny.

In the hallway, Moose glanced at a pair of carpenters wheeling a cart with a new door balanced precariously on it up to the elevator.

"C'mon," he said, his face deadly serious, "let's take the stairs. We got to talk."

"Can't we take the elevator?"

"Nope. You can't stay lean and mean riding that thing," said, Moose, holding the door to the stairwell open. Lenny shrugged, stepped into the well.

Lenny wondered what was so urgent that they had to trudge up eight floors. They climbed the first flight in silence. Moose, in fighting trim, took the stairs two steps at a time, while Lenny struggled to keep up.

As they crossed the second floor landing, Moose said, "Well, what're you gonna do about Regis?"

Surprised, Lenny stopped, then hurried to catch up.

"What do you mean 'do'? What can I do? I'm a shop steward, not a fucking lawyer."

Moose slowed his pace as they reached the third floor, seeing that Lenny was tiring.

"Ain't no one else can help him get his job back. We both know that, Lenny."

"What're you talking about? I can't get him to a grievance hearing when he's going on trial for murder."

Moose kept silent while two lab technicians, their trays laden with scarlet vials, passed them going down the stairs. His face was taut and grim. Passing the forth floor landing, Moose said, "Shit, man, all the union members come to you with their problems. You know everybody in the hospital, you go all over the place on union business. You're the only one who can do it."

"Do what?" he said, fighting to stay abreast of his friend.

"You know, get it all cleared up, like you always do."

Short-winded by now, Lenny stopped at the fifth floor landing and took in several deep breaths. His face was moist with perspiration and his legs were beginning to cramp.

"I'm sorry, I still don't get you."

A head taller than Lenny, Moose looked dead into his friend's eyes, jabbed him in the chest with his finger and said, "You got to find out who really murdered that doc."

Nine

Walter Oldenfield lay on a thin foam rubber mat inside the big hyperbaric tank and looked up at the clock on the wall. One forty-five. Dr. Galloway was late, but he was always late.

From the outside, the tank looked like a huge, squat steel egg on legs. The top of the tank formed a curved lid, that was open. On the inside it was a bit roomier than a coffin, but as cold as the morgue. Pipes from a large compressor beside the tank entered at the foot.

Galloway came bustling into the lab followed by a troupe of residents and medical students. The picture of a senior physician, he was a tall, aristocratic figure with a high forehead, long straight nose, intense hazel eyes, and a small, grim mouth.

While the group crowded around a bank of monitors on a long, white counter, Galloway pointed to various dials and displays.

"The traditional treatment for ischemic peripheral disease has been to improve blood flow to the affected limb using synthetic shunts or transplanted veins. A logical approach, since blood carries oxygen and nutrients and removes waste products."

As he spoke, a respiratory therapist connected EKG electrodes to Oldenfield's chest, oxygen sensors to his fingertips, and probes for measuring galvanic skin resistance and temperature to his feet. Finished, she spread two blankets over him to protect the patient from the cold he would experience, just as if he'd climbed to a high altitude.

From inside the tank Oldenfield asked, "Doc, are you sure this thing is helping me?"

Galloway ignored the patient as he continued with his explanation.

"Hyperbaric oxygenation of blood is an adjunct to the traditional treatment modalities, not a replacement. By increasing the barometric pressure within the chamber, we increase the amount of oxygen carried in the blood, increasing hemoglobin binding capacity by twenty percent."

A resident in a wrinkled lab coat asked, "What sort of pressures do you use on your patients?"

"On human subjects we have not gone beyond 1.85 atmospheres.

Our lab animals have sustained two and a half atmospheres without injury, and, of course, divers experience even greater pressures, but we are cautious in the laboratory, for obvious reasons. Sensory data is fed into the computer, which calculates the improvement in oxygen delivery."

Oldenfield pulled himself to a sitting position and looked over the rim at Galloway.

"Is this tank going to save my foot or not?"

Galloway turned from his audience to look at his patient. "Your oxyhemoglobin curve is shifted demonstrably to the right, Walter. I can assure you that the results are quite promising."

"Yeah, but how long does it last?"

The surgeon turned back to the group. "We are still investigating the duration of the treatment's efficacy. So far, the data is encouraging. We expect to have an article ready for the journals in a few months."

Oldenfield looked at the back of Galloway's head, opened his mouth to speak, then sank back into the tank.

The therapist grasped the heavy lid and looked down at Oldenfield. "Ready?" she said.

He frowned, nodded, crossed his arms across his chest. The therapist slowly lowered the lid, that closed with a solemn, metallic clank. Then she fastened a pair of chrome latches along the lip. She winked at Oldenfield through a little plexiglass window and withdrew to the counter to watch the patient's vital signs on the monitor.

As Galloway turned a dial, the compressor kicked in, throbbing loudly. A microphone in the tank carried Oldenfield's voice to a tinny speaker on the wall. "I'm getting mighty tired of the pain in this leg, I can tell you."

"Just relax, Walter," Galloway said into his own mike as he increased the pressure in the tank.

The residents and students silently stared at the dials as the pressure in the tank slowly increased, while the throbbing sounds of the compressor filled the room like the rumble of a descending flood.

Emerging out of breath from the stairwell onto Seven-South, Lenny asked Moose, "Do you always take the stairs? That was hell."

"Got to. Them elevators'll sap your strength." Moose stood waiting while Lenny got his wind back. "Why don't you come jogging with me? You can't stay lean n' mean without no exercise."

He pushed the food cart down the hall and began collecting the breakfast trays. Lenny took a dry mop from the utility closet and stayed close to him, sweeping the corridor.

"So, we doin' this investigation thing or not?" Moose asked.

Lenny scooped up a pile of dust and debris into a dustpan, dumping it with a clatter inside his trash bucket.

"It's a crazy idea, Moose. I'm a custodian, not a detective."

"The cops have got a scapegoat. You know they won't be looking for somebody else. Without us, Regis is a dead man."

"I realize that." Lenny stood staring into space. He puffed out his cheeks. "I'd like to be doing more to help him, but other than trying to get the union lawyer involved, I don't see what else I can do."

"We can pick up clues, that's what we can do," said Moose.

"Clues?"

"That's right. In the trash, the bathrooms, the doctors' offices…" Moose went into another room, emerging with two more trays. "Hey, just the other morning I was serving breakfast trays, and I saw there was an empty Dunkin' Donuts coffee cup on the breakfast tray of a foxy young patient."

"What did that tell you?"

"It told me somebody got in mighty early to have breakfast with the girl, or else they spent the night in her bed."

"Slick, Moose. Very slick."

Coffee cups rattled on their saucers as Moose slid a pair of trays into the cart.

"Look. Us service workers, we're invisible. The doctors and the supervisors don't hardly notice us, but we see everything."

"It's true. Look how the doctors always walk across my wet floor, even with the yellow caution signs up. They're so caught up in their stuff they don't see they're walking on a slick surface."

"That's what I'm sayin'. I could stand behind a bunch o' them doctors with a lunch tray in my hand and listen in and they'd never even know I was there."

"We're just like furniture to them!" Lenny said.

Moose brought the food cart to a stop in front of the service elevator and pushed the down button. "We could meet in Birdie's sewing room and plan our moves," he said, watching his friend's face closely. "What d'ya say?"

Lenny stood and rubbed his chin, felt the stubble that was always there, even an hour after shaving.

"I'm sorry, Moose, but I think Regis needs a Johnny Cochran, not a Jim Rockford."

Ten

Kate Palmer sat in a large, empty lecture hall going over her notes for an anatomy exam. She chewed a peanut butter and jelly sandwich, having made one for her daughter and another for herself that morning. Her eyes drifted away from her notes as she thought of her little girl in school biting into her sandwich and chattering away with her best friend, Wendy.

She glanced at her watch and frowned. Jennifer was supposed to meet her so they could study together, but she was late, as usual.

As Kate finished the last of her sandwich, Jennie came rushing down the aisle, a red leather satchel hanging on one shoulder. Her cowboy boots, elegant with heels and embroidered ankles, dripped melting snow along the floor.

"Sorry I'm late."

"It's okay. Do you have your notes with you?"

"Somewhere in this mess," Jennie said, plopping down beside Kate and opening her bag. "I need someone to micro-manage my life." She rummaged among notebooks, medical journals, makeup kit and cellular phone. Finally she pulled some papers out with a flourish. "Ta-Dah!"

Kate began, quizzing her friend about the layers of the skin. Jennie countered with the cross section of the arteries and veins. They went on to nerve fibers and motor end plates.

"Katie, did you ever hear any more about poor Randy Sparks?"

"Not much. Latterly said that the initial tox screen came back negative, but you can never trust what he says." Kate took an apple from her lunch bag and bit into it. "I wonder if the police have any suspects yet."

"Don't even think about it," said Jennifer. "It's too creepy."

"But don't you want to know who killed him and smuggled his body into our lab? It has to be someone awfully clever."

"You mean someone like Letterly."

"I don't think he's *that* smart," said Kate. "His father's a big shot on the medical board, so he thinks he's hot stuff."

"Don't you hate it when someone rides on somebody else's coat tails?"

"It's the pits," said Kate.

Jennifer brushed back her long blonde hair and thumbed through a page of notes. "If I don't do better than a seventy-five, I'm in big trouble."

"You'll do fine. Just don't get rattled by the first question. It's always impossible. They do it just to unnerve you."

"Don't I know it."

Kate turned her notebook to a blank page, saying, "Let's get back to work." She told Jennifer to draw the hip and groin without referring to her notes. Jennie drew the skeleton and muscles with an artist's eye.

"That's great, Jen," Kate said.

"Now you put in the internal organs," Jennie said.

Kate drew the liver, pancreas, kidneys, spleen and the tiny appendix, then overlapped the stomach and intestines. The drawing was more of a draftsman's sketch than Jenny's artistry, but all the parts were neatly arranged.

Jennie jabbed Kate's sketch with a finger and exclaimed, "Ha, you forgot the adrenals!"

"Oops," Kate said, hurriedly adding the tiny structures to the kidneys.

As the other students began to drift into the hall, Jennifer leaned closer to her friend and whispered, "Has anybody said anything about…you know, me and Randy?"

"No," Kate whispered, "not a peep. I still think it would give you an air of distinction. It's not like he was dead when you slept with him."

"Oh he was alive all right, believe me. I just…"

A trio of male students with Letterly at the lead filed into their aisle. As Kate tucked in her legs to let them pass, she heard the tall, beefy student saying, "Did you hear about the guy who went to his GP because he fainted every time he saw a beautiful naked girl?"

"What happened?" the second student asked.

"The GP told the guy to go into the examining room and strip from the waist down, then he said to his nurse—a gorgeous platinum blonde with huge tits—'Sherry, I want you to take off all your clothes and go in the examining room'. So she did. As soon as the guy saw Sherry, he got a giant erection, his dick jumped up between his legs and smacked him in the forehead and knocked him out cold.

"The GP wrote in the patient's chart, 'Diagnosis confirmed'."

The three male students exploded in laughter.

"Honestly," said Kate, "you men think the whole world revolves around your sex organs."

"Well doesn't it?" asked Letterly.

"Ha, ha," Jennifer chimed in.

"Seriously," Letterly said, "Don't you girls feel…"

This Won't Hurt A Bit

"Save it for later," Kate said. "It's test time."

Letterly dropped the smirk from his face, as the crowd grew suddenly silent. Jennifer rose and moved two seats away, one of the rules that discouraged cheating, while the men drifted into scattered seats.

"Good luck!" Kate said in a stage whisper.

"Thanks."

As the clock on the wall at the front of the room clicked on the hour, a young bearded instructor stepped up to a podium on the stage and tapped the microphone. "All right, people, put everything away but your brains."

Joe West's beeper went off. He found a phone and dialed the operator.

"West!" he growled.

"This is Sternbach. I thought you'd like to know we picked up your boy Devoe this morning."

"Did he give you any trouble?"

"Nah, it was routine. He's on his way to the Round House as we speak."

"Excellent. All the public defenders in the world won't be able to help him, " West said.

"You got that witness for us, don't you?"

"Nothing to worry about, she 's in my pocket."

"She better be. I'm on my way over to your hospital. Put her on ice until I get there."

"She'll be ready to sing like a bird as soon as ...."

Click. Officer Sternbach had hung up.

Eleven

While he waited for Mr. Oldenfield to return from the vascular lab, Gary Tuttle sat at the nursing station sorting the laboratory slips into alphabetical order in order to file them in the charts. He looked up to see Dr. Priscilla Gandy approaching him. The urologist was a tall, boney woman with thin lips and a pale, bloodless face. A severely tailored black velvet suit hung on her like clothing on a rack.

She pulled out Mr. Louis Anderson's chart and thumbed through it. "I don't see the resident's history and physical. Didn't he do it yet?" she asked, not looking up from the chart.

Gary flinched at hearing her voice, which rose and fell in pitch like a dentist's drill burrowing into his teeth. He recalled how often Gandy had asked him why something hadn't been done that was clearly the responsibility of the resident or medical student. He was not the house staff's nanny or supervisor, but Gandy persisted in asking him to call the person and see that a task was completed or a piece of information obtained. Once she had refused Gary's request to write an order in the chart for Tylenol, telling him, "Get the resident to do it, he needs the practice."

Gary said, "If the H. & P. isn't in the chart, I suppose that he didn't do it yet," He continued sorting and checking the laboratory slips.

"But he must have examined the patient by now!" She scowled at him, deepening the creases that ran down her cheeks like old scars. "You did notify him of the admission, didn't you? Because if he wasn't called there'll be hell to pay."

"Yes, I notified the resident," Gary said. "He wrote the admission orders, they're in the chart, all taken off."

She scanned the orders. "Did Mr. Anderson get his late breakfast?"

"Dietary sent a tray up, but I don't think he ate much of it."

"I want a strict calorie count on him. Tell the dietitian she has to see him today."

Gandy turned and stalked down the hall, her high heels clicking on the marble floor like the stick of a prison guard along the bars of the cells.

Gary felt his anger building like the blood pressure of a hypertensive patient in crisis. As he squared the stacks of lab reports on the counter, he imagined telling Gandy what she could do with her calorie count.

During Gary's encounter with Dr. Gandy, Alex Primeaux, a family practice physician wearing a rumpled corduroy sports coat with leather patches on the sleeves and an open shirt with no tie, had been sitting quietly at the station. "It's such a shame, carrying on like that," Primeaux said in a soft Southern drawl. "She doesn't understand you can catch more flies with honey than you can with vinegar. People like Gandy just create more problems."

"I wish more of the doctors could be like you, Alex."

"That's just the way my momma raised me, ah guess," said Primeaux, his warm brown eyes full of sympathy. He thumbed through the nursing notes. "I see you were able to get Mr. Dotterer in the tub yesterday. That must've been quite a struggle."

"It certainly was. He was so stiff from the Parkinson's that he couldn't bend at the waist. The poor man looked like he was half-way through a sit-up."

The physician chuckled as he began to write in the chart. "I wish ah' could've seen that." He signed off his note. "How is Mr. Oldenfield coming with his hyperbarics?"

"I don't think he can tolerate many more of them. He wants Dr. Galloway to amputate the foot."

"He's suffered with that foot a long time," Primeaux said, taking out a stack of three-by-five cards and looking over the names. "How's Mrs. Rosemond doing? Is her CBC back?"

"Here it is." Gary handed him a lab slip. "She's complaining about the liquid diet in a loud and persistent voice. She even asked me to call the supervisor when I told her I couldn't give her any solid food without your direct order."

Primeaux sighed. "I just don't understand why that woman has traces of blood in her stool. I've done every study I know, even a bleeding scan."

"Maybe she's a vampire," Gary said.

"I thought of that, but the teeth are all wrong," said the doctor, his neatly trimmed mustache lifting in a boyish smile. He rose from the chair, buttoned his sports coat and ambled off to see his patient.

As Kate and Jennifer were filing out of the lecture hall, Jennifer said, "I think I did really good this time. I really do."

"I'm sure you passed," said Kate. "You just need to spend more time studying, that's all."

"God knows what I'd do without you." Jennifer glanced at a clock on the wall. "You have time for a break? I'm starved. Exams always make me hungry."

"I had a sandwich in the hall, but I'll have coffee with you. Can we stop at the mailroom? I'm expecting a package."

"Sure."

The two made their way to the student mailroom, where Kate found a note. Jennifer, a head taller than her friend, looked over her shoulder.

"Uh-oh," said Jennifer. "It's from the dean. Those are always bad news. What does it say?

"You better check your box," Kate said, looking at her friend. "They want me to go to the office ASAP. What time is it now?"

"Eleven-ten," said Jennifer, who had bent down to open her own mailbox. "Yup, I got a note, too. Damn, what do you think it's about?"

"I'll give you one guess, and it's floating in a formaldehyde bath," Kate said. "Let's go."

They rode the elevator to the penthouse, stepping out onto a carpeted hall with recessed lighting and soft music. The dean's office had large, ornate wooden doors with large brass handles.

The secretary looked up, saw the pair and told them, "The dean is expecting you."

As the two students followed her back into the bowels of the office, Jennifer whispered to Kate, "She knew who we were without asking. That's a really bad sign."

Kate shrugged. They stepped through a door which the secretary held open for them and then quietly closed at their back.

The dean, a balding man in his fifties who wore bifocals and a bow tie, looked up but did not stand. With his eyes he indicated that they sit in two straight-backed, wooden chairs.

Seated in comfortable, stuffed chairs were two men dressed in rumpled suits, their raincoats draped over the backs of the chairs.

"This," said the dean in a clipped voice, "is Detective Sternbach." The Detective, a big, loose-limbed man slouched in his chair, looked from Jennifer to Kate, then focused his eyes on Jennifer.

"And this," the Dean went on, "is Detective Williams."

The second detective was a black man with a receding hairline and a scar down the middle of his chin.

"We have some questions we'd like to ask you," Williams said. "About that body you were cutting up."

Twelve

At noon, the patients lucky enough to have teeth and to be on a regular diet were in for a treat: chicken cordon bleu. Fat, juicy breasts of chicken stuffed with tender smoked ham and cheddar cheese and covered with a sweet cream sauce. The vegetables were boiled until they lost all taste and color, and the milk was vaguely sour, but the chicken was heavenly.

Moose Lennox pushed the food cart onto Seven-South and began serving the lunch. With a tray in either hand, he strode into a double room intending to slide the meals simultaneously onto the overbed tables, but he found a tall, blond doctor dressed in a pinstriped suit sitting on the edge of the bed and using the overbed table for a writing surface. Moose served the patient in the first bed, then placed the second tray on the window sill beside the bed where the doctor was perched. Turning to leave, he noticed the doctor close the chart, slide his hand down and squeeze the woman's leg.

It seemed like an awfully friendly squeeze to Moose.

He went back to the cart to serve the rest of the trays. When he was done, he took the stairs to the next floor, where another food cart was waiting.

A few moments later, Dr. Robert Radcliff, the physician who had been sitting on the bed writing, strolled up to the nursing station. He looked like a soap opera star with his strong jaw, striking blue eyes and blow dried blond hair parted in the middle. Putting the patient chart on the counter, Radcliff said to Gary, "See that Mrs. Grey is brought to my office at one-thirty sharp."

Gary put the patient's name, destination and time on the transport board.

"And see that she gets lunch. She has no appetite, but I want you to encourage her to eat."

"Very well."

Dr. Radcliff removed an electronic pocket organizer from his pocket. Opening the tiny computer, he scrolled down checking his appointments. He had micro-managed his time so efficiently that he knew exactly where he had to be every minute of the day, with an ample amount of time set aside for play, of course.

Closing the electronic toy with a satisfying snap, he strolled briskly down the hall toward his next appointment.

Assuming that Mrs. Grey's lunch tray had not been served, Gary went down the hall to the food cart, only to find it empty. Puzzled, he went to the patient's room to investigate. He found the lunch tray on the window sill, while the patient sat silently in bed staring out the window.

Forcing a smile onto his face, he asked, "Feel like a little lunch?"

"No, just some tea is all," she said in a toneless voice.

Gary placed the tray on the patient's table. He dropped a tea bag into the cup of hot water, pushed the button on the hand control to raise the head of the bed, and left the room muttering, "Doctors. Stupid, stupid doctors."

"Mmmm, da hmmm-mmmm...in the House of the Lorrrd."

Betty pushed her housekeeping cart down the middle of the Seven-South hall humming an old hymn. Brooms, dustpans and rags hung from its sides, while a silver-colored cross hung from the handle close to her hands.

As she advanced down the hall, an automated delivery cart approached and stopped a few feet from her cart. A red light on top of the robo-cart flashed menacingly. Betty glowered at the machine.

"Don't wink at me, you devil!"

Since the machine, that followed a track of magnets embedded in the floor, could not move sideways, Betty had to push her cart around it. She headed for the utility room at the end of the corridor, just before the double doors that connected her floor with Seven-North. Opening the utility room door, she found Lenny seated on an upside-down bucket attaching a new mop head to a handle.

"Hello, dear heart," she said.

"Hey, Boop. What's up?" he said. The room smelled of pine oil, ammonia, and wax.

"I just pray the Lord will see fit to get me through to Friday is all I've got to say!"

"Tell me about it. I've had a hell of a week already, and it's only Tuesday," he said. "I always thought that being a shop steward was tough, but now Moose wants me to help him investigate this doctor's murder. He thinks it's the only way to get Regis Devoe out of jail."

"Sounds like a awful slender thread for Regis to hold on to, but you know the cops won't look for anyone else. They got a scapegoat and that's all they care about."

"Why does everyone keep reminding me of that?"

This Won't Hurt A Bit

"Prob'bly cause you're the only one that has a chance of straightening this mess out."

She took some rolls of toilet paper and boxes of tissues from a shelf and put them in her cart. "Will they let you visit him in jail?"

"I think so. He's being moved to the Detention Center today. I'm gonna call to make sure."

"You be sure and tell him Betty's praying for him every day, won't you?"

"Of course." He stood up and hung the mop on a hook on the wall, then turned to the door.

She pushed her cart out into the hall and resumed her rounds, humming as she walked.

After mopping the patient rooms and the hallway, Lenny stepped into an empty room and closed the door, then picked up the phone. With no patients in the room, the phone was supposed to be turned off, but the operators were so busy with all the pages that they never got around to disconnecting phones between admissions.

Besides, leaving the phones switched permanently on saved the operators from having to listen to irate family members who pounded on the switchboard door demanding that their phone be turned on. When the nursing supervisors protested loudly about all of the local calls that the staff made from the empty rooms, the union answered that they should get unlimited local calling, but the administration was too cheap. They liked to bill each patient for every call.

Dialing the union office, he followed the prompts that led him past layers of union bureaucracy to the legal department. When he finally heard a human voice, the secretary told him that all three of the union lawyers were out of the office; one on vacation and two in court. Lenny left his work number, home number, and pager number, explaining that it was an urgent matter concerning a worker who had been fired and then arrested.

The secretary asked if the arrest was related to the firing. Lenny said, "Not exactly. I mean, it *might* be connected. The murder victim was a doctor in the hospital and the arrest was made the same day he was fired. Can you get somebody to call me today with an answer?"

The secretary told him she didn't think there was anything the union could do, but she would leave a note on one of the lawyer's desks. Lenny would just have to wait and hope he got a call back.

He didn't have Regis's phone number, but remembered that he and Salina had recently bought a house in East Mt. Airy. Checking new number information, he got the listing, dialed the number. After several rings, he heard a low, throaty woman's voice.

"Hello?"

"Hi, Salina? This is Lenny. You talked to Birdie and..."

"Lenny! I'm so glad that you called, I've been going crazy worrying about my Regis. I guess you heard the cops took him to the Round House."

"I heard. I'm sorry. I don't know what I can do to help him exactly. I left a message with the union legal department. It doesn't look like they'll be able to help. It's not, strictly speaking, a union matter."

"You always pulled him out of a hole before, Lenny. Can't you help him with this?"

"He needs a good lawyer, not a shop steward. Is money a problem, 'cause if it is I could start a fund raiser. Sell raffle tickets, hold a cabaret, but..."

"My uncle's a lawyer. He's not a lawyer who defends people. He's more like for property and taxes and stuff, but I'm quite sure he can find me somebody. I just need somebody to tell me what I should do!"

"Well, the first thing is, don't talk to the cops. Period. Wait until you have a lawyer, and then never talk to the cops unless your lawyer is with you. Can you do that?"

"Sure I can. My mouth is shut."

"Good. The other thing you can do is be supportive of Regis. He's gonna be scared, though I'm sure he'd never show it, and he needs you behind him one hundred per cent. Are you okay with that?"

"Of course, he's my Regis."

"Fine. Now, after I talk to the union lawyer I'll tell you what he says. All right?"

"Uh huh. I'm gonna stay with my folks for a while. I don't like being here by myself. I'll call you tonight."

"That'll be fine. And try not to worry too much, I know it's hard, but we'll get him out of this. It's just gonna take time."

"Okay. Bye Lenny."

The click of the phone was like the lock of a jail cell closing.

Thirteen

*L*enny's afternoon began in relative peace. Only a hundred co-workers approached him to ask for advice about the retirement package, or the policy on education benefits, or to see if he had a form for taxes or vacation. Freddie drew him into one of his knock-knock jokes that wasn't as bad as usual.

He was almost ready to believe he would get through the shift without another crisis, when he saw Moose walking toward him with his Serious Look on.

"So," said Moose, stepping up to him. "You working with me on this murder thing, or do I have to do it all by my lonesome?"

"It's a crazy idea, Moose."

"Crazy never stopped you before."

"Yeah, but there's practical joking and there's murder." He looked at his friend, saw the iron conviction in his eyes. "I hate the idea of West setting Regis up, you know I do, and I feel bad for his wife. I called Salina already, but…"

"You know how much West hates your guts and wants to fire your ass?"

"Yeah. So?"

"So, we pull this off," said Moose, "you'll have West off your back, permanent. No way he can harass a hero."

"That's true."

"Besides which, it'll really piss him off."

Mischief and reluctance fought in Lenny's brain. Mischief won out.

"Fuck it, let's do it. I was gonna visit Regis in jail anyway. I'll ask him what evidence the cops came up with in the arraignment. They've got to have something to justify an arrest."

"Good," Moose said. "We better try to find out everything we can about Sparks."

"Like, who he was working with when he disappeared, who he pissed off, that sort of thing."

"A nurse would know that, or could find out," said Moose. "Why don't you ask Gary?"

"I don't know. Tuttle's a nice guy and all, but he seems awfully caught up in that professional bullshit."

"You got a better candidate?" Moose asked.

Lenny thought about it, shrugged. "You're right. I'll talk to him. I'll tell Betty and Celeste, too. You try to track down Bobby D—that guy goes everywhere."

"I'll find him, trust me. What about Freddie?"

"I don't know. He's been written up so much for his absences. All those years on the bottle. I'll speak to him on the side."

"I need time to pick up the lunch trays. I'll see you at the time clock?"

"Yeah. I won't be late."

The elevator bell rang and the door opened. With a nudge from Moose, the lunch cart rolled into the elevator. "We'll have to figure out how the body ended up getting di-sected," he said.

"That's true," said Lenny.

Moose stepped in beside the food cart and tapped a button. As the elevator doors slid shut, he said, "You watch. We're gonna cast our line and catch us a big fish."

Lenny walked down the hall to the nursing station and spotted Gary.

"Hey, Tuttle, what'cha doing?"

"Hello, Lenny. I'm just waiting for Mr. Oldenfield to return from his treatment."

Lenny slumped into a chair beside Gary. "That guy seems to be in pain all the time. What's going on?"

"His hyperbaric treatments don't seem to be helping him very much. I wish Galloway would amputate the leg and be done with it."

"So why doesn't he?"

"You know how it is: he wants to prove the hyperbarics work. Besides, you have to be half-way through a course of treatments before you know it the limb is going to improve." He looked more closely at Lenny. "You don't look so hot yourself. Are you feeling ill?"

"No, I'm just worn out. I tried to save one of the laundry worker's job this morning and it didn't go too well." He summarized the encounter with Childress and West, ending with the story of the arrest.

"It sounds like you're blaming yourself for his free decision," Gary said. "He chose to reject your compromise. You can't blame yourself for another man's pride, can you?"

"I don't know how free he is," Lenny said. "I mean, he's full of rage, and frankly, I don't blame him. He's always gotten shit from Childress from the first day on the job. So he has a temper. That doesn't make it fair to can him, does it?"

"I suppose the punishment doesn't fit the crime, that's true," said Gary. "What are his chances of winning his union grievance?"

"They're zip as long as he's in jail, but I'll file the papers. Not that getting his job back is his biggest concern. A murder charge—now that's something to worry about."

Lenny eyed the row of binders and folders on a shelf behind the desk.

"Say Tuttle, don't you have a list of the residents and who they worked with?"

"Yes," said Gary, a trace of irritation in his voice his voice. "Why?"

"It's kinda personal. Can you keep this quiet?"

Gary nodded, focusing his sleepy eyes on Lenny.

Lenny leaned closer to Gary and lowered his voice. "I'm trying to help Regis Devoe out with the murder charge, but the thing is, as his union delegate, I won't have a shot at grieving his termination unless I find out who *really* killed the doctor. I can't even get him to a hearing as long as he's stuck in jail."

"They wouldn't arrest somebody unless they had some sort of evidence, would they?"

Lenny looked at Gary's smooth, bland face, remembering the nurse's mindset. Like a lot of professionals, Gary believed in "the system." And why not? He was doing all right by it.

"It's not that simple, Tuttle. Sometimes the police find someone they want to have done it. They use any sort of pretext to arrest him, and then they make up the rest."

"Are you saying that the police manufactured the evidence?"

"It happens all the time. I was at a trial once. I was just there as a character witness for somebody in the union. The D.A. got the judge to clear out the jury so that the cops could literally carry a burned-out dope-fiend prostitute to the witness stand. She was their *star* witness. They had to prop her up in the witness stand with pillows, she was so whacked out, but when the jury came back in they had no idea what kind of person she was."

"Surely the defense attorney brought out the woman's history of drug abuse in the cross examination."

"Nope. Any time the lawyer started to ask about her past, the D.A. objected and the judge ruled in his favor every time. The cops wanted a neat, straight conviction, and that's exactly what they got."

"You really saw that?" Gary asked.

"With my own two beady little eyes."

Gary sat back in his chair, folded his hands across his soft belly and took a moment to digest Lenny's remarks. "And you're going to try to find out who killed Dr. Sparks because you're sure—one-hundred percent certain—that Regis is innocent?"

"That's right. I know it sounds like a fool's errand, but I don't see any other way to get Regis to a grievance table."

"Well, where do I come in?"

"I was sort of hoping you could tell me who Sparks was working with when he disappeared."

Gary narrowed his eyes, crossed his arms across his chest and said, "If you think I'm going to get involved in some illicit murder investigation, you're out of your mind."

Fourteen

Lenny looked into Gary Tuttle's screwed-down, walls-up face, knowing that he had to have the nurse's help or his murder investigation would be a still birth. He said, "But Tuttle, you don't want to see an innocent man convicted of murder, do you?"

Gary frowned, his eyes roaming about the station, avoiding Lenny's.

"I'm all for supporting an innocent man, of course. I signed the petition for Mumia. It's just that I can't go around giving out information about the doctors. I don't have a union to stand behind me the way you do."

Lenny assumed the look of a pleading puppy. "Tuttle, we're talking about a major miscarriage of justice. You don't want the real killer getting away with it, do you? Right here at James Madison?"

"I don't know, Lenny, if word got out…"

"Who's gonna know? You can trust me! I won't tell a soul where I heard it."

Gary looked into Lenny's puppy-dog eyes.

"All you want is to find out who Randy Sparks was working with, is that right?"

"You got it."

"Well, I suppose that *is* public knowledge. It's not like it involves issues of patient privacy."

"My thought exactly," said Lenny.

Gary sighed. "Very well." He stood and reached for a clipboard on the wall. "The services are posted on the bulletin board every month. I believe that you want last month's list."

Gary showed Lenny the December bulletin. "Sparks was doing a psych rotation when he disappeared. It was Friday the thirteenth. I remember the med students joking about the date. The attending psychiatrists are Dr. Radcliff, Dundee, and Myers. These are the residents and students, and there's Sparks, still on the December schedule."

"Can you tell which shrink Sparks was assigned to?"

"Not from the list, no, but I remember that he rounded with Dr. Radcliff."

53

"Radcliff…Office on the second floor, right?"

"That's him."

"Okay, what about the other months?"

Gary stared into Lenny's guileless face. He felt his appetite ebbing. "Just how far are you going with this investigation?"

The custodian shrugged. "I don't know, this is all new territory for me. That's why I have to come to you."

Gary's hand drummed the desk. It wasn't that he didn't want to help. He knew Lenny's union work was respected throughout the hospital; that the man would fight tooth and nail to help a co-worker in trouble. It was just that Gary hated to make waves, and helping Lenny with something like the Regis affair could drop him in the middle of the North Atlantic.

Rising from his chair, Gary said, "We keep the schedules in the On-Call Book. I'll help you this one time, but no more. Understood?"

"Sure."

Gary looked around the station, saw it was empty, and reached for a black binder on a high shelf. Sitting again, he opened the binder and flipped back to November. He ran his finger down each page, pointing to the Attending physician with whom Sparks had worked, while Lenny stood behind him looking over Gary's shoulder

"What kind of resident was Sparks?" Lenny asked.

"He was a brilliant doctor. Maybe too brilliant."

"How do you mean?"

"Much of the time Dr. Sparks knew more than the private doctors, and he wasn't shy about letting it show."

"So he embarrassed the older docs."

"More than once. It's not considered good form. The attendings had to respect his intelligence, but they didn't like him for it."

"How was Sparks with the nurses?"

"He was a bit of a wolf, but we liked him because he was such a good clinician."

"Tell me about the doctors that Sparks was assigned to," Lenny said, taking out a pad to jot down the names.

"Let's see—Radcliff, the shrink. His hair is always perfect. He is quite arrogant, but then, a lot of the psychiatrists are."

"I've seen him around. A regular GQ type. What about the month before?"

Gary flipped to the previous page. "November—that was gynecology: Dr. Leslie Odom. Those guys are all a little weird."

"A man's got to be strange to want to examine women all the time. Is he anything else?"

"How do you mean?"

"I don't know. Does he have a sadistic streak. Does he fly off the handle, yell and scream at the nurses?"

"He's a distant sort of person. He has what we call a flat affect. He doesn't let on what he's feeling or thinking."

"A tight ass, in other words. Okay, what about the others?"

"In October, Sparks rotated with Dr. Gandy in urology. She can be extremely labile."

"How's that?"

"What I mean is, one moment she can be a pleasant, cooperative, normal sort of person, and the next minute she's ranting and raving and ready to slice you up."

"Could she slice up a resident and leave him on a dissecting table?"

Gary shrugged. "I don't know. You're the detective."

"Detective my ass. This was Moose's idea." He pointed to the previous page. "What about September?"

"Well, in September Sparks did a family medicine rotation. I remember he rounded with Alex Primeaux. He is far and away the nicest doctor in the house. Alex moved up here from North Carolina after he got back from Viet Nam. He's polite, and he never raises his voice."

"That's certainly unusual in a physician."

"Isn't it, though? The funny thing about Primeaux is that he reads our nursing notes. Most of the doctors don't even know we write them, let alone read the things."

"Primeaux, the gentleman's doctor," Lenny said. "Okay, who's the next guy?"

"In August Sparks worked with Nathan Galloway. He's a vascular surgeon."

"Sparks was a medical resident. Do medical residents usually spend time in surgery?"

"Galloway has a lab in the medical school where he works with a hyperbaric chamber. He's got a grant to study pumping extra oxygen into diseased tissue. He treats carbon monoxide poisoning, snakebite, gangrene—stuff like that. A lot of the residents hook up with him because it gives them research experience."

"What's Galloway like?"

"Let me put it this way. Did you ever notice the black leather doctor's bag that they carry around with them?"

"Yeah."

"When they go on rounds, Galloway makes one of the medical students carry his bag."

Holding his hand out, Lenny said, "Boy, hold this."

"Exactly."

"Hey, thanks a lot," he said, tucking his pad away in his pocket.

"That's all right. After I lose my job I can probably get another one with an insurance company doing executive physicals."

Putting a hand on Gary's shoulder, he said, "Don't worry, Tuttle. Nothing's gonna happen!"

Fifteen

Seeing that the shift was nearly over, Lenny decided to file Regis's appeal and leave it with Childress's secretary. He hung up his mop, rinsed out the bucket, and placed them in the dirty utility room ready for the next day.

Betty came in to settle her cart down for the night.

"I'm gonna punch out after I stop at the office," he told her.

"I'll see you at the time clock," she said, unhooking her cross from the cart and placing it in her pocket. She took out a pocket bible, sat on an old metal chair and began to read.

He walked to the Seven-South elevator intending to ride down to the basement to punch out, but then he recalled Moose's words about the elevator sapping his strength. "What the hell, it's downhill anyway," he grumbled and began the descent.

Reaching the basement, he went to the housekeeping locker room, opened his locker and took out a grievance form from a tattered file folder. He kept the wording simple, knowing that the more you put in a grievance form, the more the lawyers had a chance to catch you on a technicality. He wrote, "The HSWU hereby requests a Step 2 hearing in the matter of termination of Regis Devoe."

He signed the form, changed into his winter boots and pulled on his coat and wool cap. He closed the locker and ambled out to the office, where he found Courtney, Childress' sexy secretary, sitting at her desk talking on the phone. She wore a tight fitting sweater and stretch pants that clung to her dangerous curves. Her fingernails were painted in elaborately colored patterns with rhinestones stuck to the nails on each little finger. Lenny knew how she'd got her position.

"I've got a grievance to file," he told her, holding out the form. She glanced at it as if he'd used the form to clean up dog shit from the sidewalk. With a bored look she slowly reached out and grasped it by a corner, then dropped it onto her desk.

"I'd like it stamped," he told her. She frowned, picked up the form and jammed it into a machine that stamped the date and time. Lenny knew that in the past, the bosses had lied about when they received a grievance form. If it was received past the 3-day time limit stipulated in the union contract, they could refuse to hear the grievance. And did.

After asking for and receiving a copy of the form, he joined a line of workers waiting for the time clock to click over to the half-hour so that they could punch out. The line stretched from the outer office into the hallway. He took his place on line. At two-twenty-nine, the first worker in line placed his card lightly in the mouth of the machine. At the precise instant that the minute hand jumped to the half hour, he pressed the card down, punching the time, then pulled it out with a smile. It was a popular ritual, being the one to have 15:30:00 on your card. It meant that the boss hadn't gotten a single second of unpaid time out of you.

As Lenny's turn came, he, too, smiled, thinking of the time that Regis had squeezed a whole tube of Krazy Glue into the time clock. It had taken three days to replace it, maddening to Childress, who had to let the workers sign in. Not nearly so accurate a measure of their time as the hated clock.

He clocked out without running into Moose, who was probably waiting for his wife Birdie, and then went to the gift shop to buy a Daily News. He walked past shelves of stuffed animals, wilting flowers, get well cards and colorful balloons. At the cashier's, he dropped fifty cents on the counter, saying to the elderly volunteer at the register, "How's the arthritis, Doris?"

"I think it's a little better. It only hurts when I walk…or stand…or sit. Sitting's a bitch."

"What does that leave you?" Lenny asked.

"Floating in a hot tub. That feels good."

He bid Doris good night, and made his way to the main entrance. Buttoning up his coat, he walked down the broad marble steps littered with rock salt to melt the January ice. He continued past the doctor's parking lot located beside the hospital entrance to the employee lot.

Getting in to the old Buick, he pumped the gas pedal a few times and turned the key. The old V-8 turned over, rumbling a deep throaty growl. Lenny smiled at the familiar sound. The car had been his father's pride. Together they had tuned the motor and rotated the tires.

"The old rear wheel drive is not as good in the snow as the front drives, but a back yard mechanic can work on it," his dad used to say. "I'd go back to points and rotors any day."

When his dad died, his mother bought a new Toyota and Lenny inherited the Buick.

While the motor warmed up, he scraped frost from the windows and thought about Regis stuck in a cold jail cell. His car seemed almost toasty in comparison to that.

This Won't Hurt A Bit

He drove to the gate, ran his parking card through the scanner and drove out onto Germantown Avenue. He decided to take Greene Street to avoid the avenue's cobblestones that could be slippery in the cold. He turned onto Walnut Lane and followed it to Wingohocking Place, a narrow street of two-story row and duplex houses. Several porches were sagging. One abandoned house had been boarded up by the city to keep out drug addicts and dealers.

He parked on the opposite side of the street with the car facing traffic, an old Philadelphia tradition that confused out-of-towners but never drew a ticket from the cops. Passing through the enclosed porch to the front door, he unlocked it and stepped into a small living room crowded with two ancient stuffed armchairs, a sagging sofa covered with an old quilt that Margaret's mother had made for them as a wedding gift, and a stained coffee table. A ceiling-high book shelf made from old roofing timbers was packed with books, stereo and records, and odd bits of pottery.

He dropped his coat and gloves on the sofa, picked up the phone and dialed the union headquarters, again following the prompts to reach Althea Burns, the area representative for James Madison Hospital. He got her voice mail saying she was either out of the office on assignment or away from her desk. He left a message about Regis, adding a request that she ask one of the union lawyers to call him at home ASAP. If he wasn't there she could reach him on his beeper. He slowly recited all three phone numbers, then hung up.

Going into the kitchen, he realized he was ravenous, having eaten only a peanut butter and jelly sandwich and a pretzel all day. He crossed through the dining room to the kitchen, a small, efficient little room that he and Margaret had redone. She had picked out the wallpaper with pink and blue flowers and birds on the wing; he chose the cabinets, simple solid oak units with brass handles.

He opened the fridge, finding it nearly bare. Two Yingling Black and Tan beers, six eggs, some old cheese and crackers, a jar of grape jelly with purple splotches running down the label, half a loaf of Stroehman's white bread and a stick of butter. He threw out the celery that had turned black in the vegetable tray, but left the potatoes that had started to sprout.

"Refried beans and eggs," he mumbled, pulling out three eggs, butter and the loaf of bread. He dropped a slice of butter onto a frying pan and turned on the burner, then he opened a can of refried beans and poured them into the pan, now bubbling with hot butter.

While he waited for the beans to brown on the bottom, he felt fatigue taking over, like an undertow dragging him down. Every day there was some stupid abuse that some supervisor visited on a worker. Answering the constant call for help was draining.

Once the beans were done, he scraped them onto a plate and re-buttered the pan. He cracked three eggs into the pan, covered it and waited for them to firm up, then he slid them onto the plate beside the beans and carried it, along with the beer, into the living room.

He twisted the top off the Black and Tan and drank deeply from the bottle. As he ate the food he reflected, as he had so often, that he could handle the job and the union work if he didn't miss Margaret so much. She had been the best antidote for the blues. When she'd put her arms around him and hugged him, the fatigue melted away. It was as if her touch and her voice gently recharged his battery, restoring his strength and lightening his mood.

Sometimes he thought it was because she always laughed at his jokes. Sometimes he thought it was because she always turned him on, coming to bed in a skimpy little teddy and no panties. A little perfume, a hand laid gently on his chest playing with the buttons of his pajamas and he was a goner. Tired? Who's tired? He was charged up and hot to trot.

As he finished his meal, he chased away thoughts of Margaret. He unfolded the paper and began reading from the back, the way his dad had always done it. Starting with the sports and going toward the middle, the financial section—which had the better gossip than the celebrity pages—the cartoons, and then on to the front section and the so-called news.

He drained the black and tan in a long gulp and went to the fridge for the other bottle, placing the dirty plate on top of several others just like it. After finishing the beer and the paper, he carried a pile of uniforms down to the basement and dumped them into the washer, then returned to the living room. While waiting for the clothes to finish the cycle, he took down a book on home improvement that had come in the mail and began reading about building a deck. Since the little slab of cement in the back yard had become cracked and pitted, he'd toyed with the idea of putting in a wooden deck.

As he looked over the step-by-step pictures ("So simple a child could do it!"), his mind kept returning to Regis and the arrest. He knew that the cops would gather and massage the evidence to make their suspect look guilty. West would love to get back at Regis for all the stunts he'd pulled, like the Krazy Glue in the time clock. His snitches wouldn't be above perjuring themselves, either, for that matter. It would guarantee them a supervisor position once the trial was finished.

Unable to concentrate on the book, he put it down and trudged up to bed, feeling tired enough to sleep through the winter.

Sixteen 🙵

*I*n his sleep, Lenny heard the far off sound of a bell. He wondered who kept pulling the rope; why didn't they stop ringing the damn thing? It rang again, and then again, invading his sleepy mind. Reluctantly he opened his eyes, realized he was home in bed and that it was his telephone ringing.

Reaching for the cordless phone on the night stand, he croaked, "Hullo."

A woman's soft voice asked, "Will you accept a collect call from Mr. Regis Devoe?"

"Regis? Yeah, sure."

Lenny glanced at the clock: five-o-seven... A.M.

"Christ," he mumbled, sitting up now and yawning. He rubbed his chin, felt the coarse stubble.

"Hey, Lenny, is that you? It's me, Regis!"

"Hi, Reeg. How are things in jail? Are they treating you all right?"

"I'm okay. I don't sleep too good, it's so noisy in this place, it never quiets down. But yeah, I'm okay. They're fixin' to transfer me out to the detention center tomorrow."

"I'm glad to hear you're okay. Every one's been worried about you."

"How's Salina? She pissed?"

"I think she's more worried than angry. I spoke with her yesterday. She's going out to her folks to stay. She said she was scared staying alone in the house."

"She's always running to her daddy when things get rough. She always told me I got to learn to control my temper. I hope she don't change the locks while I'm in here."

Lenny sat on the edge of the bed. The wooden floor was cold beneath his feet. "How did the arraignment go? I'm sorry I couldn't be there. I had to work."

"It was okay, I guess. That prick Joe West was sitting right up there with the prosecutor, like he was one of them."

"He's an ex-cop," Lenny said. "Right away I figured he had a hand in getting you arrested. He's been trying to bust you ever since you put that

Krazy Glue in the time clock." He chuckled, remembering the incident.

"I got him good that time, didn't I?"

"You sure did. The bastard knew it was you but he could never prove it."

He stood up, opened a dresser drawer looking for a fresh uniform, found there were none. He silently cursed, remembering he'd left a load of laundry in the washer. "Listen, does your lawyer sound like he knows what he's doing?"

"Yeah, he's cool. He says the case is piss-poor. He might be able to get it thrown out before the trial gets going. He's supposed to file some papers or something."

"That sounds good." Lenny dug through the overflowing laundry basket in search of a uniform. "Regis, what's this I hear about you arguing with Randy Sparks?"

"That was nothin'! I was just blowing smoke is all."

"Yeah, but you must have said something. You didn't threaten the guy, did you?"

"Course not. That punk doctor thought it was funny, the guard going through my bag. Had a big grin on his face like his shit don't stink, and he was all the time walkin' out the door with a hospital scrub suit on. Anybody could see he was stealin' it."

"I'd be pissed off, too, Regis, but it looks kind of bad, the fact that you threatened him."

"It was just talk, you know that!"

"I know it. The problem is, what's a jury going to believe?" Lenny found a shirt and pants and tried shaking the wrinkles out of them. "Have the cops got anything else on you?"

"Nothin', man, they got nothin'! Just my mouth gettin' me in trouble, is all. I told 'em they oughta go out and find the bastard that really did kill that punk doctor, but they didn't pay me any mind."

"They won't look any further. As soon as they decided you were suspect number one they started looking for evidence on you, not for who did it."

"You mean unless the murderer walks up to a cop and tells him, 'lock me up, I'm the one,' they're gonna keep looking for shit on me? Is that it?"

"I'm afraid so," said Lenny. He dug out a pair of clean white socks and fresh underwear. "Just hang tight and things should work out all right." He felt cold standing in the bedroom in just jockey shorts and a T-shirt. "Listen, Reeg, I've got to get ready for work. I'm gonna try to come visit you after my shift today."

"They gonna let you in?"

This Won't Hurt A Bit

"I'll call before I come out to make sure, but I think I can get in being your union delegate. Is there anything I can get for you?"

"Yeah, a key and a fast car."

'Wouldn't a helicopter be better?"

"Ee-ther, eye-ther," Regis said. "But listen—talk to Salina. Me'n her, we've been goin' through some changes, and I don't want her doing something stupid, like moving back with her folks or somethin'."

"She wasn't talking about leaving you before all this shit happened, was she?"

"Yes and no. She's kinda unpredictable. You know how women are, always changing up on you. Go see her for me, Lenny. You got that sweet way of talking."

"Sure, Reeg, I'll do it. I promise."

Lenny said goodbye, hung up the phone and put it on the dresser. The surface was so thick with dust he briefly considered planting corn. Times like this he missed Margaret the most. He missed her sense of order. They'd always split the housework, but she had been the organizer. The neatnik.

Since he liked to cook—it was a way to unwind from the pressures on the job—and Margaret liked a clean kitchen, she usually did the dishes. She even dried them by hand and put them away, then wiped down the stove, always splattered with sauce or grease.

"I won't have any mice getting a free meal in my house," she would say.

Until Margaret came along, Lenny's idea of getting dressed up to go out had been fresh blue jeans and a colored T-shirt with a breast pocket. After they'd married, she bought him nice clothes, including a wool suit for weddings and other affairs. He'd last worn the suit at her funeral a year ago.

He showered and shaved, then dressed and shuffled down the stairs to the kitchen. He packed the espresso maker with coffee and placed the demitasse cup under the spout. Then he took a frozen bagel from the freezer, pried it open and dropped it in the toaster. He frothed the milk, adding it to the coffee in an old mug. He dipped the bagel, unbuttered, in the hot liquid and took a bite. The strong, bitter brew nearly scalded his tongue.

Turning the big Buick onto the hospital entranceway, Lenny noticed the employee parking lot was already half full. The third shift workers hadn't left, while the first shift was already beginning to come in. Parking the car, he walked past the doctor's parking lot, that had only a half-dozen cars in it. Residents on-call during the night, the attending physicians not having yet arrived.

He entered the building and made his way downstairs to the housekeeping office. He punched in at the time clock, then went to the locker to get ready for work. He found Abrahm Vorchensky, the burly Russian, sitting on the bench between the lockers.

"Abraham Lincoln! How's it going?" he asked, smiling broadly.

"And how are yew, George W'ushington?"

Lenny chuckled at their old joke as he sat beside his friend. Abrahm removed a pair of soft leather walking shoes polished to a high gloss and held them up for Lenny to see.

"Do you see these shoes? Three soles they have had. Three! They are from Armenia. Is very good leather in Armenia."

Abrahm lovingly placed them in his locker and put on black work shoes. "It is such shame, taking that young man into the jail. You will help him become free?"

"I'm not sure what I can do. I left a message for the union lawyer to call me. I even gave him my beeper, but those guys are impossible to get a hold of. Maybe they can help with the case, it's way past what I know about."

"You are tough with the bosses, Lenn'ye. You would make a good lawyer."

"Sure, Abrahm. I'll just attend Temple law school at night for like thirty years and then take the exam. I'll be the only guy in a pin stripe suit who can buff the floors and object to a question at the same time."

"Why not? Lenny Moss, he can do *anything*."

Lenny left his friend. Riding the elevator to his floor, he wondered again at the confidence that some of the workers placed in him.

Seventeen

In the hall just down from the Seven-South nursing station, Dr. Nathan Galloway was conducting morning rounds with a group of medical students, residents and fellow. As the entourage was gathered in a semicircle around the surgeon, the first-year resident was reporting on Mr. Oldenfield. The young physician, a handsome young Polish fellow with a disarming grin and informal manner, was stumbling over the lab values.

"Let me see, his potassium was five-point-two…no, I'm sorry, it was three-point-two, so I ordered a potassium supplement. By mouth. His phosphate level was…"

"What about his lactate?" Galloway barked.

"Sir?"

"His lactate. You know, lactic acid. The stuff your cells produce in abundance when they switch from an aerobic to an anaerobic metabolism?"

"Yes, of course, lactic acid. Let me look in the chart."

The young man nervously turned the pages of the chart, searching in the lab section for the relevant item. A few loose lab slips that had not yet been mounted on the pages fell out of the jacket. Quickly bending down to gather them up, he said, "I'm not sure we drew lactate level today. I will have to go to the computer to see if…"

"These numbers should be coming out of your mouth, not your ass," said Galloway. "You should know all the lab reports!"

"Yes, of course you're right," the resident said.

"Never mind, we can check the labs later. What about your physical exam?"

The first-year resident took a deep breath and collected his thoughts. "I appreciated a doppler pulse on the affected dorsalis pedis and the posterior tibia," he said, more comfortable with the information he could obtain with his own eyes and ears.

"What about the other foot?" Galloway asked.

The resident hesitated.

"You did compare the operative side with the non-operative side, didn't you?"

The resident screwed up his face trying to recall whether or not he had felt a strong pulse on the other foot or had heard it only with the amplification of the doppler.

"Good pulse, he had a good pulse on the left," he answered, relieved to recall the exam at last. "The foot is cool but has brisk capillary refill in the toes. Sensation is intact, reflexes are normal."

"All right. Now that we have that information, let's go on to Mrs. Rosemond, the GI bleeder without a bleeding source. Her bleeding scan and CAT scan were negative: what does that suggest?"

The tribe moved slowly down to the patient's room and occupied it. Galloway briefly examined the woman's abdomen, finding no signs of tenderness, masses or abnormal bowel sounds. He led the group out of the room. As the group drifted down the hall, it split in two to flow around the big food cart that Moose was pushing. Once reunited on the other side, the team continued off the unit.

Moose carried the breakfast trays into the rooms, one tray in each hand. Nadia, the nurse's aide, and Gary opened the trays and set about dipping tea bags, spreading butter and jelly, and fetching dentures from cups or wads of napkin, depending on how fastidious a patient happened to be.

As he passed out the last tray, Moose caught sight of Lenny. "Gonna meet me for break?" he asked.

"Definitely. We have a lot to talk about. Let's meet in the sewing room."

"Gotcha," Moose said, closing up the cart. He opened the door to the stairwell and headed down to retrieve a cart for another floor.

A short time later, Lenny was called to clean the floor in Mr. Dotterer's room. The old fellow had developed a runny, foul-smelling diarrhea and stumbled into the bathroom, leaving a trail of stool along the floor. Lenny mopped up the floor, adding some ammonia to the soap solution to control the odor. He sprayed the room with deodorizer, then knelt down and scraped some sticky substance off the floor. He thought it was food, but couldn't be sure.

He was walking out of the patient's room with his head down looking for more spots when he nearly collided with a heavy, immovable object in the middle of the doorway.

Joe West stood in the door glaring at him, arms folded across his barrel chest. Two Philadelphia detectives stood behind him.

Lenny looked at the squarely-built figure, saw the flat-top haircut, the thick arms and the broad shoulders like roofing joists. Two dour-faced men, one white, one black, sporting drab raincoats stood behind West.

This Won't Hurt A Bit

The security chief put his face inches from Lenny's nose, as he had in the housekeeping office when Lenny had tried to cut a deal for Regis. "I'd like to introduce you to two friends of mine, Moss. Police detective Sternbach and detective Williams."

Lenny fought back the urge to ask to see their badges. He didn't want to get them pissed at him. It could lead to a lot of questioning.

The two police officers nodded glumly at Lenny. The first one said, "I understand you were a friend of Regis Devoe."

"I defended him a couple of times on union matters."

"Do you have any information that might bear on a murder investigation?"

Lenny's face presented a beguiling innocence. "No, why would I?"

"Don't play games," West interjected. "Everyone with a sob story comes to you. You're an overflowing toilet of misinformation. We want to know what Devoe told you."

"I'm sure it's nothing he hasn't said to the police," Lenny said. "He didn't kill anybody and he doesn't have any idea who did. Neither do I. But if I did know, you guys would be the first to hear about it."

"If you think you can help that little twerp, forget it," West said. "There's a lot about Devoe you don't know about. Enough to fry his ass in the chair 'til he's good and black…charbroiled. He…"

"Here," said the second detective, a black man with a receding hairline and a scar along his jaw. He pulled a business card from his pocket and handed it to Lenny. "Call me at this number if you hear anything that pertains to this case, Mr. Moss. Concealing evidence from a police investigation is a serious offense."

Lenny tucked the card in his shirt pocket.

As the detectives turned to go, West stood his ground. "I've got my eye on you, Moss," he said, fingering the steel handcuffs dangling from his leather belt. "If I catch you off your unit poking your fat nose in my business I'll cuff your hands behind your back and use your head to open a fire door."

He turned and strode quickly toward the detectives, already half way down the hall.

Lenny was sure that West knew he was investigating the Sparks murder. The bastard had snitches in every department.

"Shit," he grumbled, standing alone in the middle of the hall. "It's bad enough having West always on my ass, but the cops, too?"

Eighteen ❧

After the patients finished their breakfast, Betty helped Nadia, the nurse's aide, collect the trays and return them to the cart. Wheeling the big wagon down to the pantry, the pair began scraping the uneaten portions of food into a large ziplock plastic bag. Seeing Gary stop in the doorway, Betty said, "My dogs're gonna be eating good tonight, praise the Lord. You know it's a sin to waste food. Yes it is."

"You must have the healthiest pets in the city," he said.

"They're happy creatures, I can tell you that," she said, grinning.

Lenny poked his head into the pantry.

"Boop, I'm walking down the stairs to the cafeteria to get some soup before we meet in at Birdie's."

"I'm not takin' no stairs with my knobby knees," she said. "I'll meet ya."

He walked down the stairs to the basement and made his way to the cafeteria, where he poured soup from a huge black kettle into a styrofoam container, covered it and put a garlic bagel on top. He paid for his food, dropped them into a paper bag and hurried out to the sewing room, where he and Moose had arranged to meet.

He knocked once on the door and entered. Birdie was seated at her sewing machine surrounded by a clutter of burst pillows. A large bag of foam stuffing was open at her feet. Betty sat across from her on an old metal folding chair eating curried goat and rice from a Tupperware container; Celeste had a large green salad with sprouts and croutons.

Several plants on a high window sent trailing vines down almost to the floor.

Lenny looked over Birdie's old sewing machine. It was a beauty. Black, with gold leaf around the edges of the platform and along the round body. The machine was as solidly built as his old Buick.

"That's an industrial sewing machine, isn't it, Birdie?"

"Uh, huh. Hospital got it when Stenton Mills closed. In North Philly, on Girard? Yeah, it's a fine old machine."

The needle fluttered like a hummingbird as Birdie fed fabric across the machine.

"Have you heard from Regis?" she asked.

"He called me this morning. Do you believe, he's more worried that Salina won't take him back than he is about the charges?"

She looked up from her sewing. "You think he's gonna get off, Lenny?"

"I hope so. He kept saying there was nothing but words between him and Sparks, but there's got to be more to it."

Finishing with the pillow, Birdie bit the end of the thread and tossed it into a box beside her, then started on another.

"I wish you could be his lawyer," she said.

"Hah!" Lenny snorted. "I've got enough problems being his *delegate*."

"Did you tell him you and Moose are gonna try and find out who really killed Dr. Sparks?"

"No, not yet. I don't want to get his hopes up."

While Birdie worked, Lenny examined a pair of sketches hanging on the wall. One was an effective caricature of Security Chief Joe West dressed in a Nazi uniform. The other depicted Birdie in a Hawaiian outfit dancing on a beach.

"That Moose's drawing is getting better and better. I love what he did to West. He's really good."

"That's my Moose. I've been tellin' him for years he should go to school for illustration, he's so talented."

As Birdie was speaking, Moose came in with a bag that smelled of fried food. He greeted Lenny and Betty, kissed his wife, then pulled up a chair and straddled it, resting his big hands and chin on the back.

"How's my baby? They treating you right?"

"You know nobody bothers me down here. It's just me and my plants."

"Moose, you're drawing is really getting good," Lenny said. "Why don't you go to art school?"

"I'll get to it when the money's right. Right now the kids gotta get through school." He picked up a pillow and squeezed it. "What about you? You said you was gonna take s'more college courses."

"Yeah, right. I haven't got time to scratch my ass. I've got to get Dr. Primeaux to write a letter explaining why Freddie was out for two weeks on a medical leave, the part-time transporters want me to represent them in a class suit over their benefits…the shit goes on and on. Where am I gonna find time to go to school?"

"You got to make the time. You don't wannna be a custodian all your life, do you?"

"What's wrong with being a custodian? *And* a damn good union rep?"

"Yeah you're good," Moose said. "The best. It's just you're too smart to push a mop forever, that's all. In fact, if you was smart, you'd go out with my second cousin, Vernice."

"Hey, when I feel like going out on a date, I'll pick the date. Okay?"

"Nuff said." He opened the bag and took out a container of fried chicken and French fries. He poured hot sauce on the chicken, sprinkled salt and pepper on the fries, and held out the food to his wife. "You want some, baby?"

"You know I'm on a diet again, get away from me with that greasy stuff!"

"You can't fatten a thoroughbred, ain't that right?" said Moose, chuckling and popping fries into his mouth.

"I don't know," said Lenny, "I never owned a horse."

On the fourth floor, Abrahm was cleaning Dr. Gandy's examining room. He had emptied the trash, swept the floor and wiped down the counter tops. There was a commode chair with a collecting bottle beneath the seat that siphoned urine into an instrument that measured its flow and a tall, metal instrument that looked like it had been designed for torture, with a pointed instrument that burned through flesh—a laser.

In the waiting room, he emptied the trash, returned the magazines to a rack on the wall and unplugged the coffee machine, though it was turned off. He wiped down the smooth fabric covering the sofa, then he pulled up the wide pillows to clean beneath them. Sometimes he found loose change or subway tokens there. Today he found bits of paper, two pennies, the barrel of an empty syringe and a small needle in a milky white plastic cap.

He carefully picked up the needle and syringe and stepped into the examining room to deposit them in a sharps container, but stopped. Why, he wondered, was there a needle and syringe in the sofa? That was where patients waited to go in for their treatment, not where they were treated.

Recalling what Lenny had told him about the murder investigation, he placed the two items in a ziplock specimen bag, pushed the bag into his pocket, returned the pillows to their place, and slipped out of the room.

Nineteen

Kate pulled Mrs. Grey's chart from the Seven-South rack and turned to the section for lab results.

I'm not letting that pompous ass Odom get the best of me, she thought, running her fingers down the column of numbers. *Maybe I won't raise it on rounds, but I'll be damn sure the residents hear about it.*

She had read up on endometriosis and pelvic inflammatory disease at home. She found that that there was no blood test that could confirm the endometrial disorder, but inflammation of the pelvic organs—even chronic swelling—caused a rise in the white count with a shift to the right, and an elevated sed rate.

Mrs. Grey's lab results had none of those signs.

She glanced up at the clock on the wall. She had just enough time to look in on the patient. She couldn't exactly apologize for the way that Odom had examined her in front of his entourage, but at least she could be supportive.

She closed the chart, put it back in the rack and walked down to the room. As she walked, her nose crinkled at the funny odor in the hall.

Bobby D came into the sewing room, his black leather satchel on his shoulder.

"Hey hey, we're all gonna play today," he said, lowering the bag to the floor. He opened the satchel and pulled out a portable CD player still sealed in plastic. "Who's the lucky person gonna take this Discman off my hands? Brand new. Even got the warranty, and the price, you won't believe when I tell you."

"How much?" asked Birdie.

"For you, my dear Birdie, forty-five…no, special today, thirty-five dollars."

"Does it come with batteries?" asked Moose.

"Batteries? You cheap mother. Buy your wife some batteries and let her enjoy some music while she works," he answered. "What about you, Lenny?"

"No thanks, I have a CD player at home."

"Ah my friend, but you can't take it with you to work, can you?"

"I'll get written up if I have anything hanging on my ears."

"Forget about your ears," said Moose, licking hot sauce from his fingers. "Let's talk about what we're gonna do about Regis."

Lenny told them about the phone call from Regis, then he showed them the list of physicians that Gary Tuttle had given him.

"Filling the body with pickling juice—now that would definitely take a doctor," said Birdie.

"Could be an undertaker," Moose put in. "They handle dead bodies all the time."

"Yes, but could an undertaker make those wounds that look like a car accident?" asked Lenny.

"Why not?" Bobby said. "They fix up bodies that are all banged up. Make them look normal. They could change it the other way around, too."

"Except how could an undertaker sneak a body into the medical school anatomy lab?" Lenny asked. "And even more important, why would an undertaker kill a young resident? I think we have to look at the motive. Why would somebody murder Randy Sparks?"

"He was probably kicking in somebody else's stall," said Moose.

"A jealous husband?" Lenny asked.

"You got it. Husband finds out Sparks was banging his wife. Cuts him up, wheels him across the street on a stretcher just as natural as you please, keys Mr. John Doe into the computer and Boom, he's in like Flynn."

Lenny opened the lid of his soup and dipped his bagel in it. "We should start by finding out everything we can about Randy Sparks," he said. He chewed on the bagel and looked at his friends.

"All I know is, he was smart as a whip," Celeste said. "I heard him talking with the attendings lots of times and he was doing *all* the talking."

"I can tell you he liked CK cologne and fragrant body oils," said Bobby. "Bought em from me all the time."

"What sort of body oil?" asked Betty? The kind you give a massage with?"

"You could use it like that, sure, but I think the reason he liked it was it was the flavored kind…the stuff you lick off."

"Sounds like an oversexed guy," said Lenny. "That fits in with a jealous husband or boyfriend. What about the doctors? Do we know anything about them?"

Celeste said, "I know that Dr. Primeaux is the only doc who remembers national secretary day. He brings me a big bouquet of roses every year. I can't see somebody like that killing anyone."

"Tuttle told me Primeaux is the nicest doctor in Madison. We can't cross him off our list for that, but it's something to keep in mind."

"I saw the shrink being awful fresh with one of the patients on your floor yesterday," Moose said. He described how Radcliff had squeezed Mrs. Grey's leg. "Patting the knee, I can see that," Moose said, "but the thigh? That's too close to home plate. He's got fast hands, trust me."

"Speaking of hands," said Lenny, "I had a little run-in with Mr. Handcuffs himself." He described his encounter with West and the two detectives.

Birdie said, "Maybe you better lay low for awhile, Lenny. That mean Joe West is bad enough, but you don't want to mess with no po-lice."

"What'd the cops want?" Moose asked.

"They were asking if I knew anything about the Sparks murder. I told them I didn't know anything, which I'm sure they didn't believe. Then I told them they arrested the wrong guy. That's when West made a lot of noise about knowing some shit about Regis that was going to get him the electric chair."

"Bull shit!" said Moose.

"Of course. Oh, and West finished up by saying how he was gonna kick my ass if he caught me sticking my nose into 'his business.'"

"You're not getting out of the ring, are you?" Moose asked.

"No, of course not, but I do have to be better about covering my ass."

"We'll block for you," Moose said. "That West is—"

Knock, knock knock.

The rap on the door silenced the room as everyone turned to look at the door, nobody wanting to ask who it was.

Twenty

Sandy, the hospital's oldest security guard, poked his head inside the sewing room.

"This a private party?"

"Yeah, no Green Berets allowed!" Lenny answered.

"Well, then I guess I'll come in an' sit awhile. I ain't got Joe West with me."

Sandy was a beefy, light-skinned black man with a flat, bulldog face and a thick mat of silver hair. He spoke in a soft, musical voice that had a hint of the Caribbean.

"Did you know we're looking into the Sparks murder, trying to help Regis get his job back?" Lenny asked

"Why d'ya think I'm here?" the guard said, unfolding a battered chair. He stretched his left leg out and slowly eased himself down. Birdie kept several extra chairs in the little room for the workers who came in to visit and hear the gossip.

A needle danced across the fabric as Birdie fed it through the sewing machine. She asked, "Are you gonna tell us what you heard or sit there like an old mule?"

"I was just gettin' comfortable," he said, shifting his hips on the chair. "Anyhow, this morning in the ER an officer from the Twenty-fourth Precinct told me Regis had a very expensive watch exactly like the one that Dr. Sparks was wearing when he disappeared."

"The Rolex!" Lenny exclaimed. "He showed it to me when I was representing him in the office, but I figured it was just a cheap knockoff."

"Nope, it was the real thing."

"You don't arrest a man for wearing a watch!" Moose said, balling his right hand into a fist.

"There's more," Sandy answered. "Just before Sparks disappeared he got into a big shouting match with Devoe. Mason—he's that guard who's bucking for promotion—while he was searching Devoe's gym bag at the main door, Sparks walked past him wearing hospital scrubs. Devoe wanted to know why they didn't arrest the doctors for taking hospital property when they were always searching the workers."

"He's right, there's a double standard," Lenny said "They fire us if we're caught with hospital property on us, even a fucking toothbrush, but they let the doctors walk out with anything they want. Last month I defended a secretary in radiology. A doctor who was retiring from her department walked off with a computer on his last day and the boss wanted to discipline the *secretary* for letting *him* take it! I don't blame Regis for getting hot."

"Hot, that's okay," Sandy said, "but when Sparks told Devoe to mind his own business Devoe threatened to meet Sparks in the parking lot, and right away Officer Mason went and told Joe West about it."

Birdie looked at Lenny. "They can't find him guilty on something stupid like that, can they?"

"Not for an argument, no, but give the cops a scapegoat and they have ways of manufacturing evidence. Besides, West was bragging that he knew things about Regis that I don't. I have a bad feeling they've got more evidence than we know about."

"So we'll get our own evidence!" Moose said. "Where do we go next?"

"I think we should first find out everything we can about Randy Sparks. Who was he friendly with, who was he sleeping with."

"Who'd he piss off," said Moose.

"Right. Then, we see if any of the doctors he worked with had something to hide. It'll have to be big, so we'll have to dig deep, but it looks like that's our best shot at coming up with a suspect."

"And when we find him," said Betty. "What do we do then?"

Sandy slowly rose from his chair. "That's when you page me and I'll come and put the cuffs on him. Right Lenny?"

"That's right. I'll page you when and if we uncover the murderer."

With that promise in hand, the security guard left.

"We better get back to work, too," Lenny said.

Going out into the hall, Betty, Celeste, and Lenny walked at various paces to the elevators. Moose, turning down the corridor toward the kitchen, said to Lenny, "Take the stairs, it's good for the legs!"

"That's easy for you, Moose—dietary's in the basement!"

Moose strode away toward the kitchen. Lenny looked at the elevator doors, shrugged, told Celeste and Betty he'd meet them on the ward and walked to the stairwell.

He was lost in thought as he trudged up the steps thinking about Randy Sparks. Dead. Bruised and battered, lying on an autopsy table. How did he get there? He was a bright doctor. Confident. A bit arrogant, even, but that could hardly invite murder.

The way the body had been made to look like an accident victim was slick. And slipping it into the anatomy class to be cut up must have been the killer's idea of a joke. A sick joke, but a smart way to get rid of the body. The killer had thought through the crime, step by step, so it probably wasn't a crime of passion.

He was convinced that the killer was a doctor. Who else knew how to pickle the body so it wouldn't rot away between the time of the murder and the start of the anatomy class? Who else would know what the automobile wounds looked like? Who else could enter the right computer codes and set the body out as a John Doe?

He continued slowly up the stairs, so immersed in his ruminations that for a long time he did not hear the fire bell ringing. When he finally stopped on the fifth floor landing to catch his breath, he listened to the long sequence of rings—three bells and a pause, meaning it was in the main building; seven rings, which meant it was for the seventh floor; and one bell distinguishing the south from the north side.

"Shit, it's Seven-South," he said and bounded up the remaining steps. "My fucking floor's on fire!"

Twenty-one

"Emerging out of breath from the stairwell, Lenny rushed onto the ward where he found patients milling about in the hall while the nurses directed them through the double steel doors to safety on Seven-North. A stream of thick, acrid, black smoke was pouring out of the patient lounge and billowing along the ceiling.

Lenny heard Marianne at the nursing station call out, "Gary! Go pull twenty-seven and twenty-nine out on their sheets!"

Gary came charging up the hall yelling, "I'll get them as soon as I shut off the oxygen!"

Lenny yelled to Tuttle, "I'll get it! The shut-off valve is next to my closet!"

He ran the short distance to the wall panel, jerked open the plexiglass window, and pulled the green handle shut, then looked toward the lounge, where the smoke was getting thicker.

As he began searching the rooms for bedridden patients, he nearly bumped into Kate Palmer, who had been in the next room interviewing Mrs. Grey.

Kate said, "I thought the alarm was another drill until I smelled the smoke. Is it a patient room?"

"No, it's coming from the lounge," Lenny said.

"Thank god for that. Let's see who needs help getting out."

"Okay!"

They found a middle-aged man in bed paralyzed from a stroke. Using the bed sheet as a sling, Lenny and Kate lowered the man to the floor.

"I'll get him," she said, wrapping the ends of the sheet around her wrists to get a sure grip. "You get somebody else."

"Gotcha!"

He stepped through the door behind Kate as she dragged the patient out of the room. She was slightly built, but strong, pulling the weight easily over the marble surface and protecting the man's head at the same time. There was something appealing about the way that she knotted up the sheet in her hands and went to work.

Focusing on the task at hand, he passed Mr. Oldenfield, who was holding on to a grab bar on the wall and hopping down the corridor on his good leg, saying, "Is this goddamned hospital on fire? What the hell is going on?"

Lenny said, "I'm not sure, but the smoke is real."

Overhead, the alarm clanged incessantly. The black smoke drifted down to the nursing station, sending out black fingers wherever a draft pulled it. The open door to Seven-North was like a vacuum pulling the smoke toward it, as patients walked, hobbled and were dragged through to safety. Mrs. Gold, head bent to the floor, led Mr. Dotterer through the doorway. As he leaned forward and progressed with stiff, unsteady steps, she told him "Just keep on walking, Gerald. Just keep on walking."

Lenny found a tiny, frail old woman strapped to a chair and talking to herself. He pulled apart the knots, picked her up fireman-style, and carried her out into the hall. Just then Moose burst out from the stairwell across from the lounge. He grabbed an old, water-filled fire extinguisher mounted on the wall and ripped it from its mounting strap. Grinning wickedly, he pulled out the pin as he marched into the lounge, black smoke billowing about his head.

From the lounge came the sounds of Moose's mad laughter and water hissing on fire. Moments later he emerged from the room, fire extinguisher in one hand, a smoldering trash bucket in the other.

"Cigarette fire, that's all it was. Paper caught it, burned a bunch of styrofoam cups. That's what threw up all the smoke."

The staff slowly drifted back down the hall. Lenny slapped his friend's back. "Moose, you're my hero!"

As they walked together back to the nursing station, Joe West marched onto the ward wearing a hard hat and speaking into a walkie-talkie. He ordered Moose to put the smoldering bucket down.

"Put that back in the lounge, the fire chief will want to make a full investigation."

"Of what?" Moose asked. "Patient dropped a butt in the waste basket, that's all."

"That's not for you to decide. Leave everything as it was."

West strode toward the lounge speaking into his walkie-talkie, while the staff congregated at the nursing station. The sound of a fire truck siren came up from the street, then slowly died as the truck came to a stop in front of the hospital.

Lenny said, "I better get my mop and bucket and clean up the water in the lounge."

Gary piped in, "Didn't West ask that everything be left as it is?"

"He didn't mean the water on the floor. I can't leave a mess like that. What if a patient stepped in the water and fell?"

A few patients were peeking through the fire doors, asking if it was safe to return to their rooms. Kate slipped past them and entered the ward. Seeing her, Gary grabbed Lenny's arm and drew him closer.

"You know who that is?" he asked in a whisper, pointing at Kate.

"Cleopatra? How should I know?"

"That's the medical student who discovered Randy Sparks in the anatomy class."

"Really?" Lenny's eyebrows arched in delight. "Why Tuttle, I thought you didn't want to get involved in the investigation."

"I am not *involved*. I'm just passing on some hospital gossip. That's all."

Lenny walked quickly after Kate, who was headed toward the nursing station. He considered how best to approach her. He had a feeling that she was an open kind of person who would probably respond best to directness.

Catching up with her, he asked, "That was great the way you hauled that patient out."

She stopped and eyed him, noting the blue custodian's uniform.

"We medical students aren't completely useless, despite what people say about us."

"No, I didn't mean it that way. I didn't know they taught rescue techniques in medical school, is all."

"Actually, my dad's a fireman. I guess it's in the blood."

"In Philly? Which station?"

"He's in Center City. He used to be in the northeast, but he got a promotion."

Lenny looked down the hall, gestured toward an empty room.

"Could I talk to you a minute?"

Puzzled, she walked beside him into the empty room.

"Listen, I know it's none of my business, but, aren't you the student who found that doctor's body in the anatomy class?"

Kate studied his earnest face. "Actually, it was my lab partner Jennifer who recognized him. I was busy doing the dissection."

"Do you mind if I ask you about it?"

"I don't know you from Adam," she said, eyeing him suspiciously. "What's your interest?"

Twenty-two

Lenny looked at Kate, saw the mistrust in her eyes, but also something else. Curiosity? He wasn't sure, but he had a good feeling about her.

"See, the police arrested a laundry worker—Regis Devoe—but I know he didn't do it 'cause he had no way of getting the body into the school, or faking the identity. I hear there was a lot of computer stuff involved in making Sparks a John Doe."

"It's true, you would have to be familiar with the data entry system to get the cadaver into the lab without arousing suspicion. Maybe your friend had an accomplice."

"I don't think so. He doesn't know anyone in the medical school. Besides, he doesn't know anything about preserving bodies with embalming fluid."

The crush of work had given Kate little time to think about Randy Sparks, but she had wondered how the body had ended up on her table. Jennifer had suggested it was some kind of sexist joke, because Kate was tops in her class, but she had shrugged the idea off.

"An undertaker would know how to prepare the corpse," she said.

"But not how to falsify the identity. You have to log all the bodies in the hospital computer and account for them."

Kate looked with new intensity at Lenny. She was struck by his dark eyes that seemed to notice everything about her.

"I really shouldn't be discussing this with anyone," she said.

"I understand, and it's not like I *want* to pry into this sort of thing. Believe me, I'd much rather be in a grievance hearing trying to win somebody their disability pay. The problem is, the only way I can help Regis get his job back is to prove that he *couldn't* have murdered Sparks."

Kate looked again into Lenny's face. He seemed earnest and attentive. The blue uniform had misled her. This was no ordinary custodian.

"Who are you?"

"Didn't I introduce myself? How rude of me." Smiling, he held out his hand. "Lenny Moss, custodial engineer and Hospital Service Workers' Union representative."

This Won't Hurt A Bit

Kate took Lenny's hand in a firm grasp. "Kate Palmer, first year medical student."

Studying his face more, she decided to trust him...provisionally.

"I probably shouldn't tell you this, but one of my classmates has an in at the Medical Examiner's, and he says Sparks didn't die in a car accident. That his wounds were faked."

"Yeah, I heard something about that."

"Did you know that his hair was dyed very dark, almost black? He was really blond."

"No, I didn't." Lenny drew closer to Kate. "Anything else?"

"Let's see. In addition to the phony accident, they say his hands were badly bruised."

Lenny said nothing, waiting for more. He was surprised at how open she'd become. She seemed different from the usual medical students. More down to earth. Did he know her from somewhere?

Having grown up in Philadelphia, a city of close neighborhoods, he often ran into people he'd gone to school with years ago. Once, when filing a petition with the National Labor Relations Board, he found the government lawyer eyeing him suspiciously. "Don't I know you from somewhere?" the lawyer had asked, then he exclaimed, "Rosa Parks Elementary! We were in Mrs. Feingold's homeroom!" Lenny recognized him then. Roger Billstein. They had attended the same elementary school in Germantown twenty years before. Roger had put on a good thirty pounds and was going bald, but he was still the nerdy kid who used to sit in the front row and always raise his hand.

He asked Kate, "What sort of a guy was Sparks?"

"Randy was super bright. A unanimous choice for chief resident. They say that he had the highest board scores ever recorded from his medical school."

"I heard he showed up a few of the older docs, made them look stupid."

"That's true, he could get under a private doctor's skin, but we all admired his brains."

"Did he have a girlfriend?"

"I never heard there was anybody special in his life," she said. "They say he played around quite a lot."

"I see. Well, did he have any special type of medicine he was interested in?"

"It's funny you should ask. Randy was always saying that ninety-nine percent of all diseases are genetic. That we either inherit them, or we get them from chromosomes that were damaged in the womb."

81

"Is that true?"

"Nobody knows, but there's more evidence coming out about it every day, from cancer to schizophrenia. He used to say he was going to invent a gene that would let him live forever and splice it into his DNA."

Glancing at her watch, she said, "I've got to get to class."

"I appreciate this, Kate, I really do. If you hear any more, will you let me know?"

She eyed him again. His face was earnest, but now his eyes were light-hearted.

"I'll consider it."

As she walked away, she wondered why talking with him had been so easy. She hadn't been on guard, as she was with the professors and the attending physicians. Conversing with him was almost as comfortable as talking to her family.

She shrugged and walked off on to class.

Lenny went to the housekeeping closet and wheeled out his mop and bucket. As he mopped up the dirty water in the lounge, he recalled Kate's slim figure dragging the patient down the hall on the sheet. A gutsy woman. A lot like Margaret, though Kate didn't look like her.

He stopped mopping a moment. "I must be losing my mind," he muttered. "She's gonna be a doctor. What am I doing thinking about her?" He wrung out the mop and continued soaking up the water.

Lenny's mop caught a small piece of metal in its thick, cloth fingers. He bent down and untangled it from the mop. It was the head of a disposable cigarette lighter with shards of the plastic body attached.

He ran his fingers through the mop head until he found the remaining pieces of the lighter.

A cold shivering sensation ran down his spine. He realized that someone had broken open the lighter and poured the fluid in the trash bucket to whip up the fire.

"Son of a bitch," he muttered. *It wasn't a cigarette fire at all. Somebody set the trash on fire.*

Dropping the pieces into his shirt pocket, he thought of the acrid smoke that had poured out from the lounge, and of the elderly patients in their beds. "What a prick," he muttered. "What a soulless, arrogant prick."

Lenny squeezed out his mop and stood watching while the floor of the lounge slowly dried. He had worried about Regis, stuck away in a jail cell, and West jumping on his ass, and now he had this crazy person setting fires. It seemed as if the whole hospital was turning to shit, like a giant toilet overflowing.

This Won't Hurt A Bit

A part of him wished the whole mess would just go away, but another part wanted to pull the bastard out of his hiding place and beat the crap out of him. Leave his face in worse shape than the body in the anatomy lab.

Kill the bastard.

Twenty-three

After West looked over the remains in the trash bucket with the firemen, he allowed the patients to return to their rooms. Once the ward was back to normal, Marianne said to Gary, "I really need to go have a cigarette."

She opened a cabinet door behind the nursing station, pulled out her purse and rummaged through it, then she dumped it out onto the counter and fished out a crumpled pack of cigarettes. With the pack in one hand, Marianne continued looking through the contents.

Lenny strode up to the nursing station. "Really desperate for that smoke, huh Marianne?"

"No, that's not it, it's my wallet. It's gone!"

"Are you sure it's not in your coat pocket?"

"Positive! I always put it in my purse, zip it up, and stow it in the cabinet under the station."

Marianne reached for her stethoscope, which she'd set on the counter by the phone just before the fire alarm had sounded. It, too, was missing.

"I don't believe it! My brand new scope. That's a hundred-dollar instrument!"

"Isn't that the one Justin just gave to you?" Gary asked as he helped look for it.

"It sure is. Oh, God, he's gonna kill me when he finds out. I've got to find it."

Lenny leaned toward Gary and asked in a whisper, "Who's Justin?"

"That's her new boyfriend," Gary said. "He's a second year medical student. He's kind of short, but nice looking." He added, "I hear he's got money."

"That's not true. He told me his grandfather has money, but he's not even sure he's in the will. Justin's sweet, and he takes me to nice clubs."

"And buys you expensive toys."

"Yeah, but no ring yet," she said, holding up a left hand with no jewelry on the fingers.

Sandy, the security guard, approached them.

"I'm glad you're here," Lenny said. "Marianne just had her wallet and stethoscope stolen."

"Damn, another one? Every time there's a commotion something ends up stolen. We must have a dozen incident reports down in the office by now. This ain't no homeless guy off the street. It's an inside job."

From his pocket Lenny pulled out the pieces of the cigarette lighter. "Look what I found on the floor in the lounge." He showed Sandy the head and pieces of the lighter.

"Well I'll be a mother's uncle. Some sicko broke the lighter and sprinkled the fluid into the trash can."

"That's how I figured it," Lenny said.

"You know I'll have to turn this over to Joe West. It's evidence."

"Sure," Lenny said, dumping the items into Sandy's outstretched palm.

Turning to Marianne, Sandy said, "You'll have to make out an incident report. I'll come back later to pick it up."

"Okay."

Moose came up to the station and picked up the diet sheet for the next day's orders. As he approached Lenny and Sandy, the guard said in a low voice, "Let's step around the corner."

They walked down the hall to the dirty utility room and stepped inside. Seeing that no one was in the hall nearby, Sandy confided, "I just remembered something else about the murder. When the police came to examine Sparks' things, I opened up his locker for them, but I didn't need a key. It was unlocked."

"Did they find anything?" Lenny asked.

"Nope. Just some old scrub suits and a couple of books. And you know, when they examined his car in the parking lot, that was open, too."

"That's nuts," Moose said. "Nobody owns a car in Philly leaves it unlocked. Looks like somebody was looking for something."

"It's possible," Sandy said. "A thief might not bother to lock up after he was inside the car. What does he care if it's stolen?"

"True," Lenny said, "but then again, he might want to lock it up to cover his tracks. Make sure nobody knew he was nosing around."

"Maybe," Sandy said. "Ain't no way to tell till the police get the fingerprint report."

"That won't help us any if we can't see the police files," said Lenny. "If the bastard who killed Sparks was looking for something, it would have to be small enough to fit inside a locker."

"Now there I agree with you," Sandy said. He took a ziplock plastic bag from the specimen tray and dropped the pieces of lighter into it. He closed the bag carefully and shoved it into his pocket. "I was just thinking…

Remember that time Freddie was out on sick leave for four months with hepatitis?"

"Sure I do. I had to file a grievance to get him his time off. We had a third-step hearing with Freely and the rest of them. The whole nine yards. What about it?"

"Well do you remember who it was stood in for Freddie helping Doc Fingers do the post mortems?"

Lenny looked at Moose, frowned, furrowed his brow over worried eyes.

"Shit!" he said.

"That's right, it was our boy…"

"Regis Devoe," said Lenny. I'd forgotten he worked in the morgue back in ninety-one. Still, it doesn't mean anything, you know that."

"*I* know it. The problem we got is, *West* knows it, and you *know* that he told the police about it. Prosecutors love to take shit like that and tar and feather somebody in front of a jury."

Lenny put his hands in his pockets and blew out his cheeks.

"What's done is done," he said. "No use crying over spilt beer. We just have to bust our butts and find out who really killed Sparks."

"And who set the fire and's been stealin' all over the building," Sandy said, as he turned and ambled off to join West in the lounge. "Prob'bly the same individual."

Turning to Moose, Lenny said, "Listen, I know it's been a hell of a fucked up day, but I told Regis that I'd try and make a run out to the Detention Center after work to see him. Any chance you can come along?"

"Sure I can," Moose said. "Lemme go down to the sewing room and give Birdie the car keys."

"Okay," Lenny said, looking at his watch. "I've got to get the unit back in shape. Let me finish up my work and I'll meet you in the parking lot after I punch out. Okay?"

"You got it," Moose said and went off.

Twenty-four

While Lenny and Betty picked up the debris left by the hurried exodus of patients, Celeste brought the patient charts back and began putting them in the rack.

"It sure is a mixed-up situation when saving the hospital records is more important than saving people," she said.

"I agree with you," said Gary, who was helping straighten up the station. "I told Miss Burgess that we should get all of our charts on the computer. That way we won't have any hard copy to have to carry around."

"Think they'll go for it?"

"No, it's too expensive. But maybe someday…"

"Someday we'll all be dead and the charts they store in the sub-basement will be growing mold."

The phone rang. Celeste picked it up.

"This is the HSWU legal department," said a woman's voice. "Is Leonard Moss there?"

"Sure, I'll get him," Celeste said and pressed the Hold button.

When Lenny picked up the phone, the union secretary said, "I have a call from Mr. Granger. Hold please."

In a moment the union lawyer came on the line.

"Moss? Fred Granger. Listen, I got your message about the laundry worker who's in jail facing a first degree murder charge, and I have to tell you that I can't do anything for him in an official capacity. The union has no legal standing in a criminal matter."

"I didn't think you could defend him, but I was hoping you could advise him on finding a good criminal lawyer."

"Officially I can't even do that, but unofficially, sure, I know several good men in the city. Have him call my office and I'll leave a few names and phone numbers."

"They won't let him have his cell phone in jail," Lenny said. "I'll tell his wife Salina to call your office later."

"That will be fine. I have to run. Goodbye."

After getting the ward back into order and mopping the corridor, Lenny walked wearily down the stairs to the basement, but instead of going to his locker he went in the opposite direction. He was soon in the old section of the hospital, its damp walls peeling old paint and a permanent smell of mold in the air.

Coming to an intersecting hall, he turned left and came to a battered metal door with a tarnished metal sign reading **Morgue**. Lenny pushed open the heavy door and stepped in to a chilly, damp, low-ceilinged room. His senses were hit with the powerful stench of disinfectant, formaldehyde, and blood.

Freddie was hosing down the big stainless steel platform where the bodies were dissected. Gutters along the sides of the platform carried the blood and other bodily fluids to a sink with a collecting trap. One of the sliding drawers was open, feet protruding from the opening.

"Hey Fred, you busy?"

"Yo, Lenny, come on in. You just missed a good one. Doc Fingers cut this bad boy here from stem to stern. You should've seen the juice that flowed out of him. It was like a sewer main broke and flooded the streets."

"Yeah, I'm really sorry I missed that." He came closer to Freddie, avoiding the cadaver with the feet sticking out of the opening in the big refrigerated unit. "How've you been doing?"

"That new lab supervisor's been stepping on my dick," he said. "Every time I turn around she's coming around asking me what I'm doing, where am I going. She gets up in my face real close trying to smell my breath."

"Subtle bitch. If it keeps up I'll threaten to file a grievance for harassment. You've been sober for, what, year and a half?"

"Twenty-eight months, two weeks and a couple of days," he said, his stooped shoulders rising for a moment in pride.

"I'm really happy for you.... Listen, can we talk about something private?"

"Talk away my man, there's nobody here but you and me and the stiff on the slab."

"Okay. You heard how Moose and me are trying to help Regis get the charges dropped, right? We're trying to find who killed Randy Sparks. I know Regis didn't do it. It's not his style. It's too complicated. Too much planning, you know what I mean?"

"Damn straight he didn't do it. The John Doe and the fake wounds—no way a laundry worker could do something like that."

"Could you do it?"

Freddie stopped spraying the table, turned off the hose, and slowly coiled it up.

"I'm not accusing you, understand me," Lenny said. "I'm just speaking hypothetically."

"I know. I'm thinking about it. It's a good question."

Lenny waited while Freddie straightened out the room.

"Draining the blood and filling the cavities with formaldehyde...okay, I could do that. It wouldn't be easy, but I could do it. But the wounds? I'd be guessing what they look like. How deep to make 'em, how hard to hit the chest and the face. I couldn't do that. Not so's it would be convincing."

"What about the computer stuff?"

"The John Doe? I don't know squat about computers, but somebody who knew about them could make out a ticket. It's just an entry in the system as far as I know. Shouldn't be *too* tough."

"Okay," Lenny said. "Thanks. Oh, I got one more thing to ask you."

"Go ahead."

"It would help us a lot if I could find out what was on the autopsy report. You think Dr. Fingers knows about it?"

"More'n likely he does. He's got friends in the medical examiner's office. Talks to them all the time. He might not see the actual report, but he probably heard about it. I'll put a little squeeze on him. Let you know what I find out."

"Thanks Freddie. I'll check with you tomorrow. I've got to punch out."

"Right-o. Tomorrow."

Freddie pushed the tray with the fresh cadaver into the refrigerator and closed the door. Lenny was curious by the way he did it. He didn't slam the heavy metal door, but closed it gently, as if he didn't want to wake the dead.

Twenty-five

*L*enny made his way to the locker room, opened it and put on his hat and coat. Punching out at the time clock, he walked out the main hospital entrance and continued past the doctor's parking lot to the employee lot, where he saw Moose waiting by the car.

"Thanks for coming with me," Lenny said.

"Ain't no big thing."

Lenny unlocked the passenger side for his friend, then crossed to the driver's, unlocked it and climbed in. The soft bench seat was cold but comfortable. The young guys could have their bucket seats; he'd take a bench with a woman snuggling up beside him any day. Not that he'd had a woman beside him for a while, but still...

He fired up the V8, turned on the headlights and the defroster.

"Why're you blowin' cold air on us?" Moose asked.

"My father taught me that. Even though it feels cold, and right now, okay, it *is* cold, but even before it gets really warm it still pulls a lot of moisture off the glass. See what I mean?"

"You just like to hear my teeth rattle."

Lenny put the car in reverse, eased out of his spot and pointed the nose toward the exit. As the car approached the gate he said, "Hey Moose, d'ya ever get an impulse to smash through that stupid gate? I mean, it's only a hunk of wood. It wouldn't even scratch the Buick."

"All the time."

Lenny inserted his parking card into the slot and waited for the gate to lift. He pulled out onto Germantown Avenue and headed for Walnut Lane. With its big wheels and soft suspension, the car barely shuddered riding over the old cobblestones and trolley tracks. The mayor had eliminated the electric trolley on Germantown Avenue, to widespread complaints from preservationists and people who liked the open air cars. The noisy old trolleys had often got stuck behind double-parked cars, raising the tempers of the riders, but the trolley was a beloved part of Philadelphia's history.

A coterie of wealthy diehards in Chestnut Hill had managed to keep a short section of the line rolling in their neighborhood for a time, but that, too, would soon be gone.

Turning onto Chew past the all-night deli, Lenny said, "I wonder if the cops really do have something on Regis, like Joe West was telling me."

"Got to be. West is one guy who don't bluff. When he puts those cuffs on you, he's on solid ground. Trust me."

"I hope not, for Regis's sake," Lenny said. "Catching the killer is a million-to-one long shot. Besides, I'm not sure how much more snooping around I can get away with."

"That West's been after your ass for years."

"Don't I know it. Every time he walks past me he fingers those damn handcuffs of his."

"Once a cop, always a cop," Moose said. "But you know what? I don't think the killer set the fire."

"No, why not?"

"Stealing wallets is penny ante stuff. The killer's too slick for that. Look how he faked the car accident and got the body in the classroom to be cut up. He's too smart to stick his head out over some credit cards, maybe a little cash."

"I think you're right," Lenny said. He turned onto the Roosevelt Expressway and crossed to the through lanes that avoided some of the lights. The big car seemed to stretch out, easily cruising at 65.

Moose turned on the radio. KYW announced a chance of flurries, a high of thirty-six, the low around twenty in the city, down in the teens in the suburbs.

"It never snows in Philly anymore, you know that?" Moose said.

"We haven't had a good blizzard since, when was it, eighty-one?" said Lenny.

"That's the one. I told my kids about the time the snow was up to my waist and they wouldn't hardly believe me."

Moose asked if he could change the station, switched to the Temple jazz program. The throb of the car's big V8 seemed to harmonize with the music.

Lenny glanced at the gas gauge. Three-quarters full. He liked to keep the level up in the winter to keep moisture from condensing in the tank.

After driving in silence for a few minutes, Lenny said, "I know you're just trying to help me out, Moose. I know that."

Moose watched the stores on Roosevelt Expressway pass by, their Christmas lights still up and splashing the night with color.

"That's a shame, they closed that big Sears store. I always loved that place."

"Me, too. And now even Heckinger's is gone."

"Your only choice is Home Depot or the local hardware store," said Moose."

The radio announced upcoming jazz concerts. He stretched his big frame, looked at his friend.

"Hey Lenny, 'member how you started out kinda lukewarm about this murder thing?"

"Uh-huh."

"You sorry you took it on?"

Lenny shrugged. "I was just thinking what my dad would say if he were alive. I've told you about him being a labor organizer…?"

"Yeah. Lots a' times."

"In his day they 'd do what they had to do to win a strike. Once a bunch of them put on women's clothes and slipped past a line of cops delivering food to some strikers, only they didn't just have cake and cookies."

"Sounds like your dad was a fighter."

"He was. What I'm doing is pretty tame compared with the stuff they did in his day."

"You've taken a few punches and you're still on your feet."

"It's not the same," Lenny said. He pointed to an exit sign. "Here's Cottman. We'll be there soon." They turned east and drove through a large industrial section, with old warehouses squatting in empty lots, closed down gas stations, their pumps removed and old tires piled haphazardly in the corner of the lots.

They passed a large sign that warned against trespassing. Down a short decline, then up for a brief stretch, they passed Holmesberg Prison and continued on to a new, modern red brick building. Surrounded by a low fence, the facility looked like a UPS depot, but was the The Philadelphia Detention Center.

Lenny turned to Moose. "They might not let you in without union ID. You okay waiting in the car?"

"Sure. You do what you have t' do."

At the guardhouse, Lenny showed the officer his union identification and driver's license. Moose showed his hospital ID and license. The guard looked over a roster of visitors.

"Your buddy's ID don't say he's a union rep."

"He's just been elected shop steward, his card hasn't come through yet. I'm showing him the ropes. It's awful cold out here. Can't he come in with me?"

The guard looked from Lenny to Moose, blew a stream of vapor into the cold air, and turned back to Lenny. "I hope you've got a sleeping bag in the trunk. Your friend's gonna need it."

The guard ducked back into his guardhouse and closed the door. He spoke with someone on the phone, then he pulled a switch. The gate swung open.

Lenny slowly rounded a bend and came in sight of the prison. It was an ugly stone and brick edifice, thick-walled and brooding. An electrified fence surrounded it, while another guard station stood at the foot of massive steel doors. Lenny thought of Robin Hood going over the wall of the castle and of the evil Sheriff of Nottingham, but he knew Regis wasn't going anywhere for a while.

Maybe for a long, long while.

He parked the car, left the key in the ignition and the engine running, and stepped out. His boots crunched on ice and gravel as he approached the guard station at the door.

The high, stony walls jogged loose a childhood memory. He was a little boy of perhaps eight. He had come with his father to meet his Uncle Julius, who was being let out of jail. His mother had objected to Lenny's going, but his father had prevailed, saying that he wanted his son to know that being in jail was no shame, but a badge of honor when you were arrested for sticking to your principles.

Lenny didn't remember what prison they had visited. His father had waited patiently at the gates. When Julius came out they had hugged, then his uncle knelt and shook Lenny's hand. He told Lenny he was a brave boy to come to an evil place like this. Lenny didn't feel very brave; he was just happy to get out of school and ride with his father in the car, but he accepted everything his uncle said as truth.

Lenny never learned what crime had sent his uncle to prison. When his father died years later, he found old newspaper clippings about the McCarthy trials, and figured that Julius had been arrested in the witch hunts for refusing to testify about the communists in the labor unions.

Lenny pushed the memory aside and stepped up to the gate. A large sign with the picture of a finger pointing at him said, **WARNING: NO BEEPERS, CELL PHONES, CAMERAS OR ELECTRIC DEVICES. NO EXCEPTIONS!** Below the sign was a metal box with a label declaring, "Contraband" where people left any incriminating items they didn't want discovered on them.

He again showed his union ID to a guard. After the guard opened the big door, Lenny placed his keys in a plastic tray. He took off his shoes and gave them to the guard, who bent them looking for weapons and ran a wand over them searching for metal. After Lenny passed through the metal detector he was escorted to the visitor's area, where he signed in and waited.

There were a dozen other visitors sitting on chipped plastic chairs. The room was thick with cigarette smoke. There were no windows.

Twenty-six

After a forty-five minute wait, a prison guard wagged his finger at Lenny. Lenny went to him, but instead of escorting him into one of the cubbyholes where visitors looked at the prisoner through plate glass, the guard led him down a corridor. A sign on the wall with an arrow pointing straight ahead said "Infirmary."

"What's the matter, is my friend sick or something?"

The guard ignored the question, passing several offices with iron grates on the doors, then he opened a heavy gate. Above it a sign read, "**WARNING. NO SHARP OBJECTS ALLOWED IN INFIRMARY.**"

The guard walked through another metal detector, stopped, turned, and beckoned Lenny through it. Satisfied when it made no warning BEEP, the guard led him into a high-ceilinged room with two rows of cots lined up military style along opposite walls. In the corner was a nursing station enclosed in thick plexiglass. Through the glass he could see two nurses with sour looks on their faces writing in charts.

The guard tapped on the plexiglass, getting a nurse's attention. He pointed at Lenny and said "Devoe," then walked back out of the room.

The nurse spoke through a microphone as is done in a fast food outlet. "Bed six," she barked, pointing at one of the rows of cots. Lenny followed the numbers taped to the ends of the beds, and found Regis lying on a cot. His face was bruised and lacerated, the areas around his left eye purple and swollen shut, and the top of his head swathed in thick bandages.

How can I help this guy? he asked himself. One night in the Detention Center and he was already in trouble.

Lenny stood beside the cot, saw there were no chairs, and sat gently on the edge of the bed.

"Hey, Regis, what happened?"

Regis opened his good eye, smiled at Lenny, then grimaced. His jaw was swollen and his teeth were caked with blood.

"Lenny, they let you in!"

"What the fuck did they *do* to you?"

"I said something to one of the guards. Didn't mean nothin' by it. He called in his buddies and they worked me over with their sticks."

"Oh Reeg, I'm sorry man. Those bastards. Does your lawyer know about this?"

"Yeah, I called him already. He's gonna file a bunch of papers or some shit." He sat up in bed, the springs creaking under the weight. "How's things with you?"

"Moose and I have been looking into the murder. We figure the only way to get you back is to prove somebody else killed Sparks. It's kind of a long shot, but—"

"Man, I *know* you and Moose can do it. I'll be back with you all inside of a week."

"Don't get your hopes too high, Regis. These investigations take a lot of time, but I think we're getting somewhere."

Lenny related what he had uncovered to date, including the list of suspects and the mysterious fire on Seven-South and the broken lighter he'd discovered on the floor beside the trash can.

"Fire—that's no joke in a hospital," Regis said. "A man does that will do anything."

"It looked intentional, that's for sure. I mean, I'm no fire investigator. I didn't sniff the ashes for petroleum products, but it looked pretty much like somebody sprinkled the lighter fluid into the waste bucket and lit it."

"Damn!"

"Somebody's been taking advantage of the emergencies to steal stuff. I think he set the fire to start a panic. A nurse had her wallet and her stethoscope stolen in all the commotion."

"You're up against one nasty mother."

"Think he's smarter than me?" Lenny said.

"No way. You n' Moose'll bring him down."

"I'm not sure how smart we are, but we have a lot of good people pulling for us back in James Madison."

Regis asked Lenny to hand him his cup of water. He took small sips from the straw. "I can't eat no solid food. Just pudding n' stuff on account of the loose teeth."

"Listen Reeg—that argument you had with Sparks. Did you really threaten him?"

"I was just blowing smoke is all. I get pissed when those prissy white kids from the Main Line walk out in hospital scrubs and we get searched for nothin. I *hate* that shit."

"I can't stand it either, but what did you say to Sparks?"

"I don't remember. He was acting all superior, and I said something like say that shit to me outside, but I didn't mean it. I'm not stupid enough to fight a doctor on hospital property."

"I know you're not. I just worry what a lawyer can get a jury to believe."

Lenny shifted his weight on the cot, looked over his friend. "Regis, what else do the cops have on you?"

"Nothin. They got nothin' on me!" he said, shifting in the cot and making the springs groan. Then he rubbed his ribs in pain.

Lenny studied the young man's swollen face. He let a moment pass until Regis had calmed down.

"You know, in my union work I've found that sometimes things that make a person look guilty actually point the finger at the real culprit if you know how to look at it. You follow me?"

"Not exactly."

Lenny folded his arms, thought a moment.

"Take the fact that you worked in the morgue when Freddie was out on sick leave. The cops must know about that by now. Joe West filled them in I'm sure, and they'll probably make a big deal about it if you go to trial."

"I'm not goin' to no trial! My lawyer's filing' those papers, remember? Besides, you an' Moose are gonna grab the fucker's ass that killed Sparks and haul it in."

"Sure we will. The point is, if you look at the morgue time you had in another way, the killer might know about it, too. And if *he* knows that you had the argument with Sparks he'd feel pretty confident that the cops would finger you and not even bother come looking for *him*."

Regis slowly sat back in bed, the pain forgotten as realization dawned on him.

"Ohhh, yeah, I get it. You're sayin' somebody set me up. I know that bastard Joe West is in the middle of it, helping the killer, if he didn't actually do it himself."

"Probably so. What I'm thinking is, if the killer was really slick, he might drop Sparks's expensive watch down the laundry shoot in the off chance that you, of all people, would be the one to find it...see what I mean?"

Regis pulled the pillow up against the metal headboard and leaned back, his eyes guarded, his voice silent.

"Regis, if I'm going to help you, I have to know everything, even the bad stuff. Otherwise I'll be wandering around without a map. Okay?"

"Okay," he said, a sullen look on his face.

"I mean it Reeg. The truth. All of it."

Lenny looked into Regis's eyes and waited.

"Does Salina have to know?"

"No, Regis, Salina doesn't have to know. It'll just be between you and me."

"Fair enough," said Regis, settling back into his bunk.

Twenty-seven

"I need to know about the Rolex, Reeg. Did you really get it on the avenue?"

Regis reached for the cup of water and sipped from the straw. A few drops dribbled down his chin onto his chest. He ignored them. "Nah, I found it in the laundry just like you figured, but I didn't know it came from a dead guy!"

"And you couldn't admit where you found it because it would get you fired for stealing."

"You know it."

"All right," Lenny said, "we still go with the story that you bought it."

He looked at his own watch, a Timex that Margaret had given to him years ago for his birthday. He liked the expanding band that let him pull it up his arm almost to his elbow when he had to wash his hands. Often he'd forget he'd moved it there. When Betty or Moose would tease him about it, he'd claim to be starting a new fashion trend—"arm" watches, instead of "wrist" watches. "Everyone'll be doing it eventually. It's cutting edge chic," he'd said, and gone the rest of the day wearing his watch just below his elbow.

He waited for Regis to tell him more, but his friend kept quiet. Lenny considered that the young man must be worn out from his ordeal, but he had a few more nagging things he had to get through.

"Have you ever been near Sparks' car?" he asked.

Regis shook his head, winced at the pain. "Shit," he hissed through clenched teeth. "Why would I do something stupid like that?"

"The cops found it unlocked. Somebody had been in it. They went through his locker too."

"Not me! I don't even know what his car looked like!"

"And his locker?"

"No, I'm clean! I swear it man!"

"Okay, Reeg, I believe you. Calm down."

Regis tried to plump his pillow. It was as heavy as wet sand.

"How's Salina? She still mad at me?"

"I hear she's more worried than angry. Birdie promised to call her and go over."

"Worried—that's good. As long as she doesn't change the locks."

"Have you and her been arguing or something?"

"Kind of, yeah. You know how it is with women. She's all hot to get married and have a passel of kids. Ball and chain. I told her, "look, I'll give you a child, and I'll be a good father. Really be there for him, you know? But I don't see no need to tie that knot around my balls."

"You told Salina that? In those words?"

"Not exactly those, but close enough. After a while she sort of backed off on the marriage thing. I think she was thinking I'd change up when she got pregnant, and maybe I will. I'm not sayin' I'll never do it, it's just not my time is all."

"She's a terrific woman, Reeg. I hope you stay together."

"Sure we will, we're just like ice cream and cake. We'll always be together."

Lenny looked at his watch. "Jeez, I forgot. Moose is out in the car waiting for me! I'll be out of gas if he has to wait there much longer in this cold. I better get going."

Lenny stood, looked down at the young man.

"What's the matter?" Regis asked.

"I just had a shitty thought. I wonder if West had anything to do with you getting beat up."

"Why'd he do something like that?"

"I don't know, distract me maybe, throw me off the trail. West was a cop. He probably has friends in the prison system."

"They did jump on me for nothin," Regis said.

Lenny shrugged. "Do you need anything? Something to read? I could get some chocolate at Asher's."

"Nah, that' okay. I'm cool."

As Lenny stood by the bed, Regis held out his hand.

"Thanks for comin' t' see me, Lenny. I won't forget."

"That's okay. It's gonna be a scream when we get you back on the job and Joe West has to eat his words. He's gonna be one stopped-up asshole."

"Yeah, and I know just how to jerk his chain," Regis said, grinning and showing his wired jaw. The word "chain" reminded him of where he was and his face stiffened.

Lenny said goodbye, then he retraced his steps to the outside world, accompanied by the same guard. In the parking lot he found Moose sitting in a cold car with the engine off.

This Won't Hurt A Bit

"Moose, how come you didn't run the motor? I had plenty of gas."

"Wasn't cold. How's Regis?"

Lenny told him about the injuries, none of which seemed life-threatening. He added his worry that Joe West had sent a signal to the prison guards to hurt Regis.

Moose balled his big hands in fists. "I wish I could get West alone somewhere outside the hospital. Make him pay for all the shit he's done."

Lenny drove through the dark streets. When they reached Roosevelt Boulevard he switched on the radio. For a while the only sounds were the low hum of the motor, the wheels on the smooth asphalt, and the cool jazz.

"Moose?"

"Yeah?"

"I was wondering, why is it you were so hot to do this murder investigation. I mean, I'm a union delegate. I sort of have to do something for Regis."

Moose looked at the stores as the car sailed along the Boulevard, not turning to Lenny. He took in a deep breath and blew it out slowly onto the window, forming a frost. He ran his finger along the frosted window, making a heart shape.

"When I was fifteen I got into a jam. Went riding with a buddy in a stolen car. I didn't know it was stolen, I was just going for the ride. Cops pulled us over n' my buddy up and ran for it. Bein' young, I thought I was in the clear. I didn't steal the car, so I just sat there and talked real polite to the cops."

Moose drew letters in the heart.

"What happened next?"

"They beat the crap outta me. Beat me good and sent me to Juvey Hall for eighteen months."

Moose rubbed out the heart on the window, settled back into the seat.

"When I turned eighteen they wiped my record clean and my cousin Eunice helped me get this job. I met Birdie there and been workin' in the hospital ever since."

"I'm sorry, Moose."

Moose turned to his friend. "So I know what Regis feels like, stuck in a cell for something he didn't do, and I guess I'll just have to help him get out of it."

As they passed the empty Heckinger's building, Lenny asked, "You want to stop? You need anything for the house?"

"I promised Birdie I'd watch the kids so she can go out. How about you come jogging with me Saturday morning, then we go to the hardware store?"

"What, jog in this freezing weather? I'd freeze my balls off."

"The cold won't hurt if you warm up first. Come on, be good for you."

"I'll let you know, Moose. I'm beat to hell. I need a day to lie around and chill out."

"Okay."

Lenny dropped Moose at home, then he stopped at a Wa Wa deli to pick up the Daily News. He drove through frozen, half-empty streets. With a gray, leaden sky and no snow for the children to play on, the winter cold drove most Philadelphians inside.

He pulled up to his row house, happy to get a spot right in front of the door. The street lights had not yet come on, and in the failing light the porch was in shadow.

"Dark," he muttered to himself, opening the porch door. "So fucking dark."

Twenty-eight

Lenny stepped into the porch and walked wearily toward the inner door, unlocked it, stepped into the house, and flipped on the lights. He threw his hat and coat on the sofa and passed on in to the kitchen. Too tired to cook anything, he poured cold cereal into a large bowl, filled it to overflowing with milk, sipped the milk from the bowl and set it on the dining room table.

Opening the newspaper, he flipped through it, looking for news about the Sparks murder and Regis's arrest. There was a short article buried in the middle of the paper that quoted Joe West, who described Regis as a "violent, antisocial type who was continually in trouble with the hospital" who had "quarreled violently" (how can you quarrel violently, he wondered) and threatened Dr. Sparks. An unnamed source in the police department reported that the arrest had been made "in a house in a quiet section of East Mt. Airy known for its youth gangs and drug sales."

His bowl empty, Lenny grew more and more disgusted at the news coverage. He'd hoped the reporter might have at least given a single line to Regis's lawyer, but there was no hint that he had even tried to call him. The account briefly reviewed the discovery of Sparks's body in an anatomy lab at James Madison's School of Medicine.

Putting the paper down, he realized that the news would be a likely source of information on Randy Sparks as well. He wasn't sure how long it had been since he'd tied up a bundle of newspapers and set them out to be recycled, but he knew there was a pile of them in the basement, as well as several issues lying on the floor in rooms around the house. He scoured the upstairs bathroom, the bedroom, and the kitchen until he had collected every copy of the paper.

Setting them in order by date, he found the earliest one, dated December 23. He recalled cleaning up the house before going out to the shore to visit his mother and aunt over Christmas. They didn't celebrate the holiday, but he had it off and it was a good time to go, since he didn't have Margaret to celebrate with him.

There was no mention of Randy Sparks until the discovery of his body, which was only logical. Up until then it had been a simple missing persons case. Sparks hadn't been wealthy or a powerful figure in the community, so his disappearance barely raised a tiny ripple in the news community.

During the third week of January, when Kate and Jennifer had discovered the body, there was front page coverage, with the photo of a smiling young Randy Sparks, probably taken from the security ID photo required of all hospital employees. The photo was cropped into a corner of a larger photo of James Madison Hospital over a caption, *"Dead Doctor Cut Up by Students...Grisly Discovery Shocks the Medical Community."*

It described the discovery of the body of a physician in training, Dr. Randolph Sparks, in the medical school of James Madison School of Medicine and Dentistry. The reporter spoke of Sparks as a bright young resident who had been highly respected by his peers, with a promising career in inherited diseases. The usual quotes from the chief of staff and a pair of residents followed. The cause of death had not yet been determined.

Questioned about how a murder victim could be included among the cadavers that had been legitimately donated to the anatomy class, the dean of the medical school swore that security in the school was "first rate" and "state of the art," and that a full investigation into the processing of cadavers was underway. A medical student, who asked not to be identified, commented on the ironic disposition of Sparks's corpse, and stated that the perpetrator, perhaps a disgruntled patient or family member of a deceased former hospital patient, must have been making a statement about the medical establishment.

There was a brief summary of the victim's career, beginning with an undergraduate degree in biology at Haverford and medical school at Penn, followed by his two years of residency at James Madison. His parents had died when he was in high school. He had lived with an aunt in Bryn Mawr until going to college, and lived on his own after that. He was not married and had no brothers or sisters.

Lenny couldn't' find the following day's edition. By the next day the story had been pushed back to the metro section. It reported that autopsy results were inconclusive, and that samples had been sent to a "federal laboratory in Washington, DC," for further tests. The following day contained no mention of the case, and that brought Lenny up to today's story.

All together, the paper revealed little that helped him. Aside from the description of Regis's argument with Sparks, there was not a single sentence that pointed toward another suspect.

He clipped the relevant articles out and slipped them into an envelope, which he labeled and placed on the table, then he put out the lights and dragged himself up to bed. He took off his shoes and uniform and wrapped himself in the comforter. Although dog-tired, his mind was racing through the events of the day.

Lenny wrapped the comforter more tightly around him. Certain that he would be awake half the night, he closed his eyes one last time and fell into a deep sleep.

Twenty-nine

As Lenny slept, an anemic winter sun cast a pale light through the bedroom window, cloudy with frost. Dirty clothes were piled in a corner, old newspapers yellowed on a bedside table. Three coffee cups, two with mold growing in the bottom, sat unnoticed on the floor between bed and wall.

He awoke with in a state of arousal, dreaming of Margaret. Drifting on the edge of sleep, he imagined her soft, smooth body beside him. Imagined her thick, fragrant hair falling on his face. He reached a hand out to the space beside him in the bed.

It was empty.

He listened for the sound of her breathing.

There was only silence.

His desire ebbed…Expired. He felt cold, hungry, and depressed. His head ached as if he'd been drinking bourbon and coke half the night. He hated sleeping alone, not just for the lack of sex, but wanting the warmth of another person. He missed the weight of another body pushing against him. Missed wrapping his arms around her and sleeping like a baby, his face pressed against her back.

He poked his feet out from beneath the covers, felt the cold air. He pushed himself up, scratched his hair, which was oily, then stumbled into the bathroom. He brushed his teeth and showered. The single towel on the rack was damp. Lenny used it anyway.

Back in the bedroom he opened the closet and searched the high shelf. He found an old uniform, its blue color faded from too many washes with bleach. "At least it's clean," he mumbled and began dressing. Buttoning his shirt, he looked up at the brown stain in the ceiling. *Got to get up on the roof before the Spring rains*, he thought. *God, I hate roof work.*

He shuffled downstairs to the kitchen and poured a tall glass of orange juice. He dropped two alka seltzer tablets into the glass—his usual treatment for a hangover—and chugged it down. The mixture didn't lift his spirits much, but it did begin to ease his headache.

He followed the juice with a bowl of cornflakes and a cup of espresso. Donning a woolen watch cap and navy pea coat, he bit into an apple and fished in his pocket for his keys. He had his hand on the front door knob and was just turning it when the phone rang.

He froze, considering his options. He didn't want to talk to Regis again this early in the morning.

Brring-bring.

"Shit," he mumbled, releasing the door and stepping back into the living room.

"Hullo?" he said.

"Lenny? It's Salina. I hate to bother you this early in the morning, but you said you were gonna see Regis yesterday, and I figured, you know, better to catch you at home than bother you at work and all…"

"It's okay, Salina. I saw Regis, and—"

"You saw him? Is he okay?"

"Ye-ah…" he said, drawing out the one syllable, "I mean, as good as can be expected."

"What do you mean? Is my baby all right?"

"He's fine, he's gonna be okay. He…"

"*Gonna* be? What happened?"

"A couple of the guards worked him over a little bit, but he's fine, nothing's broken. He's in the infirmary and he's getting very good care."

"Oh, my poor Reegie. Did he say anything about me?"

"He asked me to give you a big hug and a kiss, which I can't do over the phone, and he wanted me to say he loves you."

"Oh, that's so sweet. Thank you Lenny."

"How are you doing? You okay? You were said you were sick the last time I talked to you."

"I'm starting to get my appetite back. The doctor says I won't be showing for a while yet, but…"

"Showing? You mean like *pregnant* showing? Is that why you couldn't eat anything?"

"Oh, Lenny, I wasn't supposed to tell anybody yet. Regis is going to kill me, but yeah, I'm expecting. It's my first time. Isn't it wonderful?"

"I'm very happy for you, Salina, and Regis, too, but why didn't he tell me when I saw him yesterday?"

"You know how he is. He's very private."

"He's got to start trusting me if I'm going to help him."

"He will, Lenny, give him time!"

"I know," he said, glancing at his watch. "Speaking of time, I have to run or I'll be late and Childress will be suspending me. Did you get him a lawyer yet, 'cause the union said they have somebody they could recommend if you didn't."

"My uncle is an attorney. He's found us a Jewish lawyer who's a real shark."

"Uh, well, as long as he knows what he's doing. I have to run. I'll try to call you tonight. Are you gonna be at your parents?"

"I think probably so. I'll call you, okay?"

"Fine. Take care of yourself, Salina."

"Bye Lenny! I'm gonna give Regis lots of hugs and kisses when I see him."

Hanging up the phone, he thought, hugs and kisses. That's just what Regis needed right now, along with a good lawyer, a solid alibi, and a new suspect.

He stepped outside onto a dark, silent street and breathed in the cold morning air. The street lights formed yellow circles in the frosty air. He unlocked the car and settled in. The big V-8 in the Buick turned once, hesitated in the cold, then caught in a low-pitched growl. He loved the car. Parts were hard to get, and it burned a lot of gas, but it would hold up against a bus in an accident, and it cruised the highway as smoothly as the cue ball on a first-class pool table.

Driving toward the hospital, he considered what to do next. He was in the dark and he knew it. He needed information, but where was he going to get it? Hopefully, Fred would get something out of Dr. Fingers on the autopsy. The pathologist had stuck by Freddie at the arbitration hearing, testifying that the man's drinking hadn't impaired his work performance, though Lenny knew that it had.

He wanted to look at the gynecologist, Odom. Gynecology could mean pregnancy. That could mean fooling around, having somebody else's baby, all kinds of nasty things.

Then there was Radcliff, the shrink with the fast hands. Psychology wasn't exactly a picnic in Fairmont Park, either. Those guys learned a lot of dirt on people. If Sparks sat in on some raunchy sessions or read through some private notes and learned something that threatened someone…

Not that he could rule out the others. If only he could interview them the way he did in a grievance, but in this investigation he had no standing. No authority. He was just going to have to rely on the cunning of his friends and hope they came up with something.

Thirty

Betty walked down the basement corridor toward the housekeeping office to punch in, her red rubber boots squeaking in the marble floor with each step. As she came up to the office, Mr. Docksett, the assistant director, had her time card in his hand.

"I'm pulling you to the third floor offices," he said, handing her the time card.

"You didn't have to pull my card to tell me that."

"I wanted to be sure I caught you. You can return to your unit after your done."

"Do I got to do the clinic, too?" she asked.

"Of course. Everything on the third floor."

"Well, then don't even think about the sorry state Seven-South will be in by the time I get up there, 'cause it's gonna be a solid mess."

As she trudged on to the women's locker room, she saw Lenny, who had just punched in himself. "They're pulling me to the third floor," she told him.

"That's a bitch," he said. "I guess I won't see you till morning break."

"You got that right. This poor old body will be nothing but creaking bones by the time this day is through."

"I'll take care of the soap dispensers and paper towels."

"Thanks," she said, stepping toward the door to her locker room.

"I'll tell you about Regis later. Moose and I went out to see him last night. He looked okay."

"Praise the Lord," she said, disappearing behind the door. "Praise the righteous Lord."

Lenny entered his locker room and sat down on a bench to remove his boots. Abrahm, already dressed, was sitting reading a Russian language paper.

"Tell me Len'nye, you are asking about that young dok-tor who was killed, yes?"

"You heard about that, too?"

"Moose tells me about it. The reason I ask you, yesterday I see something not right in Dok-tor Gandy's office when I clean it. Come look."

Abrahm retrieved a piece of formed plastic that had once contained a sterile syringe and needle. Beside it was a long needle in a milky plastic cap.

"What's so odd about them?" Lenny asked. "I sweep up junk like that every day."

"Sure, sure," Abrahm said, "it is not what I find. Is where I find it. I find them under the cushions in the sofa in the waiting room, outside from the examinating room. Also I find four little white squares between the cushions. The squares are dried out, but once they were wet with alcohol."

"Is that unusual?"

"Yes, yes, very unusual. The injection is given in the little room where the dok-tor examinates you, not in the waiting area. You see?"

"I think so. You've never found any needles in the waiting area."

"Never."

Lenny looked more closely at the container and needle. "Can I keep them?"

"Of course." Abrahm deposited them in Lenny's hand, then he laced up his work shoes and closed his locker. "You will help Mr. Devoe to be free from prison, yes?"

"I hope so. Me and Moose are working on figuring out who really killed Randy Sparks, but right now it looks like a long shot."

As Abrahm rose to go to work, Lenny grabbed his arm. "Wait a second. What were you doing cleaning underneath the cushions in Gandy's office?"

Abrahm shrugged. "You see, at home my wife, she tells me to clean under the cushions, so when I come to work, I clean always the same way."

Lenny released his friend's arm. As he watched the stolid fellow amble out of the locker room, he thought he must have forgotten what it was like to be married.

Nathan Galloway was making early rounds with his staff on Seven-South. The doctor placed the metal tip of a doppler on Walter Oldenfield's diseased foot and listened intently for a pulse. The instrument could amplify the weakest pulse. It could even transmit the beating heart of an immature fetus in the mother's womb and broadcast the sound from its speaker. But even with the doppler's amplification, Galloway could not hear the crisp "whoosh-whoosh" that indicated a healthy flow of blood through Oldenfield's artery. The foot was cold, the nails, gray.

The surgeon put down the instrument and turned to his entourage.

"The graft is clotted off. Sipowiecz: call radiology and tell them you'll bring the patient down for arteriogram and declotting STAT." The young resident began writing the instructions down on his clipboard.

"See that he's NPO. Stop the heparin and run lactated ringers at eighty an hour...Make that one-hundred. And have radiology page me with the results."

The resident scribbled furiously as Galloway ran off the instructions.

"Got it," he said, and hurried to the station to make the appropriate phone calls.

Mr. Oldenfield threw the blanket over his foot. He looked up at Galloway, the web of lines in his face deepening with apprehension.

"You said the last operation would fix my leg."

Galloway focused his unblinking hazel eyes on the patient's forehead as he spoke. His small mouth was set in a grimace. "I said that there was a high probability that the last procedure would provide adequate perfusion to your leg. There are no guarantees with vascular disease. You know that Walter."

"I only know that I'm tired of all the pain and the drugs and the damned hospital. Cut the thing off if you have to. I want to be done with it!"

"Amputating the leg is not a cure-all. It will start you on a whole new round of treatments and physical therapy. I've explained all that."

Opening the patient's chart, Galloway entered a sentence in the progress notes written in neat, block letters any calligrapher would admire: "Pulse absent; A-gram to declot."

Finishing his orders, Galloway went to insert his pen in his inside jacket pocket but missed the clip. The pen fell to the floor and lay there in a sparkle of gold. Six medical students bent down simultaneously to pick it up for the surgeon. Two of them hit their heads. A woman student was first to the pen, which she plucked up and handed to Galloway.

Without a word, the surgeon handed the chart to the senior resident. "Call the OR and put Oldenfield's name in for an add-on. We'll do him after the last case." He picked up his black doctor's bag and held it out to one of the medical students who had struck his head, then he stepped briskly out of the room. The entourage narrowed to a funnel shape, squeezed through the door, and caught up with the surgeon like a slinky expanding.

When he reached the nursing station, Galloway picked up the phone and dialed the operator. As he listened to the ringing, he pulled another chart from the wall and scanned the lab results, then scrawled a hasty order.

He listened to the phone ring, then held it out in front of him and turned to Gary Tuttle. "Eighteen rings! I just dialed the operator and she didn't answer after eighteen rings. There's no excuse for that!"

Gary, anxious to get his insulin administered before the breakfast trays came up, shrugged his shoulders.

"Who were you trying to reach, doctor?"

"I wanted her to page Primeaux. I'm declotting Oldenfield's leg this morning."

Gary pulled out a blue 3-ring binder labeled "Physician Referral List", opened it, and thumbed through the listing of Attending Physicians.

"The list is alphabetical, doctor. Alex Primeaux's beeper number is right here beside his name. All you have to do is enter the code for page, dial his number and enter the number you're calling from."

He punched the sequence into the phone so hard the plastic cover popped off the face of the phone.

"I can't be bothered with looking up every damn physician's number!" he said, frowning deeply. "That's what we have operators for."

Gary rolled his eyes and went back to drawing up his syringes. As he worked, he thought of a series of sarcastic retorts and scathing observations he would like to make to Galloway, Gandy, and a few other physicians.

Thirty-one

Galloway left a message with Primeaux's answering service that he was ordering the declotting procedure for Oldenfield for later in the day, and that Primeaux could reach him in the OR if he had any questions.

Priscilla Gandy, who had just examined Louis Anderson, had walked up to the station with the patient's bedside clipboard in her hand. A gold-colored stethoscope stuck out of her smart, lavender suit. She scanned the vital sign record, then looked over at Galloway.

"Hello Nathan. How's that woman with the cold right foot I sent you last week? Were you able to help her?"

"If the fool would stay off the cigarettes and consent to the hyperbaric treatments she'd be fine, but she claims to be claustrophobic and won't lie down in the tank."

"Nothing that a little Valium won't cure," she said, as the two walked on to the nursing station.

"That and a second insurance carrier. Have you seen how much they're cutting the Medicare rates? What do they expect us to do, practice medicine out of a tent in Fairmont Park?"

"We've been cut, too," Gandy said. "You're lucky. You can pull in research money with your lab. We decided to turn our practice over to a managed care group. It was either that or bale out and go to work for Falcon Pharmaceuticals. Do you believe they're actually hiring physicians for their *sales* department? What is this world coming to?"

"A fate worse than death," said a new voice from behind them. Robert Radcliff, who had ambled up to the station, stood with coffee cup in hand. "Don't tell me you'd consider wallowing in the backwaters of industry," he added while searching for a chart.

"Why, Robert," Galloway said, "you look hale and hearty this morning."

"How are you, Nathan? Priscilla."

Radcliff retrieved a chart from the rack and opened it.

"We were just bemoaning the new Medicare rates," Galloway said. "I'm thinking of going into real estate and Priscilla here is thinking about working for industry."

"Research?"

"Drug Sales," Galloway said.

"They pay better than the HMOs," Radcliff said. "The drug companies have deeper pockets than the feds. Look what they charge for Ameliatrax. Two dollars a pill. You won't have much prestige working for them and they'll keep the copyright of anything you develop, but the hours are good and the benefits are first-class"

"I'd miss seeing my patients," Gandy said. "Wouldn't you?"

"Of course," said Radcliff. "That's why we're all in it. For our patients." He stood up, bid his colleagues pleasant day, and sauntered off to see his patient.

Gary Tuttle, who had been in the medication room, had stuck his head out and heard the last part of the conversation.

Seeing him in the doorway, Gandy said, "Gary, I don't see Mr. Anderson's weight on today's flow sheet. Aren't you people weighing him?"

Gary stabbed a syringe into an intravenous bag and injected medication into it. He removed the needle, looked at the sharp tip and eyed the tall, severe woman standing at the station. He dropped the syringe into the sharps container.

"I'll have to check the log, Dr. Gandy. Just a minute."

He stepped out and hunted for a large worn leather notebook among the charts and scattered papers on the desk. He opened it, ran a finger down a column.

"Here's his weight. Nadia hasn't entered it in the chart yet. He's one-hundred twenty-seven pounds."

"One-twenty-seven? Don't you feed him his meals?"

"Of course we feed him, but Mr. Anderson just has no appetite. The dietitian's been in to see him twice, but it hasn't done any good."

"Tell the resident to start him on Enpros injections," she said as she scrawled a note in the chart. "That will reverse his catabolic state. And tell Mr. Anderson if he doesn't eat I'll tie him down and put the gastric tube in his nose."

Under his breath Gary muttered, "I know where I'd like to put that tube," but to her he only nodded as he returned to mixing his medications.

The physicians went their separate ways, with Galloway's retinue following behind him like a choir of eunuchs.

In the gynecology suite on the third floor, Betty checked each of the bathrooms to be sure there was plenty of toilet paper in the holders and paper napkins in the dispensers. There was actually little work for her to do. The trash buckets were empty in the examining room. Whoever had covered the area the previous afternoon had done a good job of tidying up. She had only to pick up a few stray bits of paper, dust off all the hard surfaces, and see that there was plenty of facial tissues and paper hand towels.

One of the examination rooms had some trash. She bent down to the bucket, pulled out the clear plastic liner, and was about to drop it into her trash container when she hesitated. Why would all the trash buckets be empty except this one? Wasn't Dr. Odom's office closed Wednesday evening? She was sure it used to be, though she couldn't be sure it still was.

She put the liner back and stepped next door to the clerk's reception desk. Jessica was there pulling charts for the morning appointments.

"Hey, Jessica. The office still closed Wednesday afternoons?"

"Yes, that's right. Dr. Odom has hours in the Center City office, and Dr. Duranyi is in the clinic. Why?"

"Oh, just wondering about something, that's all," she said.

Betty returned to the examining room. *Okay*, she thought to herself, *the office was closed Wednesday afternoon, so nobody should have been seeing patients*. Recalling that Lenny had asked her to keep her eyes open for anything suspicious, she thought, *might as well poke around*.

She put on rubber gloves and fished through the contents. There were several blue sterile drapes, which she knew the doctors used to cover patients during procedures. There were the plastic bubble packs for several syringes as well. Among the debris was a wad of bloody gauze. Her heart began to pound in her chest. She picked up the gauze as gently as she could. Opening it, she stared down at a small, bloody lump of tissue.

"Oh Lord, have mercy," she whispered, tears welling up in her eyes. She wrapped the gauze up in a cloth dust rag and carefully placed it inside her cart among the rolls of toilet paper.

"I've got to get this to Lenny," she muttered. "If this is one of his lost souls, Jesus let me do the right thing for it."

Thirty-two

After collecting all the trash, Lenny walked casually up to the Seven South nursing station, where Gary eyed him with suspicion.

"Hey, Tuttle, how's it going?"

"Oh-kay," he said in a guarded voice. "And you?"

"Great, just great." He fished in his pocket and came out with the needle in the plastic cap and the empty syringe packet that Abrahm had given him. "What do you make of this?"

Gary took them from Lenny to examine. "It looks like an ordinary eighteen-gauge needle to me," he said. "That's the package it came in, and that's the needle that went with the syringe. Was it in one of the patient rooms?"

"No. Somebody found them under the sofa cushions in Dr. Gandy's waiting room. But wouldn't they give injections inside one of the treatment rooms?"

"Usually they would, sure. The waiting room has no sharps container. The doctor, or the nurse, would have to carry the contaminated syringe back to the exam room to dispose of it properly."

"But they could still give an injection in the waiting room, couldn't they?"

"Yes, of course. You can inject somebody anywhere, even in the hallway if you don't mind who's watching."

"I don't get it," Lenny said. "If the person threw out the syringe, why didn't they throw out the needle, too? Wouldn't they be connected?"

"They were at the time the package was opened. Since you have the needle and not the barrel of the syringe it was packaged with, they were obviously separated."

"But why would that be?"

Gary sighed, seeing that he was again being sucked into the investigation. He was amazed at the way that Lenny could start with a few innocent questions and, before Gary knew it, he was off on some complicated analysis that drew Gary deeper into the investigation.

"Come on back to the medication room and I'll show you," he said in a forlorn voice.

This Won't Hurt A Bit

They stepped back to the little room, where Gary took a new sterile syringe from a tray on the counter. Peeling open the sterile container, he pulled out the syringe and removed the milky white plastic cap, exposing a shining steel needle. Then he took a small bottle of sterile water in his hand. Deftly stabbing the rubber cap of the bottle, he turned it upside down and withdrew the plunger until the syringe was filled with water, then he pulled the needle out and carefully recapped it.

"Okay," he said, "now suppose that I've just drawn up some medication which I want to give to someone, only I'm not going to give it in the muscle. Instead, I'm going to give it just under the skin."

"Like when we get the TB test," Lenny said.

"Exactly. That's a 'sub-q' injection, meaning, subcutaneous. To do that, I have to remove the larger, intramuscular needle that comes with the syringe and replace it with a smaller needle, like so."

He twisted the needle with the milky cap until it separated from the barrel and placed it on the counter, then he extracted a small needle with a blue cap from a bin and twisted it onto the syringe.

"Now I'm all set to give the sub-q injection. After I do that," he said, dropping the syringe with the blue-capped, sub-q needle into the sharps container, "I drop it in the bucket, leaving...these."

He held the needle with the milky cap and the sterile packet in the palm of his hand. They were like the ones Abrahm had found in Gandy's sofa."

"Tuttle, you're a genius! I think that's exactly what happened. Gandy drew some kind of drug into a syringe, changed caps and stuck somebody in the ass."

"The arm or leg is more likely if she used a sub-q needle," Gary said.

"Whatever. The point is, she was giving something while they were on the sofa, which could be suspicious."

"Or it could be something the nurse does quite often. She may have given an innocent dose of some medication and dropped the needle in the process. It happens. You find needles on the floor all the time. I know, I have to sign the incident reports."

"Yeah, you're right, it probably doesn't have anything to do with the Sparks murder, but one of the other custodians showed it to me and it seemed like something I should follow up, even though I don't have any idea what it means, or if it means anything at all."

"That hasn't stopped you in the past, has it?" Gary asked.

Lenny opened his mouth to speak, then stopped, surprised that Gary

Tuttle—Mr. Professional—was busting on him. He hadn't thought the guy had it in him.

"Ouch. Good one, Tuttle."

Glancing out the door of the medication room to be sure no one was nearby, Gary said, "I found something interesting that might be related to your investigation. Lately someone's been stealing several doses of an injectable drug called Enpros. It's a cancer drug that works on the prostate and testicles."

"What's interesting about that?"

"In a non-cancer patient it produces a prolonged erection called a priapism."

"Really? How long?"

"It could last three, four, perhaps even six hours. The drug is a hundred times stronger than Viagra."

Lenny winced. "Jeez, isn't that painful?"

"It's more than painful. The priapism shuts off circulation to the penis. The tissue can become necrotic and slough off if it isn't relieved."

"Slough off? What kind of fool would take a drug like that?"

"Oh, the kind who thinks that he knows all there is to know about sexual organs and drugs. A cocky, over-educated type."

"A doctor," Lenny said.

"Exactly."

Lenny looked up at the clock, saw that the morning was rushing on, just like his life. He took down the mop with the new head, dropped it into the swirling, soapy liquid, and spread the water in wide circles. He found the work relaxing, the monotony of the motions clearing his mind, allowing him to focus on what to do next.

Henrietta Oldenfield sat beside her husband stroking his hand as though petting an old and beloved cat. She looked about the room, then reluctantly at his face.

"Ought to cut off the damn leg," he grumbled.

"Now, I'm sure that Doctor Galloway is doing the best that he can. I know it's hard to be patient when you're suffering so, but…"

"*Patient?* I've been patient as a saint, for God's sake, but I can't keep suffering this way. I want the problem fixed one way or the other."

She patted his hand, looking with weariness and sorrow at her husband of half a century. For all of the sacrifices she had made taking care of her husband for years, she couldn't imagine what it would be like living without him. She chased away the thought as if awakening from a bad dream.

This Won't Hurt A Bit

An orderly came in with a stretcher, followed by Gary with the chart. The orderly wheeled the stretcher beside the bed and held out his arm to help the patient slide across.

Helping the orderly pull the patient onto the stretcher, Gary said, "You haven't had anything to eat or drink, have you Mr. Oldenfield?"

"Nothing. I'd give up both legs for a good cup of coffee. Not the swill they send on the tray. I'm talking about a fresh cup, like my wife always makes me."

"Well," said Gary, tucking the chart beneath the patient's pillow. "The cafeteria has a new espresso machine that makes a pretty good cup of cappuccino. Perhaps your wife could get you a cup while you're down in x-ray."

"That's a marvelous suggestion," said Mrs. Oldenfield. "How long will Walter be gone?"

"The procedure usually takes about an hour and a half. Maybe two."

"That long?" she said. "It sounds like an operation."

"It is, in a way. The nurse usually calls to tell me the patient is coming back. I'll let you know and you can get the coffee."

"At least I'll have something to look forward to," Oldenfield grumbled.

The orderly pulled a sheet up to his chin, raised the head of the stretcher, and slowly wheeled the stretcher out of the room and down the hall.

As Mrs. Oldenfield began to straighten the bed, Gary approached her.

"You look tired, Mrs. Oldenfield. Why don't you go down to the cafeteria and have something to eat."

"All this worry about Walter, I forgot to take my pills this morning." Continuing to tug on the bottom sheet and tuck it under the mattress, she said, "I have to remember to take care of myself. He couldn't find his dentures in his own mouth without me, you know."

She folded the top sheet neatly at the foot of the bed, picked up an old black leather purse from the windowsill, and slowly shuffled out the door.

Thirty-three

*H*aving finished mopping the patient rooms, Lenny was pushing two hampers filled with fat, moist bags of dirty linen to the laundry shoot when Moose came bounding up to him.

"Lenny, come on! We got to go to central supply!"

"What, did they flood it again? Should I bring my mop n' bucket?"

"Bucket? Get real, man, we got ourselves some clues to investigate!"

While Moose held open the door to the laundry shute, Lenny hefted the heavy bags and sent them sliding down the shaft, then he followed his friend down the stairs toward the central supply department.

In the basement, they followed a narrow corridor of pipes and cables attached to the ceiling. The air was musty, the floor stained with oil and dirt. Reaching a battered, metal door, they stepped into a large, brightly lit room. Tall, metal shelves overflowing with supplies took up the center of the space. In one corner, several robo carts huddled like beasts of burden waiting to be packed and sent on their automated rounds.

The two men passed through another door into a hot, steamy room with glistening tile walls and floor. Women in green scrub suits, long rubber gloves and white hairnets stood along a broad counter wrapping bundles of instruments in green towels and sealing them with cream-colored tape in preparation for sterilization.

A black woman who looked older than her fifty-five years looked up as the men approached her. She finished taping the bundle before her, then stepped away from the other women. Moose approached her.

"Lottie, this is Lenny, the guy I told you about."

Lottie removed a glove and shook Lenny's hand. Her palm was callused and hard.

"Moose tells me you been looking for clues about that young doctor that got murdered."

"That's right," said Lenny, noting her stooped shoulders and sad eyes.

"He said I should tell him if I find anything unusual. At first I wasn't gonna say nothin'. What it is I found might not have nothin' to do with it, not that it's any o' my business, anyhow."

This Won't Hurt A Bit

Lenny waited. He knew when a witness needed time.

"But then I remembered how you helped Alice get her disability that time the steam pipe split open and burned her face, so I figured I ought to show you, in case it's important."

Lottie reached down to a low shelf and brought out a bundle like the ones being prepared for the steam sterilizer.

"I found it this morning in the Soiled Equipment Room outside the Short Procedure Unit."

As she unwrapped the towel, Moose and Lenny stepped closer. They saw several syringes, a pair of kidney-shaped metal basins, some long tongs and an instrument that might be used to serve salad.

"I didn't think too much about the tray when I first opened it. The needles were gone, which is only natural. But there were a few strange things about it."

"Like what?" Moose asked.

"For one thing, the disposable syringes and the reusable ones were both on the tray. The OR nurses always throw away the plastic syringes."

She picked up a milky-white plastic syringe in one hand and a clear glass one in the other. "We can clean and sterilize the glass, but not the plastic. It melts."

"So," Lenny supplied, "whoever left this tray in the soiled room didn't know that. Could it have been, say, a new nurse just starting up there?"

"Could be, except there isn't anybody new. Hasn't been for years. The nurses up there are so old, they could all retire tomorrow if they had a man at home that had any kind o' life in him."

Poking around in the tray, Moose asked, "What else?"

"The cloth towels were neatly folded and left in the tray. The nurses always throw the towels in the dirty laundry bag, not send 'em down here. We don't wash towels in CSR."

"Somebody didn't know that either," Lenny concluded.

"That's why I talked to Moose. There's something not right about this tray."

Moose pointed to the instruments. "What's this used for?"

"This is a D n' C tray. It's for scraping the inside of the womb."

"Isn't that how they do abortions?" he asked.

"No, not usually. This is for when the mother has a miscarriage, or a lot of bleeding from her period."

"Then it's a tray that would be used by a gynecologist?" Lenny asked.

"That's the one," she said. "Gynecology."

Lenny thanked Lottie for sharing the information with him. They went out into the hall, where Moose said, "Think that tray's got something to do with the murder?"

"Hell, I don't know. Collecting clues was your idea, remember?"

"We'll get it together, trust me. You come up with anything?"

"Nothing definite. We have to focus on Sparks. Find out everything we can about him."

"I got a cousin works in the medical clinic. I'll go up there later and run my mouth, see what she knows about him."

"Good. I'm going to try and talk to this medical student I met yesterday."

"You still think it's a doctor that did Sparks?"

"If it was a doctor with something to hide, it would have to be something so bad it would mean taking away his license to practice medicine."

"License to print money you mean," Moose said.

"More or less. Either that, or Sparks stood in somebody's way and wouldn't move, so he had to be removed."

"That's what I've been sayin'. Sparks dug up some dirt on one of these docs and BAM! He gets it."

Lenny nodded his head, picturing Sparks being knocked in the head and dragged away from wherever he was killed.

"Let's meet in the sewing room on the afternoon break."

Moose clasped his hand on Lenny's shoulder, beaming with satisfaction. "Tell me you're not up to your nuts in this murder thing."

"It's funny, Moose, but when I was a kid my dad was always going to meetings. People would show up from out of town, other countries, even. I'd come down in the morning and there would be people asleep in the living room, snoring in three different languages."

"Your dad was all union."

"He was, not that my mother was a slouch. She's still active in the B'nai B'rith. I guess that's where I learned to fight the system. At dinner we'd have a half a dozen guests arguing about Wall Street and the military-industrial complex."

He recalled his father's stories about fighting the Pinkertons when he'd been organizing striking telephone workers in New York, and of challenging the McCarthy trials.

"I bet you wish he was here, with all this talk of downsizing and selling the hospital and all."

"He'd probably tell me to call for a walk-out," Lenny said ruefully. He had to give his old man credit. The apple hadn't fallen far from the tree. He hated what the system did to guys like Regis about as much as his father had.

Moose smiled at his friend. "You're just like a dog on a scent. We'll tree that bastard and get Regis his job back."

"Sure," Lenny said, striding toward the elevator, "if the asshole doesn't kill me first and cut me up."

"Heh, heh," Moose said. He saw Lenny heading for the elevator and gave him a questioning look. Lenny sighed and turned to the stairway, muttering, "Those stairs are gonna give me a heart attack."

"I'll come with you. I got to collect the menus anyway."

Moose began the ascent taking three steps at a time. By the third floor he saw Lenny lagging behind. He turned around, balanced on the edge of the steps with the balls of his feet, and began to climb by walking backwards, lifting his foot two steps at a time and looking down at Lenny with a big grin.

"God damn show off," Lenny said, and he grabbed the railing to help pull himself up the stairs. Moose laughed the rest of the way.

Thirty-four

On Seven-South, Alex Primeaux knocked on the open door of Mrs. Rosemond's room and stepped in. The patient was sitting in an oversized armchair, her enormous hips pressing against the sides of the chair like a mound of Jell-O in a square cup.

"Good mornin' Miss Rosemond. How are you feeling today?"

"Oh doctor, I'm a little weak today. I got dizzy when I went into the bathroom to do my morning affairs, and I had to sit on the toilet until the room stopped spinning."

"Ah see," he said, his mustache twitching as he screwed up his mouth in frustration.

"Maybe I need a blood transfusion," she said. "Wouldn't I feel better if I had an extra pint of blood?"

"Nnnn-no ma'am, I don't think that would help you a 'tall. Your actual blood count is fine. It's always been fine. It's just that trace of blood in your stool that's been a puzzle. I'm afraid I've just about run out of tests that I can do for you."

"But what's to become of me, doctor? You can't send me home when I'm so dizzy I can hardly stand up, can you? My brother says he'll beat down your door if you send me home when I'm in this state."

She pulled a raft of tissues from a box on her bedside table and began to dab her eyes, moist with tears. As she blotted her face, Moose came silently into the room to collect the menu. He saw that Mrs. Rosemond hadn't filled it out.

"How am I supposed to get better when you only feed me liquid food?" she said. "A body can't keep itself together without some real food in it."

"Ah explained, Miss Rosemond, I think you may be bleeding in your small intestines, which is very hard to see. Solid food might make the bleeding worse, so it's necessary to keep you on a liquid diet."

"I think I had a seizure in the bathroom this morning. You can't send me home if I'm having a seizure."

"Did anybody see it?" he asked.

"How could they see me when I was on the toilet?"

Primeaux remained silent for several seconds while he composed himself. "Very well, tell me what happened."

As Moose quietly stepped out of the room, he listened to Primeaux's southern accent. It reminded him of his aunt and uncle in Arkansas, whom he visited often. He realized he hadn't seen them in several years, and decided to talk to Birdie about taking the kids down there on their winter break from school.

"We can't keep you in the hospital forever, ma'am," Primeaux said. The government only allows us so much money for a given illness, and you've used up your share a long time ago. If I knew what exactly the problem was I could treat it, but as it stands now…"

"I can't go home. I'll die if I go home. You don't want me to die, do you, doctor? You don't want me to be found slumped on the floor in a pool of blood, do you?"

"Of course not. It's just that—"

"You have to keep me in the hospital until you find out what's wrong with me. My ex brother-in-law is an attorney in Bucks County and he told me to call him if I have any problems with my care, and that's just what I'm going to do."

Primeaux sighed, looked one last time into the woman's fierce eyes, stood and walked wearily out of the room. Moose, seeing the doctor, asked him, "Say doc, you from Arkansas? Reason I ask, I got family down there."

"No, ah'm from North Carolina, actually. I went to school in Durham. Why?"

"Your accent sounded Arkansas, that's all."

"Well, my mama was from a little town called Goose Neck, Arkansas, and ah guess her way of speaking rubbed off on me."

"Yeah, guess it did," said Moose, who added Rosemond's menu to the stack he had collected. "I hear Durham's a nice town. What's the name of that Triple-A ball club…the Razorbacks?"

"No, the Razorbacks are from Little Rock."

"Oh?" Moose said, waiting for an answer to his original question.

Primeaux looked uncertainly at Moose. He frowned, his neat mustache turning down.

"I was sort of a nerdy kid coming up. I never much followed sports," he said. "Excuse me."

Moose watched the doctor walk away. There was something off about him, he was sure of it. The guy was too damn nice to be a doctor.

Freddie had picked up the specimens from the GI Lab and broncoscopy suite and brought them to the pathology department to be examined. As he came into the lab, he saw Dr. Fingers hunched over a microscope examining slides from a liver biopsy. Freddie placed the specimens in one of the big refrigerators, neatly stacking them beside a tub with an entire heart in it.

When the pathologist looked up to remove the slide, Freddie said, "Any post mortems today, doc?"

"Not so far, but the day is young," he replied.

"I wish I was young," Freddie said.

"Don't we all." Fingers placed another slide under the microscope and peered through the lens.

"Hey Doc. You hear anything about what killed that guy Sparks?"

Not looking up, Fingers said, "The initial finding was cerebral edema."

Freddie came closer to the doctor. "That mean like his brain was swollen up, right?"

"That's right."

"What could do that?"

Fingers looked up from his microscope, feeling a hint of suspicion.

"You didn't know Randy Sparks, did you?"

"No doc, it's nothing like that. I had a feeling you wanted to do the post mortem and I just figured you'd talk to the ME about it."

"It's true, forensic pathology is one of my passions. The toxicology report was particularly interesting."

"How's that?"

"It was negative for opiates, alcohol, and sedatives. Whoever killed Sparks did so without drugging him, and without any external signs of trauma, save for some superficial abrasions on his hands. It's a very intriguing case."

"Sounds like it's right up your alley, doc."

"Indeed it is. I'm going to follow it closely."

"Whatever floats your boat, doc."

Freddie walked out, noting that the doctor had returned to his slides apparently unconcerned about the questions.

Thirty-five

Kate Palmer sat at the Seven-South nursing station looking for the MRI report in Mrs. Grey's chart. So far, all the lab values were normal, which contradicted what little she knew about infections. She had so much to learn. The amount of information they crammed into a semester was unbelievable, plus she was in a journal club and was supposed to summarize six articles a week.

Maybe I'm not cut out for this, she thought. I can master the material, okay. I proved that with my grade point, and I can stand up to the other students. Most of them are kids, they haven't been out in the world, raising a child like I have, but...why do the attending physicians have to be so damn patronizing? Like Odom—a short man's syndrome on top of a physician's arrogance. Am I going to end up like them, busting some poor student's butt just to show him I've arrived?

And then there was the time away from her daughter. "It's the quality time," her mother had tried to reassure her, "you know you have that. I can put in the quantity. You just study hard and make us all proud."

As Kate sat musing, Lenny, who had finished mopping the patient bathrooms, caught sight of her. Pushing his bucket of soapy water closer to the station, he wet the mop and let a puddle of soapy water flow close to where Kate was sitting.

"Excuse me. Mind if I mop under there?" he asked.

She looked up, saw Lenny, and smiled. "Hello Lenny. Sure, I'll move to the other side."

She pulled her chair back and crossed to the other side of the station, where she stood looking over the chart.

He wrung out his mop, immersed it in the rinse water and ran it over the area, soaking up the soap and dirt, then he stood leaning on his mop, like an ancient hunter on his spear.

"That Mrs. Grey is a nice woman, isn't she?" he said.

"Uhmm," Kate said, immersed in the chart.

"Did you know one of her daughters got a scholarship for singing in the choir. A little private college down south, I think she said."

"No, I didn't know that," she said, turning from the chart. "We medical students don't get time to talk much with the patients. We're supposed to just be reviewing the charts and learning physical exams."

Stepping closer to her, he asked, "I don't suppose you've heard anything new about the Sparks murder, have you?"

"Not about Randy Sparks, no, but..." She closed the chart, stood up and came around the station to stand beside him. "I did hear something, but it probably doesn't have anything to do with your case. This med student Letterly. His father's a big shot attending here at James Madison who sits on the Medical Board. Letterly said he heard that the board gave Radcliff a slap on the wrist for being too fresh with one of his female patients."

"Psychiatrists aren't supposed to touch their patients, is that it?"

"It's not only taboo, it's illegal as hell. Pennsylvania has strict laws against psychiatrists having sex with their patients. Their patients are very vulnerable, and they can be abused and think it's somehow therapeutic."

"What did they tell Radcliff?"

"Just to keep his hands to himself, or as Letterly put it, whatever part of his anatomy he was waving around."

Seeing that the floor was dry, Lenny pulled the chair back for Kate to sit down.

"No thanks," she said. "I only have a few minutes between classes. I have to run, but how is the investigation going?"

"Not too well, actually. These doctors don't advertise their failures. It's pretty tough figuring out who was involved with the victim."

"You still believe that it was a doctor who killed Randy Sparks?"

"Yeah. I mean, it would have to be somebody who could move through the hospital without attracting attention."

"That could be anybody," Kate said. "A nurse, a PA...a custodian, even."

"I'd look awful funny with a dead body tucked under my arm, wouldn't I?"

"Not if you were dressed in a scrub suit," she said, then added with a smile, "although with your face I suppose some people might take notice... unless you wore a surgical mask"

"What's wrong with my face?" he said, adopting a hurt expression.

"Nothing. It's just distinctive, that's all."

"Oh?" Becoming serious, Lenny looked into her eyes. "You didn't hear anything else?"

"No..."

He waited, looking into her face. She broke out in a smile.

"But if I do, yes, I'll pass it on. I have to run to class now."

This Won't Hurt A Bit

"Okay, thanks," he said, watching Kate hurry down the corridor and through the double doors to the elevator. He liked her. He knew he was a fool to even think it, but he liked her.

After mopping the hallway and the patient rooms, Lenny decided that he needed to take the bull by the horns if he was going to get anywhere with the investigation. Sparks had been working with Radcliff when he disappeared on December 13th. Lenny reasoned that if Radcliff had been having sexual relations with one of his patients, Sparks might have found out, and the shrink killed him to cover up his affair. If he could get a look at the psychiatrist's appointment book, he might get some idea of the women he was seeing at the time Sparks disappeared.

He hurried down to Radcliff's office on the second floor. As he strode down the corridor he wondered what excuse he could use to get into the office and nose around. He passed a utility room, where Abrahm was emptying a bucket of dirty water into a large, porcelain sink and approached him.

"Hey, Abraham Lincoln—how's it going?"

"Hullo to yew, George W'ushington," he replied, grinning broadly.

Lenny spied a battered old vacuum cleaner leaning in the corner.

"Say, Abrahm—you think I could borrow your vacuum cleaner for a little while?"

Abrahm pointed to the machine standing in the corner.

"Sure, Len'nye, take it."

"Thanks. Bring it right back."

Lenny grabbed the vacuum cleaner and marched back across the hall to Radcliff's office. He knocked once and opened the door on a tiny waiting room with soft leather chairs, a rack of glitzy magazines and a black lacquer table. Classical music played softly from hidden speakers.

Behind a counter sat a heavy-set woman with thick, pancake make-up, plucked and penciled eyebrows, and frosted hair. She looked suspiciously at him from her desk, where she was typing something from a Dictaphone. Pulling the earphones from her head, she asked in a frosty voice, "May I help you?"

"Hi. No, I can manage, thanks. Dust patrol. Won't take long."

Seeing the skeptical look on the secretary's face, Lenny added, "We've been getting complaints of excessive particulate matter in the carpeted areas of the hospital. Personally, I think the baffles in the hot air exchangers should all be replaced, but who listens to a simple custodian?"

When the secretary continued to look at him with mistrust, he explained, "We're supposed to vacuum all the rugs."

The secretary made a silent 'O' with her lips and resumed typing. Lenny plugged in the vacuum cleaner, which let out a boisterous clatter and whir. He gingerly moved the machine around the office.

Finding that the noise made dictation impossible, the secretary pulled the earphones from her ears and threw them onto the desk. She rose from her chair and yelled over the racket, "I'm going for a cup of coffee! Close the door behind you—the lock's on!"

Lenny nodded and moved down a narrow corridor, trailing the electric cord behind. Out of the corner of his eye he watched the secretary retrieve her purse from a drawer and step out into the corridor. The door closed automatically behind her, leaving Lenny alone in the psychiatrist's office.

Thirty-six

Lenny pushed the vacuum down the hallway, which was made narrower by a tall row of filing cabinets and a bookshelf on the left. Opposite them were two doors. A full length mirror took up the wall at the end of the hall.

He knocked gently on the first door. "Custodian. Got to vacuum." Getting no reply, he turned the knob and peeked in, only to discover the cleanest, brightest bathroom he had ever seen at James Madison hospital. Not only were there real cloth towels hanging on a wooden rack instead of the standard brown paper dispenser, but the water in the toilet bowl was aquamarine.

"Tidybowl," Lenny mumbled appreciatively.

He went on to the second door, knocked. "Custodian. I've got to vacuum."

Silence within. He tried the knob, found it locked.

Returning to the reception area, he turned off the vacuum cleaner and surveyed the secretary's disorderly desk. Earphones lay beside an expensive-looking dual-cassette recorder. Charts were piled in trays marked "Dictation," "To File," and "Outgoing." A large appointment book open to the current week caught his eye.

Lenny closed the door to the outside corridor, then returned to the secretary's desk. He positioned himself with his back to the door so that someone coming in would have trouble seeing what he was doing.

He took out a rag and pretended to dust the few bare areas. As he dusted with one hand he turned the appointment book around with the other and flipped the pages to the second week of December, when Sparks had disappeared. There were patient names accompanied by those of the referring physicians. Other times were tagged with notes such as "Cntr City Office" or "Fl Conference."

A few names had pencil lines through them. After scanning several pages he determined that the canceled patients had been rescheduled a week or two later.

To the right of each name were initials of various insurance plans, most of which Lenny could decipher. There was HSWU, his own Hospital and Service Workers' Union, the BP&F, Brotherhood of Police and Firemen, BC/BS for Blue Cross, and one or two he didn't recognize.

One of the appointment slots had been whited out. He flipped forward and back, but saw no other names had been plastered over.

Curious.

He held the book up to the desk lamp and peered through the page. The name started with a 'V.' Vivian? No. Virgi… Virginia. The last name was tougher. It began with an 'R'. Raccoon…no. Racing…no, that didn't fit. 'Racine.' That was it. Virginia Racine.

Why would the secretary white out that one name and no other? He paged forward and back but could find no other entry with that name. She hadn't been rescheduled, like the names with the line through them. Was it significant? Maybe not, but the date was suggestive: December 11th—two days before Sparks disappeared.

He heard the sound of a key turning the lock in the outside door. Keeping his back to the door, he began dusting the edge of the desk with vigor. Suddenly he felt a sharp tap on the shoulder, turned and found himself looking into the penetrating blue eyes of the psychiatrist, Robert Radcliff.

Radcliff looked past Lenny at his secretary's work area, saw right away that the appointment book was turned around and that the page was open to the previous month. "What were you doing?" he asked in a commanding voice that could have sent troops into battle.

"I was just giving the desk a quick dusting," Lenny said, tucking the rag into his back pocket.

"I meant," said Radcliff, studying the name embroidered on the custodian's shirt, "what were you doing looking in my calendar?"

Putting on a simple look, Lenny said, "I wasn't looking at anything, I was trying to work around the mess. It's not easy keeping surfaces clean when they're all cluttered up."

He felt Radcliff's blue eyes looking through him as if he were transparent. Feeling his bluff collapsing, he turned away to avoid the staring eyes and unplugged the vacuum cleaner, then he slowly coiled the electric cord around the handle.

"You aren't our regular custodian," Radcliff said.

Lenny fiddled with the vacuum, avoiding the doctor's face.

"I'm on the dust patrol. We've been getting complaints about excessive particulates in the air."

Lenny could see the psychiatrist watching him, and as he moved toward the door, Radcliff blocked his path.

"I'm going to check up on you, Mr. Moss."

This Won't Hurt A Bit

"Be sure and tell my boss what a good job I did on your carpet, okay?"

Lenny's smile was more a grimace as he waited for Radcliff to let him pass. The psychiatrist stared at him for a long, agonizing moment, then abruptly turned and strode down the short hallway to the second door. He took out a ring of keys and unlocked it, looked back once more at Lenny and entered the inner office. The click of a lock followed the door closing.

Lenny was wheeling the vacuum cleaner out of the office when the secretary nearly ran into him returning from her break. After she brushed by him, she placed a powdered donut and cup of coffee on the desk and settled into her seat.

On his way out the door, Lenny glanced back to see the secretary busily typing away, appearing oblivious to him, as well as to the powdered sugar on her chin and sweater.

As Lenny returned the vacuum cleaner to the utility room across the hall, he realized that his hands were trembling. He doubted that the psychiatrist believed his story about dusting, but he didn't see how Radcliff could link his nosing around to the Sparks murder.

Going down the hall, he muttered to himself, "I should have my head examined for letting Moose talk me into this murder investigation." He glanced back at Radcliff's door and thought, *Shit, I bet I already have.*

Thirty-seven

"Mmm-mmm, we are...climbing...Jacob's...ladder...mmm-mmmm..."

Betty pushed her cart along the Seven-South corridor. Seeing Lenny, she said, "Hello, dear heart. It sure is good to be back home. Thanks for covering for me."

"No sweat. I got the trash already and I filled all the paper towels."

"I'm so tired of going to the GYN clinic. Childress has been pulling somebody every day for the last two weeks on account of Mattie is still out sick."

"The circulation in her legs is bad again. I'm afraid she's not gonna make it to sixty-two."

"You can't get her no disability?"

"I'm trying. Dr. Primeaux in the Employee Clinic is all for it, but the insurance company's HMO doctor wants to send her back on light duty."

"Sshhuh," Betty snorted. "Ain't no such thing as light duty in this department and Childress knows it."

"It'll go to arbitration. We'll have to wait for a hearing."

"Speaking of a hearing, how's Regis? You heard any more from him?"

"I went out to see him yesterday after work at the detention center. I'm afraid he got into it with one of the guards and they worked him over pretty good. One eye is swollen shut. He says the doctor told him he'll be okay, but I'm worried about him."

"Of course you are. He acts hard as nails but he's too young. He doesn't belong in a place like that, full of hardened criminals. You got to get this murder investigation going."

"I'm trying, Boop, believe me, but it's slow. I mean, these doctors don't leave their dirty linen hanging out on the line."

"You know what they say—doctors bury their mistakes six feet under."

"Don't I know it. If they'd done the right tests on Margaret early on..."

"Now dear heart, there's no use looking back at what might have been. The Lord took her to His bosom and we have to just accept it, just like we did when she lost the baby. We have to look ahead. Every day is a new promise of salvation."

This Won't Hurt A Bit

Lenny said nothing. He had told Betty years before that he was an atheist and knew he couldn't change her beliefs. He turned to go when she caught his arm with a grip as strong as any man's.

"Wait a little minute, I got something on my cart I need to show you."

She reached into her cart and withdrew a small bundle wrapped in a cleaning rag. She peeked out the door to be sure no one was in the hall nearby, then placed the bundle on top of her cart.

"You told me how I was supposed to keep a lookout for anything suspicious like, you an' Moose looking for clues and all, so I thought maybe I better show you this."

Lenny stared at the bundle.

"Go on an' open it," she said.

Lenny peeled open the cleaning rag. Inside it he found a wad of gauze. Pulling apart the layers of gauze, he uncovered a lump of blood-caked tissue no bigger than the tip of his little finger.

"Where did you find it?" he asked, looking perplexed.

"In the trash bucket in Dr. Odom's office this morning."

"What is it?"

Betty shook her finger at Lenny. "They think Betty's dumb! They think Betty won't notice somethin' evil like this. Lemme tell you, I know when the devil's at work, and this is a sign of his evil, so help me God!"

"You never find tissue like this in a doctor's office, is that it?"

"No, that ain't it. Listen. Yesterday was Wednesday, and on Wednesday the GYN office closes after lunch. This morning when I was putting up paper towels and toilet paper, I noticed all but one of the trash buckets was empty, which told me that the housekeeper who got pulled there yesterday—I think it was Gladys—that she emptied all the trash, but the one waste basket in Dr. Odom's examination room must have been used during the night!"

"Couldn't Gladys have missed one of them?"

"No, she couldn't miss one. You know how the guy-nee doctors complain if their offices aren't perfect. Childress loves to write us up for stuff like that when we get pulled. It's like adding an insult to an insult."

"Maybe the doctor keeps evening hours?"

"Evening hours? You crazy? That man only sees patients on Wednesday morning from ten to twelve and Thursday from two to four. I know. My niece works days and wanted to see him after five. No way, Jose. She had to take off half a day from work!"

"So the bundle was there this morning, but there were no patients scheduled last night…What do you think it means?

"Man, you're the detective, you figure it out. But as soon as I saw it I got scared that Dr. Odom was doing the devil's work on some poor unbaptised soul."

"Abortions."

"It sure looks that way to me."

Lenny stared at the tissue lying on the gauze, wondering how, or if it bore on the Sparks case. He silently wrapped it back in the cleaning rag.

"Is it okay if I take this to the pathology lab later? Maybe one of the techs can tell me what it is."

"Sure," Betty said, "but Lenny, you be careful. This is the Devil's work, make no mistake about it."

She turned her cart around and pushed it down the hall, humming to herself, "In the house of the Lorrrrd."

He carried the bundle back to the housekeeping locker room and hid it on a high shelf behind a gallon bottle of ammonia, then he went back out onto the ward.

They had found a suspicious D&C tray in Central Supply. Now Betty had found what might be the result of an abortion in Odom's examination room. Maybe the murder was about love and sex and an unwanted baby.

Later in the morning, Gary went to the pantry to fill a pitcher with ice for one of his patients when he found Betty scraping leftover eggs and hot cereal into a ziplock bag.

"My dogs'll be sleeping good tonight with all these eggs," she said, sealing the plastic bag and slipping it into the refrigerator.

"They must like ketchup," he said.

"Sure they like ketchup. And mustard, too! And peanut butter? Why they lap that stuff right up, praise the Lord."

Gary filled the pitcher with ice and was carrying it to a patient's room when he saw Lenny striding toward him.

"Hey, Tuttle, got any specimens you want taken to the lab?"

"Thank you, Lenny. There's a sputum specimen and a couple of routine urines in the messenger tray."

"I'm gonna take my morning break. I'll drop them off on my way."

He picked up the specimens and hurried down to the utility closet. Glancing up and down the hall to be sure nobody was watching, he stepped into the room and retrieved the specimen from the shelf. He tucked it in with the other specimens and went to the service elevator, which he rode down to the fifth floor.

Like Betty, he had a bad feeling about the specimen he carried. There had been rumors about late-night goings on in the gynecology suite, but the hospital had always turned a deaf ear. Lenny realized that he risked opening a real can of worms.

Thirty-eight

At the nursing station, Marianne, a petite strawberry blond nurse dressed in white painter's pants, white turtleneck and sneakers, dropped her medication book onto the counter and sank into a seat beside Gary.

"Man, that Mrs. Rosemond is so stubborn!"

"What did she do this time, refuse to bathe?"

"No, worse! She says that she won't take her meds unless we switch her back to solid food. She clamped her big fat mouth shut like this."

Marianne sucked in her lips until her crimson lipstick disappeared, leaving only a slit between chin and nose.

"I told her, 'Mrs. Rosemond, if you don't take your pills, that big bad medical student will come up and put the rubber tube down your nose again. You wouldn't want that, would you?'"

Gary leaned back in the chair and listened, hands clasped across his soft stomach.

"Know what she did then? The bitch pulled the blanket up over her head and started to snore like she was asleep!" She tossed her head back and laughed, flashing teeth as white as neon lights. "I'm going for coffee," she said, still chuckling. "You want a pretzel?"

"That would be lovely," Gary said. "And please remember…"

"I know—don't forget the spicy mustard."

As Marianne left the station, he decided he needed a double shot of Maalox. He rose from the station and stepped into the little medication room, where he found Dr. Primeaux rummaging through a cabinet.

"Can I help you with something, Alex?"

"Oh, no thank you, Gary." Primeaux stood and looked sheepishly at the nurse. "I have a little bursitis today is all. I thought I might find some extra Motrin. I'll get something from the pharmacy, thanks."

"Wait, I think Mr. Oldenfield had some, but it's been discontinued. Gary poked in the pharmacy return basket. "Here it is, six-hundred milligrams. Take the bunch."

He handed the doctor a ziplock bag of pills. Primeaux thanked him, took one pill out and swallowed it without water.

This Won't Hurt A Bit

"How are things with you? Is Gandy still raking you over the coals?" he asked in his soft southern drawl.

"I haven't seen her today, knock on wood." Gary rapped his knuckles on the counter. "To tell you the truth, I'm worried about Mr. Oldenfield. I don't know how much more he can put up with if they can't open up the graft."

"Those shunts are tricky things. I'm glad I only have to handle the medical side. Not that we have any great drugs for circulation."

Primeaux pocketed the bag of pills. "Thanks for the Motrin, Gary. If you ever need a script for something let me know."

"Thanks, Alex."

The doctor walked softly away. Gary shook a bottle of Maalox, poured some into a medicine cup, swallowed it down. As he shuddered at the taste, he wondered if he should tell Lenny about finding Alex poking around the box of medications.

Probably not important, he decided. Not when it's Alex.

Lenny dropped off the sputum specimen at Microbiology and left the urine samples in the Chemistry Lab, then he carried the bundle that Betty had found to the Pathology Lab to the last laboratory at the end of the corridor.

The Pathology Lab was a large, cold, brightly-lit room that harbored the sickening smell of formaldehyde and decaying flesh. A pretty technician in a powder blue scrub gown and crisp, white lab coat sat at a black marble counter looking over a stack of slides. On a cutting board at the end of the counter lay a scalpel, tweezers, and lumps of pink and gray tissue.

Along the opposite wall stood four huge refrigerators with glass doors that housed myriad jars, buckets, slides, and test tubes. Specimens of various size, color, and shape filled the containers. A sign on each glass door proclaimed in bold letters, **"NOT FOR FOOD STORAGE!"**

Lenny cupped his hands over one of the refrigerator doors and peered in, saying over his shoulder, "I heard you've got the brain of a psychotic killer in one of these, is that true?"

"Hi, Lenny," the technician said, looking up. "What brings you to the ghoul's icebox?"

"Hey, Leslie, how ya doing?" He walked up beside her. "How's your mom?"

She looked up from her log book, brushing her long brown hair back from her face. "She's okay. The poor thing still isn't used to not having to go to work."

"You mean after I busted my butt helping her get early retirement she still misses coming to this rat hole?"

"You know how it is. Mom threw out the alarm clock, but she still wakes up at five-thirty every morning."

"Well I can't help her with that problem, I've got enough to worry about, with everybody coming to me with their problems. Why don't they bug the other reps?"

"Because you tell the best jokes," she said, smiling, "and because you don't back down."

"One of the many character flaws that West is forever pointing out," he said, chuckling. He looked over her shoulder at the counter. "You busy?"

"No, just cataloguing some slides." She closed her log book. "What can I do for you?"

"Do you think you could look at something for me?"

"Sure. Let's see what you've got."

She stepped down from the bar stool and invited Lenny to join her at the counter. He placed the bundle down and unwrapped it.

Leslie peered at the lump. "What is it?"

"That's what I was hoping you could tell me."

Leslie picked up the tissue with long tweezers and placed it on a glass plate. From a drawer she took a large, thick magnifying glass, held it to her face and adjusted the distance from eye to lens.

After looking for a moment, she took a long stylet and probed the specimen. The color rose in her face. She flushed pink, then crimson.

He looked over her shoulder. "What is it? Can I see?"

She turned to face Lenny.

"Where did you get him?"

He pulled back, surprised. "*Him*? What do you mean 'him'?"

Leslie handed the lens to Lenny. He shut one eye and looked. As far as he could see, the specimen was a shapeless piece of flesh. It could be anything.

"You're looking at the torso of a fetus that's been badly traumatized,"

"This is a baby?"

"It would have been if it hadn't been aborted."

Lenny peered through the glass again. Try as he might, he couldn't make out the features. It just looked like an amorphous lump.

At that moment he heard the sound of shuffling footsteps. Looking up, he saw a heavyset man in a long, dirty lab coat enter the lab carrying a jar with a very large and very bloody organ inside. Seeing Lenny and Leslie, he put the jar in the fridgerator and came over.

"Find something interesting, Leslie?"

"Yes, Dr. Fingers, you could call it that. Take a look."

This Won't Hurt A Bit

Dr. Fingers took the lens from Lenny and focused on the specimen. While he examined it, Lenny studied the doctor. The man was big, stoop-shouldered, and disheveled. He had dark, greasy hair and his tie was held in place by an unusual silver clasp in the shape of a snake. His lab coat was stained with various colors, and he had about him an odor like sour milk.

"It appears to be the result of a rather sloppy vacuum abortion. I'd say a gestation of eight to ten weeks."

Fingers handed the magnifying glass to Lenny.

"See the two stubs on the bottom? Those are the remnants of the legs—one disarticulated at the knee, the other at the hip. The head is gone, of course. Yes, it was definitely a vacuum abortion."

Lenny turned to Leslie. "How did you know it's a boy?"

Her color having returned to normal, she said, "You haven't got any children, have you? You never waited outside the delivery room to learn the sex of your child."

"No, Margaret had cysts on her ovaries. She couldn't have kids."

Lenny watched as Leslie opened a plastic specimen cup half filled with formaldehyde and gently slid the conceptus into it.

"It has male genitalia," she said, screwing the lid firmly onto the jar.

The pathologist took the lens back from Lenny. "Where did you find it?" he asked.

"In the trash," he said, instantly sorry he'd opened his mouth.

The doctor did a double take. "The what?"

"It was in the trash in a doctor's office wrapped up in a paper towel."

Putting out his hand to receive the specimen from Leslie, Fingers said, "We can dispose of it properly here."

Lenny stepped in front of Leslie before she could give up the specimen.

"Yeah, that's true, doctor. But I removed this from a doctor's office, and I really ought to take it back where I got it, don't you think?"

Fingers looked at Leslie; Leslie looked at Lenny. For several seconds nobody moved.

Thirty-nine

*L*enny spied a phone at the end of the counter.

"Tell you what. Why don't I call the doctor? I'll explain the situation and ask if he wants the specimen back or if he wants me to leave it with you. Okay?"

Lenny dialed the number to Birdie's sewing room.

On the third ring Birdie answered, "Sewing room."

"Hi, this is Lenny. Yes, the custodian. Listen, I'm over in the pathology lab. I found a specimen in your doctor's trash this morning, and I was wondering if the doctor wants it back in his office, or should I leave it with the lab to dispose of it.... Yes, I'll hold."

Knowing that Lenny was up to one of his tricks, Birdie kept quiet. After a suitable interval, Lenny continued, "Uh huh... I see... O-kay. Sure, I can do that, no problem. Thanks."

Fingers, reaching for the phone, said, "Perhaps I should speak with them about—"

Click.

Lenny hung up before the pathologist could finish his sentence.

"The doc wants the specimen returned to his office," Lenny said. "He didn't mean to leave it in the trash. It was a mix-up."

The custodian reached his hand out to Leslie to receive the specimen cup. She looked at Dr. Fingers, who, frowning, eyed Lenny suspiciously.

"What office were you speaking to just then?"

Lenny summoned up his most innocent face, a look long practiced in showdowns with Childress and Joe West at the grievance table.

"To be truthful, Dr. Fingers, it sounded like the doctor was embarrassed by the whole thing. His secretary asked me not to mention his name."

Fingers looked into Lenny's eyes for a long moment. The doctor slowly nodded his head, allowing Leslie to hand Lenny the specimen, which he tucked in his pocket. The pathologist picked up the jar he had come in with and left.

Lenny said to Leslie, "Thanks for helping me out. Give my best to your mom."

This Won't Hurt A Bit

"I will, Lenny. Don't be a stranger, now."

After Lenny left the pathology lab, Dr. Fingers began to wonder why a custodian would be asking a technician to look at an aborted fetus. Was he one of those rabid anti-abortion agitators trying to get some dirt on the hospital? Fingers didn't think so. Then he remembered Freddie's innocent-sounding questions about the autopsy results of Randy Sparks, and he began to wonder if there was something dangerous going on.

He went into his office, closed the door and picked up the phone.

"Operator, page Mr. Joe West in security… Yes, it's a STAT page."

In the cafeteria, Lenny purchased a cup of coffee and a steaming hot biscuit. As the cashier, a heavyset Filipino woman counted out the change for him, he asked, "Hey Marrissa—how're the feet?"

"About as worn out as my old man," she said with a doleful look, though her eyes twinkled.

He carried his food to a table in the corner, sitting between Moose and Bobby D. Celeste sat across from them. Bobby was biting into a toasted bagel with melted cheese and strips of bacon on top. He leaned back in his chair chewing and smiling at the sweet flavor.

"Mmm man, that Luisa makes a mean bacon melt. I should marry her just for her cooking."

"You couldn't afford her," said Moose, a bagel with cream cheese smothered in his big hands. "She likes fast convertibles and diamond rings. Luisa's always talking about how she had dinner at this club and dancing at that club. She probably sweats champagne when she works out at Lady-Be-Fit."

"She goes to that club? I'll have to see if I can sell her some workout clothes. She can try them on at my place any time."

"Dream on," said Lenny. "You'll be selling Lexuses before she'll go out with you."

"I wish I could afford that club," said Celeste. "Maybe I could get my figure back after those kids of mine ruined it."

"Your figure's perfect," said Bobby. "And that African print you have on today…it looks great on you. I've got a nice little gold necklace, fourteen-caret guaranteed, would go with the gold and brown you've got on."

"The only fourteen carrots you've got are from the produce market," she said. "I buy all my jewelry at Robbins 8th and Walnut."

"Anyway," Bobby said, turning to Lenny, "I was taking around some perfume to the girls working in psych and one of them told me that they fired a temp last month. A girl supposed to help them convert all their files to computer. She was a temp so they didn't actually fire her, but they let her go, and the reason was, she complained that Radcliff stuck his tongue in her ear."

"Ycchh, that's disgusting," said Lenny. "Too bad she wasn't in the union, I'd have grieved his ass."

"Hope the girl got another position," Moose said. "All these docs are the same. They got sex on the brain."

"That's not where they got it," said Celeste. "One time Galloway was walking toward me in the hall and he puckered up his mouth and stuck his tongue halfway out and wiggled it. Grossed me out something awful."

"What a dirty old man," Lenny said.

"It don't surprise me," Moose said. "My cousin Vernice, works in the Surgical Services office. She told me that Galloway's on his second wife, and she's young and sexy."

"The trophy wife," said Lenny.

"You got it. Vernice also told me that when he was a medical student out at West Chester he got a nursing student pregnant, and he was married. The girl dropped out of school and left town, and when she came back the next semester, no baby."

"She probably had an abortion," said Celeste. "I wouldn't want to carry a married man's child. You never get child support, only abuse."

Lenny told them about the D&C tray from the gynecology department that he and Moose had seen in the Central Supply department and the fetus that Betty had found in Odom's examining room.

Moose said, "Try this on for size. Suppose a woman got pregnant, only not by her husband. He goes off, finds out who the father is and terminates him."

"That's plausible," Lenny said, but it doesn't—"

"Wait!" said Bobby. "What if the husband had a vasectomy and he couldn't knock up his wife. She knows if she doesn't get the abortion her husband will see her filling out and know it had to be another guy, so she runs away to the boyfriend, but the husband finds out and kills him."

"No, you men got it all wrong," said Celeste. "What if the husband couldn't get it up anymore, so when he discovers his wife is pregnant, he not only hates the guy cause his wife is carrying another man's baby, but he's humiliated on account of he couldn't knock her up even when he wanted to."

"That's brilliant," said Moose.

"So," said Bobby D, turning to Lenny, "who killed Dr. Sparks?"

"How the fuck should I know?" he answered. Then, realizing his words had come out more harshly than he had intended, he said, "But with a team like ours, it's just a matter of time before we find out."

Forty

Gary was at the nursing station enjoying his pretzel with hot mustard when he and Marianne heard a cry from one of the patient's rooms.

"Nurse! Nurse! Help her! Help her, please!"

He ran into the hall, where he saw Marianne hurrying into Mrs. Rosemond's room. Following her in, he saw Mrs. Rosemond sitting on the edge of her bed, a lunch tray in front of her, her hands at her throat. Her lips were purple, her nostrils flaring, her eyes bulging in panic.

Marianne rushed to the patient and grasped her shoulder.

"Can you talk? Say something! Can you say something?"

The only sound Rosemond could make was a faint gurgling in her chest.

Gary hurried to the other side of the bed. He knelt on the bed behind Mrs. Rosemond and wrapped his arms around her massive girth to perform the Heimlich maneuver, but the patient was so huge, Gary could not reach all the way around.

Marianne yelled, "Lay her on her back and Heimlich her from the front!"

"Okay!"

Gary got off the bed and came around in front of Mrs. Rosemond. He pushed her shoulders until she lay on her back across the bed, legs kicking in the air, hands still at her throat. The purple color in her lips was darkening, her face growing gray.

Gary straddled the woman's legs, clasped his hands together and pressed them between her breasts, in the soft spot below the breastbone. He pushed deep into her abdomen.

No effect.

"Harder, Gary!"

He lunged forward, putting his weight into the effort and pushing with all his strength. A loud "whoosh" came from the patient's throat, then she began to cough furiously.

Marianne and Gary pulled Mrs. Rosemond up to a sitting position, and she coughed a piece of meat onto the floor.

Gary wrapped a napkin around the piece of meat to pick it up and deposited it on the patient's tray. Mrs. Rosemond noisily took in volumes of air, all the while coughing and fluttering her hands about. Tears streaked down her quivering cheeks.

He picked up the bedside phone and dialed the operator. "Page Dr. Primeaux STAT for this room, please."

Marianne looked at Mrs. Rosemond's lunch tray. It contained Jell-O, broth, tea, and two pieces of meat on a napkin. Marianne put her hands on her hips and stood squarely in front of Mrs. Rosemond.

"Where did you get this meat?"

Mrs. Rosemond's roommate, Mrs. Gold, the elderly bent-over woman who had found the shiny penny, came forward.

"I gave it to her. I'm sorry. She was so hungry, you see, and she seemed to be starving to death, so I gave her some of my lunch."

Marianne wagged her finger in Mrs. Rosemond's face.

"You shouldn't beg from another patient. Shame on you! I'm going to tell Dr. Primeaux when he comes up."

Mrs. Rosemond began to whimper. "Please don't tell the doctor. Please don't, he'll kick me out of here!" She moaned and tried to grab the nurse's arm, but Marianne walked out, shaking her head.

Lenny put down his coffee cup and said, "The problem with our investigation is, we need to find a connection. Something that nails one of them."

"Don't forget the motive," said Moose. "We got to find out who had a *reason* to do Sparks in, not just that he could've did it."

Just then Freddie ambled up to the table, a cup of milk in one hand and a cup of ice in the other.

"Hidey-ho, what's the news?" he said, setting his drink down. He pulled up a chair beside Celeste, poured half the milk over the ice and drank deeply, then he smacked his lips and dabbed his mouth with a napkin.

"Nothing like a cold glass of milk to make a man feel good," he said.

"Only thing better is mother's milk," said Bobby with a grin.

"Don't talk trash," Celeste told him. "I'm a mother, don't forget."

"Sorry," he said.

Freddie turned to Lenny. "I asked Doc Fingers about the autopsy report on Sparks. He said Sparks had swelling of the brain, but the skull wasn't cracked or anything like that. No drugs in his system, either."

"That's great, thanks Freddie. Did Fingers say the swelling was the cause of death?"

"He didn't say, exactly."

"No drugs and no cracked head," said Moose. "So what did it?"

"I don't know," said Lenny, "but I'm going to have to ask somebody with a medical background, that's for sure."

"Tuttle?" asked Moose.

"I was thinking a doctor, if I could find one who would talk to me."

"I'll ask Birdie," Moose said, standing up. "I got to pick up the late trays anyhow."

As he walked away from the table, Sandy, the old security guard with the bulldog face, came to the table with coffee cup in hand. After greeting everyone, he settled slowly into his chair, saying, "These old bones are creaking like an old rocking chair." Getting comfortable, he said, "What was the day that Sparks disappeared?"

"It was Friday, December thirteenth," said Lenny.

"That's it. I was remembering I saw something funny right around the time he got his-self killed and I figured you'd want t' hear about it."

"Oh?" asked Lenny. "What happened?"

Sandy scratched his left calf, taking time to collect his thoughts and enjoying the attention.

"It happened last December, just about the time that young doctor disappeared. About six-thirty in the evening a woman came to the information desk to get a pass to visit a patient in room...let me see, I've got it written down somewhere...Yes, Room four-oh-nine. I was in the lobby at the time. The woman was tall, blond, and she had on a black fur coat. Very expensive. The collar was pulled up around her face, even though it was warm in the lobby."

Lenny noted he stirred in three packets of Sweet n Low into his coffee and remembered Sandy was diabetic. Had been treated in the emergency room once for insulin shock and Lenny had to speak to West to get his leave time.

"The woman asked the information clerk which elevator to take and where to turn to get to the patient's room. It was time for me to make rounds anyway, so I offered to escort her to the ward, but she insisted on going up alone. Said she'd been there once before.

"But she asked the clerk for directions," Lenny said.

"That's right."

"What happened then?"

"When I made my rounds I asked Pearlie, that little rollie-pollie LPN on four-south? Did the blond woman in the fur coat find her party in room 409 all right, and Pearlie told me the patient didn't have any visitor that night.

She said the patient *never* gets visitors. All her relatives live down South and never come to see her."

"She could've gone almost anywhere," Moose said. "Did you see her leave?"

"Nope, an' I watched the lobby good after that. But I *did* do some askin' around and I found somebody who thinks maybe they saw her go past her station."

"You're kidding! Where?"

Sandy paused, all eyes on him, and savored the attention.

"Third floor, north wing."

"That obstetrics, isn't it?" Birdie asked.

"Sure is," Sandy answered. "And gynecology, too."

Lenny said, "I wonder who she was meeting…and why the story about visiting a patient."

"Ain't no way to tell," Sandy said, "but it's mighty suspicious happening the same week he disappeared."

"It's strange, all right," said Lenny. "Like everything else in this case."

Their break over, Bobby made a show of looking at his watch, its face glittered with diamond-like stones. "Back to the pits," he said.

Walking out of the cafeteria with Celeste, Lenny said, "Do you believe it's only Thursday? It seems like this week is a month long."

"Got the weekend off?" she asked as they walked toward the elevator.

"Yeah, thank God. Why?"

Pressing the button for the elevator, she said, "The way I see's it, we all better rest up good, cause this murder thing is gonna take a lot more work. For all of us."

Forty-one

Dr. Primeaux arrived on Seven-South and hurried to Mrs. Rosemond's room. His examination indicated that she had suffered no serious injury. He went up to the nursing station, where he heard Marianne recap the choking incident. Speaking in his soft, southern drawl, he said, "That woman hasn't got the sense of a mule and is twice as stubborn."

Gary asked the doctor if the patient needed anything done.

"Well, ah guess we ought to get neck films to be sure there's no tear in her esophagus. There's always the chance of laceration."

"Okay. We'll send her down to x-ray."

Gary brought the wide wheelchair from the closet. As he placed it beside Mrs. Rosemond's bed, Primeaux bent down and locked the wheels of the chair.

"Thank you, Alex. Not many doctors would think of that."

"That's all right, Gary. Happy to help."

While the doctor and nurse were speaking, Moose, who had come to collect the lunch trays, listened to their conversation. Primeaux's accent was familiar, reminding him of his uncle and aunt in Arkansas.

"Lord, that must've been quite a sight when y'all Heimliched her," Primeaux said.

"It sure was. When I couldn't get my arms around her, we laid her on her back and did the maneuver from the front."

Primeaux chuckled as he filled out the requisition for the x-ray.

"I sure wish I could find the source of her bleeding. She's still got that little bit o' blood in her stool, and she still claims she's nauseous, but I'll be damned if I can find the reason."

As Dr. Primeaux turned to leave the unit, Moose asked, "Say doc, you sure sound like you're from Arkansas."

Primeaux said, "I'm from Durham, North Carolina, lahk ah told ya."

"Gotcha," Moose said. He went back to collecting trays, feeling there was something wrong about Primeaux's story, but he couldn't quite put his finger on it.

While Moose was talking with Primeaux, Lenny approached Gary at the nursing station. "Hey, Tuttle. Anybody ask for me while I was gone?"

"No, why? Are you in trouble again?"

"I hope not. You look a little worn out. Something the matter?"

As Gary began to tell him about the emergency with Mrs. Rosemond, he saw Mrs. Grey standing at the station looking at him.

"Can I help you?" he said.

"I'm sorry to bother you, Gary, but I came out of the bathroom just now and there was a doctor going out the door of my room. I don't know why, but I had a bad feeling about it, so I looked in my beside cabinet and realized my wallet was missing. I'm sure it was there the last time I looked. It's a red leather wallet."

"What did the doctor look like?"

"I didn't see his face. He was a big man. He had blond hair and he was wearing a white lab coat."

Moose smacked his fist into an open palm. "It's that same guy been robbing the staff. You get an emergency, people running around all excited, and BANG, he strikes again."

Gary asked Celeste, who had been sitting at the station, if she had seen anybody strange pass her during the commotion.

"No, Gary, just the usual types. Dr. Primeaux, a couple of orderlies…that's all *I* saw."

Lenny pointed down the hall. "I came up the back stairs at the other end of the hall and nobody unusual passed me there."

Moose ran to the stairwell in the middle of the hall. "Come on! I'll go up, you go down."

Moose burst through the exit door and lunged up the stairs three steps at a time. Lenny grabbed the handrail and half-slid, half-jumped down the stairs. On the next landing, he opened the door and looked onto the empty corridor. There was no blond figure in a lab coat in sight. He quickly turned and rushed down another flight of steps. All the way down to the first floor there were no white-coated figures in the hallways.

At the basement, Lenny opened a gray steel door labeled "boiler room." He stepped in, paused, listened, heard a low-pitched "thump-a-tah, thump-a-tah."

At first he thought it was his heart pounding from the hurried descent and the excitement of the chase, but he realized that the sound was the rumble of the pump delivering oil to the great boiler.

Lenny moved cautiously down cement steps into a large, dimly-lit room. On his right, steam pipes ran along the wall and turned upward through the ceiling. He could feel the heat radiating out from their uninsulated surfaces.

On the opposite side of the room, three huge steel oil tanks stood on squat legs, the cement floor beneath them black with dripping oil. As he stepped onto the hard floor, the tremble of the pumps feeding the boiler rose through his feet.

Lenny crouched, trying to see under the tanks, but it was pitch black beneath them. *Wish I had a flashlight,* he thought. *A gun would be nice, too.*

He decided it was unlikely that a man in a white lab coat would hide beneath the dirty oil tanks—there was barely more than a foot of clearance—but the spaces between them was big enough. The ceiling lights between two of the tanks were out, leaving the area in darkness. He pulled the paint scraper from his belt and stepped into the dark alley between the two tanks.

"This is nuts," he mumbled, inching forward. He made his way by running one hand along the cold steel walls of the tank on his left and holding the blade in front with the other hand. The surface of the oil tank was rough with rust. Probably never been painted.

He continued, his heart pounding as hard as the boiler pump. It was cold and black as a crypt. He thought, *if I end up dead I'm gonna kill Moose.*

He continued along the tank until he felt the blade strike the cement wall. Nothing, thank God. He felt the space on either side between wall and tank. Six, maybe ten inches, if that. Nowhere near enough for a man to hide.

He turned around and hurried back out to the center of the room, finding it not nearly so dark now that his eyes had grown accustomed to real darkness.

He listened hard; heard nothing but the pumps and the soft hiss of the steam as it rushed through the pipes. He walked forward toward the boiler.

I should have sent Moose down here. He's the fighter. I could be upstairs looking down bright hallways filled with people.

The boiler stood in front of the far wall, a massive steel pot encasing a fiery fury of burning oil that was released as a fine spray and fanned by an enormous rush of forced air. Water pipes entered at one side of the beast and exited on the other as bare steam pipes so hot you could boil water in a kettle on them.

He saw an iron ladder several feet to the side of the boiler. Walking over to it, he stood at the foot of the ladder and peered up. There was a trap door in the ceiling. *Could the guy have come into the boiler room and disappeared up there? No way I'm going up that ladder.*

He listened for breathing, movement…there was no sign of anyone.

Suddenly he sensed a motion behind him. He started to turn.

Crack!

He heard the blow to his skull just as flashes of light exploded behind his eyes and lightning bolts of pain crackled through his head.

He sank to his knees, tried to steady himself with his hands on the cement floor. A second blow at the base of his neck sent a spasm down his spine. His limbs twitched, he collapsed onto the floor. His mind switched off, swallowed in darkness.

A tall, powerful figure grabbed Lenny by the shirt collar and dragged him along the floor. At the furnace, the figure grasped Lenny's head by the hair and pulled it back. The figure slowly brought Lenny's face toward one of the steam pipes where it exited the furnace. He pressed Lenny's face against the pipe and its three-hundred-degree heat.

A terrible searing pain erupted in Lenny's face and neck. The agony and the stench of his burning flesh revived him. He felt his knees on the hard cement floor and the hand at the back of his head pressing him onto the pipe.

He reached instinctively for the putty knife clipped to his belt. Almost of its own will, his hand grasped the handle of the knife, pulled it off the belt.

He drove the knife upward into the figure's belly. The man grunted and released Lenny, who fell heavily to the floor.

As he lay face down on the cold cement floor, the pain eased slightly. An overwhelming fatigue came over him. He welcomed the cool relief of the floor.

With the rumbling of the furnace echoing through the floor, Lenny thought he heard a familiar voice calling in the distance. The pulse of the furnace mixed with the throbbing of his pain, and he couldn't be sure what was furnace sound and what was inside his head.

He felt the light rap of footsteps running away from the voice, then welcomed the sweet embrace of sleep.

Forty-two

Moose found Lenny lying face down on the floor of the boiler room. As a boxer who had seen many a man knocked down and out, he knew not to panic. Gently turning his friend over, he patted Lenny's cheek.

"Hey Lenny! You hear me, man?"

Lenny slowly reached his hand to Moose's face and felt a chin, a nose, ears. As his mind cleared, the jagged thrusts of pain coursed through his head and he opened his eyes.

Moose pulled Lenny to a sitting position, then saw his friend's face. "Jesus Christ! Your face looks like it's been cooked on a grill!"

Moose felt dampness at the back of Lenny's head. He pulled his hand away. Slippery, warm blood glistened in the dim light.

"Shit, you're bleeding! I gotta get you to the ER"

He grabbed Lenny by the armpits and lifted him to a standing position. "C'mon, let's see can you walk."

Lenny tilted to one side and started to fall. "I'm gonna be sick," he said, knees buckling.

Moose grabbed Lenny behind the knees and back and picked him up fireman style, then started for the door.

"Put me down, I can walk," Lenny said weakly, but his head lolled like a drunk and he did not struggle to get down. As he rocked in Moose's arms, he said, "Ohhhh, man...Somebody get me off this boat."

Moose carried his friend out of the boiler room and up a flight of steps, around a corner and down a long hall to the Emergency Room. At the entrance, Moose eased Lenny's feet down to the floor.

"Can you stand up?"

"Can I stand up! Of course I can stand. What d'ya think?"

Lenny wobbled, his shoulder struck the door. Moose grasped his arm and steadied him, and together they entered the Emergency Room.

A young nurse took Lenny into an exam room, with Moose following, and helped him onto a stretcher. She put an ice pack on Lenny's face and a thick dressing over the back of his head where a large laceration was oozing blood.

"We'll have to get an x-ray to check for a fracture," the nurse said. "After that the medical student is going to put some stitches in this baby."

"Thanks a lot," said Lenny weakly.

"Look on the bright side. You got hit right smack on your bald spot. That means I'll only have to shave a little piece of your scalp."

"I seen guys take worse hits and stay on their feet," Moose added.

The nurse told Lenny to keep the ice pack on his face to reduce the ache, and Moose promised to see that he did.

Patience, a slender black woman, came into the room and laid a hand gently on Lenny shoulder.

"Are you all right, Lenny?" she said in a low, throaty voice. Her hair was cut short, and she wore no makeup.

"Just peachy."

"I'm going to take you down the hall for an x-ray, okay?"

Lenny started to sit up, intending to get off the stretcher to walk down the hall, but the pain made his vision blur and nausea overwhelmed him. He fell back onto the stretcher.

"No, you stay put," said Patience. "I'll push you down on the stretcher."

"Want I should help?" Moose asked.

"Thank you," she said, pushing the stretcher around a corner and down to the x-ray room. Inside, Moose grabbed the sheet beneath his friend and slid him easily across to the table. Patience folded a soft bath blanket and placed it under Lenny's head. She stopped to look at the burn on the side of his face.

"That's a nasty burn."

"It only hurts when I try to talk."

"Then you have a big problem. You have to keep your mouth shut."

He glanced at her face, saw a mischievous look in her eye, decided the whole world was bent on making him miserable.

She removed a lead apron from the wall and draped him from the waist down.

"Thank you," he said.

"It's an OSHA regulation, otherwise I wouldn't bother," she said, winking at Moose. She went behind a plexiglass screen to enter the coordinates into a console.

Lenny turned to Moose for support.

"Did you hear that? I'm the patient! Aren't I supposed to get some TLC?"

Moose chuckled. "Just do what you're told, you'll be all right."

Patience ordered Moose out of the room. She closed the door, primed the x-ray, then told Lenny to take a deep breath and hold it.

This Won't Hurt A Bit

Lenny expanded his lungs. As he held his breath, he felt bombs explode in his head.

The x-ray machine beeped. Patience stuck her head out from behind the plexiglass.

"You can breathe now."

"Thank you. That did wonders for my headache."

She pulled the x-ray film from beneath the table and held it up to the light.

"Now I'm going to find out what's really inside that hard head of yours, Lenny Moss."

"Snakes n' snails and puppy dog tails." He mustered a feeble smile, then groaned.

She cast him an affectionate look, turned, opened the door and sashayed out of the room, saying to Moose, "You can have him back now."

After the ER nurse shaved and cleaned the wound at the back of his head, a medical student who looked young enough to be in high school brought in a sewing kit and deftly began closing the oozing gap in Lenny's scalp.

While the student worked on him, Moose called Gary on Seven-South. Gary arrived just as the medical student finished the suturing. He examined the student's neat stitches. "Very nice work," Gary said. "You'd make a good tailor."

"I plan to go into plastic surgery," he said.

The student examined Lenny's burn, which ran from his temple down to his jaw. He opened a jar of white burn ointment and spread a thick layer over the wound, then covered it with a white dressing.

"This is gonna hurt like a mother by tonight," the student said. "Do you want a script for pain medicine?"

"Nah, I'll be all right."

Gary said, "You don't have to be a macho guy, you know. It will help you sleep."

"Somehow, I don't think falling asleep is going to be a problem," said Lenny. "Waking up—now that's another story."

He slid off the stretcher, touched the back of his head. It felt about three hat sizes bigger. He went to the station to sign his discharge papers, wanting nothing more than to go home and put his head on a nice soft pillow. As he scrawled his name on the discharge order, a hard object jabbed him in the back. Turning, he was face to face with Joe West.

Forty-three

"Somebody didn't hit you hard enough," said Joe West, eyeing Lenny's battered face with satisfaction.

"What do you want?"

West held out a sheet of paper that was all too familiar to Lenny.

"This is a written warning. You were away from your station today twice, and it wasn't union business. What were you doing in Dr. Radcliff's office?"

"There's no hospital regulation that says I can't help a co-worker after I finish my work. I was doing a little vacuuming for Abrahm."

"Shove it up your ass, Moss. You weren't there to clean anything. You've been sniffing around James Madison thinking you can help your buddy Devoe."

"You got an overactive imagination, West."

"Dr. Fingers called me from the pathology lab. He told me about the specimen you brought down there. I'm giving you a written warning for being out of your work area. One more violation and it's a three-day suspension."

"Great. Three days off is just what I need, and when I win the grievance, it'll be three days back pay."

West leaned to the side to get a better view of Lenny's burned neck.

"You keep on with your dumb-shit interference in police business, you'll get time off from your life," he said, then turned and strode out of the emergency room.

Gary, who had witnessed the conversation, pleaded with Lenny to back off the investigation, at least until West had cooled down.

"No can do," Lenny said. "My dad always used to say, it's a good thing to be attacked. It's a sign you're becoming a threat to the power structure. We have to keep pushing until we beat this thing. West will never let up. Never."

They came out of the emergency department into the waiting area just as Moose arrived.

"I told Docksett you were in the ER and he signed you out," he said. "You got to make out an incident report."

"I'll do it tomorrow, the ER record will cover me," Lenny said, struggling to put on his coat. He told Moose about his encounter with West. Gary repeated his hope that Lenny would lay low for the time being.

"You rattled his chain," Moose said. "Got him nervous. We're on the right track, trust me."

They had stepped through the automatic door leading to the driveway. When Lenny fished for his car keys, Moose said, "What the hell you doin'?"

"I'm going to drive my ass home and go to bed."

"Are you crazy? You can't drive the way you've been slammed. I've taken some punches in the head, I know. Give me the keys."

Lenny held the keys in a fist, but Moose easily pried his fingers apart and took them.

"You're coming home with me for dinner. You'll stay the night, too. I'll drive."

"He's right, Lenny," Gary said. "You're not fit to drive."

Lenny followed Moose out onto the driveway and up the ramp toward the employee parking lot. "C'mon Moose, give me the keys, I'm okay."

Lenny stumbled at the curb, Moose and Gary caught him by the arms and held him up.

"Bullshit! You can't hardly walk, how you gonna drive?"

Lenny groaned. "I do feel a little sick," he said. The promise of resting on a sofa and being served one of Birdie's wonderful meals heartened him. "Okay," he said, "but I'm sleeping in my own bed tonight."

Moose invited Gary to join them. He said that he would try and come over after dinner, but his wife was in class that evening and he had to watch the kids.

After letting Lenny into the passenger side, Moose slid behind the wheel of the Buick, his big frame filling the seat. When the old motor turned over with a growl, he grinned. "Nothin' like a big old V8. Smoothest power there is. And you got real gauges, not them idiot lights. No wonder you held on to your dad's car."

"Margaret used to say that I loved the car more than her, but I always said, Listen, do I bring it flowers?"

"When did you ever bring your wife flowers?"

"*Every* Valentine's day."

"That's cause you knew you'd never get in the door without 'em, heh-heh."

Moose turned the steering wheel effortlessly at corners, keeping a light touch on the gas pedal. The car cruised smoothly over the cobblestones on Wayne Avenue into Mt. Airy and soon came to a stop in front of an old stone twin. The enclosed porch was filled with leafy plants. Children's hats, coats, and boots were thrown in the corner on the floor.

In the house, Moose settled Lenny on the couch. He brought his friend a pillow and a fresh bag of ice to put on his head. Heading toward the kitchen, he asked if Lenny wanted a beer.

"Christ, I need a lobotomy, not a beer."

"Thought they did that already. Heh-heh."

The living room had thick carpeting and heavy drapes. A tall, walnut breakfront held a wrought iron candle holder, a crystal vase and family photos in heavy, carved wooden frames. There was no television set.

Moose passed back through the living room to join Birdie in the kitchen.

Lenny lay back, closed his eyes. The throbbing in his head beat at him like the base guitar in a rock concert. The sweet scent of meat cooking drifted in from the kitchen and made him nauseous. He turned his face to the back of the sofa to shut it out.

He pushed through the pain and the odors to concentrate on what had happened. Was the attack on him the work of a desperate thief, or was it somehow connected with the Sparks murder? He didn't see how they could be related, but the attacker was cruel enough to have killed him, of that he had no doubt. If Moose hadn't come along…

Could the killer have learned about Lenny's pursuit and lured him into a trap? It was an odd coincidence that all the suspects seemed to know what he was doing, and this afternoon his face was put on the barbie.

And then there was the head of security, who knew he was knee deep in the Sparks affair. He and West had sparred for years over countless union grievances. West hated him, but would West have the nerve to do this? No, he'd use his authority in the hospital to drive him out. He'd claim Lenny had resisted his order to leave the building and get in a few licks. That was West's method.

In the pain and the fatigue, the clues became a jumble. The whole investigation seemed like a fool's errand. He was a union delegate. He knew the contract, the supervisors, the workplace. He knew nothing about murder, hadn't any access to police files, autopsy reports… couldn't interview the suspects…didn't even know for sure which one of the doctors *were suspicious*.

Birdie came in with a pitcher of juice and poured him a glass. "You need a good meal and a night's sleep," she said. "Why don't you lie down, put your feet up and close your eyes? I'll call you when dinner's ready."

"Maybe I will." He pulled off his shoes and settled into the sofa. Moose and Birdie went back to the kitchen.

This Won't Hurt A Bit

As Lenny closed his eyes, the images of the day began to blur. Even the reason for his involvement was out of focus, and he drifted into a fitful sleep.

He dreamed of Margaret, sick with cancer, vomiting uncontrollably. Lenny was fishing in the vomitus with his fingers, trying to save the premature little baby that had died in childbirth.

She couldn't stop throwing up, burying the little baby deeper in the vomit. Lenny dug feverishly, terrified that the infant would be lost, and sick with the knowledge that he was losing the only child that Margaret would ever bear.

Forty-four

"Yoo-hoo, sleepy-head. Feel like some dinner?"

The images of Margaret and the lost baby faded as Lenny was called back from sleep. He awoke sweaty and exhausted. The content of the dream vanished, like smoke from a dying fire, leaving him with a weeping sense of loss.

He opened his eyes. Birdie was sitting on the sofa beside him, her face a portrait of tenderness and humor.

"Huh?"

"You were moaning in your sleep. It looks like that head of yours isn't quite as hard as it's cracked up to be."

"No, just cracked!" Moose contributed from behind her. He mouth was grinning, but his eyes betrayed his worry.

Birdie offered to bring Lenny a tray so that he could eat at the sofa, but he declined. Rising to a sitting position, he squinted, felt the thick bandage on his scalp.

"The doctor didn't remove the top of my head, did he?"

"No," Moose told him. "He just drew off the evil demons. Can you walk?"

Lenny put on a hurt expression. "Can I walk? Ha! I've been hit a lot harder than that and still stayed on my feet."

He raised himself to a standing, if not exactly upright posture, and shuffled over to the dinner table.

They took their places at the table just as Birdie came in with a huge platter of baked chicken and sweet potatoes. Moose began heaping Lenny's plate with food.

"Wait'll you try this. Birdie spoons the chicken juice on the potatoes in the oven. Sweet as honey. Mmmm, mm."

Lenny was relieved that the nausea had passed. He took a tentative bite of chicken, chewed slowly, let it slide down his throat.

Moose poured him more juice. "Birdie said you got to drink a lot of fluids."

He took a long drink, realizing that his mouth had become very dry.

This Won't Hurt A Bit

He felt weakened and drained. He finished the glass and asked for a refill from Moose, who was looking hard at him.

"You okay?"

"I'm just hunky-dory. No, I was just thinking that I'm wandering around in the dark like I was still down in the boiler room. I really don't know what the fuck I'm doing."

"You're not quitting on me, are you?"

"I didn't say I was giving up, I just said I was lost, that's all."

"Well don't even think about getting out of the ring. We can't do shit without you. You're the one everybody talks to."

"Let them bend somebody else's ear. Mine is half burned off."

Moose sipped his beer, studied his friend.

"You been beat and you're hurting. It's only natural you get discouraged. By tomorrow you'll be back on top. Trust me."

"If I live till tomorrow."

"What would your old man say?"

Lenny chewed on the question, sipped his drink.

"He knew when to make a tactical retreat, that much I'm sure of. Of course he wouldn't quit. *I'm* not gonna quit. I just don't know what to do next."

"That's why we're gettin' together tonight. Two heads are better than one."

"I feel like I already *have* two heads."

They ate and talked of life outside the hospital—of children and schools, the neighborhood and the city. The food eased Lenny's pain, and everyone was glad to be on any subject except the murder.

Just as everyone was taking their last bite, Gary came in. He apologized for being late as he handed his coat to Moose.

"I'm really sorry Miriam couldn't make it."

"Dessert's comin' out of the kitchen now. Sit yourself down and don't worry about it."

Gary sat beside Moose, who told the story of the x-ray and stitches, putting special emphasis on how Lenny's bald spot had made the stitching a lot easier.

As Birdie carried away an armful of dirty plates, she asked Moose to bring out his sketch pad.

"Now, Bird', they don't wanna see that old thing."

"Of course they do. Go on an' get it while I serve the dessert."

Moose brought out a large pad and placed it on the dining room table as Birdie brought in apple brown betty with a white sauce. Dishes were passed around, and all talk ceased while spoons traveled from bowl to mouth.

Birdie opened the sketch book and began leafing through it.

"You should see what Moose has been doing. It's wonderful!"

She held up a drawing of Dr. Priscilla Gandy, who was dressed in a witch's costume. She had a long, beaked nose, and rode, instead of a broomstick, a huge syringe across a full moon.

Everyone gathered around the pad to look at the caricature. Gary, chuckling, said, "Moose, if you tried for a hundred years, you could not have captured Gandy's personality any better. This is perfect."

As they looked over the drawing, two young children came quietly into the room. After sniffing the apple brown betty, Moose's and Birdie's daughter, who was ten, stood beside her mother. Her younger brother stood next to Moose.

He put an arm around his boy. Looking stern, he asked the child, "Homework done?"

"Yes, Daddy."

"Get yourself a bowl…you, too, girl."

Both children hurried to the kitchen. Returning to fill their bowls, the boy asked, "How come you don't ask Sakira if she did her homework?"

Birdie answered, "Because she always does hers as soon as she gets home and you don't. You know that, Tyrone."

Moose wagged a finger at the children.

"Upstairs. This is grown-up time."

The children took their bowls, arguing over what TV show they would watch as they ascended the stairs.

Lenny asked if Moose had drawn any of the other suspects.

"I did all of 'em. Have a look."

Moose turned the pages to reveal sketches of each suspect. Odom, dressed in a butcher's apron, was holding two huge meat cleavers that dripped with blood. Radcliff was in a Dracula-style cape, his arms extended, vampire teeth glinting in the light. Galloway was a mad scientist, complete with an old-fashioned laboratory and hunchbacked assistant.

"This one's my favorite," Moose said, turning the page. It was a sketch of Alex Primeaux in a flowing robe, with wings and a halo around his head—an angel among the clouds. Peaking out from beneath his billowing robe was the handle of a gun.

"Moose, this is fantastic! I didn't realize you could do the faces of all the doctors," Lenny said.

"It's just like I said, they don't notice us serving their special lunches in the doctor's dining room, but we see everything."

Lenny asked if the pages could be removed and laid out on the table. "We can get a better look that way."

This Won't Hurt A Bit

Moose carefully pulled out the sheets and arranged them neatly on the table while Lenny moved the dishes to make room. Birdie poured coffee as they all studied the drawings.

Sipping his coffee, Lenny looked intently from one sketch to the next. "You know, these could be more than just cartoons."

"What are you suggesting?" Gary asked.

"I mean, we could be looking at the face of the killer right here in one of these sketches."

Everyone crowded around the table to examine the suspects, trying to draw some telltale clue from the curving lines and shaded surfaces of the five doctors.

Forty-five

Priscilla Gandy unlocked the door to her office, opened the door and slipped inside. A small night light cast a pale glow around the outer office, leaving most of it in shadow. Crossing quickly to the examining room, she turned on the ceiling light and opened a cabinet. She withdrew a syringe, and a small needle, broke open the plastic bubble pack and removed it, then she switched off the light.

As she turned back to the waiting room, the office door slowly opened and a face peeked around it.

"Am I late?"

"Lock the door behind you, Letterly," she said in a clipped voice. "Do you have it?"

"Sure do," said the medical student. He secured the door and sauntered into the middle of the room. His eager eyes shone brightly in the pale light.

Gandy grabbed his belt and tugged him toward her. She pressed her mouth fiercely against his lips and thrust her tongue into his mouth. She felt his arousal growing.

Pulling away, she said in a hoarse whisper, "Drop your pants and give me the Enpros." She stepped backward, felt the sofa with the back of her calves, and sat down.

While he unbuttoned his pants with one hand he withdrew a small vial from his pants pocket with the other and handed it to her. As he hurriedly undressed, Gandy bared the needle of the syringe and plunged it into the rubber nipple of the vial. She filled the syringe, withdrew it and recapped the needle, which she unscrewed. She dropped the needle on the floor, then she attached the smaller needle to the syringe.

"Have you got a tourniquet?" Letterly asked, expecting that she would want to inject the drug into a vein in his arm.

"No need," she whispered. She uncapped the new needle and touched the sharp tip with her finger. The prick of pain sent a hot tide of desire flowing through her.

As Letterly stood naked before her, she reached around his hips and drew him closer.

"Don't move!" she whispered in a hoarse voice.

"Where are you going to inject me?" he asked, his voice edged with fear.

"Where it will do the most good," she said, smiling wickedly.

She jabbed the needle into his swollen organ and injected.

He let out a moan.

Gandy lay back on the coach and pulled him to her.

"But Lenny," Gary said, "you haven't found any link between one of *them* and with Sparks' murder, have you?"

"Okay, we haven't got any hard evidence…"

"Or motivation, opportunity, method…"

"We do have a lot of clues," said Lenny. "Freddie found out Sparks had swelling of the brain, but he wasn't hit in the head. What would do that?"

"Well, other than trauma, some types of brain cancer can cause edema, but I don't suppose there was any evidence of disease?"

"He didn't say, but I don't think so."

"We see swelling in a drug overdose. Drowning victims can develop it too."

"Sparks didn't have any drugs in his system, and I doubt that he drowned in the hospital."

"We need to keep digging," said Moose. "It'll come. Just gonna take time is all."

Lenny turned his attention to the sketches. "If we could just find out what Sparks could've done to one of them to get himself killed…"

Gary sat back, considering Lenny's remarks.

"I think Lenny is right about one thing. Moose has captured the personalities of all the suspects. Perhaps we should consider who is mean enough to murder someone."

They looked over the witch, butcher, vampire, mad scientist, and angel.

Birdie pointed to Odom.

"He takes the lives of unborn children. Wouldn't it be just as easy to take the life of a man?"

Gary studied the butcher. "I'm not sure you can equate an abortion with a murder. Besides, all of these doctors take life one way or another.

"What do you mean?" she asked.

"Take the 'no code' order. When a physician writes that on his order sheet, he's telling the nurses not to do anything if the patient's heart stops or they stop breathing."

"But isn't that only for a terminal patient?" she said.

"It's supposed to be, but who decides if the patient is really terminal?"

"The doctor," she said.

"And sometimes he isn't," Lenny added. "Terminal, I mean."

"That's right."

"Well," Lenny went on," we know from the fetus that Betty found in his office that Odom is doing abortions late at night."

"Doin' it on rich bitches from the suburbs," Moose said.

"Why kill someone over an abortion?" Birdie asked.

"Moose thought the husband might have had a tubal ligation, or be impotent. Either way, he would be mad as hell if he discovered his wife was pregnant when he couldn't possibly be the father."

"You men think the whole world revolves around your penis." Birdie said.

Gary said, "Moose might be on the right track. If the killer had a weak ego, he could go into a jealous rage at the thought of his wife bearing another man's child."

Moose pointed to the sketch of Primeaux.

"You see him? He acts like a saint, but I don't trust him."

"How do you mean?" Lenny asked.

"It's his accent. He told me he's from Durham, but he sounds more Arkansas than North Carolina. "

"Did you ask him about it?" Lenny said.

"Yeah, he said his mom was born in Arkansas. Said her accent must have rubbed off on him."

"That sounds plausible to me," Gary said. "I can't believe that a perfect gentleman like Alex Primeaux would intentionally kill anyone."

"Just because he's a nice guy doesn't mean he can't lie," Lenny said, setting the sketch off to the side. "Let's consider Primeaux a long shot." He picked up the picture of Radcliff. "I'm putting my money on Radcliff. He was the last to work with Sparks. What do we know about him?"

Moose said, "We know he can't keep his dick in his pants. They got rid of that temp in psychiatry when it was him that was pawing her and sticking his tongue in her ear."

Lenny said, "There were complaints from a few of his patients that he was too touchy with his hands that the Medical Board hushed it up."

"There have been rumors in our department about Radcliff as well," Gary said.

"Tuttle, you never mentioned that."

"I didn't want to pass on gossip. I think a murder investigation should be based on facts, and what people say—"

"We have to look at everything," said Lenny. "A lot of rumors have a kernel of truth to them. No detail is too small to be ignored. Agreed?"

Forty-six

Lenny said, "We can't just go on clues. We have to develop a psychological profile on every one of the suspects to figure out who is capable of murder and who isn't."

"Since we're on the subject of personality," Gary said, "I know it doesn't prove anything, but the other day Radcliff told me to get a patient her lunch and the tray was on the widow sill where he could easily have served it."

"I remember that tray," Moose said. "The guy was using the table, I couldn't serve the lunch."

"That's Radcliff for you, " Gary said. "A true narcissistic personality."

Pointing his finger at the sketch of Radcliff in vampire's attire, Lenny said, "I want to know who Virginia Racine is and why he whited out her name. All the other cancellations were crossed out, but hers was the only name that was covered over."

"Couldn't the secretary have done it?" asked Gary.

"A secretary only does what the boss tells her to do," Moose said. "I say Virginia Racine slept with the shrink, got pregnant and had an abortion with Odom. Sparks found out and was blackmailing Radcliff, so Radcliff killed him."

"To keep the husband from finding out?" asked Gary.

"That's it," said Moose. He stabbed the sketch with his finger. "I say we make him the number one suspect."

Gary said, "We don't even know that she *had* an abortion, only that she had an appointment with Radcliff. Maybe she never went near Odom's office."

"Whoever did go to Odom did it at night rather than during normal office hours," Birdie said. "Why would she do that unless she was having something done she wanted kept secret?"

Gary said, "This is all speculation. I don't see how you can catch a murderer this way."

"We've got to make a few assumptions here, Tuttle. We can't expect proof to jump up and bite us on the nose."

Birdie laughed. "Especially your nose, Lenny. A man would be a fool to mess with something that scary."

"At least I've got less hair on my lip."

She pointed a finger accusingly at Lenny.

"That's because you shave and I don't. You have more hair on your body than a werewolf."

"Might make a good picture," said Moose. "Lenny with fur and fangs."

Lenny picked up the picture of Gandy in the witch's outfit. "What about her?"

"She's labile enough to do almost anything," Gary said. "Plus there's the missing Enpros. If she was having an affair with Sparks, she may have been giving him the drug to enhance their sex life."

"Maybe they had a fight and Gandy gave Sparks a lethal dose," Moose said.

"I don't know. The cadaver set-up doesn't look like a crime of passion to me. It's too well thought out. This is the work of a cool, calculating son of a bitch."

Lenny picked up the picture of the mad scientist. "Which leads us to the last suspect—Galloway. What do we know about him?"

Gary took the sketch from Lenny's hand and studied it.

"This morning on Seven-South, Galloway pitched a fit because the page operator didn't answer him by the eighteenth ring."

"What about it?" Lenny asked.

"It's just so typical of him. He thinks that everyone and everything in James Madison is there to do his bidding. It's like, anything he wants. He just needs to snap his fingers and someone will do it for him."

"Man thinks his shit don't stink," Moose said. "Look how he turned his back on that pregnant nursing student back when he was in medical school. A child would've messed with his plans to be a bigshot doctor."

Gary said, "He even has a young second wife to feed his ego."

Lenny laid the pictures out in a neat row.

"If one of the doctors *is* the killer, what could Sparks have known that was so threatening it got him killed?"

"We'll find it," Moose said. "Trust me."

Birdie and Moose collected the plates and silverware and carried them to the kitchen. Lenny looked once more at the sketches. The witch, the butcher, the mad scientist and vampire—and the angel with his beatific smile. The angel made him think of Margaret, and thinking of her fueled his anger.

"I'm getting goddamn sick of these fucking doctors!" Lenny said. He rose from his chair sketches in hand, like a lawyer holding damming evidence before a jury, and walked around the room. "First they killed my wife, then they set up an innocent man to hang for murder, then they hit me over the head, burn my face, and leave me for dead!"

"That's just the way your dad would talk," Moose said.

Lenny dropped the sketches onto the table and stared at them as if his eyes could set the paper on fire.

"One of these creeps did in Sparks," he said, "and we're going to nail his ass."

Despite his headache and his fatigue, Lenny felt that the investigation was more than a fool's errand. He was focused. On track. He heard an echo of his father's passionate voice in his words, and that passion carried him past the pain.

When it was time to say goodnight to his guests, Moose handed out coats. "There's a bad wind blowing tonight," he said. "Best button up."

Gary thanked Moose and left, but Lenny lingered at the door.

"Birdie, your cooking cured my headache," he said. He turned to Moose, "Do you mind if I borrow your sketches for awhile?"

"No problem," Moose said. "Keep 'em long as you like." He went into the dining room, retrieved the sketch pad and handed it to his friend. "You sure you're okay to drive?"

"I'm all right."

Lenny said goodnight and went to his car. The seat was cold. The old motor cranked a few times, then caught with a growl. He turned on the radio and tuned to the Temple jazz station as he drove through the empty, frozen streets.

The blow to the head, the burn, the excitement, and the dinner combined to make him sleepy, so he cracked the window, letting the cold night air revive him. He focused on the road ahead, trying to stay sharp.

As Louis Armstrong and Ella Fitzgerald came through the speakers, he felt that if he could just get one good night's sleep, he could survive anything.

It was a short ride through deserted streets to his home in the Germantown section. Parking in front of his small row house, Lenny tapped the bumper of the car behind him. He cursed the owner for taking up so much space. The engine coughed and snorted when he turned off the ignition, then died. He slid out of the car, ambled up the walk, and entered the dark porch.

"Some day I'm gonna get a timer for that fucking light," he muttered, entering the enclosed porch.

As he fumbled for the key to unlock the front door, his eye caught a movement deep within the shadows of the porch.

At once scared and completely alert, Lenny hurriedly reached to his belt and pulled out the paint scraper. In a shaky voice he called out, "Who's there?"

A street lamp's pale light reflected off the blade of the scraper. As Lenny peered into the darkness, the shadowy figure moved toward him.

Forty-seven

"Do you always greet your guests this way, Mr. Lenny Moss?"

Kate Palmer's slender form stepped into the pale light of the street lamp. Her round face, wrapped in the hood of a dark coat, was pale, almost otherworldly. Lenny felt an urge to touch her cheek to be sure that it was warm and alive.

"Jeez, you scared the shit out of me! How long have you been standing here in the dark?"

"Not very long, but it's cold out here."

He returned the paint scraper to his belt, fished out a set of keys and unlocked the front door. He found the wall switch, turned on a light, and lead her into his small living room crowded with two ancient stuffed armchairs, a sagging sofa covered with an old quilt, and a stained coffee table. A ceiling-high book shelf made from old roofing timbers was packed with books, stereo and records, and odd bits of pottery.

Lenny pulled a sweater off the couch and invited Kate to sit down. He watched her pull off her coat and fold it neatly on the back of the sofa. Then she perched on the edge of it as though she was not sure she was going to stay.

"Excuse the mess," he said. "Maid's day off."

He settled into a stuffed chair and watched Kate as she took in the room.

"You still haven't told me what you were doing on my porch. Or how you got my address, for that matter."

"Your address was in the phone book. As to why I came, I heard some disturbing things about Randy Sparks that I thought you would want to know about."

"I see."

"I also heard that someone tried to kill you today and wanted to know what happened."

"I got a few lumps is all," he said.

"May I look?"

He shrugged, came and sat beside her on the couch.

She gently teased away the dressing on his neck and examined the burn.

"This is a second degree burn. Does it hurt much?"

"Nah."

"Do you have more ointment to put on it?"

"They gave me a prescription in the ER. I'll get it filled tomorrow."

"Please do. This could become infected. The face is very susceptible to the spread of infection. It has a particularly rich supply of arteries and veins running through it."

"Is that why people blush so easily?"

"Uh huh."

She replaced the bandage and looked beneath the other one, saw the shaved area and the row of stitches.

"This one looks better, but you could put some ice on it, so long as you keep it dry."

"Thank you doctor. I'll do it when I go to bed."

She found herself close to him and pulled away. In a few seconds the silence began to feel awkward.

"You want some coffee? I've got espresso, normal and decaf. Or maybe a cappuccino?"

"I'd love a cappuccino. Thank you."

Crossing to the dining room, Lenny picked up the morning's dirty dishes and carried them back to the kitchen. The entire first floor was open; he and Margaret and a half-dozen friends had torn out the interior walls soon after they'd bought the house. Margaret wanted a modern, open look. Lenny didn't care, he just loved attacking the plaster with a sledge hammer.

While he made the coffee, Kate examined the books on the shelves. There were titles on history, many concentrating on the Civil War. Several books on the labor movement. The others varied widely, from political science to romance, home repair to natural food cooking. A whole shelf was taken up by murder mysteries.

"You've got quite a selection of books here," she said.

"A lot of them were my dad's," he called from the kitchen. "He was a union organizer."

"I see you're a mystery buff. Does that explain your interest in the Sparks murder?"

She heard the sound in the kitchen as Lenny steamed the milk. The fragrance of fresh coffee drifted into the living room.

"No, those were Margaret's. She was a nut about them. Especially Agatha Christie."

"Margaret—is she your wife?"

Lenny came in with a tray containing two steaming mugs of coffee and a plate of Oreo cookies. Kate took her cup and a cookie.

"She was. She died ten months ago from cancer."

"Oh, I'm sorry," she said.

They drank their coffee and let the silence fill the minutes. Lenny looked over his cup at Kate. She seemed light, spare, like a bird. He pictured her springing from a high board and diving into a pool, leaving only a little ripple where she entered the water.

Kate bit into an Oreo cookie, chewed, then stopped and examined the remaining cookie. "How old are these?"

Lenny picked up a cookie, dipped it in his coffee, popped it into his mouth. "I don't know. Couple of weeks, a month maybe. They're better if you dip 'em."

Kate returned her cookie to the plate. Lenny shrugged, dunked a second cookie and chewed it.

"You said you heard something about Sparks that disturbed you."

"Yes." She settled back into the sofa. "It was the autopsy report. They found several small puncture marks on his thighs and buttocks. The presumption was that he was a diabetic."

"Was he?"

"I don't think so. Diabetics don't usually inject into their buttocks. You can't see the site except with a mirror. They use their abdomen, their upper arms and legs."

"Which means that somebody else probably did the injecting. I heard that Sparks tested negative for drugs."

She gave him a look of surprise. "How did you find out?"

"We custodians have our methods," he said with an impish grin.

"With all his blood and fluids replaced by formaldehyde, I expect the ME sent tissue samples to the CDC in Atlanta. If he did, there won't be definitive results for a week or more."

Lenny chewed, sipped. Kate nestled her cup in both hands.

He saw her eye the plate of cookies. "You hungry? I've got some cheese and crackers in the fridge."

"No, thanks, the coffee is fine."

Lenny sensed that Kate was holding back. In his union work he had learned patience, that pumping a witness often raised their defenses and reduced trust. And that trust was the essential ingredient in gaining information.

Forty-eight

A man and a woman sat in a noisy bar on City Line Avenue, just over the Philadelphia border. The man, blond and handsome, was speaking in a soothing voice to the woman, who hid her eyes behind dark glasses.

"You've carried your pain for too many years, Virginia. I understand that. What you need is peace and serenity, and you will have that if you continue seeing me."

"But I'm so frightened that he'll find out, and you know how insane he gets if I have any outside friends. If he…"

"You can see me in my Center City Office. You can even use a different name."

Pulling a lavender handkerchief from his breast pocket, he lifted her dark glasses and dabbed at her tears.

"You have such lovely eyes, Virginia. It hurts me to see them tearful."

He replaced the glasses over her eyes and returned the handkerchief to his pocket, then took her hand in his and squeezed gently.

"Your pain will be gone in time…Come to my office…Everything will be fine."

"Thank you Dr. Radcliff."

"Robert. Please."

"Robert. I can't tell you how much it means to me to have a friend like you. Someone I can trust. I'm so frightened all the time. If he finds out what I've done…"

"Your secret is safe with me, Virginia. And you are safe as well."

She smiled weakly, looked down at his hand holding her.

Radcliff looked over her shoulder for the waitress and signaled her for another round of drinks.

Kate pointed to a child's drawing on the wall of Lenny's living room.

"Is that your kid that drew that?"

"No, we didn't have any children. Margaret had a miscarriage, but then she got sick. That was drawn by my nephew."

"Oh," Kate said softly.

"What about you? Any kids?"

"I have a six-year old daughter, Sarah. We live in the Northeast with my mother. It's great. I get enough time to study and time with Sarah, too."

"It must be quite a grind, medical school plus raising a daughter. When do you sleep?"

"Not very often," she said, laughing. "What with exams every week and having to go on rounds with the attendings and interview patients, sometimes it's not worth driving home. So I catch a few hour's sleep in the on-call room at the hospital."

Lenny picked up the last cookie from the plate. Kate looked into her cup, then at Lenny. "Do you mind if I ask you something?"

"After all I've been asking you, go ahead."

"I was wondering if you were going to keep working as a custodian, or were you studying for something else."

"Why, aren't I good at what I do?"

"No, it's not that. It's just that, who ever heard of a union delegate investigating a murder just to help his co-worker?"

"Maybe I should run for union president," Lenny said with amusement.

"I didn't mean that. I just think that you're cut out for another career. You could go to law school."

Lenny laughed. "Moss for the defense! No fee is too small to wrest justice from the court! My dad would turn over in his grave and throw up."

"Some lawyers are honest, Lenny. You wouldn't have to abandon your principles."

"They're whores, Kate. I couldn't do it."

"What about some other—"

"Kate, I love exactly what I'm doing right now. I don't mean the cleaning up shit, I mean fighting the system, going toe to toe with the bosses. I like to help people out."

"I know what you mean. That's a big part of why I went into medicine. To help people who are getting hurt. Only for them it's the disease that's hurting them. For you it's the system."

"Don't you ever come up against arrogant bosses?"

"Of course. All the time."

"How do you deal with it?"

She tightened her mouth, looked at her hands for a moment.

"I try not to let them mess with my head, but it's not easy…my daughter makes a big difference. She keeps me sane."

"I always figured kids were crazy. That's probably why I like them."

He glanced at an old gold watch hanging in a bell jar on the mantelpiece. "Jeez, it's nearly midnight. Look, I'm beat to hell and I have to work in the morning."

"I need to get some sleep, too. I better go."

Kate rose and put on her coat. She left the hood down.

At the door Lenny reached out his hand to shake hers. Kate's hand was small and moist and warm.

"So what would make a medical student come over and talk to me, a humble custodian?" Lenny's face showed an innocent look.

"It's hard to explain," she said, withdrawing her hand.

"Don't make it complicated. I'm the simple type."

"Well, my father is a fireman for the city—I told you that, I know—and my mother's a waitress at the Oak Lane Diner."

"I love that place! They have great omelets and home fries, and excellent coffee."

"Yes, the food is good. Anyway, I grew up among a lot of blue collar types, and I guess, being a first year student, I still feel uncomfortable around all those bigshot doctors. But around you…"

"You feel comfortable."

"That's right."

Lenny smiled, opened the door to the porch, and followed Kate out.

"Yeah, well, what can you say about a guy whose childhood heroes were the Three Stooges and Che Guevera?"

Kate stood in the porch facing Lenny. She looked into his plain, disarming face, his gentle, patient eyes.

"Lenny."

"Huh?"

"I've only been a medical student for six months, but I see the way the attendings make up their own rules and change them to suit their purposes. Sometimes they look at you—look at me, I mean—as if I were a smear on a slide that they could just wipe clean."

"At least they look at you," Lenny said. "Me, they look through like I wasn't there."

"Nobody could miss you, Lenny. Not once they've talked to you."

He shivered in the unheated porch, felt goose bumps on his bare arms. "So you think I should be careful."

"I do. Those doctors make life and death decisions every day, and they can be very mean-spirited. When somebody in a big position feel's threatened, well…"

"They get rid of the threat."

"Exactly."

She stepped out into the night.

Lenny stood in the open doorway. The bitter January air soothed his injured face. "Okay, I'll watch myself, but you have to do one thing for me. Don't scare me again like that."

"I'm sorry, Lenny. I promise I'll never creep up on you again."

As Kate started down the sidewalk, Lenny called after her, "By the way, who was the medical student who had the gossip about Radcliff?"

"His name is Letterly. His father's a physician on staff at James Madison, so he has a lot of contacts. Why?"

"No reason. Just curious."

Lenny watched Kate climb into her car. She drove away without looking back.

Forty-nine

Lenny was in a deep sleep when a car alarm began to scream in the street below his bedroom window. He buried his head under a pillow, fighting to stay asleep, but it was useless. The screeching sound awoke the wounds in his head and neck, sending waves of pain that rose and fell with the decibels of the alarm.

Disgusted, he threw off the quilt, lurched into the bathroom, turned on the shower and stepped in. He let the water run cold, sending shivers down his tired body, but also easing the pain in his head and neck, and driving out his fatigue.

By the time he'd toweled dry, shaved, combed his hair, and dressed, he felt he would live, at least through the weekend. The car alarm had stopped, which meant that either the owner had come out into the darkness to turn it off, or the vehicle had been stolen. Either way, Lenny couldn't care less.

Looking in the bedroom mirror, he saw that the burn on his neck had become swollen and red. He didn't think it needed a dressing—dressings were uncomfortable and ugly, so he left the burn uncovered. He remembered that the med student who had stitched his scalp had cautioned him to keep the stitches covered, so he peeled open a Band-Aid and carefully pressed it over the wound.

In the kitchen, he packed fresh espresso in the machine, frothed a cup of milk and made a double cappuccino. He cooked a pair of eggs in the microwave, then pried open a frozen bagel and dropped it in the toaster. When it popped, up he laid it on the plate and slid the eggs on top.

Taking his breakfast to the dining room, he set Moose's sketches of the suspects on the table and studied them as he ate. First, he looked at Primeaux, the angel with the wings and halo and the gun tucked in his billowing robe. There was no link between him and Virginia Racine, but there was Moose's observation about his accent being wrong. Not much to go on. He kept Primeaux as a suspect, but on the bottom of the list.

Next, Lenny looked at the witch, Priscilla Gandy. Gary had referred to her as 'labile.' She might have been sleeping with Sparks. There were those puncture wounds on the dead man's thighs and butt. Gandy could have been injecting him with that dick drug, but would she kill the man over their sex life? Lenny didn't think so.

Besides, the disposal of the body seemed too elaborate for a crime of passion. The disposal of the body was a cosmic joke on the medical establishment. Most important, there was nothing linking Gandy with Virginia Racine.

He put aside Gandy's sketch and turned to Radcliff, the vampire. Radcliff had whited out that one name, Virginia Racine, from his appointment book. What if she'd talked to him about having an abortion? If the father, or the husband, was linked to the murder, he could be trying to erase any evidence of her visit.

Did she go to him only as a patient, or was *Radcliff* the father of a baby that *she* had aborted? Maybe *she* was Sandy's mystery blonde who *was* seen on the same floor as Odom's gynecology office.

Would Radcliff kill Sparks just to cover up an affair with a married woman? It was weak. Besides, Radcliff had been squeamish about the smelly stool on the floor in Mr. Dawson's room. Lenny couldn't picture him dragging Sparks's body to the lab, draining it of blood and juicing it with preservative when he couldn't even stand to be in the same room with foul-smelling diarrhea.

Lenny made Radcliff number three, ahead of Primeaux and Gandy, but not on top.

Odom, the butcher with the meat cleavers and the bloody apron. He cut babies out of the womb, and he apparently did an abortion number on 'V.R.'—Virginia Racine? Doing abortions at night in his office was a secret that might ruin him, plus, as a surgeon, he had the skills to pickle Sparks and fake the motor vehicle wounds.

The gynecologist was a cool, deadpan character. He was capable of murder, Lenny was sure of that. But were his secrets explosive enough to drive him to kill Randy Sparks? Suppose he were caught. Would it end his career, or earn him a slap on the wrist? At worse, he'd have to change hospitals, maybe even move out of state. Would he kill to prevent that sort of problem?

He set Odom's sketch on the side, making him a prime suspect.

The last sketch was Galloway, the mad scientist in the laboratory. A perfect candidate. He had all the skills to prepare the body. Gary had described the man as a "supremely arrogant." Someone who felt he had a right to whatever he wanted.

If Galloway wasn't the father—a very big if—his ego was too big to accept being the cuckold. Or maybe he was siphoning money from that research lab of his and putting it in his pocket. Say Sparks found out and threatened to turn him in…

Lenny decided that Galloway's lab warranted a closer look. What's more, he had the feeling that Virginia Racine held the key to the case. He had to find out who she was and where she fit in to the puzzle, and then he had to convince her to talk to him.

He placed the sketches on a sideboard in the living room, put on his hat and coat and stepped out onto the porch, looking quickly into the corner to be sure no one was there waiting for him. He turned around to lock the front door, only to hear the porch door squeaking as it slowly opened.

Expecting that Kate had come by again, he turned around with a smile on his lips, only to find himself face to face with Philadelphia Police Detective Joe Williams.

Fifty

"Morning," Detective Williams said, stepping onto the porch.

"Humph," Lenny answered, pocketing his keys and stepping toward the door.

"I need to talk to you."

"I'm on my way to work. You don't want me to be late and get in trouble, do you?"

Williams blocked the doorway. In a gray trench coat buttoned to the throat, black scarf and black fedora, he looked like a throwback to an earlier period of hard-boiled detectives.

"If I wanted to, I could drag you down to the precinct and hold you for questioning. That would make you *really* late."

"Yeah, and I could clam up and not know anything, and you could get out the rubber hose and continue where the creep in the boiler room left off, and we'd both have nothing but a wasted morning."

The detective eyed him with a mix of hostility and respect. He'd learned a lot about Lenny in his interviews of hospital employees. From West, he'd heard that the union delegate was a pest and a troublemaker, but from others, the word was different. This was a tenacious shop steward who knew every unionized worker in the hospital. Someone who could help or sidetrack a murder investigation.

"Look," he said, stepping aside to let Lenny pass, "I don't want to be a hardass over this. We have a suspect in a murder case, and I've got to find out all I can about him. I do my job, just like you do."

"So why pick on me?"

"Because the word going around the hospital is that you've been trying to find out who killed Sparks, going on the assumption that Regis Devoe did not."

"I don't know anything you don't know," Lenny said, stepping out into the damp, cold morning air.

"You can talk to people we don't even know about. You must have picked up something relevant."

"I might have heard a little of gossip, but none of it was obviously tied to the murder."

He walked down to his car. Since it was parked against traffic, Philadelphia style, the driver's side was facing him. As he unlocked the door and opened it, Williams grabbed it with a gloved hand and blocked him.

"Listen, Moss, I know that people at James Madison tell you things. They trust you. I don't want to have to drag you down to the station and hold you as a material witness, but if you don't cooperate with me I'll have to. You don't want to spend the whole day in jail, do you?"

"Fuck, no. The room service is terrible and they don't have cable."

Lenny looked into the detective's stern, implacable face.

"Why do you guys always look so serious? Don't you ever make jokes or anything?"

Williams' face did not change.

"Look, all I can tell you is that Sparks was a brilliant guy who pissed off a lot of the doctors he worked for, but I haven't found anyone with a reason to kill him."

"What *did* you find?"

"You want me to spill my guts so you can pile on more shit against Regis. I know you'll turn anything I say inside out so that it makes him look bad."

"Bull-shit!" Williams slammed the car door shut and put his face so close to Lenny he could feel his breath on his face. "If you turn evidence over to me that points to somebody other than Devoe, you have my word I'll give it fair consideration."

"Sure, I find shit on some hospital big shot, someone with a lot of clout, and you're gonna let a laundry worker go free so you can bring in the VIP…Why does that sound just a lit-tle bit hollow?"

"Hey, I'm man enough to admit when I've made a mistake. Are you?"

"What do you mean?"

"I mean did it ever occur to you that maybe we're not as dumb as you think and that maybe your buddy really did kill Randy Sparks? He had the means, he worked in the morgue, remember? He had the method—all those ghoulish instruments they use for the autopsy—and he had the motive, the argument in the lobby. Plus, he had evidence on his person—the Rolex watch he claims he bought in the street. And he served time as a youth offender. So maybe you've been defending a guilty man."

"It doesn't wash, and if you were man enough, you'd admit it."

"Yeah? How come?"

"The murder was too sophisticated for a laundry worker. The whole thing smells of a sick, arrogant sense of humor. Come on. Using the medical school to dispose of the body for him was the sort of ironic joke that only a doctor would play on the rest of us."

Now it was Williams' turn to look doubtful. He stepped away from the car, leaving Lenny room to open it.

"I'll tell you this, Moss. My job is to bring in the bad guy, whether he wears blue overalls or pinstripes, and I take it seriously."

Lenny looked back at Williams. He didn't trust the cop, but he knew that if he didn't give him something, he'd be dragged down to the station and end up facing a lot tougher questions than these.

"I found out that somebody's been stealing a drug from the patients that gives you an erection for like three days. And a needle and syringe turned up in the sofa in a Dr. Gandy's waiting room. That looked funny to me, because apparently they usually give the shots in the examining room, not the waiting area."

Williams took out a notebook and began writing. "What was the name of the drug?"

"It's sounds like 'end-proz,' something like that. Go to the pharmacy, they'll tell you all about it."

"Right," Williams said. "About the doctor with the syringe in the sofa, would he normally prescribe this hard-on drug?"

"It's a 'she,'" he said, getting into the car, "and yeah, I think so, she's a urologist."

"I'll check it out," Williams said. "Anything else?"

"Nope." Lenny put his most innocent expression on his face

Williams gave him a hard look, folded his notebook, and put it in his pocket.

"If you find out more, I want you to call me. You kept my card, didn't you?"

"Of course, it's on my bedside table."

"Good," Williams said, stepping back so that Lenny could close the car door. "I'll be checking on you now and then. Don't drop out of sight."

Lenny started the car. He watched in the rear view mirror as the detective crossed the street to his unmarked police car, a Plymouth Fury with black sidewalls and no hubcaps.

Might as well put a sign on the door, 'plainclothes,' he thought, then he turned the corner and continued on to the hospital, looking in the mirror frequently to see that Williams was not following him.

On the drive, he considered who to investigate first. Surgeons often arrive at the hospital early to see their patients before going into the OR, while psychiatrists seemed to keep banker's hours, pretty much nine-to-five. He decided to visit Radcliff's office. If he could find a chart for Virginia Racine, he might get some idea of who she was and what her connection to Sparks might have been.

He drove through the parking gate into the employee's parking lot at a quarter to six. As he walked past the doctor's parking lot, he saw that there were only three cars there: a red BMW, a white Acura and an ancient, gray, Land Rover caked with mud. The frost on their windows suggested that they had been there all night.

That meant that Radcliff was definitely not at work.

A perfect time to make another visit to his office.

Fifty-one

*E*ntering the hospital through the loading dock, Lenny punched his time card, then he found Luis, the corpulent night custodian, half asleep in the locker room. He borrowed the night man's keys, that could open all the doctors' offices, and hurried upstairs.

He walked down a silent hallway. It would be a great time to do the floors. No bosses haranguing you; no troops of doctors and medical students scuffing up your work. They were lonely hours, but maybe that was what he needed. Maybe he was too busy with the union work. People constantly coming to him with work problems, trouble with the benefit fund paying on time. Family problems, fear of layoff, forced retirement...going without work and being alone.

Those were his hardest cases, the older workers. Widowed, children moved out of town. Without work, they had little reason to get up in the morning. For that matter, without his union work, what else did he have? An old car and a little house with a leaking roof. No kids. Even his mom and aunt had moved away to the Jersey shore.

What am I doing playing detective, he wondered. *I should be sitting in a diner eating breakfast, reading the Daily News. Instead...*

He stepped up to Radcliff's office door, looked up and down the empty corridor. Placing the key in the lock, he took in a breath, turned the key, heard the mechanism disengage. He entered, closed the door, and looked around.

If Radcliff treated Virginia Racine, he ought to have a chart for her. Lenny turned to the big filing cabinet behind the secretary's desk. It was locked.

"Damn." He stood considering the cabinet, wishing he knew how to pick a lock. He thought about the locked narcotic cabinet in the Seven-South nursing station. He'd noticed that the night nurse usually kept the keys in an unlocked drawer. During the day they had to carry it on a ribbon around their neck, in case the supervisor asked them where it was, but at night the supervisors didn't check that carefully.

Lenny opened a wide drawer in the secretary's desk. It was packed with all the things a secretary used, plus rolls of cough drops, gum, packets of sweet n' low. A plastic denture cup caught his eye. Thinking the secretary was too young for false teeth, he pried open the cup. Voila: a set of keys.

The smallest key opened the top drawer of the filing cabinet. He'd been thinking about what Gary had told him about VIP patients. Wouldn't they be the ones most likely to use Odom for a little nighttime problem-solving and then spill their story to a sympathetic psychiatrist?

Searching for the three patients who had the 'no c-g-e' by their names, he found charts for Thessalie Borders and Louise Maxwell, but there was none for Virginia Racine.

He unlocked the door to Radcliff's inner office with the secretary's key and stepped in. The first thing he noticed was the pale peach-colored carpet, thick and deeply padded. He had cleaned a lot of carpets. He could identify any stain, depression or wear pattern. Squatting down low, he found several colorless wet spots beside the reclining chair.

Lenny put his face down and sniffed the spots. No odor. He pressed his fingers into the carpet, then rubbed them together. They were neither greasy nor sticky, ruling out coffee, soup or sauce. The stains seemed to be only water.

He looked about the room for a water source. There was no faucet, pitcher, or drinking glass. Maybe the guy brought in bottled water. Or Perrier.

The walls were covered with beige and pink wallpaper. An oval mirror in a gilded frame hung on the wall. The surface of a small rosewood desk was covered by a sheet of smoky glass. A silver pen in a stand, digital clock and a phone nested in a group on one corner. Beside the phone was an inhaler with a vial of medicine in it. He read the name: Primeair.

Maybe Sparks had suffered from asthma, or maybe one of Radcliff's patients had left it in the office. He made a mental note to try and get a line on Sparks's medical background.

He tried the first drawer. Locked, and the secretary's keys didn't fit.

A large, deeply padded reclining chair was positioned in the middle of the room. It looked comfortable. Lenny pictured a patient leaning back in the chair, relaxing, talking. A small straightback chair beside it was doubtless the psychiatrist's perch.

A narrow black enamel shelf on the wall had two potted flowers in bloom. He touched the petals. Silk. There was a small painted bowl behind the flowerpots. He reached around and tipped it. Inside was a small, soft sponge. He held it to his nose and sniffed. It was musky. Strange. To clean the dust off the silk flowers? Maybe Radcliff was a compulsive neatnik. The office was spotless, the desk top free from debris.

This Won't Hurt A Bit

What did it all mean?

There were two video cameras, one on the wall, the other on a tripod in the corner, and a shelf with rows of video tapes. Each tape had a neatly printed label describing a clinical condition. Lenny read "bipolar personality," "anxiety-depressive," then gave up on the tapes.

Looking once more about the room, he noted that it was Spartan and functional, with nothing to distract the patient from the session.

Aside from failing to find a chart for Virginia Racine, the search appeared fruitless. Disappointed, Lenny reached for the door of the inner office. Even though there was no one around to hear, he quietly pulled the door shut.

Despite his caution, Lenny failed to notice the motion sensor in the ceiling. It was connected to the wall-mounted video camera.

Lenny not only failed to notice the security device, he failed to note the faint whir of the wall-mounted video camera that had begun taping him as soon as he had entered the room.

Fifty-two

After punching in at the time clock, Lenny went to the locker room to get ready for work. He found Abrahm polishing his work shoes, seated on a wooden bench that had been carved with countless names and epithets. He looked up as Lenny approached and smiled broadly, showing the gold caps on his molars.

"Len'nye, it is good to see you today. How is the investigation?"

"Don't ask, Abrahm."

The Russian leaned over to examine the burn on the side of Lenny's face.

"You have much pain?"

"It only hurts when I laugh…or cry… or breathe…"

"You have sick time saved up, yes? Why do you not stay home? Rest."

"I can't do it. Things are getting too hot," he said, opening his locker and removing his black work shoes.

"I understand. When the enemy surrounds you, it is not the time to close your eyes and sleep."

As Lenny set the work shoes on the floor, he noticed the florescent light reflecting off a dark shiny liquid in each one. Lenny picked up a shoe, held it up to the light. The dark substance spilled out of the shoe and onto his bare arm.

It was blood. Dark, thick, ruddy brown blood.

Lenny shuddered, and carefully placed the shoe on the floor. He examined the lock on his locker door. "Somebody must have picked the lock. Somebody with a cop's training…like Joe West."

Abrahm rose and stood beside Lenny. "It is a warning, my friend. Be careful."

"That's exactly what I thought I was doing."

Lenny carried his shoes to the bathroom, washed them and his arms under the shower. He put the shoes in a red biohazard bag and dropped it in the bottom of his locker, put on the winter boots he'd worn in to work and was about to close the locker when he stopped, reached in and rummaged among the papers and files. He methodically took everything out and returned the items one at a time, but he knew at the start it was useless.

Whoever had put the blood in his shoes had also stolen the specimen jar with the aborted fetus from Odom's office.

Lenny cursed, slammed the locker shut, and tramped off to the ward.

A group of medical students was selling coffee and bagels in the lobby of the medical school, raising money for a neighborhood clinic. Kate saw Jennie buying an herbal tea and croissant and went up to her.

"Jenny! Got a minute?"

"Hi Katie. Are we reviewing over lunch again?"

"Sure. Listen, I was wondering…You and Randy Sparks were seeing each other. He didn't say anything about getting in trouble or having a problem with one of the attendings, anything like that, did he?"

"No, Kate, he was his usual self. Always in a hurry and making plans. He got this hot research grant in Washington with the NIH. I knew he wasn't taking me with him when he left."

"When was the last time you saw him?"

"It was right before he disappeared. He said he had a tape he wanted to watch but his VCR was broken and could he use mine, and I said sure, I was going out to a lecture, but he could use it, so he came over to my place."

"I don't suppose he left the tape with you?"

"Katie, Of course he didn't. I'd have given it to the police a long time ago. Why?"

"Just wondering."

"That Letterly has been giving me funny looks. I think he knows I was close to Randy."

"I don't think so, Jen. He'd have blabbed it all over the school by now."

"That's true."

"He's probably…"

A trio of tall, beefy students appeared around a corner with Letterly in the middle.

"Speak of the devil," Jennifer whispered.

The students were laughing over something. Letterly said, "Wait, did you hear about the proctologist who always used two fingers when he did a rectal exam? He told the patients it gave them a second opinion."

The two companions burst out into loud guffaws. Kate elbowed her way between them and walked on to the lecture hall.

Jennifer slipped past without looking Letterly in the eye and sat beside her friend.

As she settled into her seat in the lecture hall, Kate thought about Jennifer's words, that if Randy Sparks left a VCR tape at Jenny's place, she didn't know anything about it. That didn't mean there was nothing there, only that Jennifer never thought to look.

As the lecturer strode toward the podium, Jennifer leaned over and whispered, "Meet for lunch at one and we can review before the anatomy quiz?"

"I'll be there," said Kate.

They pulled out notebooks and pens to copy the slide on the giant screen at the front of the hall, while the lecturer began, "Today, we will become familiar with the choroid plexus...."

Sitting at the Seven-South nursing station, Gary Tuttle was worried about Mr. Oldenfield. He had examined the man's foot with the doppler for several minutes, but been unable to find any pulse. The foot was mottled and cold. Even worse, the patient had developed a fever of 103 degrees, and his speech was rambling and confused.

Gary was certain that the man's foot was infected, and that the infection was spreading through the blood stream to his brain. He dialed the number for the surgery resident's pager, and sat impatiently waiting for an answer.

Finally, the phone rang. He picked it up before the first ring had finished.

"Mercer, surgery. What is it?"

"This is Gary Tuttle on Seven-South. Listen, Mr. Oldenfield's foot is mottled and cold and has no pulse. Does Dr. Galloway know about this?"

The resident said, "The on-call man last night told us about it in morning report. What do you want from me?"

"I want to know what to do for him. The man is becoming delirious and he has a fever of one-oh-three. I think he's becoming septic."

"You may be right," the resident said. "I'll make room for him on the surgery schedule. We'll have to amputate the foot. Get a blood count and type him for two units, and pack his leg in ice. I'll be up to see him as soon as I can break scrub."

"Okay," Gary said, and hung up. He felt anger and anxiety. Finally, the foot was coming off, and the lower leg as well. If only the operation eliminated the infection before it spread to his major organs. If it didn't...

This Won't Hurt A Bit

He considered calling Mrs. Oldenfield to notify her of the operation, but knew she came in early every morning and was probably in transit already. She would probably arrive before the OR called for the patient.

Fifty-three

Lenny spotted Gary, looking unusually glum, coming down the hall toward him. Before he could say anything, Gary called to him,

"Say Lenny, would you mind packing some ice into this bag for me?"

"Sure, Tuttle." Lenny took the bag to the pantry, ran the ice machine until the bag was a third full, then he brought it back to Gary.

In the room, Lenny watched Gary pull the covers back from over a canopy on the bed. With gloved hands Gary picked up the mottled leg with the purple foot and black toes.

"Put the bag there," Gary said, indicating the foot of the bed. Lenny laid the bag of ice in the bed and Gary pushed the lifeless limb deep into the ice. The nurse wrapped towels around the thigh and tied the bag tightly around them, then he pulled the covers up over the canopy.

"The ice will slow the spread of the infection until they can amputate," Gary said.

Lenny pictured the leg severed at the hip and packed like a huge fish in a tray of ice and shuddered.

Out in the hall, Gary asked what was happening with the investigation. Lenny told him his instincts pointed to Odom and Galloway but that he couldn't rule out the others. Gary stood quietly, looking pensive.

"You look down in the dumps, Tuttle. Something bothering you?"

"I can't shake this feeling that there's some disaster brewing. There's the trash can fire and the thefts from the nursing station, and the attacks on you."

"It has been pretty exciting around here."

"I wish you would turn everything you have over to the police."

"That doesn't seem too likely now. Especially since I just broke into Radcliff's filing cabinet."

"You did what?" Gary looked as though police would swoop down and handcuff both of them at any minute.

"Jeez, Tuttle, these doctors aren't going to leave their shit lying around for us to step in. We have to dig a little."

"But going through a doctor's files…"

"Come on, I wouldn't be a real detective without a little breaking and entering, would I? Besides, we go into doctor's offices all the time to clean their toilets. I just decided to run a dust rag over his charts, too."

Gary took a deep breath, blew it out, nodded. "I suppose you have to gather information, but I have to tell you, that sort of thing makes me awfully uncomfortable."

"Don't worry, I'm very careful. Besides, nobody notices a custodian." He followed Gary as the nurse left the computer station and went back to the medication room. "By the way, I found an inhaler in the doctor's office. It was something called Prime-air. What is that, for asthma?"

"Yes, it's an asthma medication. Sometimes it's prescribed for emphysema or chronic bronchitis. It's a broncodilator. It opens the airways so the patient can get a full breath."

"Did Sparks have asthma?"

"Not as far as I know. Was there a prescription label with a name on the bottle? That would tell you who it belonged to."

"No, nothing," Lenny said.

Gary closed the door to the medication room, then turned to Lenny. "Remember that urologic drug I told you about? The one that's been missing?"

"Yeah."

"We lost another pack of them sometime on the evening shift."

"See anybody suspicious hanging around the station?"

"That's just it." Gary's face took on a look of gloom. His soft features seemed to sag, as if under a burden. "I found Alex Primeaux hunting through the leftover box of meds. Doctors go through it all the time. Even supervisors dig around for pills, so I'm sure it doesn't mean anything, but I knew you'd want to know about anything unusual. Not that it was unusual, just an odd coincidence."

"You can't see Primeaux having way-out sexual escapades, can you?"

"I really can't."

"Is he married?"

"No."

"How come?"

"I've wondered about that from time to time, and I just don't know."

"Well don't feel bad, I don't understand much about this case, either." He leaned against the counter in the little room, crossed his arms, looked at the nurse. "My problem is, if I don't make sense of this case, Regis Devoe is going to spend a long time in a very small room."

Lenny left the station and turned his attention to the ward, which was badly in need of sweeping and mopping. There were long black streaks on the floor from a dirty wheel of a cart that someone had carelessly pushed though. Lenny didn't have the time to strip the whole floor and wax it, a major job that took the whole morning. He sprayed the streaks with Stainout and cleaned them up, while nurses, patients in wheelchairs, doctors, and what seemed like the entire hospital staff walked through the area.

While Lenny was at work, Dr. Radcliff came out of Mrs. Grey's room and strode toward the Seven-South station, where he found Dr. Gandy at the station.

"Good morning Priscilla."

"Why Nathan, how nice to see you. Isn't it a magnificent day?" Her face lit up like a mountain lioness who has just savored the body of a young deer.

"You're awfully chipper this morning. Did you bring somebody back from the dead?"

"No, I'm just relishing the challenges of my work. My patient with prostate cancer is responding well. His weight is up three pounds."

"That's encouraging," Radcliff said.

"I've got a TURP in fifteen minutes. Have to fly!"

She moved away with a jaunty walk, her long, slender arms swinging freely.

Radcliff noticed Gary with his back to the station recording physician orders.

"Gary, Mrs. Dawson's roommate has had diarrhea and its dribbled all along the floor. I can't interview a patient in a room that smells like that. I want it cleaned up right away."

Gary pressed the button on the ward intercom and paged Lenny to the desk. When he came to the station, Gary said, "Lenny, Dr. Radcliff has a problem with diarrhea in Mrs. Dawson's room. Could you take care of it?"

Lenny grinned at the double meaning of Gary's words and saluted the nurse. "On the double, Tuttle," he said, turning with a military precision. As he stepped away from the station he saw the penetrating blue eyes of the psychiatrist looking through him as if he were a pane of glass. He felt a wave of dread pass over him.

After Lenny left the station, Radcliff picked up the phone. "Operator, page Dr. Galloway for me."

Gary busied himself with charts. When the phone rang, Radcliff grabbed it before Gary could reach it.

"Nathan? Robert."

The psychiatrist put his hand over the mouthpiece and glared at Gary,

This Won't Hurt A Bit

who moved out of earshot. Gary returned to the medication room, leaving the door open, but the psychiatrist spoke so softly he could not hear much of the conversation.

Gary failed to hear Radcliff say, "Nathan, I had a break-in at my office this morning that I think you should know about."

Fifty-four

At ten-fifteen, Gary walked to Mr. Oldenfield's room, sat on the side of his bed, and read aloud the pre-operative checklist.

"Dentures out?"

Mr. Oldenfield opened his mouth wide, revealing bare gums.

"Check. ID bracelet on?"

The patient held up a wrist with the plastic band in place.

"Check. Antibiotic given?"

Gary looked up to note that the little intravenous bag was empty.

"Check. Didn't eat or drink anything this morning?"

Oldenfield rubbed his stomach, indicating hunger.

"Okay, you're ready. The orderly will be up in a moment. How do you feel?"

"The leg hurts. Seems like all it does is hurt."

Gary sat looking at his patient.

"Do you want me to call home and tell your wife you've gone for the procedure?"

"No, son, she'll likely be on the way here anyway. Besides, I'll get through it all right. I have to. If I die she'll have nobody to fuss over. She's the sort of woman who needs that."

"How long have you been married?"

"We're coming up to our fiftieth anniversary." He patted Gary's arm.

"You're a nice boy, Gary. Tell that doctor to cut me at the knee if he has to, just get me out of this hospital."

Gary tucked the chart half under Oldenfield's pillow where the orderly would see it.

"You know they don't listen to nurses, Mr. Oldenfield."

"I know, son... I know."

Lester, the surgical orderly, rolled a stretcher into the room. He was a tall young man with a broad, friendly face who wore his green surgical cap at a jaunty angle, like a sailor on leave.

Gary helped Lester transfer the patient over. "Good luck, Mr. Oldenfield."

This Won't Hurt A Bit

The patient grimaced, crossed his arms across his chest. As Lester wheeled him out of the room, Gary stripped the linen from the bed.

In the corridor, Lenny hardly noticed Lester pushing the stretcher down the hall. He was thinking about abortions. They were usually done in the operating room, and they were legal in Pennsylvania. Why would a woman go to Odom's office and have it done secretly at night? So the husband wouldn't find out…Because it wasn't his baby?

If Odom had been servicing some VIP types and Sparks found out about it, that could embarrass a lot of people with clout. Lenny knew about hospital politics. He knew the board of directors were the ones who ran the hospital, even though none of the workers or patients ever saw them or could read the minutes from their meetings. They liked to work behind the scenes, in secrecy.

Secrets. That's what this case was all about. He had to get behind the doctors' facades and get a look at their dirty laundry. Who they saw, when they saw them, and not the official versions. He thought of dates, appointments, hours.

As Gary come out of Oldenfield's room with a bundle of dirty linen, Lenny patted the date book in his hip pocket.

"Ya know Tuttle, I can't remember anything without looking in my date book. These doctors are going from hospital to hospital all the time. I bet they write everything down or they'll never know where they're supposed to be."

"That's true," Gary said, "their schedules must get confusing."

"So I bet Odom puts everything he plans to do in his personal datebook. Even those late night rendezvous with the women wanting a hush-hush abortion."

"Odom wouldn't be dumb enough to put an illegal abortion in his office appointment book," Gary said.

"No, not there, but I bet he keeps a personal one like this," he said, holding up a battered old leather date book, "and puts all his private appointments in it."

"How in the world do you plan to get a look at Odom's personal calendar?"

"I don't know, Tuttle, but there's got to be a way."

Lenny pictured Odom going into surgery. He imagined the man changing into his green scrub suit, hanging his suit jacket in a tall, skinny locker.

"The locker room. He's got to leave it in his locker when he's in surgery."

Lenny hurried after Lester, with Gary following behind. He found the orderly with Mr. Oldenfield waiting for the service elevator.

"Say, Les, when the surgeons put on their scrub suit where do they put their clothes?"

"Each of em's got his own locker. They don't cotton to sharing no locker with somebody else. Why?"

"I suppose once in a while one of them forgets his key, doesn't he?" Lenny asked.

"Sure. Happens all the time."

"Who in the OR has a skeleton key for the lockers?"

Lester fished out a large steel ring thick with keys.

"I do, plus the supervisor, Nellie, and Bandy, the other orderly." Lester looked at Lenny and raised one eyebrow. "I bet this has got something to do with that murder thing you and Moose are doing, don't it?"

Lenny drew Lester aside.

"I need to look at Dr. Odom's personal date book—the one he'd most likely carry in his jacket pocket. Is he in doing surgery?"

"Come to think of it, Dr. Odom just started a case a couple a' minutes ago."

"Would you be willing to let me into his locker?" Lenny asked.

"I have no problem with that. If you come up right now I can let you in."

Gary tugged on Lenny's arm.

"Are you sure about this, Lenny? You could be fired for going into a doctor's locker and the union wouldn't be able to help you."

"So I'll defend myself in the grievance hearing. I'll say I was searching for roach droppings or something."

Gary's lips were squeezed tight, his eyes squinted. "I'm serious, Lenny. Please don't do this. You can't help Regis if you're fired."

"And I can't get him out of jail unless I find out the truth. The killer isn't gonna leave clues out in the open like bread crumbs on the ground."

"But Lenny…"

"Tuttle, it's something I have to do."

Gary released Lenny's arm, took a step back.

"Well be careful," he said. "Please. Remember what Joe West told you."

"I'll be careful. No one notices a simple custodian, right?"

As Lenny followed Lester into the elevator, Gary watched with a growing sense of gloom.

Fifty-five

While Lenny stood in the Operating Room hallway, Lester went into the doctor's locker room to see if it was empty. After a moment, the orderly stuck his head out of the door and beckoned to Lenny.

Once inside, Lester took Lenny to a locker and unlocked it. "As soon as you get what you need, shut the door and it'll be locked. I've got to get back."

"Okay, I will."

"And keep an eye on that other door. That's where the doctors come in from surgery."

"I will," Lenny said softly. "Thanks."

"One for us, man."

Lester hurried through the other door that opened directly into the operating rooms.

Lenny reached into the locker and found Odom's suit coat. As he'd guessed, a thick leather book was in the inside pocket. He drew it out, gently pushed the door so that it was nearly closed but had not latched, and went into the bathroom. He entered a stall, closed the door and sat examining the datebook.

There were numerous evening appointments, some with names spelled out, others with initials or addresses. He flipped back to the second week of December. It was a busy week, with entries, some crossed out, filling every slot.

Then he found it. 'V.R.' was entered with a circle around it, and the date. Son of a bitch! December thirteen at 8 PM, the same day that Virginia Racine's name was whited out in Radcliff's appointment book. After the name there was what looked like a Greek letter—a kind of 'O' with a line across it. He had no idea what that meant.

In his years representing hospital workers he had learned that when somebody covered up a fact, the fact was always damning to him, and usually for the institution as well. He had a feeling that Virginia Racine, whoever she was, was a link in the chain.

Lenny closed the book, stood and peeked out through the crack in the door of the stall. Seeing no one about, he stepped out into the bathroom. He was halfway to the locker room when two young doctors in scrub suits, mask and caps strode in from the operating rooms, pulled off their masks and sat down on a bench.

"Man, did you see the way Galloway chewed out that poor nurse this morning in Room Three? I never saw him get *that* angry before, did you?" the first doctor asked.

"Never," said the second. "I was scrubbing at the sink and could hear him in the hall, so I went over to look and I thought for a minute he was going to kill the nurse, the way he was waving a scalpel and screaming at her."

As the doctors talked, not noticing Lenny, he bent down and began picking up the disposable paper caps and masks which had been strewn about the floor. He dropped a handful of them in the trash basket in the middle of the room while warily watching the doctors, who were pulling off their paper booties, taking their time.

"Even if it was her fault and she handed him the wrong guide wire, that wasn't what ruined the procedure. Did you see that poor old man's foot? It needs to come off. No way is he going to save those digits."

"Well, don't try and suggest anything to Galloway. He'll bounce you out of the program so fast, you'll be lucky to get a podiatry internship in Sri Lanka."

Lenny began to feel increasingly anxious. He didn't see how he was going to return the appointment book as long as these two were in the room. He glanced at Odom's locker, just open a hair, not enough to catch anyone's eye. He could wait around hoping the doctors would leave, but if more of them came in someone might notice Lenny and connect him with the locker.

If I leave now, Lenny thought, Odom will know someone was poking around his stuff, but at least he won't know it's me.

Wait or split. The doctors on the bench were taking their sweet time dressing. Lenny had picked up all the paper debris from the locker room floor and had no further excuse for being in there.

Deciding he could wait no longer, Lenny slipped the leather datebook under a pile of soiled scrub suits that lay beneath one of the benches, then he walked casually past Odom's locker, letting out a noisy cough as he deftly elbowed the locker door closed. He retreated to the bathroom, where he began pulling out the liner to the big trash receptacle there.

Suddenly a gaggle of doctors entered from the operating suite. They, too, began pulling off their masks and caps.

One young resident asked a short, stern-looking fellow, "How long

This Won't Hurt A Bit

have you been using the video-laparoscopes, Dr. Odom? They sure make it nice for us to see the field."

Walking to his locker, Odom replied, "We have had the video system for two years. Before that, we did the procedure under direct visualization."

As one of the residents bent over to remove his shoes, he noticed the leather datebook sticking out from under the scrub gowns. Holding it up above his head, he called out, "Anybody here lose an appointment book?"

Odom walked over to the resident and silently removed the book from the young man's hand. He looked first at the book, then, his locker. Wordlessly he unlocked his locker and placed the appointment book back in the suit pocket.

As Odom continued dressing, Lenny tried to walk casually by him and the other doctors. Their eyes felt like a CAT scan making images of his brain...his thoughts...his intentions. He wondered how many people knew that he was investigating the Sparks murder. Joe West certainly did. It looked as though one of the suspects was on to him as well.

He opened the door to leave and looked out of the corner of his eye. Odom was still staring at him. The doctor knew who had been looking at his appointment book, and there was nothing Lenny could do about it.

Hurrying back to Seven-South, Lenny felt for the first time that his job was in jeopardy. He had learned the art of bluffing from years of union negotiations. But bluffing a killer was a tad riskier than going toe-to-toe with Childress in a grievance hearing. His palms were moist and he couldn't trust his voice.

He wished that he could keep Moose closer to him. He wished that he had taken a lower profile. He wished that his father were alive to encourage and guide him. He wished he could go back to being a simple custodian. He didn't feel that he had the toughness to fight the way his father had done. Argue a contract? Fine. Defend a worker in front of the boss? No problem. But making as many enemies as he had done was wearing down his confidence.

As he walked down the corridor, he found Gary stuffing a handful of dirty linen into a laundry bag. The sickly odor of infected stool left a trail in the air behind him.

"Hey Tuttle, I made it back without taking any casualties. You feel better?"

Gary's face was deeply lined with worry. He told Lenny of the snippet of conversation he'd heard between Radcliff and Galloway.

Lenny groaned. "You didn't actually hear Radcliff say my name, did you?"

"No, I didn't actually hear that, but—"

"Well, I don't see how he could know about my visit to his office this morning. Nobody saw me, I made sure of that."

Looking like he was going to his own funeral, Gary took Lenny's arm, led him back to the medication room, and closed the door. He focused his pale blue eyes on Lenny's face.

"Lenny, I have a concern I'd like to share with you."

Grinning, Lenny said, "Why do nurses always 'share' their thoughts? Why can't they just say it like normal people?"

"This is serious, Lenny."

"I'm sorry, Tuttle. Go on."

"It seems to me that, as we continue with this investigation, the killer is going to get wind of what we are doing. He may very well know about what we're doing already. If he does—or she, in the case of Dr. Gandy—mightn't that spur the killer to kill again?"

"Are you worried about being the next victim?"

"No, not really. I'm worried more about *you*. But, to be truthful, I'm getting more and more concerned about Virginia Racine."

Fifty-six

"You lost me, Tuttle. You think I'm not in danger, but Virginia Racine is? How come?"

"If she's at the center of this, as you've suggested, she could become a target of the killer, don't you think?"

"I never thought about that." Lenny rubbed his chin, feeling the stubble. He remembered he needed new blades for his razor. Had needed them for a week.

"What are you going to do next?" Gary asked.

Lenny looked into the trusting, anxious eyes of his friend.

"I guess I better find her before the killer does. Any ideas?"

"I've been thinking about that," Gary said. "If Racine was ever treated by a physician at James Madison, her name would likely be in the computer data bank."

"Good thinking. Can you check it out?"

Gary brought up the outpatient file and typed in Racine, Virginia. There were no patients listed under that name.

"Maybe she had a prescription filled," Gary said. "I'll check the pharmacy file."

"You can do that?"

"I'm not supposed to have the access code, but one of the techs gave it to us so we can check on our patients' drug profiles. I can use it to access outpatients as well."

Lenny stood looking over the screen as Gary scrolled down lists of names. Racine's name failed to appear in the pharmacy list. He rubbed his chin, felt the stubble and the swollen area on his neck, which was beginning to throb again.

"Tuttle, you said the No-Charge patients were VIP's. What if Virginia Racine was a doctor's wife? They're the most VIP-ish of all, right?"

"I suppose so."

"In that case, her name would have to be in the files that the doctors fill out for their health insurance. Right?"

"Yes..."

"Well, I think I know someone who can help me check it out. And you'll be happy to know, I won't have to do any breaking in."

"But Lenny—"

Hurrying away, he called over his shoulder, "If West comes by, tell him I've gone for supplies."

He moved quickly to the stairwell in the middle of the hall. Hurrying down the steps to the Human Resources Office, he thought that, for a guy who'd been reluctant to even give Lenny a list of doctors, Tuttle was becoming a big part of the investigation. He might be soft on fighting the system, but he was turning out to be a solid friend.

He took the stairs to the first floor, crossed the main lobby, and passed the information desk, where a line of people waited for visitor's passes. Some had colorful balloons and boxes of candy. A pair of small children punched one of the balloons back and forth at each other until their mother told them to knock it off.

He turned a corner and walked down a corridor past Billing and Social Services to the personnel office, now renamed Human Resources. When they had changed the title a couple of years ago Lenny suggested that they simply call it "Wage Slaves," but the suggestion never got very far.

Just inside the door, a line of cubbyholes hugged the wall where applicants were interviewed and filled out their paperwork. He went straight back to an old desk piled with manila folders, scraps of paper, a large Rolodex and a phone with one of those rubber pieces that let you hold the receiver up to your ear without getting a crick in the neck.

Iris Modina, an elderly clerk who had worked at James Madison for decades, was seated behind the desk leafing through a stack of papers. She was a short, white woman with granny glasses, a prim, loose white blouse buttoned to the neck, and a large glittering diamond pin. Everyone assumed the pin was fake, but Lenny knew better. Once he and Iris had worked together at a union-sponsored Christmas party. After she'd had a few drinks, Iris had confided that she took secret glee in knowing that the diamonds were real. "I don't want everyone to know. They'd think I was a big show-off, but I trust you, Lenny."

Hanging up the phone, Iris smiled warmly up at the custodian. "Hello, Lenny. Are you here on union business, or just come to brighten an old lady's day?"

"You'll never be old, Iris."

"Well, my bones are getting older… every year. What can I do for you?"

"This is kind of an unusual request, even for me."

"Is it about the Sparks murder?"

"Jeez, does the whole hospital know I'm looking into that?"

"I can't speak for the everybody, dear, but there's precious little that goes on around here that old Iris doesn't hear about. How is that young man doing that the police arrested."

Lenny sat on the edge of Iris's desk. "Regis Devoe. He had a run-in with a few of the prison guards, so I'd really like to get this investigation finished and spring him."

"If I can help in any way, I will."

"Well, I'm trying to trace a woman who came to visit a patient but never got from the information desk to the ward. Her name is Virginia Racine. I need to know if she's the wife of one of these doctors." He showed Iris his list of the five suspects.

"You want me to cross-check her name against the doctors and see if she's related, is that right?"

"Right. The woman is apparently tall, and she could be a blonde, although I'm not sure of that. Can you do it for me?"

"Sure I can to it. Let me see," she said, "the maiden names would be listed in their insurance forms, and, if not there, then it might be on their tax form. Everybody fills those things out."

Iris reached for her cane and eased herself out of her chair. "Why don't you run along. It wouldn't do for someone to come along and find you looking over my shoulder at confidential files. I'll call you if I come up with anything."

"Thanks, Iris. I'll be on my floor."

She stepped over to one of several large file cabinets, leaned her cane against the side of the cabinet, and pulled out a drawer.

At the Seven-South nursing station, Alex Primeaux sat looking over Mrs. Rosemond's lab reports for the third time that day. He frowned, scratched his knee, underlined the hemoglobin value.

"I just don't understand what's wrong with this woman's GI tract," he said aloud in his soft southern drawl. "She has traces of blood in her stool but no iron deficiency, no microcytic anemia."

Gary stepped out of the medication room. "What about a nose bleed. Did you check for that?"

"O' course. I had ENT look at her. They checked under her tongue for tumors as well. I'm just plain stumped."

Primeaux closed the chart. "I think I'll mosey on down and look in on her."

"She was in the bathroom bathing the last time I was down there," Gary said.

The doctor ambled down to Rosemond's room. Entering without knocking, he saw the closed bathroom door and was about to knock, when a flicker of suspicion made him stop.

Silently he turned the knob and peeked into the bathroom. Rosemond was sitting on the toilet, her thumb in her mouth, sucking hard at it. When she saw Primeaux she stopped and removed her thumb from her mouth. A drop of scarlet blood oozed from beneath her thumbnail.

Primeaux frowned, grinned, laughed. "Why you sly old dog. You've been faking that blood in your stool all along, haven't you?"

Mrs. Rosemond burst into tears. Her massive body shook in waves of sobbing. She stood, her great body heaving like a troubled sea.

"Oh Dr. Primeaux, I'm sorry, I really am truly sorry. No one has ever found anything wrong with my tests and so I had to find something that would keep me in the hospital until they found out what the real problem was!"

Primeaux turned and walked back to the nursing station. He flicked open Rosemond's chart and wrote in the Physician's Orders: "Discharge patient immediately to home."

"Gary," he called out, "will you please ask Social Service to arrange for a cab to take Mrs. Rosemond home? I'm discharging her right now. She can wait in the lobby downstairs for her ride."

"Sure," Gary said, "as soon as the surgery resident writes the transfer orders. I need to get Mr. Oldenfield to the ICU. Did you finally make the diagnosis?"

"I sure did. That old woman was sticking needles under her fingernails and sucking the blood and swallowing it. The blood went into her stool, and that's how come she had the occult positive and the slight anemia."

"She sucked her fingers for blood? That's crazy!"

"Crazy like a fox," Primeaux said.

"Maybe we should have Dr. Radcliff see her before she's sent home?" Gary asked.

Primeaux handed Gary the chart. "She can see a psychiatrist all she wants—on an out-patient basis. She's history."

He signed the discharge order with an uncharacteristic flourish.

"I'm due in the employee clinic. If she's not gone in an hour, please call security and tell them to escort her from the building. I don't care how cold it is, she won't spend another night in here."

Moose, who had been in the little pantry across from the nursing station, had heard the doctor talking with Gary. He watched as Primeaux turned and walked down the hall and out of sight. He wondered why, if he was from North Carolina, the man knew the name of Little Rock's ball club, but not Durham's.

"He's full of shit," Moose grumbled. "And he ain't no saint, either."

Fifty-seven

Joe West leaned back in his chair and held the phone to his ear. Joe Williams, the detective, had just filled him in on the investigation, ending with his visit to Lenny Moss that morning. West said, "I may have some more evidence for you soon. I'm having someone go over the male lockers in housekeeping. I know for a fact the locker I emptied out didn't belong to Devoe."

"Don't your people keep a record of who owns which locker?"

"Sure we keep one, but they're always changing lockers, moving locks, trying to trick us. I told Docksett to get a name on every locker nailed down, and then find out which one has no name on it. If it turns out not to be Devoe's you may have to get a search warrant for the whole damn bunch of them."

"That may be a problem. There's a first amendment issue that the union will go to court over."

"That's okay. I'll have run through every locker before their lawyer gets off the phone."

"Well let me know if you find anything, but don't tell me how you did it."

"Hey, you scratch my back. Know what I mean?"

Williams hung up.

West sat forward, cradled the phone and opened a desk drawer. He took out an cigar and held it up to his nose. Even through the wrapper he could smell the deep aroma of the tobacco. He gently laid it on the corner of his desk, expecting that he would treat himself today to a good long cigar, as soon as he'd fired Lenny Moss' ass.

In the Human Resources Office, the young secretary who worked with Iris said she was going for a coffee break and did Iris want anything?

"No thank you dear, I'll hold down the fort while you're gone. Take your time, now."

As soon as the young woman had gone, Iris placed the five files which she had removed from the filing cabinet reserved for doctors and management on the middle of her desk. She opened the file for Doctor Odom and leafed through it. Odom's wife was a redhead, blue-eyed, thirty-eight years old. Five feet seven, one-hundred twenty pounds. Her maiden name was Brenda Olivette.

"That's one down," she said, placing Odom's file to the side.

She opened Primeaux's chart. The doctor was not married.

"That's two down." She set the chart aside.

Radcliff's wife turned out to be a Dorothy Higgins—a tall blonde. Judging by her stated weight of one-hundred and five pounds, she was probably anorexic. She placed Radcliff's file with the other rejects.

Iris looked briefly over Priscilla Gandy's chart. You never knew, she could have a sister whose married name was Racine. Or perhaps Gandy was her married name and she was originally a Racine. The section for next of kin listed two brothers, but no sister. She had no children. Gandy was her maiden name.

Her chart joined the others in the reject pile.

Galloway, the last file to be opened, gave up the prize. Under spouse, maiden name, it read 'Virginia Racine.'

Scanning the sheet containing biographical data, she learned that Virginia was younger than Galloway, born August 12, 1960—typical second wife. She was a tad short at five-feet six, and was a brunette, with hazel eyes. But a wig and high heels could turn her into the blonde that Sandy had described disappearing into the hospital last December.

This was the woman that Lenny was seeking, no doubt about it.

Iris looked next at Galloway's records. He was even older than he looked: born in 1937. That made him sixty-three. He came on staff at James Madison in 1980.

She noticed that where the other files were slim, this one was thicker than the others. Looking through it, she found a large number of insurance claim forms. Many of them were claims paid to Children's Hospital. Galloway's son, Jason, had been hospitalized several times, beginning soon after birth and continuing for the first several years.

The claim forms were hard for her to decipher, since she wasn't a nurse. They were filled with a lot of arcane abbreviations and terms she didn't understand. The child had had several operations, that much was apparent. The word 'cardiac anomaly' struck her eye. There was an operation on his colon, as well. The costs were incredible, adding up to hundreds of thousands of dollars.

She took the file to the copy machine. Being sure no one was about, she copied the face sheet with the vital statistics. She folded the single piece of paper into thirds, placed it in an envelope, licked the flap and sealed it, then she labeled it 'LM' and placed it in her pocket book. Finally, she locked her purse in her desk drawer and returned the files to their proper place.

A moment later, her assistant returned with coffee and a bagel. Once she'd settled into her desk, Iris said, "You know Judy, that coffee of yours smells so delicious, I think I will take a little break after all."

"I thought you didn't drink coffee, Iris. Doesn't it upset your stomach?"

"A body's got to take a few chances, doesn't she?"

She reached for her cane, slung her pocket book over her shoulder and set off for Seven-South.

When she reached the seventh floor, Iris walked slowly down the corridor peeking in the rooms looking for Lenny. She stepped away from a doorway as a stretcher with a patient rolled out of a room. She didn't see Lenny until she got to the end, where she spied him mopping a room.

Iris looked up and down the corridor. No one seemed to be paying any attention to an old lady with a cane. *There were so many of us*, she thought, *and we're not in charge of anything.*

Lenny saw her in the doorway. When she winked at him, he knew he'd hit pay dirt.

"Come on in, Iris, nobody's here," he told her, "but mind the floor, it's wet."

"That's all I need is to fall down and break my hip, thank you very much." She held onto the wall with one hand and used the cane to feel how slippery the floor was. "Good thing I have a rubber tip on my cane."

Just inside the doorway, she opened her purse and pulled out the envelope. As she placed it in Lenny's hand, she whispered, "Mrs. Galloway."

Lenny's eyes widened, his dark eyebrows knitted in a frown.

"Son of a bitch. I heard he had a trophy wife. I'll be damned."

He folded the envelope and shoved it into his back pocket.

"Thanks, Iris. I can't tell you how much this means to me. And to Regis, too. At first I didn't think we'd have much of a chance pulling off this investigation, but now I know we're getting somewhere."

"Did Galloway kill Randy Sparks?" she asked.

"I haven't got that far yet. I have to get to his wife somehow and find out what it's all about. I haven't exactly figured out how to approach her, but…"

"Everyone talks to you Lenny. Everyone who matters, anyway. Keep me posted how things are going, will you?"

"Of course."

She turned slowly and carefully around, planted her cane on the marble floor and eased her way out of the room. She gave a little wave of her hand without turning back as she went on her way.

Lenny wheeled his mop and bucket to the utility closet, where he saw Betty loading facial tissues and toilet paper into her cart. He told her what he'd learned from Iris and that he was going to go down to Galloway's lab to see what he could find out.

"Watch your back, Lenny. I know West is gunning for you."

"I will. Cover for me."

"Like I always do," she said. "And I'll be praying for you, too."

He wheeled his mop and bucket to the transportation elevators at the back of Seven-South, punched the down button and waited, scanning the hall and hoping he didn't catch sight of Joe West.

Fifty-eight

*I*f Virginia Galloway was the 'V.R.' in Odom's appointment book, she probably had the abortion. Jealousy was a powerful emotion, and Galloway had a colossal ego, not to mention a fiery temper. Doctors make life and death decisions every day. It wouldn't be a stretch for one of them to decide on someone who wasn't sick but who was in his way.

If Virginia had been having an affair with Sparks, she probably was terrified that her husband would find out. She confided in Radcliff, and somehow Galloway heard about it. Galloway became insanely jealous and killed Sparks to punish his wife.

If Virginia Galloway was the mystery woman, and if she would trust Lenny enough to talk…There were more if's and what-if's than at the beginning of contract negotiations.

He rode the elevator to the forth floor and pushed his mop and bucket out into the hallway, where he saw a sign on the wall that read **"VASCULAR LAB"** with an arrow pointing to the right. He continued on through an empty hallway with several closed doors on either side. At last, he came upon a brass plate on the door that read, **"VASCULAR RESEARCH LABORATORY. DR. NATHAN GALLOWAY, DIRECTOR."** Lenny put on his most guileless look, raised his hand, and rapped three times on the door to the lab. He heard a woman's voice say, "Come in."

He found himself facing a slender young woman in a blue scrub suit. She had short-cropped dark hair, a narrow face, and a friendly smile.

"Hi," she said, glancing at Lenny's mop and bucket. "Come to do the floors, eh? Great."

As Lenny pushed his bucket past her he read the name tag on her shirt. 'Melissa Singleton-Respiratory Therapist.'

"I'm just setting up for the next patient," she said. "Can you work around me?"

"Sure. I'll do that side of the room first. Is that okay.'"

"Great," she said, uncoiling cables from a monitor and plugging them in to an outlet on the side of the tank. She glanced at her watch. "You've got time, the patient's not due for twenty minutes." She brought linen over to the large, oval hyperbaric tank and spread a sheet inside it.

Lenny plunged his mop into the soapy water and spread it in broad sweeps along a section of the floor.

"It looks like you don't get a whole lot of traffic on this floor," he said. "Up on the ward the floors are a mess all the time."

"Some weeks are busy. Lately it's been pretty light. We might see more docs than patients down here."

"I guess that big tank is where you treat them."

"It's a big pressure chamber is all it is. Like for divers when they get the bends? We squeeze extra oxygen into their tissues. It helps wounds heal."

Lenny rinsed his mop and soaked up most of the soapy water. He stepped over to the long desk, eyed the monitors, the computer, and the files neatly arranged on a shelf on the wall.

"This is right out of one of those movies where the mad scientist transforms people into giant flies and stuff."

The therapist stepped from the tank to the counter. "We're not quite that advanced, although people do look a little weird when they're in the tank and hooked up to all the monitors."

"Can I mop around it?"

"Sure. I've got to check the lab animals. I'll be right back."

The therapist opened a door to an adjoining room from which came the sounds of a dog crying and scratching at a cage.

As he mopped around the hyperbaric tank, Lenny looked into it. He saw a thin foam pad, cables and electrodes, and inlets for the air. The open lid had a small plexiglass window. Pipes and cables ran from the tank to a large compressor and the oxygen outlet in the wall.

Lenny could not see how the research lab might be connected to the murder. If Galloway had been faking his results or pocketing grant money, Sparks might have discovered it and confronted him, but Lenny had no way to uncover that sort of thing.

Gary had said that often the treatments didn't help the patient very much. Lenny wondered if the whole setup could be a scam, and if it was, how Galloway could get away with it with the insurance companies and the government questioning every nickel the hospital claimed.

The respiratory therapist came back in. She stepped over to him, read the name on his shirt. "Say, aren't you that union rep I've heard about?"

"It's all lies and innuendoes."

"No, it was good stuff. You helped one of the other therapists when she didn't want to rotate to nights."

"Oh yeah, Phyllis. She didn't want to leave her three kids home at night. How's she doing?"

"Oh, she's plugging away as best she can."

"Like the rest of us."

Lenny began to mop a last corner of the lab. "What's your boss like to work for?"

Melissa pursed her lips. "Hmmm. He can be cranky, like a lot of the docs, and he expects a lot out of you."

"Does he ask for too much?"

"*He* doesn't think so. He's the first born son of a doctor. You know how that is. They say that his father always gave him everything he wanted." She lowered her voice to a stage whisper. "He expects the world owes him fame and fortune, but he's stuck in this little no-name hospital."

"A frustrated genius," Lenny said.

"You got it."

He stood waiting for the floor to dry. "Do most of the patients get better from the treatments?"

"Most of them, yes, they get better. Or if they don't..." She made a slicing motion with the edge of her hand. "It's 'wh'hup!' Off with the limb."

The lab door opened and a group of doctors filed in. In the middle was the mad scientist himself, Nathan Galloway.

Lenny pushed his bucket toward the door, forcing an opening through the group. "Careful you don't slip on the wet floor," he told them.

Galloway held the door open for Lenny. The surgeon's face was serene and smiling. His unblinking, hazel eyes focused on Lenny's face. "Expecting snow to fall inside the building, are we?"

Lenny looked down at his tall winter boots, then back at the physician. "The concierge hasn't returned my dress shoes."

Galloway smiled blandly as Lenny turned and pushed on out of the lab.

Fifty-nine

*L*eslie Odom bore down the hospital corridor, flanked by his entourage of residents, students, and physician's assistants. Coming to Mrs. Grey's room, he braked and changed course, heading toward her room.

As he came into the room, Mrs. Grey felt her heart beat furiously in her chest. She recited a brief silent prayer, trying to stay calm and not be afraid.

"I have the results of your tests," he told her. "You have uterine hypertrophy with Stage One endometrial changes."

She stared into his bland, expressionless face.

"Does that mean I have cancer, doctor?"

"No, not at all."

"Then it isn't serious? It won't become cancer, is that what you're saying?"

"You have early changes in the structure of your cellular DNA. You will have to be examined every year for further changes. We will know more after six months."

Turning to the resident, he said, "Start her on 200 milligrams of Revabid B.I.D. If she tolerates the dose, increase it to 400 milligrams."

As he wheeled around and stepped through the door, the others bumped into each other trying to follow him. The patient called out, "Oh, doctor, what did you mean, 'if I tolerate the treatments?"

"My Resident will come back and talk to you when we've completed rounds," he said over his shoulder, leading his group out the door.

She reached to her nightstand and picked up her Bible.

At the nursing station, Odom spotted Joe West. Telling the Resident to update his progress notes, he signaled to the Security Chief to join him. They walked to an alcove where patients and families often found quiet.

"Mr. West, I think you should know that an employee of yours broke into my locker in the operating room today and removed my personal appointment book."

"Did you get his name?" West asked.

"His first name was embroidered on his shirt. It said 'Lenny.' Do you know who he is?"

215

"Know him? He's been a thorn in my side for years. You don't have to worry. I'll take care of him. I'm going to have him picked up and brought to the office. We'll clear out his locker and pull his time card. This is automatic grounds for dismissal. When he comes into the office looking for his card, I'll terminate him."

"Good," said Odom. "I don't want to see him in this facility again."

"You don't have to worry, every security guard knows his ugly face. I'll make sure he isn't allowed in the building unless he comes in on a stretcher. Preferably dead on arrival."

Odom stared deadpan at West, who returned his gaze with equally dead gray eyes.

"I was planning on looking you up in your office anyway, doctor. The other day I got a call from the pathology lab. It seems someone found the remains of an aborted baby in the trash in one of your examination rooms. Know anything about it?"

Odom, his annoyance dissolving into a blank look, looked hard into West's dark, humorless eyes. Two poker faces stared at each other across a table of lies.

"No, I don't. The specimen was discovered where?"

"In the trash."

"We are extremely careful in the disposal of all human tissue. It could not have come from my office or from the operating suite. I suggest you speak to the clinic physicians."

"Yeah, I'll do that," West said.

Odom turned and walked stolidly back to join his group.

West followed him to the Seven-South station. As the doctor led his entourage away, West walked quickly up to Betty, who was cleaning the grab rail along the wall of the corridor.

"Where's Moss?" he barked.

"Lenny? I heard him say he was going to run down to the storeroom for some supplies. Let me ask Gary."

She stepped back to the medication room, where Gary was preparing his morning meds.

"Hey Gary, Joe West is out here looking for Lenny. Didn't he tell you he was going to the store room for supplies?"

Gary stepped out, saw West glaring at him.

"That's right. He said he was going down for supplies and he'd be back in fifteen minutes. Would you like me to tell him you were asking for him?"

"Don't bother," West growled, "I'll find him."

He turned smartly and strode swiftly away. As he walked toward the stairwell at the end of the corridor, he pulled the walkie-talkie from his hip.

"Attention, all units, this is West. We have a Code Ten. I repeat, a Code Ten. Find Lenny Moss and bring him to the housekeeping office. *Find Lenny Moss.*"

There was static on the box, then Sandy answered, "You want Lenny? Does somebody need a union rep or something? What's going on?"

"Just bring him to the office, I'll handle it from there," West snapped. He returned the walkie-talkie to his belt and hurried down the stairs, certain that Lenny had not gone to the storeroom. He had an idea where the troublemaker might be.

Sixty

*L*enny left the Vascular Lab and brought his mop and bucket to the elevator, where he punched the up button. He watched the numbers of the floors light up on the wall indicator as the elevator descended. He pictured Walter Oldenfield's severed leg packed in ice. Then he remembered what Margaret had looked like in the days before she died. Eyes sunken, voice a whisper, her bones pushing against the taut skin of her cheeks.

He always seemed to be dealing with death. Even the investigation was a search for death—for the bringer of it, the perpetrator. He was trying to keep Regis off of death row; he was trying to find what was the connection between Virginia Galloway and Randy Sparks.

From behind him a hand tapped him on the shoulder. Lenny jumped, spun around.

"Hi Lenny."

Kate Palmer stood smiling at him. "A little jumpy today, are we?"

A clutch of medical students watched them in silence.

"Hello Kate. How are things."

"Pretty good." She eyed Lenny's mop and bucket. "Say, I thought you worked on Seven-South."

"Now who's playing detective."

The other students stepped into the elevator that was going down.

"Actually," Lenny said, "I was just looking into Galloway's research lab."

"He gave us a lecture about his work. He does a lot with gangrene and spider bites. It sounded very interesting, although I don't think I'd like working for him."

"He's not the fatherly type, is he?"

"More like the philandering husband, I'd say."

Kate pushed the elevator button. "I should run, or I'll be late for lecture. But listen, my lab partner, Jennifer, happened to mention that Randy Sparks came to see her right before he disappeared."

"The information just *happened* to come up, is that it?" he asked, giving her a coy look.

"Okay, I was nosing around a bit. Hey, don't blame me if this detective stuff is catching."

"Believe me, I can use all the help I can get. People keep feeding me clues, but all I end up with is indigestion…So, what was Sparks after when he stopped by your partner's place? Did he want to play doctor?"

"That's not funny. No, Jenny was on her way out for a study group so she left Sparks alone in her apartment."

"What was he doing, his laundry or something?"

"Funny you should mention it, he did do his laundry there sometimes, but this time he needed to use her VCR. It seems his was busted."

"An educational tape?"

"It could be."

"I don't suppose Jennifer got a look at it."

"I'm afraid not. She left right after he came in."

"And Sparks didn't give any hint what was on it?"

"No. I asked if Sparks left the tape behind, and she said she hadn't seen it, but I was thinking that just because she hadn't *seen* it…"

"Doesn't mean it's not around. And you think the tape has something to do with the murder."

"I don't know, but it's worth a shot, isn't it? He disappeared a couple of days later."

"Hmm," Lenny said. "Radcliff has a lot of video equipment in his office, plus a bunch of tapes on his patients. If he was fooling around with his patients, he could be conceited enough to get it on film."

"I can't believe anyone would be that stupid."

"It happens all the time. The police found Sparks's hospital locker open. That could mean that somebody was searching for something small enough to fit inside a locker."

"The murderer, you think?"

"Could be."

The up elevator arrived. Lenny pushed his bucket inside, then held the door open.

"Listen, Kate—is there any chance I could look around Jennifer's apartment and try to find that tape?"

"You mean, can *I* get *us* into her place. I'll talk to Jennifer, we're meeting for lunch to study for a test. I'll call you tonight."

"Great, thanks."

Lenny needed to talk to Moose to work on a plan. He looked at his watch, saw it was break time, debated between the cafeteria and Birdie's sewing room, and decided Birdie's was the better choice. After leaving his mop and bucket in an empty patient room, he hurried down the steps, the *clamp, clamp* of his winter boots on the metal steps made him uneasy. He had the feeling that somebody was listening to his every step, following his every move, and that that someone was ready to kill again.

When he reached the sewing room, Lenny opened the door a crack and peeked inside. It was a relief to find Moose sitting there with Birdie.

"Thank god I found you," he said.

"Talk to me," Moose said, unfolding one of the beat-up metal chairs for him.

"I found out who Virginia Racine is." He told them about the 'V.R.' in Odom's appointment book and how Radcliff had whited out her name in his appointment book.

"She's Galloway's wife. And I think she's the blonde that Sandy saw last month."

"God damn," Moose said.

"If it *was* his wife who got pregnant, and the initials in Odom's appointment book say it was, Galloway's the type to fly into a jealous rage."

"He's got the know-how to pull it off," said Celeste.

"That's right," Lenny said. "Now if I could just—"

The sound of the door opening shut him up. Everyone looked to see who it was.

"Lord preserve all our sorrowful souls," said Betty as she came into the room. Moose unfolded a chair for her, and Lenny filled her in on what he'd learned.

"A man who walks with the devil must pay the price," she said solemnly. "Evil begets evil, mark my words."

"What goes around comes around," said Birdie, who had put away her sewing.

"If Virginia Racine got herself pregnant and didn't want to have the baby," Lenny continued, "that makes Sparks either the father or the one who threatened to blow the whistle on the man who was."

"That's a bull's eye," Moose said. "She got Odom to give her an abortion the night Sandy saw the blonde who never showed up on the floor. Her husband found out, became crazy with jealousy, and killed Sparks to teach his wife a lesson."

"So," said Lenny, "how am I gonna get to her before the killer strikes again?"

Everyone looked at Lenny, but no one had a solution to the problem.

This Won't Hurt A Bit

Sandy was covering the rear entrance of the hospital when he heard the orders from West to find Lenny. He called Seven-South, where Celeste told him that West had been there and left. He decided the sewing room was the place West was likely to check out next, so he phoned the room.

"Hello, sewing."

"Birdie? It's Sandy. Is Lenny with you?"

"Yes, he's here with me and Moose. You want to speak with him?"

"Right away."

Lenny's voice came on the line.

"Lenny, it's me. Listen, I just got a call from West on the squawk box to pick you up and bring you to the housekeeping office. It sounded serious, like he's gonna terminate you today."

"Shit," Lenny said. "I was hoping I had a little more time." He turned his mouth away from the phone, saying, "West is looking for me. He's gonna fire me today."

Moose said, "Where's West now?"

Lenny repeated the question to Sandy.

"He didn't say, but he's already been to Seven-South. Five'll get you ten he's coming your way."

Sixty-one

"*D*amn!" said Lenny said, holding the phone away from his mouth. "West is coming down."

"You got to get out of here," said Moose.

Lenny looked at his watch, saw it was just past eleven. "The employee clinic is open till noon. If I can make it there I can get Dr. Primeaux to sign me out. That'll give me the weekend to work on the case."

"Yeah, but how're you gonna punch out?" said Sandy over the phone. "Childress will be watching the timeclock like an old tom at a mouse hole, and you know you can't leave without punching your time card. Childress can fire you for that and there's no way you'll win that grievance."

"I'll work something out. Call me at the clinic if you hear West is heading that way."

"Will do," Sandy said and hung up.

Lenny repeated out loud what Sandy had said.

"I could punch you out, no problem," said Moose.

"Not you," Lenny said. "Childress knows we're working together. I'll ask Abrahm. No one will suspect him, he's a perfect employee as far as the boss is concerned."

"Okay, then I'll cover your back."

"I'll call around and try to find where West is at," Birdie said.

"Great," said Lenny. "Let's go."

Moose went to the door, opened it, and looked out. He saw George from the store room pushing a hand truck loaded with boxes and an orderly pushing an empty wheelchair, but no sign of West or any of the other security guards.

"Come on," Moose said. "You stay behind me, I'll cover you."

With Moose leading the way, they moved quickly along the corridor. Walking south to the back of the building, they passed through a double door and entered the old wing of the hospital, which was less trafficked. The inpatients and major treatment areas had all been moved to the new building in '85, and the old, three-story structure was used for outpatient services and offices.

This Won't Hurt A Bit

At a stairwell Moose opened the door and listened for footsteps. Nothing.

"Let's go," Moose said, charging up the stairs three at a time.

"Hey, not so fast," Lenny called, struggling to keep up.

"No time to waste, man. We're hot. C'mon!"

They passed no one on the way to the third floor. Opening the door to the corridor, Moose peeked out, saw an empty hallway. "No security in sight," he whispered, waving Lenny through the door, then he walked behind him, casting a look backward every few steps.

They hurried down the hall past the low prestige offices for Quality Assurance, Statistical Analysis and Infectious Disease, finally reaching the Employee Clinic at the end of the corridor.

"You want I should ask Abrahm to punch you out? Be a lot easier for me to get to him than you."

"That'd be great, Moose. Ask him to put my coat in a plastic trash bag and meet me behind the hospital by the trash station."

"You got it. What's your locker combination?"

"Zero, one, zero."

"All right," Moose said, opening the door to the clinic for Lenny. "You hide out here, I'll catch up with Abrahm. If it looks like West is comin' this way, I'll call over."

"Good."

As Moose hurried away, Lenny stepped into the clinic, a low-ceilinged room with peeling plaster on the walls and a large, ugly brown stain in the ceiling. *Their roof is in worse shape than mine,* he thought as he approached the desk.

A heavyset, gray-haired nurse with swollen ankles and a chronic cough sat at her desk with a look of terminal weariness on her face. She was hunting through a mass of folders, sticky labels with messages scrawled on them, and boxes of free samples that the drug representatives left in an effort to induce the clinic doctor to prescribe them once the freebies ran out. The old nurse looked up and smiled broadly.

"What brings you to our humble abode, Lenny? Come for somebody's records, I suppose."

"Not this time, Margie. I need to see Dr. Primeaux. Is he in?"

"He's seeing a patient, you'll have to wait a bit." Seeing the bandage on the side of Lenny's face, she rose heavily from her chair and stepped toward him.

"I heard about that scrape you got into in the basement the other day. Did the police get the fellow who did it?"

"No. They're supposed to be looking for him, but I doubt they'll spend a whole lot of time on it. West certainly isn't motivated to look very hard."

"If it wasn't him that did it in the first place, you mean."

"That thought did cross my mind."

Margie looked more closely at the bandage on the back of his head. "Want me to put some antibiotic ointment on that wound while you're waiting?"

"Thanks, but I better wait for the doctor. I'm gonna ask him to sign me out early, and he'll need to see it."

"Okay, make yourself comfortable in one of our deluxe easy chairs," she said, pointing to a trio of torn, sagging leather armchairs patched with duct tape, leftovers from an earlier era of patient care.

"Gee, you must have shopped at the same Goodwill store that I did," he said. "But listen, do you suppose that I could wait, say, in one of the examining rooms."

She squinted gray, flinty eyes at him.

"You need to keep out of sight or something?"

"Let's just say I'm feeling very modest, with my face burned and all."

"Fine, you can wait in number two. Alex is seeing a low back in the first room."

"Thanks, Margie."

He slipped into the small cubicle and closed the door, then looked with disappointment for a lock on it. Seeing that there was none, he sat down on the end of the examining table and waited.

Sixty-two

While Lenny sat alone in the clinic examining room, Moose hurried to the third floor in search of Abrahm, who usually covered the doctor's offices and the psychiatric ward. He found the stocky Russian washing windows in the hallway near the psych nursing station.

"Abrahm, we got a problem."

"Hullo, Moose. Is it about Len'nye?"

"Yeah. He needs to punch out, but he can't go to the office. Childress and West are gonna terminate him as soon as they lay eyes on him."

"Do you want I should punch the card for him?"

"Would you? I offered to do it, but he thought they'd be watching me and they wouldn't suspect you. Then he wants you to get his coat and hat from his locker and meet him at the back of the hospital behind the dumpsters. His combination is zero, one zero. Can you do it?"

"Of course. Should I go now?"

"Better give it about fifteen minutes. Lenny's in the clinic getting signed out."

"Vury well. In fifteen minutes I will go to the office and punch his card. No problem."

"Thanks. I gotta run, I'm trying to track West down."

As Moose hurried away, Abrahm looked at his watch, a plain, stainless steel Russian military timepiece with a wide leather band. He noted the time, then returned to working on the windows, smiling in a way he had not done in a long time.

After Abrahm finished washing the windows in the hall, he looked at his watch. Fifteen minutes had passed. He brought his bucket and rags to the utility room, where he dumped the dirty water into the large porcelain sink and rinsed out the rags to use again.

He went to the stairwell and walked down the four floors to the basement. Entering the hallway, he walked along the corridor until he reached the housekeeping office. Inside he saw the secretary sitting at the desk talking on the phone. Toward the back he got a quick view of Childress leaning back in his high-backed leather chair, doing what, he couldn't tell.

Abrahm went to the rack of time cards, momentarily out of Childress's line of sight. He picked his own card out so that, if questioned, he could explain that he was punching out to go outside the building for lunch. The administration, claiming that many employees took more than their allotted forty-five minute lunch break, had been threatening to enforce a new rule requiring the workers to punch out and punch in for their time off.

The union had been able to block the demeaning rule so far, pointing out that the contract required that workers use the time cards only when coming on and going off duty. The boss countered that going to lunch was going 'off duty,' and the two sides had been arguing the issue for months. Abrahm planned to say that he was confused about the new rule, should the boss question him.

Glancing at the secretary, who was facing away from him as she spoke on the phone, Abrahm went to the 'M' row of cards and ran his eye down the list. 'Matthews... Medowlark...Monsanto...Morris...Mott...

There was no card for Moss, Lenny.

He looked again, starting with the first M and going on to the N's and O's. Nothing. Puzzled, he tried the L's, imagining that Lenny might place his card in that slot as a little joke, but the card was not there, either.

He realized that, since Childress was watching for Lenny, he probably had pulled the card and kept it in his office.

Abrahm returned his card to the slot and hurried out of the office. He walked to the pay phone in the hallway, picked up the phone, fished out a quarter, and dialed the Seven-South nursing station. A pleasant woman's voice said, "Seven-South, this is Marianne. How may I help you?"

"Give me Betty, please."

He listened to the distant sound of voices, papers shifting, a door open and close, then the housekeeper's voice saying, "This is Betty. Who's this?"

"It is Abrahm. Len'nye is in trouble. Will you help me?"

"Of course. What do I have to do?"

"Call the housekeeping office. Tell the secretary that Mister Childress must come to executive office right away and see Mr. Tuesday."

"You want me to pretend to be calling from the president's office, is that it? Okay, give me a minute, I'll have to go into an empty room and use a patient phone."

"Vury good."

He hung up, walked back past the office and continued on to the locker room, where he ducked inside. He checked the time on his watch, then went to Lenny's locker, that everyone knew from the large HSWU sticker on it. He turned the combination lock, zero...one...zero. It popped open. He removed Lenny's hat and coat and placed them in a red biohazard trash bag. He did not notice that, save for the two articles of clothing which he removed, the locker was completely empty.

Carefully twirling the combination lock, he stepped out and looked down the corridor. Seconds later, Childress came rushing out of the office and hurried to the elevator.

Abrahm returned to the outer office. As he came in, the secretary hung up the phone, opened a drawer and pulled out a small red pocket book. She closed the drawer and locked her desk, then she went out. Abrahm had guessed that as soon as the boss left, the secretary would take a lunch break, since Childress would be unable to monitor how long she was away from her desk.

When the secretary's footsteps had faded in the corridor outside, Abrahm went into the supervisor's office and looked over the desk. It was covered by a bewildering mishmash of file folders, long runs of computer printouts folded haphazardly, half-empty coffee cups and a blizzard of pink message slips which began, "You have a message from..."

Beneath the mess was an old leather blotter, its corner pockets stuffed with old message slips and reminder notes. In the right, upper corner pocket was a single time card.

He picked it up, read the name, Moss, Leonard. Smiling broadly, the gold cap on one of his front teeth glinting in the fluorescent light, Abrahm took the card, kissed it, then went to the outer office and punched it out. He briefly considered filing the card in its proper spot as an insult to the boss But he realized that it would be better to allow Childress to think that he was still in control of the situation, so he put it back exactly where he had found it.

Walking out of the office with a new lift in his step and a twinkle in his eyes, he hurried to meet Lenny behind the dumpsters and give him his coat. After that, he would buy a cheesesteak hoagie with onions and hot peppers and a cocoa cola from The Cave to celebrate his successful mission.

Lenny sat on the examining table. Because he was finally still, he realized that his head was throbbing as if he were lying on the floor beside the furnace while the oil pump shook the floor. Shadowy images of being dragged along the cement surface and having his head pressed against the steam pipe haunted him, making the pain worse. When he closed his eyes, the pain pulsed on and off...On and off.

He wished it would snow so that he could lay his face on a cold, soft white blanket and make the pain go away.

Suddenly the room felt very small and airless. If West or one of the other security guards came looking for him, he had no escape route. No back-up plan. In fact, he had no plan at all except to get home, take a cool shower and go to bed.

Some organizer I am, he thought. *I don't have a fricking idea how to get this murder investigation wrapped up.*

He heard footsteps in the room outside, muffled voices. He put his ear to the thin cubicle door to listen, but could not make out any words. A sharp *rap-rap*-rap on the cubicle door startled him. He jerked his head away, calling, "Who is it?" and knowing that he had no room to run and no more glib answers.

The door to the cubicle swung silently open.

Lenny prepared for the worst.

Sixty-three

"It's me," Alex Primeaux said simply as he stepped into the examining room cubicle. "Who were you expecting, Jack the Ripper?"

"The one and only," Lenny said, glancing past the doctor. He was relieved to see that no one was behind him or in the waiting area. "Returning to his seat on the examining table, he added, "I guess I'm a little jumpy."

"It's no surprise after all you've been through. Ah heard about your unfortunate run-in with a steam pipe. Is that what brought you here?"

"Yeah, my neck is killing me. I took a couple of hits to my head, too, and I don't think I can make it through the day, so I was hoping that you would sign me out early."

"I would think you could take a week off just to recover. You probably suffered a near concussion. Let me look at the burn."

He gently pressed his finger on the swollen streak along Lenny's neck, noting the amount of fluid and the tension on the bulging skin."

"Second degree," he muttered. "That sucker must hurt like a son-of-a-bee. Are you taking pain medication?"

"Nah, the ER doc offered me some, but I turned him down."

"Bravery doesn't mean you've got to suffer," he said, opening a jar and spreading a thick white past over the burn with a tongue blade. "This silvadene will take the sting out and reduce the swelling. I'd like you to apply the burn ointment three times a day, followed by an ice pack. You'll need to keep it dressed or the medicine will rub off."

"Okay," Lenny said.

"Let me see the other wound." With a swift single motion, Primeaux pulled the tape off the back of Lenny's head.

"Ouch, that hurt!"

"Sorry, there's no painless way to take off tape when it's over hair follicles."

The doctor gently pressed the margins of the wound, noting with satisfaction that no pus ran out and that the edges were neither swollen nor red.

"This will heal nicely. I'll just apply antibiotic ointment and dress it. Y'all don't have to keep it covered when you're home in a clean environment."

"You've obviously never been to my house," Lenny said.

The doctor put an extra large Band-Aid over the wound.

"Why don't you wait in my office? I'll make out a prescription for a pain killer. It will help you sleep. I'll give you the burn ointment and the antibiotic."

"Okay, thanks," Lenny said, getting up and following Primeaux out of the examining room. The doctor pointed to a tiny office opposite the nurse's desk. "I'll be right with you," he said.

Lenny walked into the office and took a seat in a comfortable armchair opposite a small, neatly organized desk. The surface of the desk had a pen and pencil set, box of tissues, and a lap top computer sitting square in the middle. He noticed that, unlike most doctor's desks, there were no photos of wife, children and golden retriever, which seemed odd, Primeaux being such a decent kind of guy.

He looked on the walls, saw no photos, only several frames with diplomas, certifications, and such, hanging there.

He shrugged and settled comfortably into the chair to wait for the doctor.

Primeaux came into his office, prescription pad in hand, and settled in an old padded chair behind his desk.

"I'll give you a script for percocet, it's quite a strong pain killer. You can take one percocet, and if it doesn't do the trick, you can have a second. Just be careful not to mix it with alcohol. The combination can make you very sleepy."

"Okay."

As Primeaux filled in the prescription blank, Lenny said, "I don't suppose you heard that me and Moose have been looking into the Sparks murder. The whole hospital seems to know about it by now, as far as I can tell. The cops arrested a young man who works in the laundry who could not possibly have done it, and we're trying to find out who really did it so we can get our friend out of jail and back on the job."

"Yes, Margie told me about it. That takes a great deal of courage, putting your neck on the line to help out a friend."

"More insanity than guts. As we began to collect clues I came upon, among other things, a woman's name, Virginia Racine. She had an appointment with Dr. Radcliff, only her name was whited out, like no one was supposed to ever know she'd been there. Then her initials show up in Odom's personal date book on the same day as her appointment with the psychiatrist."

"A coincidence?"

"Maybe, maybe not. Next to her initials in Odom's date book was a symbol. I think it was a Greek letter. Doctors use them a lot for abbreviations, don't they?"

"That's right. What letter was it?"

Lenny drew an 'O' with a line running horizontally across it.

"Why, that's the Greek letter theta."

"What does it mean?"

"I don't know, we don't use it. It could stand for almost anything."

"Like what?" Lenny asked.

Primeaux put a hand to his chin, reflected a moment. His eyes narrowed.

"Come to think of it, theta is the first letter of thanatos, which is Greek for death."

"And abortions are terminations of life. It fits," said Lenny. He leaned forward. "This Virginia Racine also just who happens to be married to Dr. Galloway. I also found evidence that Odom has been performing abortions privately in his office at night. The reason I brought it up is, I know there's such a thing as a doctor-physician confidentiality, and I wouldn't ask you to betray something somebody told you in confidence, but do you know the woman, Virginia Galloway?"

"Do you think she has something to do with the death of Randy Sparks?" he said, handing Lenny the prescriptions and the medical leave of absence form.

Tucking the script in his shirt pocket, Lenny said, "I don't know exactly, but it's odd how her name keeps popping up among all these doctors who knew Sparks."

"It sounds to me like you believe a physician was responsible for the death of Randy Sparks."

"It's the only thing that makes sense. Who else could sneak the body into the medical school, drain all the blood and pus and fill it full of preservative?"

"Couldn't an undertaker?"

"An undertaker wouldn't know how to input the John Doe in the school's computer. He wouldn't know how to fake the wounds to look like a car wreck, either."

"I suppose that might be beyond his skills. Still and all…"

Lenny considered how to deal with the doctor's evasion. He'd dealt with many a reluctant witness. Recalling Gary's estimate of Primeaux's character, he decided to go for sympathy.

"Look, I've been threatened and I've been beat up pretty good. This morning when I opened my locker I found enough blood in my work shoes to float the Queen Mary."

"Mah God, that blood might have been contaminated with HIV."

"It was a serious threat, and I took it seriously, believe me. Now I've got Joe West breathing down my neck trying to terminate me, plus the cops knocking on my door ordering me to tell them everything I know, but they won't tell me a thing."

As he spoke he watched Primeaux's eyes, that were fixed on him and never looked away. "The point I'm getting at in my rambling sort of way is that someone, presumably the same person who killed Sparks, is after me. Now, I can take care of myself. I have friends in the hospital who watch my back, and I'm careful most of the time, but Virginia Galloway may not be so lucky. She may very well be vulnerable, and I'm very worried that she may be in even more danger than me. If you tell me what you know, it may help me find the killer, and that's the best way to protect her."

"You think my keeping quiet might put Virginia in danger?"

"Yes, I do," said Lenny, looking hard into Primeaux's eyes. "That's why I need your help. Right now."

Sixty-four

West pushed open the door to the sewing room without knocking and marched in. He saw Birdie at her work station, fabric sliding along the table of her machine.

"Where's Moss?" he growled.

"Who?" she said, not looking up at him.

"Don't be cute." He scanned the room, noted the three folding chairs sitting open around the sewing station. "He was here, don't bullshit me. Where did he go?"

"It's just me and the stuffing in the pillows. No one's been in here for hours."

"Never mind, I'll find him." He kicked one of the chairs, sending it bouncing off the tiled wall with a clatter. "And when I do, I'm going to see just how hard that head of his really is."

He turned and stomped out of the room.

Birdie stopped sewing, turned off the machine, picked up the phone and called the employee health to tell Margie that West had just left her room.

"I see," Primeaux said, sitting forward and returning Lenny's stare. "And just where do you see me fitting in?"

"The Galloway insurance form lists you as the primary physician. I figure you must have treated her at some point. Did she ever talk about how she felt about getting pregnant again? Did she say that she would have an abortion if she did? Did Dr. Radcliff tell you anything about her seeing him?"

"Hold on, now, you're goin' way to fast for this old boy. Let me tell you what I'm comfortable with discussing."

"Okay."

"First off, I did see Virginia on occasion in a professional capacity, and I did prescribe birth control pills for her. They caused some side effects—nothing we don't see very often—and I suggested that she skip one day a week to lower her blood level, but she may have stopped using them for longer, I'm not really sure."

"When did you see her last?"

"It's been a while, I'd have to check her file...Over a month ago, I'm not sure. She called on occasion to renew a prescription, but I don't believe she came to my office."

"When you talked to her, did she sound scared?"

"She was anxious. She never told me what about. I asked her if she wanted to talk to me or to someone else about her problems, and that's when she mentioned she was going to see Robert Radcliff."

He looked away from Lenny for the first time, put a hand to his chin. Lenny waited and watched, certain there was more. After a moment, he asked, "Did you speak to Radcliff about Virginia?"

"Lenny, I think this conversation is getting into deep waters."

"Look, an innocent man is facing a murder charge and Virginia may be in danger for her life. I *have* to know what Radcliff said."

The doctor looked into Lenny's earnest eyes, knowing that, of all the people in the hospital, this man was one who would not betray a trust.

"When I mentioned my conversation with her to Radcliff, he did confirm that she had an underlying anxiety disorder and that he had prescribed something for it."

"Did Virginia tell you she was scared that her husband would find out she was pregnant? Or who the father might be?"

"She never said anything to me about a baby. Neither did Radcliff. She wouldn't talk much, and she wouldn't make a follow-up appointment with me, either, though I asked her to see me again." He leaned back, his old chair creaking as he changed position. "I'm afraid that's all I know about her."

Lenny looked into the doctor's warm, brown eyes. He wondered how much he could push him...or trust him. Tuttle had spoken very highly of the man, but Moose had had doubts. He trusted Moose's instincts over Tuttle. Gary was a tad on the naive side when it came to the dark side of human nature, although he did know Primeaux a lot better than Moose.

He decided to push a little more to see if he could shake something else out of him.

"You worked with Randy Sparks for a month last year, didn't you? Did he make any serious enemies? Piss anyone off enough to want to do him harm?"

"No, not that I'm aware of. I got along with Randy beautifully. I appreciated his insights, he was a brilliant clinician. With his credentials he would never go into a humble sort of practice like family medicine, but he never denigrated my specialty." His face darkened. "Lord, you don't suspect that I was involved in the murder just because we worked together, do you?"

"No, of course not, but there's something else. It sounds kind of weird, but someone suggested that you are just too nice to be a real doctor."

"Are you damning me with praise now?"

"Maybe, but there's more. Gary noticed that you're very knowledgeable about things that nurses and orderlies routinely do, like locking a wheelchair before putting someone in it, and using the paging system the way that a nurse would instead of going through the operator the way the doctors mostly do."

"Ah worked as an orderly while I was in medical school, and while I was in Viet Nam I learned that rank had nothing to do with saving the patient. That's where I got my best medical training, serving with the marines."

"There's one thing more."

"What?" he asked, again turning his soft eyes away from Lenny.

"Moose tells me that your accent sounds like Arkansas but you say you were born and raised in North Carolina."

"My mama was from Arkansas. There's nothing strange about talking like your parents."

"No, but when he asked you about Durham's baseball team you didn't know their name, but you *did* know who the Razorbacks were, and they're from Little Rock."

Primeaux's fingers were now laced together in a taut weave. He looked past Lenny at the diplomas hanging on the wall. His face was pale, wan. The muscles around one eye began to twitch.

"You can't hang a man for not following sports."

"I'm not trying to hang you at all. I'm not saying you killed Sparks, or even that you know who did it, I just keep running into these puzzling facts, so I'm following all of them… Aren't you really from Arkansas, not North Carolina?"

Primeaux rose slowly from his chair and walked around his desk. He stepped to the wall and gently closed the office door, then stood behind Lenny. He ran his finger over the diploma hanging on the wall.

"Alexander Primeaux, grad-u-ated from…this diploma is presented to…doctor of medicine, in the year of… Ah always knew it would come out some day."

His words became stuck in his throat. He turned and looked down at Lenny, his eyes glistening with tears. "Ah always knew."

Sixty-five

*P*rimeaux stepped away from the diplomas on the wall and sat on the edge of his desk. His shoulders were slumped, his face pale.

"You see, I was a medical corpsman in Viet Nam. We saw a lot of action. Lord, we saw it all." He took a tissue from a box on the desk and dabbed his eyes. "One day our field unit was hit by mortar fire and the physician, Alex Primeaux, was killed. He was just blown to pieces. I took his tags to send home to his family, and, because we had no doctor, I did my best to fill in for him. We got a replacement finally, and when he saw how much I'd learned he treated me more like an intern than a corpsman.

"And that's how it went for six months. Out there in the jungle, sewing up wounds an' setting limbs, just like a real doctor. When I got out, I got copies of his school records and I studied real hard, and, well, I just decided to keep on bein' a doctor."

"From what I hear, you've become a damned good one."

"Ah work mighty hard at it, that's for sure. But I knew it would come out one day. I suppose I'll be arrested and have to do time."

Lenny stood up. He extended his hand to Primeaux. The doctor hesitated, took it, gave Lenny a puzzled look.

"You don't have to quit on my account," Lenny said, "I can keep a secret. Being a shop steward, you'd be amazed at some of the shit I hear, but it never gets past my ears."

Lenny released Primeaux's hand. The doctor stood up, speechless. Lenny couldn't tell if the man was going to laugh or cry.

"Look," Lenny went on, "James Madison can't afford to lose a good doctor. You wouldn't believe some of the dirt I've found out about the real ones. Doing abortions in their office, using drugs, and having sex in their waiting rooms…it's fucking unbelievable. It'd be a crime to bust you when *they're* still practicing medicine."

"Lenny, I don't know what to say."

"Well, you could start by telling me what you didn't say before about Sparks. You must know something more about the guy."

"Not really, no."

"Well, here are the doctors I'm investigating." He took out the same list he had shown Iris in Personnel and read their names. "Odom, Radcliff, Gandy, and Galloway. Is there anything about their relation with Sparks that looked suspicious to you?"

"Hmmm," he said, considering the question. "It's funny you should put it that way, because Randy did say that Nathan Galloway had put in a recommendation for him for a research position at the NIH. Galloway went to medical school with one of the big-wigs down in DC, and he apparently helped Randy find a very prestigious position doing genetic research."

"That was unusual for Galloway to do?"

"Oh, yes. Galloway works strictly on the you-scratch-my-back-I'll-scratch-yours system. He refers a patient to you for consultation, you refer one to him. Preferably two or three. He never gives anything away without expecting payment back—in spades."

"So for him to go out of his way to help Sparks get a plum appointment, Sparks must either have had something to trade him, or something on him that was a threat."

"Sounds likely."

"That may be very helpful. So far I have loose connections between Virginia and some of the docs, but nothing that makes one of them out to be suspect number one."

"Am I on your list?"

"Yeah, but on the bottom."

Lenny got up and reached for the door, but Primeaux beat him to it. Grasping the knob, he said, "It may sound funny to you, but all this time I've been afraid of being found out, so I haven't made any commitments. I felt it wouldn't be fair to put someone I love in that position, but now that you know…I feel like I can maybe take a chance." As he turned the knob and opened the door, some of his self-effacing smile returned.

Lenny walked out of the clinic, looked up and down the hallway, that was empty, and moved to the stairs. He decided to leave by a rear exit and approach the employee parking lot from the back of the building. Abrahm should be waiting with his coat, and from there it should be smooth sailing to home.

Reaching the exit without being seen, he stepped out into the biting cold and walked quickly along the building to the dumpsters, concealed behind a chainlink face with green slats running through it like crude crochet. He walked to the rear, where Abrahm was waiting wearing Lenny's coat and hat.

"Abraham Lincoln, you are my savior."

"Whut else is a friend for?" Abrahm answered, smiling broadly. He took off the coat and hat and handed them to Lenny.

"Did you have any trouble punching my time card?"

"Little trouble, not much. I had to make Childress leave the office, so I ask Betty to call and pretend she is secretary for Mr. Tuesday, and he must go to the boss's office right away."

"You sent Childress to the CEO's office? Abrahm, that was brilliant! I love it!"

"Thank you vury much…You will go home now?"

"That's the plan. I'm taking the weekend off. Hopefully by Monday I'll have a better idea about who killed Sparks. If I can solve the damn case I think it will go a long way toward saving my ass."

"I hope so, Len'nye. The hospital would be vury sad to lose you."

"I have to run. Thanks again."

As Lenny started for the parking lot he noticed that Abrahm was not walking back into the hospital, but heading for the Germantown Avenue, without a coat on.

"Hey, where you goin'? It's as cold as Siberia out here!"

"To the Cave. I am on my lunch break, remember?"

"Right!" Lenny said, and hurried on.

As he stepped over frozen grass and a sidewalk strewn with rock salt, he surveyed the employee parking lot. There was no security guard at the little parking booth, normal at lunch time. They were usually only there for shift changes. He saw no guard patrolling the lot in the little electric car, either.

Relaxing a bit, Lenny walked to his car, which was parked next to a white van. He could hardly wait to get inside, warm up the big V8, and cruise on home. Maybe stop and get a hoagie like Abrahm was doing, and the Daily News. Then a hot bath and a very long nap.

As he fished for his key in his coat pocket, a steely hand grabbed him from behind. Lenny froze, turned slowly around, saw the hard, humorless face of Joe West.

West dropped a heavy, bulging plastic trash bag onto the ground.

"Give me your ID and your parking gate card, Moss. You're fired."

Lenny looked into the deadpan face that left no opportunity for a wisecrack.

"What's the charge?" he asked.

"Don't make me laugh. The list is longer than a train schedule. We have Dr. Odom's report that you broke into his locker in the operating room, and we know that you brought a specimen you stole from a doctor's office to the pathology lab without proper authorization."

"I don't know anything about a locker. I was just…"

"Save it for the hearing. You were away from your station with a piece of hospital equipment, to wit, a mop and a bucket, in the laboratory of Dr. Galloway's, where you were not authorized to work."

"So I helped out a friend."

"You can waste your breath on someone else, I don't need to hear it. Give me your ID and get off the property or I'll arrest you and hold you for criminal trespass."

West, his coat open, fingered the handcuffs dangling from his leather belt.

Slowly, Lenny reached into his trousers pocket and removed his wallet. He took out the parking card and handed it to West, then he unclipped his ID badge from his shirt and gave it to him.

West placed the items in a plastic zip loc bag, as if they were evidence for a trial, then he kicked the trash bag at his feet. "Get this crap out of here or I'll arrest you for littering," he said.

Lenny unlocked his car door, hefted the plastic bag and tossed it into the passenger seat. He got in, turned the key in the ignition, and started the engine.

"Don't come back unless you're DOA," West yelled through the window.

Lenny put the car in gear, briefly flirted with the notion of running over West, thought better of it, and pulled out of his parking space. He waited while West took his time walking to the gate and using his card to raise it. Finally he drove the car out of the lot, thinking it might be the last time he set foot in James Madison Hospital.

Sixty-six

Lenny started for home, so tired and aching that he couldn't really comprehend all that had happened to him. He had accompanied workers out the door after their termination, Regis Devoe being the last in a long line. Had called them at home to cheer them up, picked them up for the ride to the grievance hearing, to their lawyer's office, the unemployment agency. Could it really happen to *him*, the union rep?

He stopped on Germantown Avenue at The Rib Rack, an old school bus painted bright red, and parked in front of a local Video Store. The smoke from the blackened metal chimney at the back of the bus wafted through the cold, still air and teased his nostrils. He realized he'd had no lunch, and was voraciously hungry.

Inside the bus, as crowded as a school trip, he picked up a half chicken with the 'Smack your Mama' hot sauce, and a pint of dirty rice, then crossed the street to the Wa Wa deli for the late edition of the Daily News and a six pack of Ying Ling Beer.

As he drove, he ran over the encounter with West. West had mentioned the break-in into Odom's locker, and the trip to Galloway's laboratory, but he hadn't mentioned anything about the visit to Radcliff's office. That was odd, he was sure the shrink would call West on him.

Which could only mean that Radcliff was waist-deep in the murder, either as an accomplice or, at the very least, as someone who was protecting the real killer.

Even though he was banished from the hospital, Lenny felt that he was getting closer to the truth. His mood began to brighten as he pulled up to his little rowhouse on Wingohocking Place.

"I'm gonna beat that fucker after all," he said, pulling the key out of the ignition and opening the door. Striding toward his little house, he knew in a strange and wonderful way that he was going to win. He was going to beat West, find the killer, and get Regis out of jail.

If he could just finally get a good night's sleep.

Inside the house, Lenny tossed his hat and coat on the sofa and went back to the kitchen. The answering machine on the sideboard was winking at him. He pushed the play button and opened the refrigerator door for a beer while the tape rewound.

First, he heard his own voice, "Hi, this is Lenny. If you've got a new joke, leave it on the machine, otherwise, call back when I'm not at home. By the way, did you hear the one about the traveling salesman who loved Big Macs and the organic farmer's daughter…?"

"Beep…"

A stilted, computer generated voice said, "This is Fiber-Net Communications with a…collect call from…" in his own natural voice, "Regis Devoe…" The mechanical voice went on, "If you wish to accept the call, press one now or say the word 'Yes.' If you choose to not accept the call, press two or say the word 'No.'"

Silence on the tape, then the mechanical voice again.

"Since you have made no response, Fiber-Net will not connect this call. Thank you for using Fiber-Net, and have a pleasant…morning."

"Beep."

The next voice was warm and familiar, and Lenny sat at the kitchen table to listen to it.

"Hi, Lenny, it's Kate Palmer. I have something really important to tell you. It's about the conversation we had in the hospital today, and I don't think I should leave it on a tape, so I'll call back later. Hope you're okay…bye."

"Beep."

The third and last voice was also familiar to Lenny, although not one he cared to hear very often.

"Mr. Moss, this is Detective Joe Williams. I got a call informing me of your termination. I just want to let you know that if you hear anything about the Sparks case, I'm still interested, and I meant what I said about the way I handle new evidence. I'll be in touch."

"Click."

The machine stopped, rewound, clicked and returned to recording mode. Lenny rose to turn it off, then mumbled, "Fuck it, I need the rest," and left the machine on.

He took out a plate and emptied the rice and chicken from the Rib Rack onto it, pouring the hot sauce from the bottom of the cardboard container over the rice, then sat in the living room to eat. The tender meat fell off the chicken at the touch of his fork, and the Smack-your-Mamma sauce stung his tongue. It felt good, making him forget the burn on his face and the lump at the back of his head.

He took a long drink from the beer, wondered if soaking his burn in cold beer would be soothing, decided it probably wasn't, and drank the rest of the beer.

He read the paper back to front, treating the headlines like a summary of what he'd already read. His father had read the paper that way, pointing out that the sensational and superficial coverage was up front, but the real news, if it was reported at all, was added near the end, and you had to read that part twice to figure out what was really going on.

He finished the food, licked the sauce from his lips, and carried the dirty plate to the kitchen, where it would sit in the sink until he ran out of plates and had to wash them all.

He wearily climbed the stairs, looking forward to a long, hot bath and a very long sleep. He undressed and was about to step into the shower when from downstairs came the sound of an insistent knock on the front door.

Lenny cursed, wrapped a towel around his waist, and walked to the front bedroom that faced the street. Peeling the curtain back, he looked down into the street, expecting to see Detective Williams standing in front of his Plymouth Fury. Instead, he saw the pale, hooded face of Kate Palmer looking up at him.

Trudging down the stairs dressed only in a towel, Lenny unlocked the front door and opened it a crack.

"Hi, Kate. Nice of you to drop by, but I'm not dressed for company."

She glanced down at the towel and his bare feet.

"I thought you might come with me to Jennifer's apartment. But I guess I came at a bad time, didn't I?"

"Oh no, I was just being fitted for my casket by my own personal mortician...Actually, I was gonna take a bath and crash. On top of everything else that's happened, Joe West fired me today."

"Lenny, I'm so sorry...You're still working on the case, aren't you?"

"Of course, although it's gonna be tough, being barred from the hospital." He felt icy air blowing in from the porch. The floor was frigid from the constant draft under the front door. He looked at the young woman standing on the porch, debated putting her off.

As he thought about his commitment to Regis, the weight of fatigue seemed to double. He heard his warm bed calling him. His legs felt weak, as though he'd been hit again in the head, and he yearned to lie down.

"I'm not gonna be much good for company, but come in while I get some clothes on."

She stepped nimbly through the door and into the living room.

This Won't Hurt A Bit

"I'll be right down, make yourself comfortable...Are you hungry, 'cause I could fix some..."

"I ate already, thanks."

She read the titles in the bookshelf while he ascended the stairs to get dressed.

Sixty-seven

In minutes, Lenny came downstairs dressed in jeans, navy blue sweater, and boots. He threw on his coat and hat, opened the door and let Kate out ahead of him.

"Can we take my car?" she asked, "I know the way."

"Fine."

He locked the door behind him and followed her to the car, an old all-wheel drive Subaru. As he opened the passenger door, Kate picked up a doll and a children's book from the seat and threw them in back. Lenny pictured mother and daughter sitting together in the evening looking at the pictures.

Putting the car in gear, Kate asked, "How's the investigation going?"

He told her the clues he'd collected, leaving out the secret that Primeaux had shared about his own past. He mentioned that Virginia Racine/Galloway had been seeing Radcliff and may have stopped taking birth control pills, and that he was assuming that she was the mystery blonde Sandy had reported wandering around the gynecology department.

He filled in the details of his run-in with Galloway at the laboratory, then gave her a blow-by-blow of his efforts to elude West and get out of the hospital without being fired.

"After all that, he still nailed you. What a shame," she said.

"I was kind of disappointed."

"Do you think Virginia Galloway is scared that her husband will find out about her abortion? I hear he has quite a temper."

"I don't know, Kate. I can't see a woman being that scared over a pregnancy."

She drove her little car skillfully, using the five-speed to keep the engine revving. Lenny grabbed the armrest as she threw the car around a corner. He liked the way she drove.

"What if it wasn't his baby?" she asked.

"I thought of that. Sparks could've been the father. An affair and an illegitimate child—that would certainly piss Galloway off. Besides, he's close to sixty. Maybe his sperm count was getting low and it ticked him off that he couldn't make another baby with his young wife, and that somebody else did."

"That could be a motive all right," she said.

"Especially to someone as egotistical as Galloway," he added, and told her how Galloway made a medical student carry his black doctor's bag for him.

"She could also be a battered woman, you know."

"I was thinking the same thing, but I think Primeaux would have told me if there were any bruises on her."

"That doesn't mean a damn thing. Men like Galloway know how to hurt a woman without leaving a mark. They leave internal injuries."

"Like a kidney punch," he said.

"Exactly. Or shaking someone really hard. That's how babies suffer brain damage, from the back-and-forth shaking of their head. The brain bangs against the skull, but outwardly, there isn't a mark on them."

"Bastards," he said.

They passed through the entrance of a new condominium development, parked beside a gray cube of a building with tiny terraces and sliding glass doors. Kate punched a button, listened at the intercom.

A tinny voice said, "Is that you, Katie?"

"Yes, Jen, let us in."

Above the loud buzzing at the door they could hear Jennifer asking, "Us?"

Kate and Lenny climbed the stairs, walked along a carpeted hall to a door that opened before Kate could knock. The tall, blond, and lovely Jennifer ushered them in. Then she locked the door with bolt and chain.

Jennifer eyed Lenny, looked to Kate.

"This is Lenny Moss. He's a union shop steward at James Madison," Kate told her. "And he's investigating the death of Randy Sparks."

Jennifer shook Lenny's hand, offered them a seat on a white coach. A small portable television set and VCR were against an opposite wall. Track lighting left shadows in the corners.

Kate said, "You were telling me that Randy Sparks came to visit you to use your VCR."

"Yes, that's right, but I don't know what he wanted it for."

"Is there a chance that he left the tape in your place?"

"I don't see how. You can see the apartment is pretty small and Spartan. There aren't a lot of places to leave stuff."

Lenny eyed the room. "Would it be a problem if we looked around?"

Jennifer's face stiffened. She turned to Kate. "I don't want to get mixed up in anything illegal, Kate."

"It's okay, Jen. If we find anything suspicious we don't have to say we found it with you, do we, Lenny?"

"Of course not," he said, showing his most innocent look.

"Okay," Jennifer said, "but I want Kate to look in the bedroom."

While the two women searched the bedroom, Lenny examined the living room. Finding nothing under the sofa cushions or beneath the furniture, he went to the VCR and looked at the tapes beneath it. Several of them were original exercise tapes with lean, smiling women in colorful body suits. Others were homemade copies with movie titles handwritten on the side.

Lenny recalled a famous maxim of Sherlock Holmes that Margaret had often quoted when he, the helpless husband, had been unable to find his wallet or keys: sometimes the best place to hide something was in plain sight.

He took the tapes one by one from their cartons and examined them carefully. Each tape appeared to match the title and manufacturer on the box. The homemade tapes were a generic brand; original tapes had professional labels and credits, and the logos stamped on the cartridge matched the logo on the box.

Except…

Except, wasn't the label on one of the exercise tapes curled away slightly at the corner? Not only that, but the logo stamped on the plastic body of the exercise tape did not match the manufacturer on the cardboard carton.

He inserted the tape in the VCR, switched on the television, picked up the remote control and pointed it at the machine and pushed the play button. The screen was gray for about a minute, then without introduction, the image of Radcliff's inner office appeared.

After a few seconds a black woman in a red robe and slippers walked to the reclining chair in the middle of the room and settled into it.

Lenny called out, "Kate, I found the tape!"

The two women rushed into the living room, stopped and stared at the screen.

The woman in the psychiatrist's chair was Mrs. Grey, the patient Kate had interviewed on Seven-South.

Radcliff approached the woman, sat on a small stool, told the woman to open her mouth. He placed a small pill under her tongue.

"What was that?" Lenny asked.

"Maybe one of the newer benzodiazapines," Kate said. "They're short-acting hypnotics that produce amnesia."

"A roofie?" Jennifer asked, referring to a popular tranquilizer that men dropped into their date's drink to make them compliant and produce amnesia.

"Something in that family," Kate said.

In a hushed, monotone voice, Radcliff told the patient, "The medicine will help you go into trance. Now lie back and let your body settle into the chair. Just let your body settle gently, comfortably into the chair."

Mrs. Grey closed her eyes. Her shoulders slumped, her fingers opened in her lap. Her whole body settled deeper into the softly padded chair.

Radcliff continued in his soothing voice, "You are so comfortable in your chair, so very comfortable as you let your muscles relax. And there is nothing to bother you in the chair. Nothing to think about or to remember. Just comfort and ease as you drift on the soft, comfortable cushions of your chair."

Jennifer said, "Isn't it dangerous for us to listen to this tape? I mean, couldn't we get in trouble for watching it?"

"Shush!" Kate said. "Let's see what's on it before we worry about who's going to object to it."

The patient breathed slowly, her eyes fluttered and closed, and her head lolled in the chair as though asleep. The doctor stood over her licking, his lips.

Sixty-eight

"That's good," Radcliff intoned, standing over the sleeping Mrs. Grey. "Ver-ry good. It feels so good to be relaxed and to think about nothing at all. And the only thing you wish to notice is the sound of my voice. Nothing else matters but the sound of my voice."

Radcliff leaned closer to the woman. "Now, in your mind you are going deeper and deeper into a comfortable, relaxed sleep. And in this chair you feel as if you are floating weightless on a cloud, completely unencumbered and carefree. Your arms are so very light that they begin to float above you in the air."

The woman smiled sweetly as her arms slowly rose from the chair and floated at shoulder height.

"Good, good, that's very good. Now let your arms settle back down softly by hour side... Good."

Radcliff stood, walked off camera. He returned with a small plastic bowl and sat beside Mrs. Grey, holding the bowl in his lap.

"Now, even in your sublime comfort you notice that the back of your right arm is becoming very warm. It is becoming uncomfortably warm. It is becoming hot, as if it had been out too long under a very hot sun."

The patient frowned, squeezed her closed eyes tighter.

The psychiatrist pulled a dripping sponge from the bowl in his lap.

"And wouldn't it feel so very good to take a cool, refreshing sponge and gently wipe your hot arm? To soothe the sun's heat on your bare skin with a cool sponge?"

Radcliff gently squeezed the sponge out over the bowl, then he placed it on the woman's arm and gently rubbed it up and down. Water trickled down to her hand.

The woman smiled.

"Good, very good. The sponge is deliciously cool and pleasant on your hot skin, and it feels so refreshing to wipe away the heat of the sun."

Radcliff moistened the sponge in the bowl and resumed rubbing her arm.

"Now, as you enjoy the coolness in your arm, you begin to feel another hot area on your neck. Yes, your neck is hot, it is very hot and uncomfortable, and it would be so nice to feel the cool sponge on your very hot neck."

He picked up the bowl and took a mouthful of cold water. He held the water in his mouth for several long seconds, then swallowed it.

"I am going to cool your sunburned neck with the nice refreshing cool sponge."

He bent his face over the woman's neck, opened his mouth. From his lips emerged the longest tongue that Lenny had ever seen. A curling, pink serpentine organ that curled above the woman's smooth, dark skin.

Radcliff slowly ran his tongue along the woman's neck. Then he stopped and whispered in her ear, "It feels so sublime, the coolness of the sponge against your skin."

The psychiatrist took another mouthful of ice water, swirled it around his mouth and swallowed. He pulled her robe away from one shoulder. His tongue emerged again and slowly licked her smooth bare neck and shoulder.

"Click."

The screen became dark and silent.

Kate had grabbed the remote control from Lenny's hand and turned off the VCR. She flung the remote into the corner.

"Of all the sleazy, sexist filth, this is the worst thing I have ever seen!" she said.

Jennifer crossed herself and shuddered. "I was seriously considering going into psychiatry," she said, "but after this, ugh!"

Kate turned to Lenny, tears in her eyes.

"How can you men watch this crap?"

"Indict me for the sins of my whole sex, okay? C'mon, I don't' go to porno movies. I'd rather watch the Marx Brothers."

Kate slumped into a chair. Her slender shoulders sagged. She looked at Lenny.

"I'm sorry, Lenny."

"That's okay."

"Is Radcliff the killer?" she asked.

"Well, he's got a good enough motive, and a secret like this would destroy his career and land him in jail if it was made public.

"You still sound doubtful," Kate said.

Lenny sat looking at the blank screen. His face was relaxed, thoughtful. He turned to the two women.

"Look, you both have had experience dissecting a body, and it's pretty gruesome stuff, isn't it?"

"I'll say," Jennifer said. "Finding out that the body we were working on was Randy Sparks…I mean, it was horrible."

"Okay. Now, psychiatrists don't have a lot to do with the body, right? They probably forget all their anatomy as soon as they finish their psychiatric training."

"That's true," Kate said. "They can't handle even the simplest medical problem. They always get an internist."

"Besides which, Radcliff is very squeamish about human waste. He couldn't even go into a patient's room until I'd cleaned up a load of smelly stool on the floor."

"What does that prove?" Jennifer asked.

"It's not proof of anything by itself, but it indicates that if Radcliff doesn't have the stomach for excrement then he wouldn't have the nerve to drain the blood from a body and fill it with preservative, let alone fake the wounds of a car accident."

"So you're saying that Radcliff is guilty of molesting his patients, but not of murder," Kate said.

"That's right. He may even know who killed Sparks and be covering up for him—the docs are all buddies up there—but I can't believe Radcliff did it."

"Then who's the killer?" Jennifer asked. "I feel as if I have a right to know, finding the body and all."

Lenny removed the tape from the machine, put it in the carton. "I'd put my money on Odom or Galloway. Odom was doing those nighttime abortions. Randy Sparks may have found out and threatened to spill the beans. Galloway helped Sparks land a cushy research job in Washington, DC. That could mean that Galloway owed him something."

"Maybe Galloway tried to buy Randy off with a favor," Kate said.

"That's possible," said Lenny. "But until I have something that proves Sparks was a threat to one of them, I can't come up with the killer."

He asked Jennifer if he could keep the tape. She gladly gave it to him. With the evidence tucked in his coat pocket, he and Kate left the apartment.

Back in her car, Kate asked what was Lenny going to do with the tape.

"I'm not sure. Maybe hand it over to Regis's lawyer if it might help get him off. Why?"

"I'd love to know that the filth was erased, but I was thinking of something else."

"What?"

She let the engine whine to its limit, shifted, concentrated on the road. She glanced quickly at Lenny, then returned her gaze to the road.

"I was thinking that somebody may have killed Sparks trying to get that tape, and now you've got it."

"And you think that somebody will come after me, is that it?"

She glanced at Lenny as the lights of oncoming traffic washed over her face.

"It looks to me like they already have."

Lenny sighed. "Did I forget to mention that somebody already put blood in my work shoes? I'll be dodging bullets before the weekend's over."

Kate pumped the brakes at a yellow light, cruised through, accelerated hard. She shot another glance at Lenny.

"This is serious, Lenny. You need to watch every step you take."

Lenny felt the bruise on the back of his head. "Tell me about it."

They rode the rest of the way in silence.

At Lenny's house, Kate wouldn't let him out until he swore that he would be extra careful. He pointed out that he was a lot safer in his own home than he would be at the hospital. Finally she bid him a solemn goodnight. Stepping out of the car, he returned the doll and book to the front seat, patted the head of the doll, and gently shut the car door.

Sixty-nine

On Saturday, Lenny slept until eight and awoke with a throbbing headache. In the mirror the burn didn't look too bad, so he didn't bother with the ointment. He dressed and went to the kitchen, made coffee and poured corn flakes into a bowl. The milk was sour. He threw it out and added orange juice to the bowl. "Not bad," he mumbled, crunching on the sweetened flakes. "Not for everybody, but not bad."

He attacked the pile of dishes in the sink, scrubbing week-old dirty plates and rinsing them in scalding hot water. When the rising steam awoke the pain in the burn he cut back on the temperature.

He knew that the hospital would drag out the waiting period for the grievance. They loved to punish you that way, make you eat up your savings, hope that you got desperate and found another job. If he won his case they would appeal it. Anything to keep him out of the hospital as long as possible.

Finishing the last dish, he turned off the water and wiped down the stainless steel sink. The hot water faucet went drip, drip, drip, even after putting pressure on the handle.

Needs a new washer, he decided. *I've got the time, might as well fix it.*

He dried the dishes and put them away, then he wiped down the counter tops and the refrigerator door. Walking into the living room, he looked over the place. When had he last washed the quilt that covered the sofa? Or dusted the bookshelf or the tables? He couldn't remember. He pulled the quilt off the sofa and threw it down the basement stairs, intending to add it to the wash when he brought his clothes down.

Once the first load of clothes was gyrating in the washing machine, he made a second cup of espresso and frothed the milk. He'd just sprinkled cinnamon over the milk when the phone rang. The bell made him jump.

The mechanical voice of the phone company computer asked if he would accept a phone call from Regis Devoe.

"Yes!" Lenny yelled into the phone.

He heard laughter on the line, then Regis saying, "What's the matter, Lenny, you got a bad connection?"

"Hi, Regis. No, it's those automatic programs the phone companies all

This Won't Hurt A Bit

use. You can't have a fantasy about going to bed with a computer like you can a real operator, you know?"

"Ain't nothin' like the real thing."

"That's what I mean," Lenny said. "Hey, are you all right? Are you out of the infirmary?"

"Yeah, I'm a whole lot better."

"That's great. What's the word on your case? Have you talked to your lawyer?"

"He was up to see me. He says the cops don't have squat for evidence. He thinks the only reason it got this far is Joe West pushing for it. Talking a lot of trash about my temper and all the times I've been written up."

"West never forgets an insult. Ever since you put the Krazy Glue in the time clock, he's wanted to fix your ass."

"How're you and Moose doing finding the killer?"

"We've found some un-fucking believable dirt on the doctors that Sparks was working with. I can't talk on the phone, but two of them had the motive, and the skills to pull it off, too."

"The workers trust you. They tell you stuff they wouldn't tell a priest. I'm halfway home."

"Now don't get too excited, Regis. We still haven't got the evidence to nail one of the docs. We're getting there. We're definitely making progress, but I ran into a few problems."

He told Regis about his run-in with a steam pipe, the blood in his shoes, and West terminating him.

"I can't roam the floors like I used to do. If West catches me inside I'll be sharing a cell with you, so we're going to have to rely on our friends even more."

"That's cool. You quarterback 'em down to the end zone."

Lenny told him that the union wouldn't be helping Regis with the legal case. Regis said that he shouldn't worry about it, his wife's family had got him a shark. He was in good hands.

"Speaking of Salina, why didn't you tell me she was *pregnant*? How can I get Betty to organize a shower for her if you don't tell me you're going to be a father?"

"I was gonna, man, it's just, my head's been screwed on ass-backwards with this jail thing, you know. But I was gonna tell you."

"And you didn't say anything about being in the Juvey Home either."

"Oh, man, that was way back when. I was just a kid. "B'sides, half the brothers've been behind the screen one time or another, even if they didn't do time like me. You know how the system works."

"Yeah, I know, Reeg. It doesn't really mean a damn thing. I understand that. It's just better if you tell me the worst so I'll be prepared for it, that's all."

"Yeah, well, I'm sorry man. No more secrets, okay?"

"Good."

"When you comin' out again?"

"Well, I'm out of work, so I have plenty of free time. I'll try to get out in the next couple of days. I'm trying to solve a murder case, don't forget."

"Hey, that's like the only thing I do think about, except for Salina, o' course. Tell her I was askin' for her, okay?"

"I will Regis. Take care of yourself."

"We won't even get to trial. Between you and Moose and my lawyer, I got all the bases covered."

"Did you talk to Salina?"

"Yeah, we hooked up last night. One good thing about the guards working me over, she's been nothing but warm."

"I'm glad to hear it." Lenny said he had to go. He had a lot of things to do to move the investigation along. Regis told him the next time they met it would be at the Goat Hollow over a pitcher. Lenny promised to buy, and hung up.

He was more confident that they would bring the murderer down. Maybe he was being cocky, maybe he was just being naive, but the pieces were coming together. Over the years, arguing union grievances he'd developed a sense of when a case was developing in his favor. There would be a sign, like a hostile witness who becomes evasive and vague when giving testimony, or a drop in the level of bombast from the hospital representative who knew he was no longer in control of the case.

He had developed that kind of sense. The clues were piling up. Night time abortions, sexually stimulating drugs, office visits covered up, and patient files that don't exist. And there were favors done for Sparks that must have required a reciprocal debt, or a threat. Either way, Odom and Galloway and Radcliff seemed like the most likely suspects. If he could meet Virginia Racine and get her to talk, he had a gut feeling that the last link would tie it all together.

But how to approach her. And how could he be sure Galloway wouldn't be there to throw his ass out…or shoot him for trespassing.

There had to be a way. Another cup of coffee, another load of laundry, and he was sure he'd figure it out.

Seventy

While transferring a load of laundry from the washer to the dryer, Lenny remembered that Celeste, the Seven-South unit clerk, had been off on Friday, which meant that she was probably working the weekend.

He called his old unit. Celeste answered on the second ring.

"Hi, it's Lenny."

"Lenny! It's so good to hear your voice, are you all right? We're all so upset West fired you. You'll get your job, back won't you?"

"Of course. It'll take some time, that's all."

"Are you still doing the murder investigation."

"That's why I'm calling. I need to know exactly where Doctor Galloway is this morning. If he's in the hospital, I may be able to go out to his house and talk to his wife."

"Okay, let me put you on hold. I'll dial his answering service and find out. Hold the phone."

Her voice was replaced by classical music. While he waited, he began to formulate a plan for addressing Virginia. He would have to be disarming. Draw her out. It would be tough, especially if she was frightened, which he expected she would be. He had to convince her that he could help her.

"Lenny?" Celeste was back on the line. "I got Galloway's service. He has an emergency surgery at Bryn Mawr hospital. He'll be scrubbed for a couple of hours, at least, so the coast is clear."

"Great, thanks, Celeste."

"Call me and let me know how it goes. And be careful, okay?"

"I will."

He had just cradled the phone when it rang, startling him. He waited a few rings to calm his nerves, then picked it up, afraid that it would be Detective Williams again.

"It's me," Moose said. "What's going down?"

"Oh, I'm just hunky dory. What's the word in the hospital?"

"Everybody's pissed as hell about West firing you. Betty and Birdie and me are gonna start a petition on Monday. Trust me, everybody'll sign it, even some of the doctors."

"Thanks. That won't carry any weight at the grievance step, but when it goes to arbitration it may influence the judge."

"What did the area rep say?" Moose asked.

Lenny was silent.

"You *did* call the union about your ass getting fired as soon as you got home, didn't you?"

"I'm sorry, Moose. With all the stuff about Regis and the murderer and everything, I completely forgot to call her. The office is closed now."

"Can't you beep her?"

"Yeah, but she can't do anything 'til Monday anyway."

"Yeah, well, she can fill out the grievance and have it ready to file first thing in the morning. I want you back on the job, brother. You hear me?"

"Sure, so I can get burned and beat up all over again. Thanks a lot."

"Heh-heh, you know you love it."

"Love it like hell, but I do want to bring this bastard down, whoever he is."

"And put that prick West out of the ring, too."

"Definitely."

"What are you gonna do next?"

"I'm going to visit Galloway's home and try to speak to his wife. Celeste just found out that Galloway is stuck in surgery, so this is a good time to go out."

"You're sure the doc's gonna be out of the house?"

"Positive. I'm not stupid enough to run into him in his own home."

"I'll stay on top of the guys here. Call me when you get back from Galloway's. You can leave a message at the kitchen. They're all cool."

"We'll have to meet off-site for now."

"How about the Dog Bite Cafe? It's just down the street, and they got booths where we won't be disturbed."

"Fine. Let's meet there Monday after work…I mean, after you get off. I'll have heard something from the union by then, and you may have more information, too."

"I'll tell Gary and Betty, we'll meet you there."

"Listen, Moose, I've got to run out to the hardware store. I want to file down the seats on the kitchen faucet and put in new washers."

"File the seats? You cheap son of a bitch, why don't you buy new faucets?"

"The faucet I got is fine, it's just the seats that are bad. Besides, I like to fix things. You know that."

This Won't Hurt A Bit

"Just like your old man. You'd put new soles on a beat up old pair of shoes before you'd buy a new pair."

"I'm not that bad. My boots are only three years old, and they hardly have any salt burn on them."

"Cheep, cheep, cheep," Moose said, imitating a chicken.

"Give me a call tomorrow, will you? I'll let you know what the area rep says."

"I sure will. Take care, man."

"You, too."

Lenny hung up. He sat a moment, sipping espresso, thinking what good friends he had in the hospital. He'd been there how long…Ten years? No, going on twelve. If he couldn't get his old job back it would be hard starting over again. Not that there was a hospital anywhere in the Delaware Valley that would hire him. With all the downsizing and layoffs, not to mention his reputation as a troublemaker. he didn't see much chance of landing another hospital job, but there were other jobs…other battles to fight.

Feeling the fatigue creep back into his body despite the coffee, he rinsed the cup and put it in the rack, then walked slowly down to the basement to start a second load of laundry. With the quilt in the wash and a load of clothes in the drier, he went to the living room to straighten up. As he put away books and stacked magazines to be recycled, he picked up the video tape with Radcliff's abuse on it.

Remembering that Sparks may have died for the tape, he considered where he might hide it. Hmmm. *If hiding the thing in plain site had worked for Sparks, why wouldn't it work for me?*

The woman's exercise tape seemed a bit out of place for him, so he took out one of his Star Wars Trilogy tapes he'd recorded off the television. Carefully peeling the handwritten label away, he scraped the exercise label off with a safety razor, and replaced it with the science fiction title, using Crazy Glue to hold it in place. Then he placed a blank label over the Star Wars tape and labeled it *Bootleg Star Wars* so that, should anyone play it, they would think he had a high quality copy.

Placing the Radcliff tape in with his sci fi collection, he considered that the psychiatrist would be right at home with Darth Vadar and all the other creepy evil doers. Put the shrink in a fictional evil empire and he'd probably be running it in by the millennium.

He stuffed the envelope with the copy of Virginia Racine's medical file into his pocket, threw on his hat and coat and hurried out the door. He was going to finally get to the bottom of this damned investigation.

Seventy-one

Betty was working overtime in the hospital, so she couldn't really complain about being assigned to the doctor's offices on the second floor. Pulling a huge ring of keys from her apron pocket, she unlocked the door to Robert Radcliff's office, opened it and pushed her cleaning cart into the outer office.

The first thing she noticed was that all the lights were on and there was soft music playing. That was odd. The secretary always turned everything off when she left at night. Must be the doc was seeing patients, she thought.

She emptied the trash bucket behind the secretary's desk, then she took a spray bottle and rag and dusted the lacquer table in the little waiting area. She didn't touch the secretary's desk, not wanting to disturb the mass of papers and open file folders that were scattered across the top.

"Kind of messy for a secretary," she thought, pushing her cart down the narrow hall. Opening the bathroom, she placed new toilet paper in the holder and fresh hospital towels on the wood rack. She scoured the sink and rinsed it.

Moving to Radcliff's office, she took out her keys to unlock the door, but found it was ajar. Since Radcliff was always very careful about locking his inner office, she decided he must be inside working at his desk, and knocked gently.

"Housekeeping. Can I come in?"

Silence.

She slowly pushed the door a bit further, poked her head inside. The doctor's desk was empty, the leather chair pushed up close to the edge of the desk.

As she opened the door wide, her eyes took in the rest of the room. That was when she saw Radcliff, seated in the reclining chair he used for his patients. His wrists were bound to the sides of the table with cloth tape. A roll of gauze stuffed in his mouth was dark with blood. His eyes were open and bulging, as though he'd looked upon some horrible, terrifying sight. His tongue, purple and swollen, stuck out from beneath the gauze.

Dark rivulets of blood ran down his chin onto a peach-colored shirt and lavender tie. His ankles, too, were bound with tape. A single tasseled loafer, kicked off in the death rattle, lay on the thick carpet in front of the body. The air was thick with the foul odors of blood and stool and urine.

Betty had seen many dead bodies in her years at James Madison Hospital. Had even helped the nurses wrap many of them, though that wasn't her job. Of all the corpses, dead from cancer and heart attacks and strokes, she had never seen a look of agony like the expression on the face of Dr. Radcliff.

She made the sign of the cross with her hand and recited a silent prayer, then backed out of the room and went to the secretary's desk, where she dialed the operator.

"Louise, this is Betty. You're not gonna believe this, but I'm up here in Dr. Radcliff's private office and I found him laid out stiff as a board."

"Is the doctor ill?" the operator asked.

"He's dead as a doornail. You best send security up here. And page the housekeeping supervisor, too."

"Do you want me to call a code?"

"No, don't bother with no code. Nothin' gonna help that poor soul but a lot of prayer. I'll stay here till security arrives."

"Okay."

Betty hung up. She took a fresh rag from her housekeeping cart and wiped her face, which was dripping with sweat, then she sat at the secretary's desk. Knowing she only had a minute or two to herself, she picked up the phone and dialed Lenny's number. When she heard his voice on the answering machine, she prayed that he was home but not in the mood to talk to anybody.

"Lenny, it's Betty. Call me at Seven-South later. I'm in one of the doctor's offices, but I should be upstairs in about an hour. Call me, it's mighty important."

She hurriedly hung up, then as an afterthought, she wiped the phone with the rag, now damp with sweat, and leaned back in the chair. Though she felt bad that any of god's creatures would die in such a horrible manner, she felt good about one thing. The cops would have to agree that Regis Devoe could not have committed *this* murder, and that could only help him with his case. They would have to look for someone else.

Didn't they?

She folded her arms in her lap, waiting for the security guard to arrive.

Lenny drove down the Lincoln Drive, the car leaning heavily in the tight curves. He knew he'd take his time, with all the black ice on the road this time of year. As if to underscore his thoughts, a wrecked red Camarro appeared on the side of the road as he passed the crest of a hill.

As he approached the entrance for Route One, he wondered how to approach Virginia Racine, a surgeon's wife. A lot of it depended on what sort of a person she was and the cues she gave out. He'd learned from interviewing countless hospital workers that some people responded to warmth and patience, while others had to be scared, even bullied, before they'd cough up their story.

Crossing the Schuylkill River, he saw in the distance the new downtown office buildings gleaming in the sun. The old height restriction—that no building be taller than the statue of William Penn atop City Hall—had been broken, and new towering structures were giving the city a modern look.

He drove west, reaching the Bala Cynwyd suburbs in minutes. He turned right just past the commuter train station and soon found the street he wanted. It wasn't far from the Bala movie Theatre, where in the old days he'd seen many a second run film for two bucks.

Lenny parked his car in the street in front of the Galloway house, a large, pseudo-colonial affair with a circular drive, skinny trees and stubby shrubs in front, wooden fence and older oak trees behind. He walked up the circular drive thinking, *Too bad I can't say I'm here to clean her carpets or mop her kitchen floor.*

Standing before a powder-blue double door with flowery, frosted glass inserts, Lenny put his nose to the glass and looked in. Dim shapes of tables, a hallway, stairs curving away in a great arc. He knocked, softly at first, then firm, businesslike.

Through the frosty glass, he watched a fuzzy, willowy shape seem to float down the curving stairwell. Ethereally it drifted across the landing toward the door. The glass peep hole became dark, an eye behind the door.

"Who is it?"

The voice was a tremulous contralto.

Lenny decided that no scam would get him in the door the way he had done in the hospital.

"Mrs. Galloway? My name is Leonard Moss. I work at James Madison Hospital. I need to talk to you about Dr. Odom and Dr. Radcliff, and…"

He was not sure how far to go.

"…about Randy Sparks."

Lenny hung on the silence between them.

"Go away! Go away or I'll call the police."

This Won't Hurt A Bit

"But if you just…"

"Go away! I can't talk to you…Please, just leave me alone."

He stood outside peering through the milky glass thinking he had one chance to get her to open the door. One chance in a million.

Seventy-two

Lenny stood outside the Galloway house, the shadowy figure of Virginia Galloway on the other side. He had a hunch, drew to an inside straight.

"I need to talk to you about your son, too, Mrs. Galloway. It's about what happened to Jason. All those operations."

He didn't really know if the child was a factor in Racine's decision to have an abortion. Wasn't sure she'd actually had one, for that matter. None of the odd things they had found in the hospital pointed to Racine's child, but Lenny had a hunch that the child's frequent hospitalizations had made the woman anxious about bearing another child.

"May I speak with you? Please."

The figure behind the glass stepped back.

"Who sent you here?"

"Nobody sent me, Mrs. Galloway. I came on my own. I'm not the police or anything like that. I work in James Madison Hospital. Look, check out my ID." He pulled the union steward ID from his pocket and held it close to the peep hole. "It's awfully hard to explain through a door."

She looked at him again through the peep hole.

"I can't talk to you. Go away."

Lenny stepped away from the door.

"Look, I can hear in your voice that you're frightened, and I understand that. But you're certainly not scared of me. I mean, you can see me through the door, right? And I'm sure not a scary person.

"I know about the procedure you had, Mrs. Galloway, at night in Dr. Odom's office. And about seeing Radcliff, and I know that you're in trouble. If you'd just hear me out for five minutes I believe that I can help you."

After a long silence the door opened a crack. Lenny could see two tearful eyes peering through the narrow opening.

"What did you say your name was?"

"It's Lenny," he said in a soft voice. "I'm a custodian in the hospital and a union shop steward, and in a goofy sort of way I got roped into investigating Randy Sparks' murder. He was a resident at James Madison Hospital. As I got deeper into the case your name kept coming up."

This Won't Hurt A Bit

"My name? Why would my name come up?"

Lenny edged closer to the door, which was still only open a crack.

"If you let me come in, I'll explain everything…Please."

She looked into Lenny's earnest face, which had the empathy of a priest.

The crack in the door widened to a gap just big enough for Lenny to pass through. He slipped in, found himself on a glossy tile floor. Fresh flowers in a crystal vase stood on a little table by the door. The carpeted stairs rose in an elegant curve to a landing with sunlight spilling through a high window.

"Hi. I'm Lenny."

He reached his hand out. Mrs. Galloway accepted it. Her hand was moist and limp.

"Virginia Galloway. I guess you know that already, don't you?"

Lenny looked her over. She was a very attractive woman in her mid-thirties, dressed in a soft, pink sweater and black pants. Slim. Athletic. Probably had a pool in the back. Her hair was dark, almost black, and fell to her shoulders in a luxurious splash.

She led him to a large living room, with straight-backed, uncomfortable-looking furniture and a great hearth with a carved wooden mantel. A picture window looked out on the broad front lawn.

Lenny sat on a wing-backed chair with little pillows on it, Virginia on a love seat facing the fireplace. He glanced at an antique clock sat on a white marble mantelpiece. A pair of wooden duck decoys, weathered and old, stood beside the fireplace. The room had a light, pleasant smell of herbs, a potpourri probably.

Lenny looked at Virginia's face. She had lovely hazel eyes red from crying, and black, arching eyebrows. High cheekbones and a small mouth.

"I'm a shop steward at James Madison Hospital in the housekeeping department. The way this all started, Mrs. Galloway, is, a resident named Randy Sparks was murdered and he was made to look like it'd been in a car accident. His body was sneaked into the anatomy lab at the medical school under a John Doe.

"When somebody realized who the body belonged to, the police arrested a young man who works in the laundry, but I'm sure that he didn't do it. Not because he's in the union, but because he wouldn't know how to preserve the body in embalming fluid or fake the signs of a car wreck. He'd have trouble with the computer records, too. Every body has to be accounted for. They don't buy them from guys off the street like they used to."

Seeing that his attempt at humor was useless, he pressed on.

"Being a union rep, I was asked to try and get the laundry worker his job back, but I couldn't do that as long as he was in jail facing a murder rap, so I agreed to see if I could find the real killer."

Lenny watched her face for response. It was taut, fearful, and gave him nothing.

"I know it sounds goofy, even to me, but, if you spent any time with me you'd know that I sometimes do goofy things."

Virginia's face was still enigmatic. Lenny glanced at the wooden decoys by the fireplace, then back at Virginia. He felt like he was talking to them.

"Anyway, during the months before Sparks was murdered, he worked with several doctors, including your husband. As I followed the trail, your maiden name showed up, first in Dr. Radcliff's appointment book, then in Dr. Odom's. Then you turned out to be married to Dr. Galloway."

"Doctor's wives have a small social circle," she said. "There's nothing odd about my visiting physicians on staff where my husband practices."

"I realize that, but your name came up in unusual ways. It was whited out of the psychiatrist's book..."

"Secretaries use white out all the time, don't they?"

"All the other cancellations were crossed out. Yours was the only one covered over."

Lenny took a breath. She didn't look as though she knew what he was talking about, but she hadn't talked about calling the police again. She was harder to read than Childress in a grievance hearing. He wondered what button he could push that would get her to open up.

"I thought maybe you were considering an abortion and you wanted to talk it through with Dr. Radcliff first, he being a psychiatrist and all. Then, it seemed that you had an abortion in Dr. Odom's office late at night when there was nobody around to see what happened."

"I don't see what this has to do with Randy Sparks being murdered, unless you think that Nathan... you don't mean *he* had anything to do with it, do you?"

"I'm not accusing anyone of anything, Mrs. Racine, believe me. I'm just trying to make sense of it all."

She stared blankly at Lenny. He waited for another response, but she gave him nothing. He decided to turn up his last card.

"I know that your son has had a lot of medical problems since he was very young. That he was born with them. And I thought that possibly you were afraid that the same thing would happen again, with your second pregnancy. Perhaps you were worried that your husband would blame you somehow, unfairly, of course, and that was one of the things you discussed with Dr. Radcliff. About the possibility of bearing another sickly child."

He had put everything he had on the table. There were no more buttons to push. All he had left now was patience, just like at the negotiating table, when the other side asked for a recess, and all he could do was sit and wait to see if they budged.

If she would only stop staring blankly at him and react, he'd have a sense that he was getting somewhere.

Her rigid face began to quiver. Her eyes closed and spilled over with tears. She turned her face into the sofa, her narrow shoulders shuddering as she sobbed into the pillow.

He pulled out his handkerchief, then thought better of offering it to her, having used it more than once. He spotted a frosted glass tissue holder and brought it to her. She dabbed her eyes with the tissue and looked away without focusing on anything in particular.

"Is it because of the problems that your son had? Is that why you went to Odom?"

She dabbed her eyes again. Her mascara was smeared. She sat with her shoulders hunched forward and her head bowed, as though she expected to be slapped in the face at any moment.

He was prepared to see pain in her lovely eyes, but he wasn't prepared for the raw, smoldering terror in them. Her pupils were so dilated he could hardly see the color in them, and they glistened with tears. Her voice was hoarse with emotion as she began her story.

"When Jason was three days old we realized how ill he was. He had congenital defects. In his heart and in his colon. The pediatrician assured me that it wasn't my fault, I wasn't a smoker or drinker, I didn't use drugs. I'd eaten well and kept all my appointments with the obstetrician."

She looked away again, crossing her arms across her chest.

"Altogether Jason had seven operations. Seven! The nurses assured me that he wouldn't remember them when he grew up, but I never believed that. I see it in his face sometimes, a kind of dread. I couldn't face having another child like that. I went to Dr. Radcliff to sort things out, and he told me that Dr. Odom sometimes offered a discretely done procedure for certain women. Special cases, he called them. So, I bought a blond wig and made an appointment with him. My husband doesn't know. He must never know."

"Please believe me Mrs. Galloway: if it's at all possible I'll keep this strictly between us."

Although he waited for more, Mrs. Galloway remained silent.

Lenny tried to look in her eyes for the truth, but she avoided eye contact. He felt that her story was true as far as it went, but it didn't connect her with the murder. Didn't give him any new information about why Sparks was killed, let alone who killed him.

The mystery woman on whom he had counted for so much had failed to clear up the mystery.

Seventy-three

*L*enny asked himself if his hopes had been too high? He didn't think so. He was sure that he was on the right track.

"Did Randy Sparks know about your abortion?"

"No. That is, I don't think he did. I only met him once, in Dr. Radcliff's office. He hardly said a word to me, but he gave me this very odd look. He asked if we had ever met before. I told him no, I didn't think so, and then he went into the room with Dr. Radcliff."

"Did Sparks sit in on your session with the psychiatrist?"

"No, he wasn't there."

Lenny recalled the mirror on the wall in Radcliff's inner office and wondered if it was a one-way window.

"What did you talk about?"

"How I felt…Scared. Confused. I know that I told Dr. Radcliff that I blamed myself for Jason's problems. He said that guilt was a destructive emotion."

"What else did you tell him?"

"That was all, really. How afraid I was of Nathan's reaction if he ever found out that I was pregnant again. I was supposed to be on the pill. That nice Dr. Alex Primeaux prescribed it for me, but the medicine was making me sluggish and bloated, so I stopped it for a while, and then…"

"You realized you were pregnant?"

"Yes. Alex did the test for me. I couldn't go through with it again."

"Was your husband really that opposed to you getting pregnant again?"

She took another tissue and wiped her nose, looked away for a moment. He felt her stalling as she weighed her thoughts. Was she constructing a story or struggling with the truth?

"You know how surgeons are known for their tempers?" she asked. "Nathan's is really something. I feel sorry for the nurses in the operating room, knowing how he can carry on so."

He wanted to ask if Galloway was the father, but didn't know how to broach the subject. He didn't think he could go that far, but if he didn't, what did he have? Just confirmation of what he'd suspected. But maybe not the whole story.

"Mrs. Galloway, if you could be sure that the baby would be healthy, how would your husband feel about being a father again? Did he want another child?"

"Definitely not. Nathan made it vividly clear to me—no more children. That was another reason I was so anxious about the pregnancy."

"So if you told him he was going to be a father again, he'd be pissed..."

"I don't want to even think about what he would do," she said.

It was as close to asking the parenthood question as he felt he could go.

Lenny considered another possibility, that Virginia knew something important about the murderer but did not herself realize it's importance. She may have confided something to Radcliff. Assuming the session had been videotaped, Sparks could have heard it later on and put two and two together, or watched it from another room...but what would it be? What did this lovely, frightened woman represent that might lead to murder?

"Mrs. Galloway, do you have any idea who might have wanted to kill Randy Sparks?"

She folded her tissues in a ball and squeezed them in a tight fist, looked past Lenny to the large picture window and the snowy yard beyond. Then she turned her tearful eyes to him.

"No, I don't. I only met him that one time...I'm sorry, I just haven't any idea."

Folding her hands in her lap, she looked as though she were preparing for a funeral. Or a long jail sentence. Lenny realized he would get nothing more from her that day.

He looked again at Virginia's lovely face, finding it disturbing. She reminded him of Margaret when she was in the last stage of the cancer. Was it because Virginia's face showed the same fear and pain?

He took out his wallet, wrote his home and work phone numbers on the back of an old grocery receipt, held it out to Virginia. "I have to get going, Mrs. Galloway. Please call me if there is any way that I can help you."

She took the strip of paper from him. They walked to the front door. She opened it wide, stood looking out over the frozen lawn, the bare trees, snowy street.

"Goodbye," she said, not holding out her hand.

He strode down to his car. She shut the front door so carefully that it made no sound, for when he reached his car and looked back, the frosted glass door was closed.

This Won't Hurt A Bit

On the drive back home, he thought about the age difference between Virginia and Galloway. She could have been having an affair with Sparks, Galloway found out, he became insanely jealous, and killed Sparks out of rage. Did he think that a beautiful young wife would keep him from aging?

How to nail down the final piece of evidence?

Knowing that his mind worked best when he was not thinking about a problem, but was doing something else, he decided to drive past the hardware store and get the new seats and washers for the kitchen sink. The work would relax him and help him get a view of the big picture. He crossed the Schuylkill River and took the Roosevelt expressway north.

While Lenny was on the road, the security guard who came to Radcliff's office made two calls. He phoned 911 and requested the police, after which he called the supervisor on duty to report the incident. Then he took out a tiny notepad and, feeling like a real detective, began to take down Betty's account.

The security supervisor also placed a call to Joe West, who realized immediately that the second murder would not only damage the hospital's reputation to the point that it's fiscal health would be in jeopardy, but it complicated the case against Regis Devoe.

He was in an ill humor as he drove to the hospital, but as the building came into sight his mood improved. He had been instrumental in building the murder case against Devoe. Had even manufactured some of the evidence. Perhaps…just perhaps he might be able to tie Lenny Moss to the psychiatrist's murder. Now that would settle a host of problems with one swift blow.

First, he would plant the remains of the aborted fetus that he had taken from Moss' locker in Radcliff's office. It had the custodian's fingerprints on it, he was sure, while West had carefully handled it with gloves. Once the police discovered it, he would describe his conversation with Dr. Fingers. That would put Moss at the crime scene.

With a little luck, Moss would be home alone playing with himself this morning. No alibi. Lock him up, work up enough additional evidence to bring charges, and another pest exterminated.

Yes, indeed, this was turning out to be a banner day.

Seventy-four

After picking up the equipment he needed to repair the kitchen sink, Lenny drove home, parked the car and went inside. The mail had arrived, early for a Saturday. Just circulars and bills, which he threw on the livingroom coffee table. He dropped the bag of supplies in the kitchen and was filling the espresso machine with fresh water when he heard a loud *knock, knock, knock* on his front door. He knew it wasn't Kate, and he knew it wasn't good news. The sound was too loud and too demanding to be anything but a cop.

Opening the door, he looked into Detective Joe William's face.

"Say," Lenny said, "don't I know you from somewhere? Aren't you the guy who..."

"Get your coat, you're coming with me."

"Yikes. Should I call a lawyer or a morgue attendant?"

"I'm not in the mood for jokes today, Mr. Moss. I have another murder on my hands."

"Really? Tell me it's Joe West, please."

"Not even close. Let's go."

Lenny took his hat and coat from the hall closet, locked the front door behind him, and followed the detective to his unmarked car.

"Where are we going, the Round House?" he asked, referring to the large, round central police headquarters just north of Center City.

"No, I'm not booking you—yet. I'm going to question you at the precinct."

Instinctively reaching for the rear passenger door, Lenny was slightly relieved when Williams opened the front and let him ride with him. Maybe the cop was being cagey, playing mind games by offering to treat him decently. Or maybe he really did want to be fair to Lenny. He had no way to tell; the man's eyes gave nothing away.

They rode down Germantown Avenue, the cobblestones and potholes rattling the old police car. In a few minutes they turned off and were at the station, a squat, ugly cement building with police cars parked at the curb and fancy sports cars in the lot. Toys of the fast-driving young cops.

Williams led Lenny past the front desk, where a tired-looking cop was half listening to an elderly woman complain about the abandoned house on her block that had become a haven for drug addicts. Down a narrow corridor past offices with ringing phones that seemed to go unanswered forever, they came to a room with a steel door labeled "Interrogation."

Holding the door open for Lenny, Williams said, "You sit at that end of the table facing the mirror."

Lenny looked across the table, saw the wide mirror covering much of the far wall. One-way glass, he was sure.

"Where's the spotlight and the rubber hose?" he asked, settling into a battered metal chair. He noticed that the chair was chained to an anchor on the floor. Protection for the police, no doubt.

"Just wait here," Williams said, and stepped out. The door closed with an auspicious click. Lenny was sure that it was locked.

The clock on the wall said ten-o-five. If the cops used the same psychological methods as the hospital lawyers during contract negotiations, they would make him wait a long time. Try to break his confidence, let the anxiety in him grow. He would have time to imagine all sorts of terrible consequences. He would start to sweat, get hungry, thirsty, have to take a leak, and they could decide when he could and could not satisfy any of his needs, including taking his bodily functions.

He decided he'd better play a game of his own, or he really would go crazy.

Getting out of his chair, he walked up to the mirror, cupped his hands over his eyes and tried to look through the one-way glass. No good.

Next, he wet his index finger and drew a large heart on the glass. It didn't show up very clearly, and he didn't have anything to draw with, like chalk or lipstick. He briefly considered scratching something in the glass, but knew they would charge him with destruction of property, so he took a deep breath and blew a stream of warm, moist air onto the glass. The mist was just thick enough to let him draw another heart, in which he wrote "JW loves RF," suggesting an attraction between Joe West and the effeminate Human Resources Director Freely.

Not much of a joke, but he operated on the philosophy that a bad joke was always better than no joke at all.

Returning to the chair, he took out his wallet and emptied it onto the table, then he sorted through it, slowly and methodically, reading each little scrap of paper. He threw away the receipts from the deli and supermarket, arranged the ATM receipts by date and made a promise to really organize his checking account.

He wished he knew origami. He could fold the scraps of paper into cute little birds and animals and decorate the room, like the bad guy in that action movie. Instead, he made tiny paper airplanes and launched them into the air. One flew well, making a loop-de-loop; another dipped down and immediately crashed.

He put his wallet back in his pocket, and glanced up at the clock. Only a half-hour had passed. He put his head down on the table to try and sleep, but that position made his head throb.

Deciding that he might as well think about the case, Lenny closed his eyes and tried to visualize the sketches of the suspects, enjoying Moose's arch portrayal of the five physicians.

In a large, comfortable house in Bala-Cynwyd, Virginia Racine/Galloway packed two suitcases, one for herself, one for her son, Jason. She collected the papers she would need: his birth certificate, her social security card, check book, and the key to the safety deposit box. Wrapping her son in a warm coat and long scarf, she walked with him out to her car.

"Are we going on a trip?" he asked, noting the suitcases that she had placed in the trunk of the car.

"Yes, sweetheart, we're going to visit my friend Angie. You remember her, the woman I went to school with? She lives in Center City in an apartment way up high. You can see the river and the Art Museum and everything."

"I remember. They have a man in a uniform who opens the door for you."

"That's right."

Climbing into the passenger side and fastening his seatbelt, Jason asked, "How long will we stay with Aunt Angie?"

"I'm not sure, dear. It depends."

"On what?"

She dabbed her eyes with a tissue, putting dark glasses on, and inserted the key into the ignition.

"It's hard to explain, dear. Let's just get to the city and I'll tell you all about it later."

"Can we get a pretzel with mustard from the man outside?"

"Of course you can, dear. And a nice hot chocolate, too."

She pulled the car out of the driveway and turned toward City Line Avenue. When she got onto the Schuylkill Expressway, she saw the city skyline, and the trembling which had rattled her arms and legs and teeth for several days began to subside.

Seventy-five

At ten minutes after twelve, Joe Williams and Detective Sternbach entered the interrogation room. Sternbach said, "All right, Moss, we have some questions to ask you and we expect your full cooperation."

"Joe Williams said you had another murder but he didn't say who. Was it a doctor? Somebody who worked with Sparks?"

"We'll ask the questions," Sternbach said. "Where were you last night between ten o'clock and two in the morning?"

"I was at home in my bed."

"Alone?"

"That's right. I've been thinking about getting a dog for a companion, but I don't know, they make such a mess and chew up the…"

"Cut the crap!" Sternbach yelled. "You think you're cute? How would you like to go down to the Round House and be arraigned on suspicion of murder? You think that would be *cute*?"

"Are you accusing me of a crime?" Lenny asked, rising from his chair. "Because if you are, you haven't read me my Miranda rights and I'm not saying a word unless I have a lawyer present who…"

"Hold it!" Williams said, putting his hands up like stop signals. He looked from Lenny to Sternbach. "I think we got off on the wrong foot here," he said in a quiet voice. "Let's begin at the beginning, shall we? Please take your seat, Lenny."

Lenny sat down, folded his arms across his chest and waited for the "good cop" to play his part.

"Now then," Williams went on in a calm, patient voice, "after Regis Devoe was arrested you decided to look into the Sparks murder with the intent of finding evidence pointing toward another suspect, isn't that right?"

"Pretty much, yeah," Lenny said.

"What do you mean by 'pretty much'?" Sternbach demanded.

"I mean, I kind of fell into it, but at first I didn't take it that seriously. I didn't really think that we'd get too far, but I figured it was worth a shot."

"You told me about a drug that the pharmacy department had reported missing," Williams went on. "A drug called enpros. Is that right?"

"Yeah, that's the one. Did you look into it?"

"We did. There have been several reports of the drug disappearing. You also told me about a needle and syringe in the sofa of a waiting area of a Dr. Priscilla Gandy."

"Right."

"We're looking into those items. I tell you that because I want you to know that our murder investigation will leave no stone unturned, regardless of where the evidence leads us. Understand?"

"Sure"

"You don't look convinced," Sternbach said.

"I'm just wondering how you're going to pin the second murder on Regis Devoe. Do you think he hired someone to do it? And by the way, who was it you said was killed?"

"As if you didn't know," Sternbach said.

"What is that supposed to mean?"

"He means, are you sure that you didn't visit James Madison last night some time after midnight and visit Dr. Robert Radcliff?"

Lenny remembered his early morning visit to Radcliff's inner office. He wondered if the night custodian had dimed on him. He didn't think it likely, but some guys broke down with a little pressure from the cops. Then he recalled the video cameras and it suddenly became clear that Radcliff probably had a motion sensor to shoot anyone entering his office. If the police had the tape, it would place him in the office, although it should also record the time, which would be Friday morning, not late at night.

"Of course I'm sure. What makes you think I was there?"

Williams reached into a canvas satchel and withdrew a plastic ziplock bag with a hospital specimen container in it. As soon as Lenny saw the container, his heart skipped a beat and he felt sweat begin to bead from his hands and under his arms.

"What can you tell me about this?" Williams asked.

"It looks like a hospital specimen cup," Lenny said.

"Don't be coy with me. We know you brought this to the pathologist at the hospital, Dr. Fingers. We have his statement, and we have your fingerprints on the container."

"Yeah, I found in while I was investigating the Sparks murder and thought there might be an abortion tied in with the motive. But it didn't come from Radcliff's office, it came from Odom's in gynecology."

"That may well be," Williams said, leaning forward and staring into Lenny's eyes. "But we discovered this evidence in Radcliff's inner office. And we also found your fingerprints on his desk. How do you explain that?"

"I'm a custodian. I was probably cleaning up."

"Bullshit!" said Sternbach. "How did the cup get into Radcliff's office?"

"How should I know? I left it in my locker and somebody stole it."

"Yeah right," Sternbach added.

"Listen, I'm not saying any more until I know if you're charging me with a crime. Are you?"

The two detectives looked at each other, then Williams said, "That depends on your telling us *everything* you know about this case. The Sparks murder. Radcliff. Everything, beginning with your list of suspects."

Lenny took a big breath, let it out. "It's not all that much, but okay, here goes. For one thing, there's a woman who came to the hospital last December around the time that Sparks was killed. She picked up a pass to visit a patient, but never showed up there."

"Who told you this?" Williams asked.

"I'd rather not name my source—for the time being. It was just casually mentioned to me and I thought it could be important."

Noticing that Williams was not writing anything down, Lenny realized the interview was being recorded, probably on video.

"Go on," Williams said.

"I thought the woman might have gone and had an abortion in secret from Dr. Odom in his hospital office."

"Why did you think that?" Williams asked.

"Because one of the housekeepers found the remains of an aborted fetus in his trash bucket."

"We know about that," Williams said. "About Odom. Didn't you get a look at his personal appointment book?"

"What are you talking about?" What appointment..."

"Don't play games with us, Moss!" Sternbach barked. "You broke into Odom's locker. West told us all about it."

"Is he out there watching?" Lenny asked.

Williams kept a deadpan face. "No. He wanted to be here for your questioning, but I explained that, as a material witness, I couldn't taint him with being a party to your examination."

"So he's here, but not outside."

"That is correct," Williams said.

"And you expect *me* to trust *you*? Come on. West has been busting my balls for years. He hates my guts. Anything he learns he'll use against me."

"And," said Williams, "anything he can do to you is pissing in the Delaware compared to what *we* can do to you if you don't cooperate."

Williams leaned closer to Lenny and lowered his voice. "And what I said at your place about being open to new evidence—that still goes. West doesn't run this investigation, I do."

Lenny looked into the detective's dark, unblinking eyes. He didn't think the police would look for another suspect...or would they?

Seventy-six

Lenny didn't know whether to believe Williams or not, but decided, on reflection, that he'd be better off telling them enough to get them off his back. Otherwise, he might be spending a lot more time in the police station, and it wouldn't be in an interrogation room.

"You know when us custodians clean the lounges we find all kinds of personal items lying around. Those doctors are real slobs."

"And you just happened to find an appointment book lying open on the floor, right?" Williams asked.

"How did you know? Anyway, I found that in December. I have the date written down at home somewhere. Odom had the initials VR written in his appointment book for the same period that that woman disappeared into the hospital, so I figured that the woman had an abortion with Odom."

"That's a mighty long guess," Williams said.

"Hey, I'm just an amateur. You're the pros."

"Next time leave it to the professionals," said Sternbach. "It sounds like you got a lot of nothing—unless you're holding out on us."

"Hell, no. You think I want to spend any more time with you guys than I have to? Nothing personal, you understand."

"First degree murder is nothing to joke about," Williams said. "I would advise you to tell us all that you know of this matter."

"That's exactly what I'm trying to do."

"So your suspect list included Radcliff, Gandy, and Odom," Williams said. "Who else, and why?"

"All I did was take down the names of the doctors that Sparks worked with and then nosed around. Those were Galloway, a surgeon, and Alex Primeaux, although he's not a suspect. I didn't find anything suspicious about him at all. Everyone says he's the nicest guy in the whole hospital."

Williams looked long and hard at Lenny's face, then he said, "All right. The man who beat you up in the boiler room. Have you any idea who that was?"

"No idea, but it could have been Radcliff."

"Why is that?" asked Williams.

"Because a patient on my floor, Mrs. Grey, told me that she saw a blond man in a lab coat disappear down the stairs right after her wallet was stolen, which fits Radcliff's description. That was right before somebody hit me."

"Did Radcliff usually wear a lab coat?" Sternbach said.

"Not as far as I saw, he was a three-piece suit type, but they're easy enough to pick up. There might even be one in his office."

"We'll check it out," Williams said. "One last question, and I want you to think very carefully before you answer it."

Lenny kept silent, waiting for the worst.

"Who do you think killed Sparks?"

"I don't know," Lenny said. "I figure that to pickle the body and make it look like it'd been in a car wreck you'd have to be a surgeon, but I suppose a medical doctor could to it, too."

"You're only considering doctors? How come?" Williams asked.

"The thing is—this is why I'm the amateur and you're the pros, I guess—but the way I see it, using the medical students in the anatomy lab to dispose of the body, I mean, that's a wicked kind of joke, isn't it? It's like hiding something in plain sight and daring the world to catch you. See what I mean?"

The two detectives looked blankly at Lenny. Although they did not comment on his theory, he had a hunch that Williams had been thinking along the same lines.

Sternbach sat still, a sullen, brooding look on his face. Williams stood up, went to the door and opened it.

"I could hold you for twenty-four hours, but I'm going to let you go. Just be sure you stay in town. Don't go *anywhere* without first clearing it with me. You got that?"

"I got it."

"We'll be talking again. Soon."

As Lenny reached the doorway, Sternbach called out, "Oh, we forgot to tell you. We executed a search warrant on your place this morning. You might have to tidy it up a bit."

He grinned a narrow-lipped snake's grin. Lenny now understood why they had made him wait so long before questioning him.

He walked alone out of the room and turned right down the hall, understanding that he was on his own getting back home.

Sternbach turned left and walked four steps, took out a ring of keys and unlocked the door to the adjoining room. An officer was rewinding a video cassette tape in a camera facing the one-way glass that looked onto the examination room. Joe West stood at parade rest, looking through the glass.

This Won't Hurt A Bit

As Sternbach came into the room, West said, "I get a copy of the tape, don't I?"

"Sure, Joe," Sternbach said, "just keep it on the QT."

West nodded solemnly, waiting for his tape to be copied.

Seventy-seven

Lenny stood outside the police station breathing in the cold air. He wished he had his car, or that Moose was home. With a shrug, he walked the four blocks to Germantown Avenue and rode a bus to Walnut Lane. From there it was a short walk home to his house. When he opened the front door, he almost laughed. The place didn't look all that different from how he left it.

First, he examined the collection of video tapes. The Star Wars trilogy seemed intact, but just to be sure, he pulled out the first one and put it in the VCR, switched on the television and waited. Instead of the rousing orchestra introduction and the giant space ship thundering across the heavens, he saw the telltale shot of Radcliff's office and the chair where his patients had been abused.

Relieved, he returned the tape to its cardboard holder and put it back with the others, then he checked the sideboard in the dining where he'd left Moose's sketches. They were still there. The cops had even stacked them neatly, probably the only thing they didn't leave in a mess. Maybe it had been a police artist on the scene.

He looked around the room, noted the quilt gone from the sofa and remembered he'd put it in the wash. Going through the dining room to the back stairs, he wondered idly if the cops had had the decency to switch his wet laundry from the washer to the drier for him.

When he turned on the gas drier, the warming exhaust pipe reminded him of his injury. He felt his face where it had brushed against the steam pipe. He knew that he was in danger and should be scared, but somehow he wasn't. He knew he should feel anger, but he was too tired for that.

Mostly he was frustrated. What if he had all the clues he was going to get? What would he do then? Maybe the clues were not really clues at all. Maybe the killer was so cunning that he had left the fetus and the D&C tray and the rest of it for Lenny to find. That he was manipulating events and leading Lenny down a garden path in order to throw him off the track.

Lenny had a sinking feeling that everything he had uncovered was worthless. Worse, that it had led him away from the killer instead of toward him.

Could the killer really be that cunning? Could Lenny be such a dope?

All that he was sure of was that Virginia Galloway was in fear of her life, and that the suspects all had something to hide. How could he identify the right one?

Lenny recalled Virginia's lovely, fearful face: her hazel eyes, small mouth, arching eyebrows. Did her face unsettle him because her pain reminded him of Margaret as she lay dying? Perhaps he simply didn't want to touch raw emotion like hers again.

He spread the sketches out on the coffee table and studied them. Each character perfectly cast in a role. Butcher and vampire. Angel and mad scientist. The wicked witch riding the syringe.

The answer was in the sketches, he was sure of it. Gandy riding the syringe, a prophetic image. Would she kill Sparks over a jilted lover affair? He didn't think so.

Primeaux the angel really was an angel. He had the secret that would ruin him, but Lenny had trouble believing that he would kill someone to keep it hidden.

Odom the butcher. Cold enough to kill? Definitely. Motive? Yes, though it wasn't the strongest of reasons. A maybe.

Moose had drawn Galloway as the mad scientist. Didn't Dr. Frankenstein create life from nonlife? Wasn't it his arrogant toying with creation that led to catastrophe?

There was something there in the sketch of Galloway that gave him the creeps—the smug little smile, the patronizing posture. The spoiled son of a doctor who was always given everything on a silver platter. Why did he help Sparks get that research assignment in Washington? Was it gratitude...or blackmail.

He thought of Sparks, who had met Virginia in the psychiatrist's office. What had she said of him—that he had looked at her oddly—was that significant? He didn't know. Didn't know anything useful, it seemed.

He lay down on the sofa, pulled his coat over him, intending to just close his eyes for a moment, and fell into a deep sleep. He dreamed of drifting snow on the city streets, and children sledding down long, gentle slopes.

On Sunday Lenny stayed in bed all morning, too tired to go out or to call anyone. He made one trip to the corner store at noon. He rarely used the little grocery store, the prices were so high, but he couldn't bring himself to get in the car and drive to the big chain store.

He bought eggs, laughing at the crudely written sign over the eggs, which said "Very fresh eggs." The small outlets saved money by buying eggs that had been in refrigerated warehouses for two, three months or more. He picked up a loaf of white bread and squeezed it: not too bad. Then he added milk and juice and the Daily News. He cast a glance at the beer, but remembered Primeaux's warning about mixing pain killers with alcohol, even though he didn't take any of them. He had no taste for a drink, anyway.

At home he cooked, ate, read the paper, and cleaned up the house a little more, dusting the rooms and scrubbing the tub.

In the afternoon Kate called. She asked how he was feeling. He told her about Radcliff's death and about his interrogation, and she offered her sympathy for him.

"How could they fire you like that?"

"It happens. I knew West had it in for me as soon as I got into this thing. Maybe I'll win it in arbitration, although that could be a year down the road. Maybe longer."

"Oh Lenny, I'm so sorry. Can I do anything to help?"

"You could ask your mom if they need someone to wash dishes at the diner. I've had a lot of experience cleaning things."

"You're not serious, are you? Maybe this would be a good time to go to school. You could take out a college loan and pay it off when you get a new job."

"Maybe you're right. I could finish my bachelor's degree. I dropped out half way through my second year. I wonder if they have a degree in custodial services."

"I'm serious."

"Still want me to go to law school, don't you?"

"No, that's not it. Whatever you want to do. It just seems like a golden opportunity, that's all."

"Well, I've got plenty of time to think about it. I haven't made any plans yet. I'm still operating on a go-to-work-in-the-morning mode."

"Of course," said Kate. "Listen, I have to go, my daughter's calling me. I'm taking her out shopping for a coat and boots. They grow."

"So I hear. Thanks for calling. Maybe I'll see you around the hospital."

"I hope so, Lenny. Bye."

As glad as he was to hear from her, the only call that would boost his spirits would be a call from Virginia Galloway, but the day slipped past without it, and he had the sinking feeling that she would never call him.

He hoped that she had taken off with her son and was safe. He wondered if he should go out to the Galloway house and check on her, but wasn't sure. He didn't want to run into Galloway and get him hopped up. He might take it out on Virginia, *if* she was still at home.

He finished his last laundry, put fresh sheets on the bed, got into the silk pajamas Margaret had bought him one Christmas, and settled into bed. Looking at the alarm clock, he was unnerved at the thought of not having to get up and go to work.

"I'll call the union in the morning," he mumbled, putting out the light. "File the grievance…make some calls…"

A lone car crawled slowly up the street and came to a stop. The house breathed and settled down for the night.

The furnace hummed gently in the basement. Lenny closed his eyes, grateful for sleep and wishing that he didn't have to deal with so much shit in the morning.

Seventy-eight

*L*enny woke up, his neck throbbing with pain. Putting on an old terrycloth robe, he brushed his teeth, then went downstairs to make coffee. The day stretched ahead of him like a long ribbon of road on a flat desert.

He knew he should call the union office, but decided he would do it after he'd had his coffee...After he'd cleaned up the place...fixed the kitchen faucet....

Walter Oldenfield lay in his bed pale and weak and wandering in his mind. He muttered something about his brother needing him at the store. He had to help his brother at the store, but he was so weak when he tried to sit up he could only lift his head a few inches from the pillow and then fell back.

For the fourth time that morning, Gary measured the patient's vital signs. His pulse was 130, blood pressure 90/50, temperature 103. The leg, now amputated below the knee, was elevated on a pillow, the thick white dressing stained brown with old blood.

Gary hurried to the station for Tylenol to fight the fever. He knew that if the doctors didn't transfer his patient to the Intensive Care Unit and give him some aggressive treatment, Oldenfield would not survive, and he had no desire to wrap a dead body today, especially not a decent man like Walter Oldenfield.

After administering the Tylenol, he called Dr. Galloway's answering service, since the doctor had not answered three pages inside the hospital. The service promised to beep him and report Gary's information.

Frustrated, Gary paged the surgical resident and described Oldenfield's condition. The resident told him he couldn't transfer the patient to the ICU without Galloway's authorization.

Gary said, "That's great. Can you get hold of him? I've paged him and left messages with his answering service, but nobody can find him."

The resident was silent for a moment. Gary said, "Look, I can barely get a blood pressure, he's in there shivering with a fever. He's obviously septic. If you don't transfer him the infection is going to spread, and then you'll have to transfer him because he'll have coded."

"All right, I'll come up and write the transfer order. Hang a liter of

Ringers Solution and run it wide open."

As he grabbed a bag of intravenous fluid and hurried down to the room, Gary asked himself for the hundredth time that morning, *where was Dr. Galloway?*

After speaking to the union representative, who promised to file grievance papers before the end of the day, Lenny sat in his living room and sipped his second cappuccino of the morning. He was fidgety. He got up and took from the shelf a book about the Flint sit-down strike that his father had given him, leafed through it and put it back.

He pulled down a stack of old *Consumer Reports*, took twine from the kitchen and bound them neatly, then placed them on the shelf to go out with the next recycling day. If Margaret were alive, she would ask him what were the chances that he'd actually *remember* to put these magazines on the curb the morning that the big truck came around. He resolved to either remember himself or throw the crap in the trash.

He retrieved a dusty pile of photographs from a high shelf. He'd been meaning to put them in frames. He selected a half-dozen and set them aside, planning to buy a bunch of frames when he went to the hardware store for the plumbing supplies.

"I could get a lot done today," he mused. "I should make a list and get all those chores done that I've been putting off."

He glanced at the drawing on the wall that his nephew had given him. It was a crude rendition of a dragon and a knight, but the knight wasn't fighting *against* the dragon, he was fighting *alongside* him, against an army of stick men. Lenny had always liked that drawing because of the way it blithely ignored the traditional antagonism between wild creature and man. Out of the mouths of babes, and all that.

He thought about Margaret's miscarriage, and her biggest regret, not leaving him children. It brought a heavy, dull ache in his chest that made the burn on his neck seem superfluous. He was not often sad or depressed, but this was one of the few subjects that brought him crashing down, down, down.

But even as his spirit sagged, a light flashed in another part of his mind. A strong white light that cut through all the loose ends and half-truths of the investigation. Suddenly he knew who had killed Randy Sparks, and, more importantly, he knew why.

The truth that struck Lenny was so repugnant that it sickened and angered him at the same time. He fought against it, tried to find the flaw in his thinking, but could not. It made too much sense to deny.

"What an ego-fucking-maniac," Lenny muttered.

His voice trembled with anger. His lips pressed together until they blanched. He didn't talk words, he hissed them, spat them out in explosive bursts. "Bastard! Sicko, rotten fucking bastard!"

Lenny pulled on his coat as he kicked open the porch door and hurried down the steps, not bothering to button up. He jerked the car door open, slid into the seat and started the motor, giving it only a few seconds to circulate its thick pool of oil. He put the car in gear and pointed the hood ornament for James Madison Hospital. He had one thing to check out to be sure that he had the whole scenario right, and then he would bring the bastard down—hard.

Gary helped Lester, the orderly, pull Mr. Oldenfield onto the stretcher. The patient moaned weakly as they lifted his leg, now packed in a bag of ice, onto a pillow.

As they wheeled the stretcher into the hall, Gary called out to Celeste at the station, "I'm going with the patient to the ICU."

"Okay!" the clerk called back. "Good luck."

He checked the intravenous to be sure that it was dripping as fast as possible, fearful that Mr. Oldenfield's shock would deteriorate until his heart arrested.

When the wheels of the stretcher bumped on the floor of the elevator, Oldenfield grimaced. His pale face was cold and clammy. Gary thought how apt the phrase was: 'clammy,' the skin like the moist, sticky surface of an uncooked clam.

The elevator doors closed, Lester punched the button for the second floor, and Gary hoped his patient would make it to the intensive care unit without arresting.

Turning the big car onto Germantown Avenue, Lenny pushed it hard as he dared, knowing that the cobblestones could be slick in the cold. Three blocks from the hospital he parked in the lot of a Wa Wa convenience store, dug an old scarf out of the trunk and wrapped it around his mouth and chin. He realized that his nose still stuck out—a possible giveaway—but shrugged it off. No time for plastic surgery. Pulling his cap low over his forehead, he walked quickly down a side street to enter the building from the back.

He circled the back of the hospital building, coming up the broad driveway toward the loading dock. There were no trucks in the bay, nobody on the platform. He walked quickly into the dock, where the macadam was

This Won't Hurt A Bit

black with the oil drippings of a thousand heavy trucks. Scrambling up onto the bay, he opened one of the big doors through which supplies were carried, stepped inside and shut the door behind him. There was nobody in the hall.

Harvey, the supply clerk, was across the hall in the store room. Lenny could see his curly red hair through the glass window. As the clerk came out of the office with clipboard in hand, Lenny came up behind him.

"Hey, Harvey, how's it going?"

The clerk stopped in midstride, turned around.

"Lenny, I hear you got fired! What are you…"

"Sssh. Keep it down, will you? Yeah, West canned me. I'm incognito."

"Cool. You gonna get the job back?"

"I'm gonna try. Listen, have you seen West around lately?"

"Nope, bastard hasn't come by."

"Good."

"You goin' inside?"

"Yeah."

"If I see West I'll call Birdie in the sewing room."

"Great."

As he set off down the corridor, he heard Harvey whistling the marching song from *Bridge on the River Kwai*. He grinned, buoyed by the man covering his back.

Seventy-nine

*L*enny hurried past the supply room, walking toward the kitchen, where the staff was busy washing the breakfast trays and beginning lunch.

He peaked in through a double swinging door, looked quickly around, didn't see Moose.

"Maybe he's on a break," he muttered. He didn't want to go to the cafeteria—too many people. But Moose could be at Birdie's.

He hurried down the corridor, peeked around an intersection, found it empty and turned into it. He came to the sewing room and tried the door, relieved to find it unlocked, and hurried inside. Birdie was at her perch repairing hospital gowns.

"Lenny! I'm so glad to see you. Do you have your first-step hearing today?"

"No, it's not scheduled yet," he said, unwrapping the scarf from his face and removing his knit cap. "I'm here to nail that bastard who killed Sparks. Is Moose around?"

"No, he's collecting the breakfast trays."

"I need to use your phone."

"Help yourself."

He dialed the Seven-South nursing station, was glad to hear Celeste answer.

"Celeste? Lenny. Where's Gary?"

"Hi, Lenny. Are you in the hospital?"

"Yeah, I need to reach Tuttle."

"He just transferred Mr. Oldenfield down to the ICU. He'll be back soon."

"Shit. Is Galloway around?"

"We've been trying to get him to answer his page to tell him we were transferring his patient to the ICU, but the page operator can't raise him. He's not in the hospital."

"Listen Celeste, would you tell Gary as soon as he gets back that I've gone down to Galloway's Vascular Lab and he should meet me there right away?"

"Sure Lenny. Is Galloway the killer?"

"Yeah, the bastard. I have a pretty good idea how he killed Randy Sparks too. I'm going to the lab to check it out."

"Okay Lenny, I'll tell him."

"Thanks, Celeste, I'll…"

"Wait! I just remembered, two people called for you. That medical student, Kate somebody…"

"Okay."

"…And a woman who didn't give her name. She was crying and all and I couldn't get her to tell me who she was, but she wanted to reach you awful bad. She said she tried your home, but there wasn't any answer."

"Damn. It had to be Virginia Galloway."

"Is Mrs. Galloway involved?"

"In a way, she's the reason for the murder. Did she leave a message or anything?"

"She said you were the only person she could trust, so I told her about you being fired and that I'd be sure to tell you to call her back if I heard from you, but I had to have her number. At first she wouldn't give it to me, but after I swore on a stack of bibles that I would only give it to you, she gave it to me. Here it is."

She recited the number for him.

"Shit, I hope she's all right," he said, writing down the number and placing the paper snugly in his breast pocket.

"Tell Tuttle to meet me at Galloway's lab. I got to go."

"Okay, Lenny."

He hung up, turned to Birdie.

"Will you track down Moose and ask him to meet me in the Vascular Lab?"

"Sure, Lenny, I'll find him, but aren't you afraid you'll run into Galloway if you go to his lab?" she said, rising from her perch in front of the sewing machine.

"No problem, Galloway's not in the hospital. I won't see him, but when I hook up with Moose we'll have to figure out how to bring the bastard down."

"You want me to tell Sandy, too?"

"Good idea. I'd forgotten about him."

She stepped to the door, opened it, and stuck her head out.

"No sign of West," she said and entered the hall. "You be careful, now."

"I will," Lenny said, feeling the sewing room door close behind him. Why did the metal door feel like a coffin closing on him?

Birdie walked swiftly toward the kitchen. Lenny made for the stairwell and began climbing, not even thinking about using the elevator.

He pulled the cap low over his eyes and wrapped the scarf around his face as he hurried down the hall. Entering a stairwell, he climbed two flights to the second floor. Hurrying down a corridor past obstetrics and labor and delivery, he entered a waiting room where expectant fathers and other relatives gathered.

He went to the back of the room to a bank of telephones and dialed Virginia's phone number After four rings, he heard a click, then Galloway's voice on the answering machine ordering the caller to leave a message.

Lenny hesitated. He didn't want to alert Galloway that he knew who Virginia was, but he wanted to warn her, too. After hesitating, he said in a voice he hoped was disguised. "Hi, this is your friend. Can you call me? I'll have my beeper if I'm not home. Thank you."

He hung up, not sure if he had made things worse for her or better.

There was a sickly feeling, like watching Margaret when she took the chemotherapy. the poisons definitely made her feel and look worse, with vomiting and diarrhea, but they might also have made her better. It was a crap shoot.

Lenny hung up the phone and hurried out of the room. In his rush to get away, he failed to notice a doctor in an expensive suit who was standing at the nursing station talking to a nurse.

Leslie Odom did not fail to see Lenny. Nor did he hesitate to pick up the phone and page Joe West, STAT.

Leaving the Labor & Delivery department, Lenny entered a stairwell and climbed one flight, then exited and turned right. Two doors down he came to the familiar door labeled **VASCULAR RESEARCH LABORATORY, DR. NATHAN GALLOWAY, DIRECTOR.** He was confident that this was the place where Sparks had been murdered, but he wanted to check something about the hyperbaric tank, and he was hoping that the friendly respiratory therapist would be there to answer his question about the tank.

Lenny grasped the knob, turned it slowly and entered without knocking.

Seated at the computer console was a tall, dark-haired man in a crisp white lab coat. Nathan Galloway.

Eighty

Kate Palmer was seated beside Jennifer in a large lecture hall taking notes in a clear, neat hand. Kate had a textbook open in her lap with an illustration of the heart and lungs and the circulation nourishing them. The principles were difficult, with pressure readings in several regions of the chest, and she referred to the book as she followed the speaker.

Suddenly, a disturbing thought intruded on her concentration. She knew with utter certainty that Galloway had murdered Randy Sparks. She didn't know why he had done it, but she was sure of his method.

Closing her book and throwing her notebook into her bag, she rose from her seat.

Startled, Jennifer looked up at her and whispered, "Kate, what's the matter?"

"I have to reach Lenny."

"But Kate, you can't walk out on a lecture!"

"No? Watch me," she said and pushed past the laps of attentive students until reaching the aisle. Then she hurried out of the hall and walked quickly to the elevator.

Without knocking, Joe West opened the door to the sewing room, stepped in, and found the room empty. "Damn," he muttered.

He looked at his watch. Too early for lunch. She could be out on the floor delivering pillows, but he doubted it. Odom had reported seeing Lenny at the pay phone in the Obstetrics Department. He could have called the sewing room and asked Birdie to run an errand for him, but what?

West yanked the walkie talkie from his belt, pressed the button.

"All units, this is West. If you see the seamstress, let me know right away."

Static filled his ear. "All stations, did you copy that?"

"Two guards spoke at once, their voices garbled in the mixing of the sounds.

"I didn't hear that," West said. "Has anybody seen her?"

"Negative," said one of the guards. "I'm in the ER. I haven't seen her or Moss."

"Me, neither," said another. "No sign of him at the front entrance."

Keep looking for both of them!" West barked and hurried along the corridor. He pressed the button on the elevator, deciding to try Lenny's home base.

Lenny stepped slowly into the Vascular Laboratory, saw the tall dark-haired figure in the white lab coat, who continued typing at the key board. Lenny stood still; the door closed automatically behind him.

The big metal hyperbaric tank stood with its lid open. In another room, one of the lab dogs howled pitifully—"Owr-oooo!"

Lenny stepped beside the tank and stared at the back of Galloway's head. The doctor's ink black hair was neatly trimmed above his collar.

"There's a cage with your name on it, Galloway."

The doctor continued typing into the computer as though he hadn't heard him. Lenny felt his face flush. It pissed him off the way the arrogant prick ignored him.

Galloway pressed a key, entering the data into the mainframe, then he casually pushed back his chair, stood, and slowly turned around.

"I have been expecting you, Mr. Moss. I'll be with you in a moment. You may have a seat, if you like."

The doctor's casual manner fanned Lenny's anger. They were always talking to him like that. Condescending, smug, in charge. It didn't matter if he was on the job or with his wife in the doctor's office, they were always the same arrogant bastards.

"You don't get it, creep. I know about Virginia. I know about Sparks—the whole thing."

Galloway turned his back to Lenny, picked up a file folder. He ran his finger along a shelf until he found the appropriate slot and pushed the file among the others.

The surgeon casually turned back to Lenny. He placed one hand in his lab coat pocket in the classic physician's pose and smiled his best office smile at Lenny.

"We know all about you, Mr. Moss, my colleagues and I. We've been aware of your movements from the beginning. But you...You know nothing."

Lenny took a step closer.

"I'll bet you treat those dogs in the lab better than you do people."

"And why not? They are so much more obedient."

Lenny took another step. His voice trembled with rage.

This Won't Hurt A Bit

"I know that Virginia Racine was adopted as a baby. I know that when she came of age after your wife died—a death that deserves investigation, I have no doubt—you took advantage of her."

Lenny looked into Galloway's unblinking eyes.

"You seduced her, then you married her."

Lenny's rage was fierce, but his desire for revenge was even stronger.

"I know that Virginia Racine was the illegitimate daughter that you abandoned when you were a medical student. You located her when she was old enough. Being a doctor probably made it easy, and you fucked her—your own daughter!"

Galloway's polished exterior remained unchanged. He stood immobile by his desk like a painting, with one hand still casually tucked in the pocket of his lab coat.

The doctor made an offhand gesture.

"And why not? She was a beautiful young woman when I first saw her—innocent, sensual, beguiling.

"I hadn't planned on loving her, only to satisfy my curiosity. Were my genes dominant? Was she like me? Was she beautiful, intelligent, masterful?

"One look into her divine face and I knew that I could never let another man possess her. She was so much like me. Where would I ever find a more perfect partner? We were strangers. I hadn't raised her, I hadn't gone through all the stupid, boring little details that a parent endures. She was the perfect mate."

Lenny stood with clenched fists. He pictured them crushing the surgeon's skull.

"She knows, doctor. Your perfect mate knows and she's taken her son and left you. You're going to jail and her suffering is going to end."

Galloway withdrew his hand from the pocket. He held a small metal device.

"I think not. No man could ever separate a perfect love such as ours. Certainly not someone like yourself."

Lenny stepped back, crouched down behind the hyperbaric tank. *Shit*, he thought, *why did I have to barge in here like the cavalry? I was so fucking sure he wasn't around.*

He pulled the paint scraper from his belt and held it in front of him, then carefully peeked out around the side of the tank. He saw Galloway standing there, tall and smug, aiming the weapon at him.

"Radcliff knew. He heard it from Virginia. Is that why you killed him?"

"Ah, the reassuring therapist. Yes, he knew about Virginia and me. He was jealous of me, in fact. Robert had a thing for young women, you see, and

I think he was just a tad envious that I had the balls to do what I did."

"So why kill him? Wasn't your secret safe with him?"

"Not as long as he had a tape of Virginia. Besides, he was getting too close to her. She was beginning to trust him more than she trusted me, and I couldn't allow that."

Galloway stepped toward Lenny, his weapon aimed directly at the name embroidered on the custodian's heart.

Eighty-one

After transferring Mr. Oldenfield to the ICU and reporting off to the nurse, Gary pushed the empty stretcher along the hallway. He had said good luck to the patient, but Oldenfield was so weak he could not form any words of parting.

Returning to Seven-South, Gary stopped at Oldenfield's room to strip the linen from the bed. He stuffed it in a laundry bag in the hall and was walking toward the nursing station when Mrs. Grey called to him from her room.

"Gary! Could I see you for one little second please?"

Gary stepped in. "How are you Mrs. Grey? Feeling any better?"

"Yes, I feel ever so much better, thank you. I just have to ask you one thing."

"Yes?"

"Do you think I should continue seeing Dr. Radcliff after I'm discharged? He's offered to take me on as a patient, and I think I've gotten something useful from him, but I'm just not sure I want to continue with him."

Gary wanted to tell Mrs. Grey what a beast the psychiatrist had been, but made it easier for her instead.

"I'm sorry, Mrs. Grey. I suppose you didn't hear about Dr. Radcliff?"

"Hear what?"

"I'm afraid that the doctor has died. They found him Sunday morning. I'm sorry to be the one to tell you."

"Oh dear," she said. "Was it a heart attack?"

"I don't know what the cause of death was." He watched her face become contemplative. "Would you like me to see if his colleague would be willing to speak with you?"

"No, I don't believe so. I think I'll just see how this medicine helps me. Thank you."

As Gary left the patient's room and walked slowly down the hall, he saw Celeste waving to him from the nursing station. Puzzled, he continued on toward her.

In the Vascular Lab, Lenny crouched behind the hyperbaric tank. His only weapon, the paint scraper, was no match for the device in Galloway's hand. Why had he been stupid enough to come down here alone?

He estimated the steps to the door. Three, maybe four. If he could get through it quickly enough…

Lenny grasped the scraper by the tip of the blade and peeked over the rim of the tank. Bringing his arm back, he hurled the scraper like a throwing knife at Galloway, then spun around and leaped toward the door.

He was two steps away from escape, then one. He grabbed the handle, turned the knob.

The device in Galloway's hand clicked. A dart leapt out, tethered by a slender metal thread. It struck Lenny in the back. Four hundred joules of direct current swept through his chest. His heart muscle contracted in an agonized spasm and then stopped.

Lenny's entire muscle system had been shortcircuited. He could not even take in a breath or make a sound. His leg muscles buckling, he fell to the floor, paralyzed.

The electric device in Galloway's hand recoiled, bringing the dart back.

Galloway walked casually over to Lenny.

"How do you think we subdue the animals in the lab, eh? Handy little device. It has a much more rapid onset than a tranquilizer dart."

The doctor grabbed Lenny's shoulders, lifted his torso and dragged the limp body to the hyperbaric tank. Galloway heaved, forced Lenny's head and shoulders over the lip of the tank. He lifted Lenny's hips to the rim. Galloway lifted Lenny's legs and pushed him over into the tank.

His body fell like a cadaver without bracing. Lenny's burned face erupted in pain as it struck the bottom of the tank. His right arm was pinned beneath him, wrenching his shoulder. He lay on his side weak, helpless, able to move only his eyes.

A shadow fell across Lenny's face. Galloway was grinning at him exactly like Moose's mad scientist as he lowered the lid of the tank. The lid crashed down with an ominous *clank*.

A pair of latches clicked shut. The chamber was sealed. Airtight.

The surgeon stood over the tank looking at Lenny through the small plexiglass window, then he turned and walked out of Lenny's line of vision.

A moment later, Lenny heard Galloway's voice from a tinny speaker inside the tank.

"Congratulations, Mr. Moss. You are only the second human being who has volunteered for this unique hyperbaric experiment, although, to be precise, it is actually a hy-PO-baric experiment."

This Won't Hurt A Bit

Just as Lenny had suspected, the chamber was capable of not only pumping in higher pressures of air, but it could also suck the air out.

A sound of air rushing through a narrow opening filled the chamber.

"You see, human beings have survived climbs up to nineteen thousand feet, perhaps a bit higher. But do we really know the absolute limit of human endurance in terms of barometric pressure? How thin must the air become before the cardiac and pulmonary systems are unable to supply the tissues? Randy Sparks found out. Soon you, too, will enjoy that same knowledge."

Lenny's muscles were slowly regaining some of their strength. His heart had resumed beating seconds after the electric shock. Hey found he was able to turn his head weakly from side to side. His diaphragm drew in large quantities of air, but the air was thin and growing thinner.

With his free hand he pushed against the floor of the tank, lifting his torso. Pain shot through his shoulder where his arm was pinned beneath him. He gritted his teeth, lifted his chest. Through the agonizing pain he pulled his arm out from under him, then he rolled onto his back. He opened and closed the hand. It was numb, but functioning.

Placing both palms against the lid, Lenny pushed with all his strength.

It was useless. A tank that was designed to withstand several atmospheres of pressure easily withstood his feeble efforts.

He looked around the tank. Beneath him was a thin foam pad. He peeled back the edge hoping to find something helpful underneath, but found only rivets and steel.

He felt along the sides. At the feet there was a white plastic lever with red letters on it: **EMERGENCY RELEASE**. Relieved, he grasped the lever as he would a lifejacket in a stormy sea, closed his eyes and pulled the lever as hard as he could.

The lever pulled away from its hinge. Disconnected. Useless.

Eighty-two

Moose was on the fifth floor collecting lunch trays when he heard his name called. The ward clerk was holding a phone up in the air and gesturing to him.

"It's for you, Moose—it's your wife. She says it's important."

Moose slid a tray into the cart, walked over to the desk, and took up the phone.

"Hi sugar. What's up?"

"Moose, Lenny's looking for you. He said he was going down to the Vascular Lab to check something out. He said he knew that Dr. Galloway is the killer and that after he got through with the lab he was going to talk to you about how to bring him in."

"Where's Galloway?"

"He's supposed to be out of the hospital. Nobody can find him."

"But he wants me to meet him in the lab. Right?"

"That's what I'm trying to tell you. He said Galloway's not in the hospital so it would be okay for you to meet him there. He wants to show you something about the case."

"Okay, I'll get right down there. I'll call you later."

Moose hung up the phone, turned to go. Suddenly there was a loud crash from the patient's room across from the nursing station. Moose and one of the nurses hurried into the room.

An elderly woman had pushed her lunch tray off the bedside table. It had fallen to the floor, shattering the porcelain dish and cup, and spilling coffee and milk and spaghetti across the floor.

Turning to the nurse, Moose said, "Listen, normally I'd help you clean this up, but I promised to meet somebody and it's real important I get downstairs."

"Oh no you don't!" the nurse said. "This is your department. You help me clean up this mess or I'll call your supervisor and report you."

Moose looked at the mess on the floor. Birdie had said that Galloway was not in the lab. It wasn't like he had to rush the way he had done when they were chasing the killer down the stairwell and Lenny got hit in the head. It wasn't an emergency.

This Won't Hurt A Bit

"Okay, you go get some towels. I'll pick up the pieces."

The nurse walked out of the room, stopped at the doorway.

"Don't forget to get under the bed. It's probably a mess there, too!"

Moose cursed under his breath, looked up at the confused patient. The woman smiled, happy and serene in her confusion.

There seemed to be a thousand pieces of crockery to pick up.

Now the air in the hyperbaric tank was getting thin enough to notice. Lenny panted, hungry for oxygen. He found himself pursing his lips in an unconscious effort to build up the air pressure in his lungs. His heart pounded so hard that he could feel it lifting his chest as it strained to compensate for the poorly-oxygenated blood that it was pumping.

He beat his fists against the plexiglass window. He knew that Galloway had killed Randy Sparks in the tank, had probably stunned him with the same electric dart. Now Lenny knew why Sparks had bruises on his hands.

He beat at the plexiglass window with the emergency release handle, but it was plastic and didn't even scratch the surface.

There had to be some way out of the damned tank. Sparks had failed to find it. Lenny pulled at the small speaker attached to the wall. It pulled away. He yanked desperately at the wires hoping they might follow a channel to the outside and let in some air, but they did not.

He bent his knees and braced them against the lid, pushed with his hands and legs with all his strength. He strained against the lid until his limbs trembled and became rubbery and fell by his side.

Waves of nausea swept over him. In a panic, he feared he would vomit. His wife had vomited moments before she died—a foul-smelling, ugly brown vomit. The nurse had cleaned her up but the foul smell hung about the bed, soiling his last memory of her.

He didn't want to die in his own throw-up. He felt cold in his legs and arms. Even his nose and ears were chilled, as though frostbitten. It was just like being on a mountain top, except there was no wind.

There wasn't even enough air to blow on his hands to warm them.

Lenny whipped his belt off his pants. He scraped madly at the plexiglass window with the metal tongue hoping to crack it, but the metal left only superficial marks. He scraped and stabbed at the window. His arms grew weak, refusing to follow his will. They became useless—a dead man's arms.

Then the pain and the straining of his heart eased. The cold sensation left his limbs, and he felt himself sinking into a sweet embracing sleep.

In his sleep Lenny was warm and at peace. An inviting breeze lulled him. He floated effortless on a cloud. A bright smiling sun embraced him. He smiled. He was warm and comfortable and asleep.

When Gary reached the Seven-South nursing station, Celeste was on the phone taking down admissions. She asked the admission clerk to wait a moment, pressed the hold button and said, "Gary, Lenny asked me to tell you he was going down to the Vascular Lab and he wanted you to meet him there."

"How long ago was that?"

Celeste glanced at the clock on the wall. "Oh, maybe ten minutes ago."

"Did he sound urgent?"

"Uh huh. He said that Galloway was the guy who killed Dr. Sparks and that he was going down there to check something out."

"Galloway hasn't answered his page, has he?"

"I don't think so. The operator's been paging him for the last hour and he hasn't answered."

"Okay, tell Marianne I left the floor again, will you?"

"Sure will," she said and returned to the admissions clerk.

As Gary walked toward the elevator, he saw Joe West striding briskly toward him. He felt his stomach begin to knot up.

"Where's Moss!" the security chief growled. "I know he's in the building."

"I haven't seen him," Gary said, glad that he did not have to tell an explicit lie.

"But you've heard from him, haven't you?"

"No, I haven't spoken with him," Gary said.

"When I find him I'm going to arrest him for trespassing."

West looked over Gary's shoulder, saw a young woman who meant nothing to him standing in the hallway. He fingered his handcuffs as though stroking himself, then marched off, squeezing the button on his walkie talkie and growling low into the mouthpiece.

Gary turned to go, saw Kate Palmer watching him.

"Have you heard from Lenny?" she asked.

"He left a message. He's gone to the Vascular Lab. That's where I'm going now."

"I'll go with you."

They hurried to the elevator and punched the down button. The bell chimed, but the elevator was going the wrong way. The sense of impending catastrophe that Gary had been feeling for days came back.

We better take the stairs," he said.

"Good idea."

They walked to the exit and began to descend. With each step he took his feeling of doom increased. As anxiety gripped him, Gary quickened his pace until he was running down the steps, gripping the railing for support and jumping onto the landing. Kate was leaping down the steps right behind him.

Eighty-three

Galloway was sitting at the control panel reading the pressure gauges. He noted the time on his watch, estimated it would take five more minutes before Lenny's death was assured. Perhaps he would give the man an extra three minutes, just to be certain. The fellow had proven himself rather resilient.

The surgeon rose and stepped to the tank, looked in through the window, saw that Lenny's chest was no longer rising and falling. Good, he thought. A few more minutes, and then he would hide the body in one of the empty cages. He would cover the cage with canvas and attach a sign saying that it was being fumigated. No one would disturb it as long as they thought it was being deloused.

He would return tonight and remove the body. Not to the anatomy lab again. No, Lenny's face was too distinctive—that large nose and those bushy eyebrows. He would have to dismember it and carry out the parts in separate containers to dispose of later. He would take his boat out on the Delaware Bay and feed Lenny to the fishes.

Galloway returned to the computer station to check the pressure readings one more time.

Suddenly, there was a loud *bang*. Moose had kicked the door open and barreled through. He stood in the doorway and scanned the room with a practiced eye accustomed to sizing up opponents.

He spied Galloway standing on the other side of a large, evil-looking metal tank. In an instant, Moose realized that Lenny was in the tank. He stepped forward, saw the weapon in Galloway's hand and froze in place.

Galloway pointed the stun gun at him.

Moose turned sideways to present the narrowest aspect to his opponent—an old fighter's trick. He focused his eyes on Galloway's extended arm and shoulder, ignoring his enemy's face. Moose was relaxed, ready, just like in the ring.

The doctor's arm jerked slightly as he squeezed the trigger. The jerking motion gave Moose a fraction of a second to respond. As he bent backward at the waist, the dart, far slower than a bullet, sailed past him and struck the wall.

In two giant leaps Moose closed the distance between himself and his opponent. Galloway raised the stun gun to use as a club. Moose dodged to the side, the gun striking him on the shoulder.

With his left hand Moose jabbed twice at Galloway's chin. The doctor stumbled backward. Moose raised his right fist and sent it down in a hammer blow that broke Galloway's collar bone. The force buckled the surgeon's knees, putting him down for the count.

As Galloway collapsed, Gary and Kate rushed into the room.

"What's going on, Moose?" Gary asked. "Where's Lenny?"

"He's in the tank!"

They all rushed to the chamber.

Moose frantically unscrewed the clamps which held the lid down. He bent his knees and pulled on the lid with all of his strength. His neck bulged and his face contorted with the effort, but the lid would not open.

Kate pointed to the pipes running from the chamber.

"It's the vacuum. You won't be able to open it until you restore the internal pressure."

Gary said, "I'll check the controls!"

While Gary scanned the dials on the console that directed the pressure and flow of air through the tank, Kate peered through the plexiglass window at Lenny.

"Hurry, Gary, he's not breathing!"

"I'm doing the best I can. Let me see: influx, oxygen-CO^2 mix. I think...wait a second... this might be the one..."

Gary turned several dials. The sound of gas rushing through pipes could be heard as the vacuum of the tank sucked in the air. Gary watched the pressure gauge rise slowly from a negative number toward zero—still not atmospheric pressure, but getting there.

"Okay Moose, try it now!"

Straining once more at the lid, he pulled up fiercely. With a loud whoosh the lid came free.

Gary bent over the rim of the tank, placing his ear above Lenny's nose to listen for breathing. At the same time he laid one hand lightly on his friends chest to feel for the rise and fall of respiration.

Lenny was not breathing.

Eighty-four

"Shall I do chest compressions?" Kate asked, looking down at the motionless figure in the hyperbaric tank.

"Not yet," said Gary, kneeling beside the tank. He pinched Lenny's nose, pressed his mouth against Lenny's and blew two deep breaths. He watched as the chest rose and slowly fell. He felt at the neck for a pulse. It was slow and feeble, but a pulse was there.

"He's alive!"

Gary forced two more breaths into Lenny's lungs, waited, saw no spontaneous movement of Lenny's chest, and administered two more breaths.

They watched and waited to see if Lenny would breathe on his own. Slowly, his chest rose, fell, rose again. He stirred, opened his eyes and slowly looked around him. He saw Gary, Moose, and Kate standing above him.

"What's going on?"

Moose bent over him.

"You were dead, man. Gary gave you mouth-to-mouth."

Lenny brought his good hand up to his mouth and rubbed his lips. He stuck out his tongue.

"Yccchh, that's disgusting! What about Galloway?"

"I put him on the mat," Moose said. "The cops'll have to carry him out of here."

Lenny reached up to the lip of the tank and tried to pull himself to a sitting position, but as soon as his head lifted from the mattress, a blinding pain shot through his skull. It was worse than when he'd been hit in the basement and burned on the steam pipe.

"Jeez, what a headache! What hit me?"

Gary bent down over Lenny. "You've got brain edema from the lack of oxygen. The swelling should go down in a couple of days."

"Get me out of this tank, will ya? Randy Sparks died in this thing!"

Gary and Moose lifted Lenny out of the tank and eased him to a sitting position on the floor with his back against the metal.

Galloway moaned, stirred on the floor beside the counter. Moose stood over to him.

"Try and get up. Go on, try it!"

The doctor opened one eye, looked warily up at Moose, ceased groaning and lay still.

Sandy, the silver-haired security guard, came into the lab. He quickly scanned the room, saw Galloway on the floor, turned to Lenny. "He the killer?"

"He's the one. He even tried to kill me!" said Lenny.

Sandy pulled the handcuffs from his belt and clapped them on Galloway, saying with a grin, "Sir, I am arresting you for the murder of Dr. Randy Sparks. Any shit you say I will gladly repeat in court if it will help to fry your ass."

Sandy chuckled and winked at the others. "Birdie paged me and told me to get my butt down here," he said. "Soon as she said it, I knew Galloway was our man."

Moose put his arm around Lenny and pulled him up to a standing position.

"Come on, I'm taking you to the ER You need to have that head checked out again."

"No way am I letting another doctor mess with me. No fucking way."

"Don't be stupid," Gary said. "You're suffering from the same cerebral edema that killed Sparks. You have to have it treated."

"He's right, Lenny," Kate said. "Your brain has been insulted. You may need a CAT scan."

"I'm not getting in another goddamn box!" he said.

Gary wrapped Lenny's arm around his neck. With his friends on either side, Lenny had no choice but to be half-carried, half-dragged to the ER.

"Ooooh," he moaned, "find me a hole and throw some dirt over me somebody. I feel worse than when I was sand-bagged."

"You can't die yet," Moose said. "You haven't dated my cousin Janice. She's got a cute little red sports car. Heh heh."

"Just what I need, a nice bouncing ride around the city to clear my head."

Lenny smiled at his friends despite the pounding pain in his head.

Eighty-five

After Lenny had been treated and released from the Emergency Room, he promised to meet his friends after work in the sewing room. With time to kill, he went to the gift shop and browsed among the magazines. He was sneaking a look at *Consumer Reports* when he heard a tap-tap-tap on the tall glass window that looked out on the lobby. Kate was standing and waving at him. He put back the magazine and went out to her.

They began walking slowly through the lobby.

"So, Kate, now that you won't be wasting your time helping me, I guess you'll have more time with your daughter... Sarah, isn't it?"

"That's right. Tomorrow we're going to get up early and go out to the Star Diner for breakfast and visit my mom. Sarah loves their homemade pancakes."

"I like their coffee. Especially the real cream they put out instead of that plastic junk a lot of places give you."

"Their coffee can't compare to the expresso that you make, Lenny."

They had stopped at a juncture of two hallways. Lenny looked at Kate, noted her slim figure, her short hair, her direct way of looking at him.

"Maybe you could come over for dinner some weekend. You could bring your daughter."

"That would be nice, Lenny. Maybe after midterms. I'll give you a ring."

"Good." He looked wistfully at the corridor she would take, feeling clearly that their budding friendship would soon dissolve. "Well, I'll see you around the hospital."

Kate walked to the right. Lenny watched her go, then he walked in the other direction to the exit and descended to the basement.

Entering the sewing room, he found Birdie at her machine repairing patient gowns. The sleeves of some had been cut by doctors or nurses when intravenous tubing or other entanglements had made removing the gown difficult. Others were missing snaps that had been ripped out by a hurried nurse or an out-of-control patient.

Moose was seated at her side while Birdie worked.

This Won't Hurt A Bit

Lenny took a chair beside Moose.

"Moose, I hate to think what would have happened if you and Gary hadn't come into that lab when you did. Those fuckin' medical students would be dicing and slicing me on their anatomy table."

"Nah, you're hide's too tough. Need a chain saw to open you up."

"Moose Lennox, shame on you," Birdie said, "talking about Lenny that way."

Lenny said, "That's okay, Birdie. Any man that saves my life without kissing me can say anything he wants—anything."

Gary came into the room.

"Greetings, all. How are you feeling Lenny?"

"Like a pile of dog shit on the frozen ground, but happy to be alive. Very happy."

Gary picked up an old armchair missing a broken arm that was in a corner and carried it to where the others were sitting.

Lenny pointed at the chair.

"See! See! You picked up the chair and carried it across the room. How come the other nurses have to drag 'em along the floor and scuff up my clean floors?"

Gary looked at the chair as though it was a fascinating specimen.

"You must be speaking about the scratches that we make pulling furniture along the floor. Is that right?"

"Yeah. The nurses are always tearing up my new wax."

Gary settled into the chair. He stretched out his legs, folded his hands across his belly and considered Lenny's problem.

"Lenny, the armchairs on our floor are old and heavy. Most of the women aren't strong enough to pick them up and carry them from one room to another. Especially the new high-back ones with a steel frame."

"Why don't they get someone to help them?" Birdie said. "Two women can easily lift a chair."

"Do you know what our staffing has been like lately? We're down two nurse aides, one LPN and an RN. Often times we can't just dig somebody up to help move a piece of furniture. We're busy as Hell up there."

Moose picked up a soft, thick bath blanket.

"Put something like this under it, it'll drag easier. Save the floor, too."

"That's a good idea, Moose. I'll suggest it when I go back to the floor."

Betty came into the room, her face beaming. "Hello, hello and God bless us all. This looks like a prayer meeting to me!"

"Hi, Betty," Birdie answered. "We were just talking about the murder case. C'mon in."

"Thank you, dear heart. Now that we've chased that Devil Galloway from the temple, we can all rest easier."

"How are you feeling?" Lenny asked. "Was it a shock finding Radcliff's body in his office. I heard he looked like he'd seen a ghost."

"My dear, the devil himself came for that man's soul, believe you me. The look on his face, only the fires of hell could scare a man that much."

"So it didn't bother you?" Moose asked.

"Why should the devil bother me, I have the Lord on my side," she said. "And all of you, besides." She laughed, carefree.

Gary pointed to the sketch of Security Chief West on the wall. "You know, Moose, it looks like your sketches of the suspects helped break the case."

"They were the key," Lenny agreed. "When I met Virginia Galloway-Racine her face was so familiar. It was eerie. It took me a while to put it together, but then I remembered that story of Galloway's affair with the nursing student back when he was a medical student. How she came back without the baby. I thought about Galloway's son with the birth defects, and then I remembered that Sparks was going to specialize in genetics.

"But you know what really put me on to him? My nephew drew this picture of a knight and a dragon. I was thinking about what a funny pair they made, how unnatural it was for them to be together. Virginia was the right age to be his child, and it just popped into my head. The only thing I wasn't sure of was if Galloway's hyperbaric tank could be reversed to create a vacuum."

"I figured it to be Galloway from the beginning," Gary said. "A physician who makes a medical student carry his little black bag for him is capable of anything."

Moose and Lenny looked at each other. Lenny said, "Is that what your Zen detecting came up with? A little black bag?"

"I was leaning toward Radcliff," Moose said, "'cause most of them shrinks are crazy anyway, until he got himself killed."

Ring-ring.

Birdie picked up the phone. "Sewing, how may I help you?" She listened a moment, then handed the phone to Lenny.

Pressing the receiver to his ear, Lenny took a deep breath, felt his stomach tighten.

"Lenny, it's Virginia."

"Oh, hi. I tried to reach you last night but your answering machine was on. How are you? And your son—Jason?"

"We're okay. We've been staying with a college friend in Center City.

I was thinking about going home, but I'm not ready to face it just yet, even though I know Nathan's not there."

"I understand."

There was silence between them for several seconds. Finally, he said, "Virginia, how long have you known who your husband really is?"

He pictured her lovely face. Felt her pain as he had felt Margaret's suffering.

"I didn't know with Jason," she said. "I just had this feeling after he was born that something was wrong with him, and I thought it was my fault. I thought I was the problem.

"The pediatrician assured me that I had nothing to do with it. I was relieved, but then this feeling started to grow in me that it was about him. It was about Nathan."

Her voice was overcome with sobbing. Lenny waited.

When her sobs had grown softer, he said in a gentle voice, "Can I tell you something? A little over a year ago, a doctor told me that my wife had cancer of the ovaries and that it was too far along to be cured. What he didn't say was that for months and months they told her that she'd be okay, that it was just gas pains or PMS or endo-something or other. I know a *little* something about suffering, Virginia. Not like you know it or the way my wife knew it, but something. And I know that you had nothing to do with your husband's crime. Nobody can blame you for what he did."

"I hope not," Virginia whispered. "Do you have to tell anybody about it?"

"I won't if I don't have to, but when the murder goes to trial I may not be able to hold back the truth."

"I just want us to stay as far away from him as we can."

"I understand."

He considered Virginia's future. "Maybe when it's all over you'll want to find your mother."

"I've been thinking a lot about her. I *would* like to try and find her, for Jason's sake as well. After it's all over."

"Of course. After it's over," he said.

"Goodbye, Lenny. Thank you. I don't even know you, really."

"I'm just a guy trying to help a friend get his job back."

After hanging up the phone, Lenny turned to the others. There was no need to explain what he had said.

Eighty-six

The door to the sewing room opened and Freddie, the old morgue attendant, came in carrying a tray with cups of coffee on it.

"Hey, now, coffee time!" he called out.

"Freddie, it wasn't your turn to buy the coffee," Moose said, "it was Lenny's."

"That's okay, after all the boy's been through, I figured to spring for him this one time."

He handed cups around, then pulled up a battered folding chair and settled down.

"You'll never guess what ol' doc Fingers told me today," he said.

"Is it about Radcliff's murder?" Lenny asked.

"Nothin' but. Fingers got the preliminary tox screen on the body. It would take a genius to figure out what it was that actually killed him dead."

"Cocaine?" Lenny asked.

"Nope."

"A paralyzing agent," Gary put in.

"Uh, uh... He did have some tranquilizer in his system, but that wasn't what did him in. His blood was loaded with a drug they call a beta...beta blacker?"

"A beta blocking agent," Gary said. "That's a drug that inhibits adrenaline. We give it to patients with heart disease to slow their pulse rate down. It's usually a very safe drug, unless the patient has asthma."

"That's what Doc Fingers said. That Radcliff had a real bad form of asthma. They looked up his medical records and he's got prescriptions for a couple of different asthma medicines."

"That explains the inhaler I found in Radcliff's office," Lenny said. "I thought it might have belonged to Sparks, or one of Radcliff's patients, but it was really his!"

"And the beta blocker set off his asthma by causing his airway to constrict," said Gary. "What a gruesome way to die."

"Yeah," Freddie went on, "they say his face was all screwed up, like he suffered real bad before he died."

This Won't Hurt A Bit

Birdie looked up from her sewing machine. "Speaking of Radcliff, what did you do with the tapes that he made?"

"Ah, the tape," Lenny said, "Remember Nixon's Watergate tapes? Radcliff's tape got erased somehow."

"Good for you," Gary said. "They would be painful for the women on them to see if they had to be played in court."

"That's what I was thinking," Lenny said.

A knock on the door, and Sandy, the elderly security guard, stuck his head in.

"I know there's always a party in Birdie's room." He came in and walked up to Birdie.

"Have you started working on my suit, darlin'?"

Birdie smacked him in the stomach.

"Get away from here, you old cheapskate! I've got my hands full with my work, and two children to clothe as well."

Sandy turned to Lenny.

"You remember all those thefts we've been having on the wards? The ones that always seemed to happen during a code or a fire, or some kind of emergency? Well, old Sandy decided the only way to catch the perpetrator was to go undercover."

The group waited in perplexity.

"There was a code called this morning, see, so I left off my hat and put on a white lab coat I borrowed from the lab. A disguise, you see? I went up to the floor—it was Five-North—and hung around where all the activity was, looking busy, and don't you know I spotted this medical student slinking around the patient rooms.

"I waited at the door of the room he went in, and when he came out I grabbed him. Sure enough, he had the patient's wallet in his shirt. I put the cuffs on him and he came along like a kitten."

"Sandy, you're my hero!" Lenny said.

"Not only that, but the patient who reported her wallet missing identified him as the one who was going from room to room. Oh, his goose is good and cooked, you can believe it."

"That's the creep who decked you," Moose said. "Has to be."

"Of course he is. When I was searching him for evidence I saw this big old bandage on his belly and I knew right away that was where Lenny got him with his putty knife."

"You are a regular Sam Spade," Lenny said, standing and offering the guard his chair. "What was the student's name?"

Sandy lowered himself into the chair and stretched out his legs.

"His name's Letterly. I hear his father's a bigshot doctor. I opened up his locker. It had a bunch of drugs in it. Something called 'In-press' I think it was, and a key to the nurse server drawer."

"That explains the missing meds," Gary put in. "No doubt Letterly was selling it to the other male students."

"Now why couldn't the police go after somebody like him," Birdie asked, "instead of that poor Regis Devoe."

"Speaking of Regis," Lenny said, "I called his lawyer and he said it should only take a day to get the papers filed and Regis out of jail. I'll try to get an emergency grievance hearing scheduled for next week. He should be back on the job, *with* all his back pay by then."

"What about your job?" Birdie asked.

"The area rep already talked to Freely. They're working on a deal to take me back. I'll go on medical leave and come back when I'm good and ready, as long as I agree not to sue their ass."

"Right on," Moose rejoined. Putting his arm around Birdie, he said, "Let's go out and celebrate. I know a perfect place, the Dog Bite Cafe."

"I don't know if I'm up for drinking," Lenny said, "the way I've been knocked around."

"A little alcohol will do you good," Gary said. "It will reduce some of the swelling in your brain."

"For real?" Lenny asked.

"Of course. Alcohol is a natural diuretic. It makes you pee extra water." Gary reached into a plastic shopping bag, coming up with a tray from the meat section of the supermarket. "I was grocery shopping the other day, and on an impulse I went in and bought these pigs feet. I understand dogs love to chew them."

"That was mighty thoughtful of you, Gary," she said. "Thank you, but, uh…"

She looked at Lenny, who began to laugh, as did Moose and Birdie.

Perplexed, Gary turned to Lenny, who said, "You see, Tuttle, Betty doesn't really have any dogs. She's raising three grandchildren. Her daughter, well, she has an addiction problem, and while she's getting herself straightened out the children are staying with their grandmother. She takes that food home to make soup and stews and stuff. For the kids."

"We can use the pig's feet. Don't think it'll go to waste," she added. "They make a wonderful stock for black-eyed peas. Thank you so much."

Embarrassed, Gary handed the plastic shopping bag to Betty.

"You're welcome," he said.

"Okay," Lenny said, "we'll go out to the Dog Bite Cafe and kill a bottle of bourbon…and Gary can be the designated driver."

"Not me," said Gary. "I'm getting sloppy drunk."

"Yeah, sure," said Lenny, "and I'm Sherlock Holmes."

TIMOTHY SHEARD is a veteran critical care nurse and a prolific mystery writer who has published over 100 short stories, plays, reviews and articles. His short mystery stories have appeared online in Blue Murder, Galway Writer's Electric Acorn, and Webdreamer. His plays have been performed by Stage Shadows at the NY Museum of Television and Radio, and at the Pulse Open Lab on New York's celebrated theatre row. He currently lives with his wife and two sons in Brooklyn, NY.